-Books by Ryan Clark-

Warden

Warden

Tech Hunter Book 2

Ryan Clark

Published by Ryan Clark
www.ryanclarkbooks.com
Cover design by Ryan Clark
ISBN 978-1-7336702-3-4

Edited by Courtney Andersson
www.elevationeditorial.com

To my Mom and my Aunt:

You are sisters of mirrored similarities, and of drastic differences;
you are both inspirations to me in your own incredible ways.

Table of Contents

Candles

She made her way about the room, feeling the age in her knees as she lit a number of small candles along the walls. The dim flickering cast a kind of glow simply not achievable by electricity or emergency chem lights. It was the kind of light that stimulated the mind to wander, to explore the recesses of the past or touch upon the possibilities of the future.

She knelt with a grimace, setting her knees upon the small mat of rubber-coated cables. Not for the first time, she wondered which line of thought was more difficult to entertain. The past was painful, with the sum of its years in full view to her, but the future was more worrying than ever before, and was steadily growing out of her reach as her own remaining years declined.

A bead of sweat formed on her forehead, and it found no easy path down her aged and wrinkled skin. She closed her eyes, willing the heat of the candles to guide her thoughts, but a change in the lighting of the room distracted her. She opened her eyes, expecting to see that some of the candles had gone out.

Instead, her data pad was glowing.

She picked up the device.

The new message on it was small, just a few words, but to her it said a great deal; it meant she had found someone else to carry the torch.

Someone else who could light the future ablaze.

Chapter 1: Offsending

Baxel set his gloves against a flat section of steel, then paused before pulling himself over the ridge. He rechecked his scanner for any changes in gravitational fields, as the last thing he wanted was to fall up into a broken mess of jagged metal. With a smooth motion, he applied pressure against the ridge and floated out past the wreckage and into the wide expanse.

The chill down the back of his neck had nothing to do with the regulation systems of his suit. He had checked over every connection before passing the habitat barrier, just the same as he had on every expedition. No, the feeling was spawned out of contrast. Only minutes before, he had been edging his way through tight corridors within the superstructure. Now, the next solid structure in his path was within a scattered shell nearly a quarter mile away. Beyond that, there was nothing but stars.

It would take several minutes to reach the other side, based on how hard he had pushed off. The slow pace was deliberate; it would ensure he had enough time to compensate if his course was wrong. That thought was what had sent the chill down through his spine. He was at the outer edge of the orbital wreckage—the edge next to the vastness of space—and if something went wrong with his vent jets, the section on the far side would be his last chance to grab onto anything. Past that, solutions would have to get creative to escape the prison of his own drifting momentum.

"Making my way across now," Baxel said into the comms within his helmet. As he spoke, the front glass fogged up a bit from the weak seals of his inner face mask. "Three point two meters per second, relative."

"I see you," a voice rattled into his ear. Tymon's transmitter had been messed up since he nearly cracked his helmet on their last run. "You should kill your lights. Some of this looks habitable."

"My thoughts exactly," Baxel said, tapping his helmet to kill the glow scattering forward into the sheets of dust. He was suddenly left drifting through thick shadows. Only the farthest spread of cables hanging off toward the void reflected the fading sunlight.

"We're not allowed to make contact, Bax. I don't want to be confined to Hab again."

"I know!" Baxel said irritably as he glanced back to where Tymon's scanning pad made a small point of light in the dark. "But that last one was on you."

"Yeah, whatever. Just get your ass to the other side so I know you didn't just float off away from the fleet. Oxygen, sixty percent."

"Sixty-three," Baxel sounded back without so much as a thought. Their coordination had fallen firmly in place in the two years since their start as a duo exploration team. Of course, that was not to say team Firebrand handled the risks as well as the search coordinators preferred, but traversing shifting gravitational fields was the same as trying to please the coordinators: difficult, slow, and often a pain.

The area only grew darker as he neared the far edge of the fleet. The false orbit brought them into a six-hour cycle with the sun, of which they now were entering the dark phase. If they had not been on the space-side of the fleet, they could have watched the steadily receding sunlight shift across Earth. Instead of the rolling stars Baxel watched now, the lights above would be in the shells of cities long gone. Much like the systems that continued to maintain the low orbit of the fleet, Earth continued an existence unaware of the absence of its human population.

The last traces of sunlight slipped from the far tendrils of loose cables, the voluminous glow faded from the atmospheric edge, and the area plunged into the brink of complete darkness. Had the strut he aimed for not been square against the backdrop of the stars, he would have been left with no distinguishable visual to adjust his course.

Rather than use the system to guide his landing, he tapped the visor again and pushed the control onto his right hand. One flick of his thumb produced multiple jets of air from the left side of his suit and set him moving to the right. Baxel tapped his lights back on and realized that in his impatience, he had overcorrected his course. He was forced to use more of his air supply to realign himself for a final approach.

Baxel pulled up his legs and made a smooth circle with both arms as he neared. The rotation slowly carried him around and brought his feet firmly against the metal. One more tap on his helmet engaged the magnetic locks on his boots. His feet connected smoothly to the surface, thankfully without any of the temperamental quirks of the system.

"I'm across," he said as he looked around. The large section of outreaching metal turned out to be nearly twenty long steps across. Baxel leaned to look over the edge. Of course, it was only a matter of perspective, but he still felt the exhilarating span of what he perceived as a drop-off into infinity. The moment passed as his mind adapted to the illusion. Years spent in and out of the artificial gravity zones of the habitats had ensured that the moments of exhilarating disorientation were each more fleeting than the one before.

Baxel turned, and his suit continued recognition of his steps, causing the magnetic pads to release and attach as he moved forward.

"I'll keep on and give you a point to jump closer to the bulk of the wreckage."

"And what is our reference to get back to this side? I already placed my last nav beacon in the interior, remember?"

Baxel glanced back to Tymon, who was now a half mile straight above him in relative position. "We can head back if you make the call."

"Look around since you're already over there," Tymon finally said. "Just don't find anything too interesting."

"Oh, wow!" Baxel exclaimed in wonder.

"What is it?" Tymon asked in a moment of excitement. It was the latter half of the same moment that he realized his mistake. "Oh you . . ."

"A shuttle! Marked with the Warden's symbol, no less!"

"Shut it, Bax. I swear . . ."

He chuckled to himself, but more importantly in Tymon's ear, as he continued along the arching twist of metal. The thing about growing up together in one of the smaller habitat levels of Safe Harbor was that they had years of practice in stepping on each other's toes. It all amounted to nothing serious, especially outside of the habitat barriers, but Tymon was due a few more jabs than usual for what happened on their last run. They'd been kept off the search for two weeks after Tymon filled his tanks outside the habitats with an unexamined oxygen supply. They had found a living tree in the sealed section, though apparently that was not enough evidence to satisfy the safety concerns of the coordinators.

Baxel frowned as his boots attached again at an inconsistent angle with his direction. The path he was walking along was beginning to have distortions in the surface. While damage was obviously commonplace amongst the orbital wreckage, he had never seen anything quite like this. As he continued, now giving less attention to his thoughts and more to his surroundings, it became more apparent that the steel had taken on a wavelike pattern. He raised his head and looked forward with his lights. As far as he could tell, the recesses and peaks only became more severe farther on.

Now, curiosity drove him forward. It was as if the metal had been heated and blown across, much like a breath over a container of water. The ridges continued to build higher until some showed strands of the metal hanging out from the peaks of the waves. He moved carefully, knowing that the stagnant ribbons could be sharp enough to tear a hole in his suit. Misshapen metal was nothing out of the ordinary in the Remnant Fleet, but this increasing pattern almost had the look of being made long after the initial destruction.

The ridges turned to violent shards where the stretching metal had broken off or burned away during the intense heat. When it became difficult to lift his leg safely over the next wave in the metal, Baxel decided he would have to move over the top. He bent his knees slightly and tapped his helmet. A gentle push with his legs brought him up, and the release vents on his shoulders stabilized his position. He leaned forward, and the system provided for his momentum over the tops of the ever-increasing distortions. When the peaks would have been rolling over his head if he were standing, the large strut finally joined in with the main structure of the orbital ship. That was where the far edge of his lights revealed a large repulsor engine that had buried itself deep into the wreckage.

As far as Baxel could tell, some point after the repulsor engine became lodged, the repulsor overloaded and spewed out an immense torrent of heat and particles strong enough to push against the molten steel for nearly a hundred yards.

Baxel engaged his jets to get around another large cross-running support strut. It was then that he realized that the ten-foot repulsor engine stuck into the steel was only a piece of the entire shape. Caught in a tangle of inner structures and struts was the rest of a ship larger than anything functioning in Safe Harbor. The entire length of the hull was crinkled from the crossing metal that had it securely trapped. The paint on the exterior, a mix of orange with accents of grey, was a different pattern than anything he had ever seen amongst the Remnant Fleet, especially when compared to the bent and stripped metal that surrounded the crashed ship.

Before exploring ideas of how it came to be, his first instinct was to start mapping it out. A first glance over was for a way in. Any tears in the hull appeared to be clogged by the surrounding structure, and he could not see an obvious exterior hatch. One of the numerous dents where the orange and grey paint had been scraped away might serve as a weak point for entry—provided they did not cut into somewhere vital. He then spotted, near the top of the craft and inverted from his own perspective, a long rip in the hull of the ship.

Without a second thought, he pushed off. His heart raced as he drifted at a fraction of a meter per second toward the opening. The gash looked as if the ship had pulled against the heavy metal support of the orbital fleet ship after the support pierced the smaller ship's side. Baxel cautiously pulled himself in along the support enough to stick his head through. He glanced around with the lights of his helmet on and was left breathless.

The dead exterior of the ship was a stark contrast to the various system lights and slow pulsings of caution warnings in the dark interior. Perhaps the most striking of all were the six glass-faced pods glowing gently into the dark of the ship through their coating of ice. Baxel's excitement was interrupted by Tymon's voice in his helmet.

"Baxel," Tymon rattled through, "get back across. Now."

"But there is . . . it is possible this is—"

"We need to pick up the beacons and get back to the inner zones."

"It can wait, Tymon." Baxel glanced at his oxygen. "You'll never believe what we found."

"It doesn't matter. Safe Harbor has called for an all-return. On open broadcast."

Baxel let out a breath. Forcing himself to leave the cryopods behind, he edged his way back out of the ship and looked up and into the distance, where Tymon had turned on his own helmet lights. Baxel gave him a questioning look, though his expression did not matter without sharing his facial sensor data. "What is going on? Why would they signal a return?" He tapped his helmet and kicked off through the twist of steel. Once he hit open space, he gave another pulse of his leg jets for good measure.

"Bad news for us, at least. I don't know about Safe Harbor."

"I hear you," Baxel replied. He made a quick check of his reserve before he kicked on another burst of thrust. "Oxygen, forty-seven and inbound."

"Oxygen, sixty percent."

Several minutes later, Baxel used a few twisted grates and split rails to pull himself along behind Tymon as they entered a tighter stretch within the orbital wreckage. The number of gravitational fields increased as they moved farther into the wreckage, each pulling at different directions and with varying intensities. It took a series of strong pulses from their suits to counteract a gradient as they neared a dangerous and ripped entrance to a hallway.

When they passed the threshold of sharp edges, Tymon released his suit and dropped down to the surface below. Baxel followed, touching his boots to the downward face of the hall without the need for the magnetic locks. He rolled his shoulders to help transition his perception; for the next twenty yards, they would have a set direction to call down.

Tymon crouched and unclipped the small navigation beacon from the floor. As the blue rings of light disappeared, Baxel's own display made a small sound to notify him that a signal had dropped off. Oftentimes, exploration teams would leave their beacons to return to the same place on their next outing.

"Perhaps we can actually leave the trail next time," Baxel said as Tymon put the beacon into a pouch.

"And play within the search coordinates?" Tymon teased, although an odd mix of additional sound in the transmission made it difficult to understand. When Tymon stopped speaking, the jittering audio continued.

Baxel hit a fist against the side of his helmet, but the loud click and impact did not stop the noise. "Is that Flerin?"

Tymon looked above them, past the deformed steel jammed through and pressing against the cracked window of the hallway. "Some of these fields may be disrupting Flerin's signal."

Baxel's exterior visor dimmed as Tymon glanced past him with his helmet lights.

Tymon tapped his data pad against his open hand. "Damn, I wish I knew how to clear it up. You think Flerin is trying to tell us something about Safe Harbor's open signal? About the all-return?"

"Only one way to find out." Baxel took the lead, and they started through the interior passages at a redoubled pace. It was nearly fifteen minutes of clawing and kicking their way through passages with varying gravitational forces before Tymon picked up their final navigation beacon.

As they left the last artificial gravity zone behind them, the distant lights of the first Remnant colony came into view. The habitats were shored-off structures set deep into either side of the split that ran the length of the massive orbital ship known in the logs as the *Firmament*. The orbital ship had supposedly carried millions of people up from the planet, though now it held the entirety of Safe Harbor and the majority of the population of the fleet. The ruins of a smaller ship, the mile-long *Fortuna*, acted as the center of the colony and was anchored into the widest part of the split in the *Firmament*.

"Where is everybody?" Tymon asked. "Do you see any returning shuttles?"

Baxel blinked to no avail and studied the area hard with one eye. Normally there were the blue lights from repulsors traveling from one entrance to another as people were shuttled between the separate habitat zones. As Baxel and Tymon passed through the actual border of Safe Harbor, several orange lights along their arms powered on as part of the automated precautions to avoid collisions. Baxel then realized that there were also no other Remnants making their way about in suits. The all-return was already in effect.

"Try and get ahold of Flerin," Tymon said.

"Screw that! He's going to be unbelievably—"

"Bax," Tymon interrupted, "I want to know if we are floating into a trap."

Baxel tried to look over his shoulder, though he could not immediately tell where Tymon was. "All of Safe Harbor a trap?"

"It has been evacuated before."

Baxel shook his head.

It was then that a transmission broke through, and this time it was very clear. "Team Firebrand, respond. I repeat, exploration team Firebrand, respond. I swear, if you make us send out another damned signal to the entire damned fleet . . ." Flerin, their coordinator, trailed off and finally let up on his transmission. Baxel held a hand up to his helmet, since he was the one with the undamaged comms system.

"This is Firebrand Two, responding."

"Baxel, you and Tymon . . . just report to the Hall of the Warden as soon as you can. I'll send you which barrier to meet me at."

"Wait, what has happened?" Baxel asked as a location popped up on his helmet display. It was one of the airlocks to the central vessel. "Why not return to the SE-S?" Baxel asked. The Outset Protocol passed down for centuries by the Warden's Vigil required any long-range expedition to return to the barrier of their departure. In normal circumstances, Flerin would meticulously check over their systems before letting them reenter the airlock of the SE-S; the Search and Exploration Sector.

"Dimarka has died. The initial call went out several hours ago for an all-return. The dignitary is getting a full send-off."

"Hours?" Baxel asked. He could nearly feel Tymon's glare burning a hole in the back of his helmet as he slipped up.

Flerin let out a breath, likely to keep in his pent-up curses. "Just get to the hall. Everyone is waiting on me to account for your return. You've already caused enough trouble forcing me to blast a distress signal to the fleet. The scavengers will take notice, and now the exploration teams will have to . . ." They both received a ping informing them that their search coordinator had terminated the connection. Somehow, his anger resonated more than the pleasant tone of the end notification.

It put a nervous urgency into things when over twelve thousand people were waiting on you to get back to the rest of their wake cycle. Actually, with the importance of Dimarka to the Remnants, it was possible everyone else in the sectors had been awakened to observe his departure. There were very few in Safe Harbor that could claim his level of influence, and fewer still his accomplishments. The old man's careful plans were the only reason Habitat Three had regained partial functionality through intensive reconstruction. Baxel had grown up watching layers open up and new families move in from the overcrowded Habitat Two because of Dimarka's foresight.

"I bet this has got the Vigil standing stiff," Tymon said. His orange lights sped ahead of Baxel.

"Why is that?" Baxel asked.

"Because they might actually have to think about the conversation of expansion."

It was not just an expansion of the search coordinates that Tymon was speaking about; the coordinators changed the search coordinates for their teams relatively often. It was a simple matter of adjusting the Safe Harbor communication relays to enable clear communication with the search teams in different areas. But when compared to the wide ranges of the orbiting wreckage, the search coordinates only encapsulated a small portion of the entire fleet. Now, realizing that Safe Harbor would no longer be bullied by Dimarka into sticking to their traditional ways, Tymon was thinking of an expansion of their population itself. It had been over four hundred years since their people had made a home anywhere other than Safe Harbor, and Baxel and Tymon knew there was an entire fleet waiting out there.

"You don't really think they will allow expansion farther into the fleet, do you?" Baxel asked. "Dimarka always said taking more than the Warden gave us was the same as betrayal."

Tymon paused a moment. "But he's not here anymore to press that point, is he?"

"Suppose not."

Dimarka's argument was for the sake of preserving resources for future generations. However, even with all the destruction from the initial wreckage, there could be vast stores of resources yet untouched in the fleet beyond the horizon. Just before he started to make that comment to Tymon, Baxel had a thought a little closer to home. "You think the reconstruction will continue? I mean, in the years to come. Will Habitat Three ever be finished if we decide to look farther?"

Tymon paused as if shaking his head as they continued floating through the zero-space, the area of space between the sectors of Safe Harbor where the coordinates of Safe Harbor's navigation and search grid were near the center of origin, zero. "What are you asking me for? That's something not even the next Warden could know, let alone the Vigil."

Baxel said nothing in reply as warnings in his suit began sounding off. With the extra push to get them to the hall, his oxygen had finally dropped into the single digits. He knew he still had minutes left, though the usable concentration would continue to degrade once it dropped below zero. With luck, Flerin would be too rushed to check their systems.

Tymon's voice rattled, "I have a connection with the habitat barrier. Still getting a slight gravitational pull, but your momentum should carry you through."

Each of the airlocks had a system in place to counteract the gravitational fields of Safe Harbor, though very few of them could be kept perfectly balanced. As he drifted toward the open outer doors of the airlock, Baxel felt the slight change in direction. He set a foot forward, just to make sure he would catch the edge of the platform. Tymon pushed a hand into his chest to help stop his momentum once inside. Tymon then tapped his helmet, and the outer doors closed.

As air filled the chamber, a readout on the sidewall showed the oxygen levels increasing. It was only a couple of points off from his own external sensors. Baxel set two hands on his helmet and removed it when the pressure hit around 70 percent. He couldn't stand to wait any longer to wipe the sweat from his face with the back of a glove. He then gripped his gloved fingers below his eyes and along the bridge of his nose and pulled down the inner face mask. After a moment, his helmet pulled down against his other hand with an increasing weight as the gravity fields readjusted.

The interior doors opened a few seconds early, causing a gust of air to flow in. Their search coordinator, Flerin Arterrus, stood on the other side with his arms crossed sternly over an abnormally formal outfit. The gathering of their people called for an air of formality, but the uncomfortable fit of the button-up uniform was apparently all the formality Flerin would stand for; he still had the dark shadow of a second-day's stubble.

Next to him and standing a few inches taller was Coordinator Reyson, who looked entirely too pleased with himself over their late arrival. Reyson was the coordinator for another team that was always in competition or at odds with Firebrand. Behind the both of them was a small crowd who had gathered as part of the all-return. An uncomfortable number of the people were looking their way, appearing irritated at the wait.

"You two alive?" Flerin asked.

Baxel glanced to the side as Tymon pulled down his own inner face mask. Baxel experienced an echo of his earlier worry. Normally, the systems of their suits would be checked meticulously before they were even let out of the airlock. After that, an inspection of the exterior surfaces of the suits for chemicals and hazardous materials and several tests of the various suit sensors and releases were mandatory for the long-range teams such as themselves.

"Two of two for Firebrand," Tymon said with a shrug.

Flerin flicked a hand up to the thin wire that wrapped around over one brow. Baxel could see the projection shift over his eye as he put their return into the system.

"Stay within the *Fortuna*," Flerin growled, "and keep quiet." At that, he glared at Coordinator Reyson before striding away through the thin crowd.

"We're all glad for your return," Coordinator Reyson said with a smile formed entirely wrong for sincerity. He turned to follow Flerin without a second glance back.

It took Baxel and Tymon several moments before they finally stepped away from the airlock barrier and into the larger room. They both tried to avoid eye contact with the closest individuals, though there was no avoiding the agitated tone of the murmurs going around.

"What do you think about going to the Trade Sector?" Baxel said, leaning over to Tymon as they continued through.

"You don't think it will be shut down as well? Come on, we'll find someplace here to lie low."

Baxel shrugged and followed. Even though most of the furnishings had been stripped down, if not removed altogether, their remains were still evidence that the *Fortuna* was once a passenger transport ship. It explained the many airlocks lining the sides with seemingly no other possible purpose than shuttling passengers in and out.

Tymon led the way through an opening reinforced with assorted steel pieces; the actual door had been repurposed elsewhere. They stepped into a long hall, finding it empty of all but a few people talking amongst themselves. Flerin was nowhere to be seen, most likely having moved farther toward the center of the ship via one of the other openings down the length of the hall. Tymon led the way to their right. So long as they were stuck in the *Fortuna*, Baxel was glad they were not simply going to stare at the same walls.

"Might as well set your suit to refill," Tymon suggested as they walked past a shut and sealed door. The patchwork of welding sealing the door and keeping them separated from the vacuum of space barely influenced Baxel's agreement. They'd lived in similar conditions for as many cycles as they could remember. If there were open arcs of electricity, it was common knowledge to not touch them. If one's hair and clothing pulled at a pressure difference, a quick report to the Maintenance Sector would get it fixed, or the section would be closed off if it was not necessary to the functioning of Safe Harbor.

Baxel tapped at the pad on his arm, causing a hum on the top side of his shoulder as the surrounding air was compressed into his reserves.

The path veered to the side through a cut-out part of the wall, as the original hallway dead-ended at a destroyed section. A few steps had been added to get up to the level of the next passage, where long pipes ran both below the grating underfoot as well as along the walls. Baxel tapped the back of his glove on one of the larger pipes, causing a hollow ting. It was possible that some of the pipes had been repurposed for moving water about the various sectors in the ship, though the one he had tapped sounded unused. It was likely on the list should another sector need a pipe for repairs or construction.

A small door to the left was open. Because the controls had been stripped out, the door was jammed halfway open by a welded band across one corner. They could hear voices from that direction and edged through the gap. This room looked as if it had once been joint quarters, but now the stacks of crates in the bed racks touted it as storage. They stepped out into another hall and found a small group of people watching a flickering holographic display.

"—the passing of loyal Dimarka, and may the Warden's guidance reach us all. Forever shall the effects of his actions be felt within Safe Harbor, and—" the voice of one of the high-ranking Vigil priests continued.

Over the shoulders of the few people watching the display, Baxel could see that the Hall of the Warden itself was filled with hundreds for the offsending. He had never seen a gathering so big. Near the front was a line of Vigil, each with their uniform and white band hanging over one shoulder to touch the floor in the front and back. Baxel started to look closer to see if he could make out any faces, but Tymon nudged him with an elbow.

"Bax, let's keep on."

A few of the people glanced back, but only the two playing a data pad game gave them a second round of attention. "Exploration team," one of the stock workers said, "am I right? I heard your sector had something to do with the wait."

"Yeah," Baxel said. "Something like that. We are—"

Tymon motioned with his helmet in hand to keep moving, and Baxel started to obey. Even though this batch did not look entirely aggravated by the extended break, Baxel knew it would be best to keep their names from being talked about any more than they already would be.

"You're welcome to watch here," the man said with a motion to the display on the wall. "Or the Hall of the Warden is that way," he said, now motioning to one of the other rooms along the passage.

Tymon all but pulled Baxel through into the small room the man had motioned to. The back wall had been cut out of the room, leading to a temporary walkway made over the top of a huge storage room. Here, some larger containers of supplies were kept, though storage was hardly the specialty of the *Fortuna*, since the Food Storage and Supply Sector was located within the main structure of the larger orbital ship.

Baxel and Tymon received passing glances from the shipping workers down below as they made their way over the room. Many of the workers were just sitting on top of or against the transports, waiting for the order to stay inside the habitat barriers to be lifted.

As they made their way through the haphazard halls of the sector, the paths began to clear out into the more organized original passages of the vessel. Displays began to show the way to various sections of the ship, though just below them were the written names of what they were actually called now. Baxel motioned as one projected display read *"Hangar 01."* Below it, painted onto a section of heavy plastic wired to a bent rod, were the words *"Hall of the Warden."*

* * *

Flerin Arterrus used his rag to wipe at his forehead again as he finally made it to his place in the crowd while the Head Vigil continued speaking. Flerin stood three rows back in the center, which on most offsendings would just have started into any heads of the various sectors in attendance, with the family in front. But seeing as Dimarka had no remaining family of his own, the first rows were filled with those most influential to his life, which also meant the most influential to Safe Harbor—the heads of the sectors. The likes of Nendra Halimuth, head of the Production and Research Sector, Dannil Wardenson, head of Safe Harbor's Transmission Sector, and many others all stood in the forward rows. The only exceptions to the formality were a few of the oldest leaders who had brought their own seats. They, along with Dimarka, were born in Safe Harbor before the attack.

"Now," Algan Treys, the Head Vigil, said from the front of the room, "we will perform the final step before Dimarka is taken from the hall for his offsending." He adjusted one of the two white sashes that rested over either shoulder. "The Warden's Rite, as she herself used and as was passed down through our generations." The old Vigil clasped his shaking hands and looked to the side. "Nendra, you have prepared?"

The woman moved forward and took Algan's place at the head of the container holding Dimarka's body. The leader of the Vigil moved to the opposite end, and they both placed a hand on top of the container. The room fell into complete silence until the Head Vigil spoke, moments later.

"Speak of his name."

Nendra turned to face Dimarka, but spoke loud enough so that most of the hundreds in attendance could hear. "Dimarka. His forename abandoned to honor the end of his lineage."

It was a sad business. Flerin ducked his head. After Sarthyl betrayed their people years ago, many families had all but ended. If there was to be no continuation of a line, the last member took the family name as their one and only title.

"Speak of his heart."

"Wounded," Nendra said. There was a stiffness in the air that Flerin knew everyone else could feel. "Wounded, and repenting for a loss shared by many."

"Speak of his actions."

"The rebuilding of Safe Harbor. The reconstruction of the habitat sectors."

Flerin had been too young to remember, but Sarthyl had attacked the habitat sectors first. Dimarka had spent his life since then trying to repair them, though it would still be many years before the reconstruction was complete, and many more before their population could regrow to fill the original, abandoned sections.

"Speak of his cause."

"Loyalty to the Warden and to those of the fleet."

In particular, Dimarka held on to the idea that Safe Harbor had been given to them by the Warden to preserve the resources within the rest of the orbital fleet. Flerin, as a coordinator and past member of an exploration team, understood that everything the Remnants found was limited. In his younger years, he had seen areas all but cleaned of anything useful to Safe Harbor. He himself had found immense, unruptured oxygen stores in the depths of the wreckage that, after years of use from Safe Harbor, had become empty clusters of long tanks in the dark. Dimarka wanted the Remnants to survive as long as they could with the resources they had around Safe Harbor out of fear of overexpanding and burning through the resources of the fleet like a cascading electrical fire.

"Speak of his legacy."

"In place of his family, he took the Remnants, the fleet, and Safe Harbor."

Algan paused to let the thought sink in. A legacy left for Safe Harbor was not usually a material gift or the teachings of the deceased— it was normally the deceased's family. In the case of Dimarka, everything he had worked to leave behind was for everyone still alive, as they had replaced his family as his lasting legacy.

"Speak of his memory."

"Stubborn," Nendra said. She gave a small smile at that. "Well needed, to deal with all of us." There were scattered chuckles and a fair share of humored nods passed around by those who had often butted heads with the old man. While the Vigil took the same stance as Dimarka, saying it was the Warden's wish that they stay well within Safe Harbor, many knew that the loudest voice on the matter was Dimarka's.

"Speak as he would wish."

Any levity in the air was crushed by the tension. If there was to be trouble and bad blood in the offsending, this was the moment. While Dimarka had been overbearing enough to keep most everyone working on his project of repairing the habitats, he and Nendra had often been at each other's throats regarding the prospect of pulling in more resources. Now, she had been asked to speak on his behalf.

"Never stop rebuilding Safe Harbor," Nendra said.

Flerin noticed a few glances exchanged by the other Vigil in attendance. Though she said his words, by her tone it appeared Nendra would not be easing up on the issue. It would leave the Vigil needing to impose the Warden's will, one way or the other. Flerin shook his head like many others, knowing that it was going to be a mess before it got better.

Algan held a hand up and cleared his throat to reclaim the attention of all in attendance. "And finally, speak on our behalf."

"May the Dimarka line forever live on in the memory of the Warden." Nendra and Algan pulled their hands from the container. "And may grief never find you in the arms of space."

Chapter 2: Sky Flare

The shuffling of steps echoed through the dark under-levels of Norclave. The pace of the steps was cautious, and the figure paused at the merging of walkways, just on the edge of one of the few lights still left this deep. Allek Skaves acted as if he knew he was being followed, but that knowledge could only have come from the fear of his own circumstances; Kara knew she had given no sign of her presence.

The tech hunter crouched low to avoid being silhouetted as the man looked over his shoulder as he crossed under the dim light. She could see the beady reflection of sweat hanging onto the man's forehead. His eyes flicked rapidly against the dark. He had good reason to be afraid, coming to the lower levels alone to join the last pieces of a group that had already failed to seize the city. And perhaps more troubling for Allek Skaves was that he had attracted the attention of the Cryo of Norclave herself. Kara was sure she could go on, but it wasn't his fate she was worried about; she really only care about where Allek Skaves was headed.

"Please, sir," a weak voice said from just ahead. Kara frowned as her target turned his dim light on an old man sitting along the walkway. She cursed under her breath as she watched a third man in heavy rags stand up behind Allek. The lowlife was raising a jagged piece of railing over his head.

"Just a few tokens and I could . . ." the first continued.

Without waiting for the end of the sentence, Allek suddenly took off running down the walkway. Kara pushed herself up and started forward as quickly and quietly as she could manage on the rusty grating.

"All you had to do was hit him!" the first of the two shouted.

"You were supposed to keep him there!"

Things had turned grim in the back alleys of Norclave since Olana Nuand seized control. Many of the more vocal supporters of the Overlord or the administrators were stripped of their possessions, and many of the mercenaries who had rallied during the revolution were now forced to scrounge for a living. The situation had led to an influx of low-level criminals and a large sum of outcast individuals simply trying to stay out of Nuand-patrolled streets. Areas that Kenneth had told her were originally uninhabited due to the swarms of rubble mites now contained a surprising number of inhabitants. Things had only gotten worse as the continuing raids by Nuand filled the cells and aided in the influx of more of the nipping insects.

The last of the noise from the beggars faded away as she followed her target around several more corners. She knew he was lost, but all she could do was stay close until he eventually found his way. The man took another sudden turn, steering away from a stretch of wider path lit by checkered moonlight. Nearly twenty people were sitting along the edges of the large area. She followed him, always making sure to keep the pace of his footsteps at the forefront of her attention. He would probably keel over in fright if she ran into him.

Kara stopped as he met another intersection and paused. The ceiling there was lower, and looked like the underside of a large container. It was likely a storage building on the second level. Kenneth would know exactly where they were, but her own guess was that the man was getting closer to where he was going. If she were to advise him, she would tell him to find a small flight of stairs and go up. At this hour, very few of Norclave's soldiers would be patrolling the streets.

A small area in front of the man lit up as he looked at his data pad again. Kara ducked under one of the railings and stepped onto a supporting strut off to the side. The man spun a few circles as if trying to find his direction, then took off at a jog back the way they had come. Kara held her breath as the light passed over her, but thankfully he was too absorbed with his data pad to notice another shape in the dark.

Once she was sure he had his direction, she slipped up onto the rail and tailed him back. Her eyes narrowed as he turned another corner. He was making his way straight through the gathering of people. Anyone could alert him of her presence, and if he saw he had a tracker, odds were that he would abandon his meeting with the remaining administrators from the Norclave rebellion.

"Keep moving!" one of the people sitting on the floor growled to her target. "I don't need any more freerunners trying for my meal packs."

Kara was forced to start along a different alley as her target pushed through the square. She moved quickly and with a touch less caution as she hurried to intercept his trail again. It bit at her to let Allek out of her sight, but she could not risk anyone noticing that she was following him—especially when she was worried that someone in the group of people would be looking for him as well.

Her boots scraped across the grating as she hurried past a few scattered pairs of people. Her attention was diverted momentarily as she brushed past a father, who pulled his two sleeping children in closer. Kara shook her head in disgust at their situation. Jance had a hell of a lot more work to do to set Norclave back on its feet.

She slowed to a stop and glanced around a corner, then spotted the familiar glow of the data pad. When it started off again, Kara ducked low and made her way forward through the dust-filled shafts of moonlight. The beams were uneven here, filtered through multiple layers of pipes and hanging cables. She froze in place as three other figures crossed an intersection between her and Allek and hoped that if they did look her way, they'd mistake her for another lost soul hiding in the night.

Kara stood up to move again just as a shout sounded from around the corner. She had her shocklance out in an instant, knowing what was about to happen, though after a moment's hesitation she kept from charging it up. The crackling of electricity would give her away in the dark, and that was a risk she could not make herself take, even though she knew Allek was now someone else's target.

Kara cautiously slipped up to the next corner. As she looked around the bend, the long hall lit up with a bright flash of orange. The deep punch of the pulse cannon was drowned out by a loud scream.

"Get the data pad!" one of the attackers shouted.

In their lights, Kara could make out Allek lying on the walkway. He weakly kicked against the grating with a heel and pulled himself toward the edge of the walkway with one elbow. Just as one of the three men rushed forward, she saw the flick of the data pad being tossed off the walkway. Kara looked under the walkway and watched as the glowing light of the pad bounced off another level ten feet below, then dropped down out of the under-levels of the city.

"What was on it?" the first man to reach Allek yelled. The man's hair was cut short enough that the many scars across his head were visible in the others' lights. He pressed the heated metal at the end of his pulse cannon against Allek's shoulder, causing another groan of pain and a sharp hiss. "What were you sending to the administrators, Skavely?"

Her target let out a rough, fluid-filled cough. "This is our rebellion. Stay out of . . . the way."

"You lost your chance as soon as the Nuands moved in!" The heated the inner coils cast a warm light on Allek's face as the brute leveled the weapon to finish him off.

The leader of the three stepped forward. "Enough!" he shouted. He was a thinner man with jet-black hair and a dark tint to his skin. At first glance, he did not seem to fit the mold of the common thugs; there was something deeper about him that she could not quite place.

The scarred, nearly bald man gripped the weapon with a rage eager to boil over. "They caused this. Their attempt at overthrowing the Overlord . . ."

"He is dead. Leave him be," the leader ordered. It was just enough to get the man to lower his weapon. "Go back and tell Travend to have the others search the scavengers on the lower levels for a fallen data pad."

The brute lowered the pulse cannon and gave Allek one final kick in the ribs before storming off toward Kara. She climbed down farther, resting her feet on a small pipe that was dripping water onto another walkway below.

"You really think we can get it back?" a third voice asked quietly as the brute walked over her.

"If nobody leaks that we are looking for it? Then possibly," the leader of the group replied. "Otherwise, the scavengers will start stealing any piece of scrap they could think to scam us with."

Kara shook her head. Years before, she had hunted for and traded tech, hoping it would be enough for her next meal pack. But she couldn't imagine how different things would be now. For about as long as she could remember, the strategy of selling veritable scrap as tech had worked on the Overlord, but that line of trade had died with him. She never would have thought at that point in time, holding a handful of broken wires and a few pieces of melted plastic, that one day her greatest find would set into motion all the chaos now in Norclave. She pulled herself up onto the walkway and pushed old thoughts to the side. Right now, she was hunting for any new information available. As the others left the area, she started toward Allek Skaves.

"You still alive?" Kara asked, stepping closer. She did not need to roll the man over to know that the superheated discharge from the pulse cannon would have burned a hole into his back.

"Who . . . are you?" Allek asked, pushing through the bubbling in his speech.

Kara took out a tube of medi-seal and held it where he could see. She had no plan to use it on him—no amount of it would do any good—but it was the easiest way to convince him she was trying to help.

"I'm with the administrators," Kara lied. "Can you tell me what information you were trying to get to us?"

The man looked confused. "You don't . . ." he said, glancing back at the medi-seal before giving Kara a fearful look. "Information. From the inside . . . too many plans. Too many sides."

Kara looked over her shoulder as the loud echoes of somebody running reached her. "What kind of information?"

"Conversation. The Cryo. Nuand. Norton needs to . . ." He coughed weakly. It was full of a secondary noise, and he did not continue his explanation.

He was starting to slip away, and Kara knew she had no more time to stay with him. She produced a small silver square from a pocket with the same double cross marking as the medi-seal. She held it to the side of his head, and the device emitted a harmless pulse that caused his eyes to roll back as he slipped into a coma. Anyone else would have woken after a time, but he would be spent before then. It was all she could do to help, and it would also keep him from giving her away.

Just as another round of lights and shouts from a Nuand patrol flooded the hall, Kara was rounding the next corner. She cursed at her own failure before slowing to disappear into the rusted folds of Norclave.

* * *

A wandering haze reached up from the surrounding forest as the orange glow of the sun filtered through the thick air. The morning winds scraped across the hundreds of abandoned spires to the south, bringing streams of dust high over the forests and an uncomfortable twinge to each breath. Through the tangle of the city, Kara could hear the puttering rumble of a transport taking off at first light. Olana Nuand had placed a strict policy against any usage of the docks during the night in a vain attempt to stifle the underground movements in Norclave.

Kara rubbed her eyes and glanced around. She had spent the rest of the night tucked away on a large cross-running support beam on the back side of a row of container houses. She was toward the edge of the city facing south, far from the rubble mites, the conflicts of the rebellious groups, criminal movements, and the overlook of the interior of the starscraper. Kara tucked a segment of her red hair back into her hood and placed the shocklance back against its magnetic plate on her thigh.

She stood up as another transport fired up its repulsors on the landing pad just above her. As she climbed up onto the streets, she noted that she was amongst the first wave of people up and about this close to the docks. Transport pilots were looking for an early start at running supplies, and the scowls on their faces showed that they had likely been awake for hours, waiting for the restrictions to lift with the sun. And odds were that they had an empty haul while heading out, as Norclave was hungry for all the supplies it could get.

As Kara moved farther in toward the heart of the city, the activity in the streets shifted toward smaller merchants moving armloads of supplies toward their temporary stalls in the trade center. By the way two women carrying sacks of clothing over their shoulders greeted each other, Kara could tell the routine of bringing their wares to the center had existed for years. After all, unless you were someone who owned a building near the trade center, your unprotected goods would be lost to the night.

The soldiers at their morning posts gave Kara suspicious looks as she passed. Tech hunters like herself had never been completely trusted by most people, and she knew the Kamriek mercenaries had been given orders to watch for anyone who might stir up trouble.

While the Norclave soldiers were allowed to keep their gear, along with the signifying diagonal red stripe crossing their chest, they had no authority. Each group of Norclave soldiers was led by one of Olana's followers, evident by a shoulder piece made of wraith steel. The amber-colored material was laced on the inside with a grid of solar-absorbing tech and had once made up the massive windows of the starscrapers. The large deposit on the north face of the starscraper served as the center of the economy of Kamriek's Grove.

Kara stepped out into one of the upper levels of the trade center and looked down through the war-torn walkways crossing the center. There had been heavy fighting on this level when the administrators tried to take over the city, but it was still nothing like the seventh level. Jance had workers repairing the walkways through the middle of the trade center, though there were a few walkways that had been so torn up that they would have to be dismantled. Just the day before, the workers had finally stopped the broken heap of a transport resting on one of the inner docks from smoking, though the remains had yet to be sent down to the scrapsmiths.

Norclave was a mess in more ways than one. There was no denying that. Even though Kenneth had told her that he would follow wherever she went, her gut was still telling her to stay in Norclave. Not that it was entirely appealing, but with Jance trying to keep the peace and Kenneth doing his part by fixing transports, staying seemed her best option. She tugged on a corner of her hood as she stepped past a merchant trying to sell her something before he even had his stand completely set up.

The rest of her journey up to the seventh level was uneventful, thanks in no small part to the paths she took. She stayed out of the main streets but also avoided the potential dangers of the narrowest paths.

The black grime that clung against the buildings of the seventh level was evidence of the explosion that had happened on the far side, and many of the houses—large salvaged cargo containers—were riddled with holes. Other storehouses, built with arrays of rusty, cracked, and dented panels, were simply opened up like canisters. The walkways were uneven in places where heavy chunks of the buildings had fallen onto the streets.

The one thing the level still had going for it was the lack of confinement. Instead of being trapped in the heart of the unplanned mess of Norclave, the sky was nearly open. The only boundary above was the shell of the fallen starscraper Norclave was built into the side of, but as it was easily hundreds of feet to the nearest section of the structure, the only effect the shell had was to temporarily block the sun for parts of the day.

Kara was finally stopped as she started up the large steps leading to what was once the Overlord's complex. Whether the large structure of plates mixed with containers continued to be called the Overlord's complex or not would ultimately be determined by whether Olana decided to assume the title of Overlord.

"Hold there, tech hunter." The soldiers guarding the main entrance all had the starscraper glass shoulder plate, but also varying pieces of flight armor that had been ground down to a rough shine. Each held a spear with some sort of tech at the top. A quick glance told Kara that with the batteries hooked to them, the spear points would provide quite the jolt.

"I am here to speak with Ambassador Lorège," Kara said. She partially wanted to see if they would recognize Jance by her title instead of only as "the Cryo."

The man started to hold a finger up to his visor to ask for her clearance, but his motion was interrupted by a woman stepping out of the entrance. She had dark hair and a bright smile.

"No need for all of that," Sora said. Instead of her usual overly burdensome bag of data pads and other storage devices from the Norclave Library, the archivist simply had a smaller bag on a sling over her shoulder. It appeared to be quite full, however. "This one is permitted at any time."

The man stepped to the side, and Sora motioned with a smile for Kara to follow her.

"I'm sorry for the inconvenience," Sora said as she led the way through the drab hallways. The only accents were the lights bolted onto the steel, the bullet holes, and patches of retempered metal from errant repulsor shots. Kara could still make out dark lines in the edges that most others would miss. She guessed the blood had not been easy to clean away.

Sora continued, "While I agree that there is reason for the extra caution, it is still quite the hassle that Olana has given so little trust to the soldiers that actually know the people of Norclave. I feel like I am explaining everything to every one of her underlings."

Kara glanced cautiously at the soldiers as they passed another checkpoint within the building. Sora waved at the only Norclave soldier in the group.

"I see no difference," Kara said. "It's the same for me as when I brought information to the Overlord in the first place."

Sora rolled her shoulder as she pulled a bit of her dark hair out from under the strap of the bag. "I almost keep forgetting you are not part of the city, especially with all you have done for us." When Kara said nothing in reply, Sora continued like there was no pause, "I suppose if we can wake up a Cryo from six hundred years ago and give her near the highest position in Norclave, we could just as well make room for a tech hunter."

"I'm not sure who is more out of place."

Sora gave a quiet laugh. "Nobody has said you have to stay. If I recall correctly, you were the one who offered to play tracker." Sora was referring to the night before, when Jance had spoken to Kenneth, trying to learn more about who she could trust. The man she had tracked down, Allek Skaves, appeared to have adjusted some records to place himself higher within the ranks of officials during the transfer over to Olana. But Jance had found some suspicious inconsistencies in Allek Skaves' records in her accounting of personnel.

Jance was being very thorough as she installed the regime of Olana Nuand over the existing Norclave structure. It was more work than Kara would have ever agreed to, managing that many people, but the number of profiles to manage did drop when you considered how many of the old Norclave administrators had been killed in their failed attempt to overthrow Overlord Obrourke in the first place. Of course, it was Kenneth and Kara that had ended up chasing down and killing the Overlord to save Jance, though Nuand was continuing the purging of the administrators from Norclave.

Kara followed Sora around a corner and through a room being stacked full of crates. She was surprised to see several plants growing out of dirt held in the lids torn from meal packs.

"Jance told me about the floral displays they used to have in the starscrapers," Sora explained. "I thought maybe just a touch of home would help her continue her work."

Kara said nothing. The gesture was kind, but Jance was not just homesick. She had stood in the same starscraper that Norclave was built into when it was still being used as the Council Building for the United World Coalition. If anything, Jance would be longing for a world that had been destroyed in every way, and reminders of that destruction would always be around her.

Sora led the way past another pair of guards at a heavy door and into a large room. Kara had been here once before, when meeting with the Overlord. The walls of the Norclave Library were lined with shelves piled full of data pads and other scraps of tech that had information on them. Much of the light in the room came from hundreds of devices and the many terminals throughout. Many of the larger pieces of tech had been raided during or after the fighting.

Toward the back of the room, a table of the highest luxury had been set up. It was a sleek white with a trim of blue light that emitted a decorative glow beneath it. The table hovered above the distortion base at whatever height the user designated. With the projected screens stabilized midair, and without so much as a hint of distortion, the table itself was a testament that some pieces of the world had survived unscathed. However, the grand display was still nothing compared to the woman who sat behind the desk. Jance Lorège had been forced into cryostasis just before the world tore itself apart, and though she looked like a woman in her thirties, she was actually nearing six hundred years of age.

"There you are, Kara," Jance said, swiping a few of the projections out of her way and shifting her visor back to display over one eye. "Have a seat, if you wish." Jance motioned to one of the chairs in front of the floating desk. They had the simple look that came with being made in Norclave.

"Where is Kenneth?" Kara asked, glancing about the room. These days, when he was not working under a transport he was often here.

Sora turned a seat to face Kara and Jance and sat down. "He should be here shortly."

Jance gave Kara a concerned look. "Is everything all right? How did tracking Allek go?"

Kara looked to the side. "I should never have gone. Allek Skaves is dead. The resistance got to him first, and the data pad he was using dropped out of the city."

Jance looked at her as if searching for more answers. "Did anyone see you?"

Kara shook her head. "Nobody that matters."

"Then you did as well as you could," Jance said, still leaning forward. "Tell me more."

Kara unclenched her jaw and took a step forward. "I should have stepped in! It was my fault. I knew what was going to happen, and I just . . ."

Jance stood up and gave Kara a reassuring look. "We cannot change the past, no matter how long we try to do so." She slid her hand along the edge of the table in thought. "Our work is here. Tell me about what happened."

"There were three men. I could pick their voices out if I heard them again. They had to have been waiting for him, for Allek, to pass by."

"Did you catch any names?" Jance asked.

Kara paused a moment as she thought. "One referred to Skaves as Skavely. I think they knew each other, though there was no friendship. And later, the leader told him to go back and tell someone named Travend to have the others search the scavengers for the data pad."

"Travend?" Jance asked. When Kara did not appear to have an answer, she turned to Sora. "Do you know this name?"

Sora pulled in a breath. "There is nobody that I know of that worked for the Overlord with that name." She motioned back toward one of the terminals. "I can check in the records, or ask around Norclave."

Kara shook her head. "If you start asking, he will run."

"I will bring it to the attention of Olana," Jance said. "Perhaps we can get more eyes looking for movement when we decide to spread the word that we're looking for him." Jance touched a finger up to her visor in a motion far more natural than anyone else Kara had seen trying to use the things. The door to the room slid open as Jance gave the signal.

Kara turned and felt a slight pull in her breathing as Kenneth entered the room. She tried to hide her attachment to the man with the others in the room, but she still found her heel lifted off the ground, ready to take a step toward him. Sometime in the night, he had shaved away the course stubble from his jaw and washed the nearly ever-present grime that clung up to his elbows. She had to admit—only to herself, however—that she still felt an urge to wrap herself in those arms when he gave her a smile.

When she noticed the strip of cloth with the slight stain of dried blood tied around his knuckles, she gritted her teeth. If he had been forced into a fight or had been attacked by . . .

Kenneth glanced to his hand and wiggled his fingers. "Punched a transport. Pry bar slipped." He gave her a look up and down. "How are you? Is something wrong?"

"I am fine," she replied. "I . . ." She trailed off, thinking of how to best explain how her night had went without worrying him again. "Norclave is full of complications right now."

Kenneth nodded. "That's an understatement." He brushed his hand down her arm as he made his way to one of the chairs. "The first pieces of the defensive array are nearly ready to bring online. A couple of test shots should be enough to stop the Kessians from pushing against the borders much farther."

Kara moved to stand behind Kenneth and rested a hand on his shoulder while she listened.

"Good," Jance said. "Maybe the touch of security for the city will put Olana at ease."

Kenneth gave a short laugh. "I doubt if anything could do that, but it may help. And things should get moving quicker once the next two caretakers arrive."

Kara smiled as he said caretaker, the new name for the riftwalkers. It was actually the original name for the worker mechs, according to Jance. While Jance had been putting a great deal of effort into learning the local descriptions, Kenneth seemed determined to mess her up by using the original names.

"Just make sure to keep Olana from putting weapons on them," Jance said. "Caretakers work best with both arms free for lifting."

"I've already stripped the repulsor cannons from the three here in Norclave," Kenneth said. "Luckily, she had not seen them yet."

Without warning, Jance's expression darkened in the blink of an eye. She flicked the visor back across both eyes and started pulling up a number of projections—some she left flat, and others she pulled up from the surface of the desk to hover translucently in the air.

"What is it?" Kara asked.

Jance pushed one of the displays as far forward as the desk would allow and flipped it so that it was the correct direction for her and Kenneth. "Is this a threat?" Jance asked sharply.

The image was a wide view of the top of the starscraper and past the forest of the impact valley. Kenneth leaned forward to get a better look. "Which direction is this?"

"To the east," Kara said. "Toward Reclaim." She recognized the pattern of the broken spires to either side. As they watched what Kara could only describe as a sky flare, the object dropping out of the sky left behind a long and striking trail of red. The object itself was nearly too small to see, though the trail it left was clear. That in itself led Kara away from thinking it was a weapon.

"Can this magnify any further?" Kenneth asked.

Jance tapped the desk and the image shifted. The view had a difficult time tracking the object as it fell. There was a bright flare of blue, and the object disappeared from the projected display. When the camera mounted atop the starscraper found it again, the object had lost an outer layer, and an array of blue spears burned brightly beneath it, slowing its descent.

"That looks like some sort of container, but like nothing I have ever seen," Kenneth said. "You've not seen this before?" he asked Jance. When she shook her head, he asked Sora if she had come across anything in the records. The archivist had seen nothing like it either.

"You do not believe it is a weapon though?" Jance asked.

"Too obvious," Kara said. "And it seems to be slowing down to avoid an impact, though we will see when it touches down."

Jance held her hand up to her visor and started giving a brief report of the situation to Olana. If it landed in the borders of the Rift Hills, Norclave's first priority would be to find out what it was. If it was an object from the wreckage of the Orbital Armistice Fleet, the contents could be invaluable—or at least have enough mystique to allow them to bluff against the other zones.

"That is landing way out," Kenneth said. They watched it fall for a long while before it finally slipped out of view. The massive trail of red dust continued to hang solidly in the air, as though the dust's downward drift came at an unnatural rate.

"That is in Reclaim territory," Kara agreed. "Even if we redirected a transport already in the sky, we would never get to the Steel Valley before them."

"It would start a war if we tried," Kenneth said, glancing to Jance. "Just like the Overlord's hunt for your cryopod."

There was a long moment of silence as they considered the idea of further hostilities. At a time so unstable for Norclave, conflict with the other areas would undoubtedly make things far worse for the people, who were barely managing to survive as it was.

"Unfortunately," Jance said coldly, "that is not our decision. Olana Nuand has taken the Overlord's mantle."

Chapter 3: Silent Preparation

"Alright, so tell me about this thing we found. This ship."

Baxel glanced to the side to make sure nobody was listening to them. After finding the entire Hall of the Warden packed well beyond capacity, he and Tymon had moved into the Hall of the Vigil. When they had arrived, the clean hallways lined with decorations of colorful hanging cloths and projections were entirely empty. Now, groups of returning white-sashed Vigil continued past, though their attention was caught in their own conversations regarding the shift in leadership in Safe Harbor in the wake of Dimarka's death.

Baxel turned his shoulder to shut out any passing looks. There were no hard restrictions against entering the Hall of the Vigil, though Remnants were generally expected to stick to their own sectors unless their service required otherwise.

"We have to go back there," Baxel said, adjusting his inner face mask from where it hung around his neck.

"Okay. Well, we know where it is for when the search coordinates are eventually adjusted."

"No, you don't understand. This is too big to risk not beating team Redemption to it." Baxel leveled a very serious look at Tymon as a large group passed by. "Keep this between us. Only us."

"Okay, Bax, enough with your cryptic hype crap. What was it?"

"A shuttle. Inside were cryopods."

Tymon let out a sigh and replied in monotone, "Oh my, you got me twice now. I cannot believe I fell for that a second time." Tymon narrowed his eyes. "I'd better keep my guard up for when you say you have found the Warden herself!" Tymon bumped Baxel in the shoulder with the helmet in his hand. "Come on, stupid. Let's go find something to eat."

Baxel held his arms out, one hand open and the other holding his helmet, and sent a frustrated look at the back of Tymon's head. He jogged a few steps to catch up. "Hey, listen to me, you cargo mite. I'm serious."

"Cargo mite?" Tymon pulled to a stop and raised an eyebrow at Baxel. About a year ago, they both saw a swarm clinging to the inside of a sealed container after they opened it. The hibernating insects were one of the main reasons the Food Storage and Supply Sector quarantined supplies. While extremely rare, there was no eliminating an infestation when the creatures could simply pop back up from the cracks after centuries of exposure to the vacuum of space.

Baxel grabbed Tymon's shoulder with his free hand and shoved him to a side corridor, away from everyone else. "The way it was trapped in the wreckage—that had to have happened recently. Who knows what we could find in there? And the Vigil will want those pods."

"You're serious? We actually found pods? It's been, what, several centuries since anyone has actually found a pod to bring back in?"

"I'm absolutely serious. At least one was open, but the others looked functional."

"Baxel . . ." Tymon lowered his eyes to the floor before looking back up. "You still know the game. We cannot bring them to the attention of anyone with it being outside the coordinates. They'll pull our suits for that. And possibly for good this time. We just have to wait until they shift the coordinates again. It may take years, but it's not like the pods are going anywhere."

Baxel started to argue, but Tymon moved a gloved finger over his lips, and Baxel fell quiet as another group turned the corner and started toward where they were standing.

Most of the approaching group had the standard single cloth over their shoulder marking them as members of the Vigil, but one man toward the back of the group wore more normal clothing and tapped at his visor absently as the Vigil continued their debate. However, the seemingly unassuming figure in his late thirties was far more than one would guess at first glance. Baxel had seen Varnil Williams a few years ago, when the man was led around the SE-S and informed of their safety procedures for the first time. Although Varnil was now permitted unbarred access to any sector within Safe Harbor, he was not actually a Remnant himself.

Varnil was the current Reawakened of Safe Harbor, meaning that he was born some six hundred years prior, somewhere on Earth.

In a tradition ranging as old as the second appearance of the Warden, a single individual was brought out of cryostasis periodically to aid in the continuing preservation of the others cryogenically suspended within the Preservation Core. At one point, Baxel had heard numbers ranging from three thousand to several tens of thousands of cryopods, though the matter was not often discussed outside of certain circles.

When the last Reawakened had decided to return to stasis after nearly thirty years of service to the Remnants, the Vigil elected to bring another out of stasis. After one failed attempt and another who simply could not grasp the change to their world, Varnil was the one that accepted. It had only been three years since the man took the position of the Reawakened, and he still apparently had a difficult time in keeping neutral on matters within the Remnants.

"There will be dissatisfaction if we do not side with this movement of reaching out for more resources," one of the Vigil said. "We should have taken Dimarka's side before the idea of expanding caught so much traction."

Varnil laughed. "Perhaps your Warden can see that expansion is not such a danger."

"With all due respect, Reawakened," the Vigil said, "without intervention from the Warden, we are left to treat it as such. Mistakes can be very dangerous amongst the Remnant Fleet. May I remind you that we have many years before we recover, in population alone, from the last time we strayed from the Warden's guidance?"

The Vigil was referring to Sarthyl and his attempt to control the Remnants. He had all but split the Remnants in half by reshaping centuries-old customs to push for aggressive expansion. Where the offending of Dimarka had marked the end of a man so dedicated to undoing Sarthyl's destruction, the day also marked the reoccurrence of the same argument that had started it.

Varnil rolled his eyes. "While you look to your Warden, I will be listening to Nendra Halimuth, her Production and Research Sector, and your own Head Vigil. The question at hand is not whether we will expand from this colony—which is falling apart—but when."

Baxel and Tymon both watched wide-eyed as the group continued their debate down the length of the hall. Baxel finally turned to Tymon, fully intending to drive his point home. However, Tymon beat him to the argument.

"Baxel," Tymon said with a gloved finger pointing toward him, "all that means is that we can wait. As they said, it is inevitable. That should make us more patient."

"Patient? Coordinator Reyson will be stabbing at our heels to find out where we went. How much time do we give Redemption to maneuver?"

"Baxel, it's not worth it. If we get a suspension for holding up Dimarka's offsending, fine. But reporting something that far outside the search coordinates—"

"Do you even know how much gloating Checkra will do when Redemption finds those pods in, what, two or three years? We will live the rest of our *lives* listening to it."

"Dammit, Baxel!" Tymon said, clenching his helmet and shaking his head at the floor.

"All I'm asking, Tymon, is that we go back. Who knows what else could be there?"

Tymon thumped his helmet against the chest of Baxel's suit and gave him a dark glare. "You say nothing about this to anyone else. It's going to take more than one trip for us to move whatever valuable items are in there into the search coordinates. That will mean going out on our own after our normal exploration shifts."

Baxel couldn't help but give him a grin.

"Wipe that stupid look off your face. If we're going to move things without involving the other teams, we'll need supplies, and plenty of oxygen to keep moving quickly."

* * *

Flerin raked his rough-cut hair back over his ears as he entered the room. At one point in time, the place would have been the control deck overlooking Hangar 01, but now the space served as the Hall of the Warden. The windows were gone, and a railing had been put up long before his time to replace the consoles, which had been sent to other parts of Safe Harbor.

There were already two of the heads of the SE-S waiting, as well as three other search coordinators besides himself and a couple of the more experienced of the exploration teams. Flerin nodded to Greely Reyson, a fellow coordinator, but did not get so much as a cold stare back. There always was some form of competition between the coordinators; everyone wanted to have their teams mark a discovery first. Not that they kept any of what they found. Everything was sent to Food Storage and Supply, or Production and Research if it was an unknown object. Even still, Flerin knew there was resentment against Baxel and Tymon because of Firebrand's traditional disregard for the rules. That resentment was exacerbated by how their team of two managed to compete against the larger operations, like the four groups making up the twenty-suit operation of Redemption, or even the senior groups in the other teams. Granted, Baxel and Tymon rarely did the retrieval of larger items themselves, but for sheer exploration, there was no match.

It had been nearly twenty years since he himself had gone out as part of an expedition. A few weeks before he wore the mark of Firebrand on his arm for the last time, two members of his team were killed in a pressure collapse.

Flerin looked over to the blue-lined uniforms of Sol and the mismatched greys of Redemption and knew this meeting was going to be rough. One of the heads looked as if he was supposed to be in his sleep cycle, and the experienced teams never took lightly to Baxel and Tymon showing them up. There were always complaints about the two failing to deliver on common supply marks, instead only shooting for more interesting finds.

"Oundara will be here shortly," Coordinator Reyson said with an unrevealing stare toward the entrance.

Flerin moved to take a position against the back wall as they waited. Out of any of the heads of the SE-S, Flerin put his odds on Oundara taking up more of the room at the top, even at her younger age. She had transferred from rationing supplies throughout the sectors to directing the searches she blamed for not bringing in the proper materials. It had created quite a stir, but it gave her an angle the others had to respect.

The attention of those in the room pulled toward the door as Oundara stepped in. Her deep brown eyes matched the color of her skin, and her wavy hair was cut short, almost to the scalp. She looked around the room and nodded as if finishing a count.

"Right," she said with a half smile, "looks like enough of us are here."

Flerin was almost expecting some jab at waiting for Baxel and Tymon.

"Firstly, I would like to say that the Search and Exploration teams, coordinators, head advisors, everyone, is saddened at the departure of the ever-loyal Dimarka. Both the family and the man. Whatever conflict of belief he had with others, it did not diminish his unwavering resolve to make Safe Harbor better."

A few murmurs of agreement passed around.

"And whatever changes may happen, now that those differences are weakened, it is up to our teams to make sure the Remnants are well-equipped to the challenge. I will be working closely with Food Storage and Supply to ensure we are up to whatever task the Warden has in store for us."

"And I," Dermuth Fraight, the eldest of the advising members added, "will be in touch with Mrs. Halimuth, as well as the Vigil, to ensure the quickest action upon the Warden's instruction. If we need transports to, dare I say, Earth, we shall be fully prepared to supply that need."

"Redemption already has some promising marks," Greely Reyson said, trying to downplay his push for his team's nomination by raking a hand across his wiry beard. "And with an expansion of the search coordinates, I'm sure we can get what is needed."

The third SE-S head, Quervin, nodded. He was a thin and, in Flerin's opinion, rather shrill man. "I will clear it with Wardenson and see that the transmissions will be approved for a range increase." He sent a meaningful glance over to Flerin. "Wouldn't want to lose track of our exploration teams, would we?"

"No, of course not," Reyson agreed without hesitation. His straight stare had not changed yet. "I prefer frequent checks with my team while they are out. It could turn dangerous otherwise."

Flerin could feel the heat rising from the back of his collar. Even their teams with years of experience were scared to go to half the places Baxel and Tymon would. And that was just the places Flerin knew about.

"That . . . brings about the next order of business," Oundara said with more hesitation than she normally would. She met eyes with Flerin but quickly diverted them to the ground and took a breath. "I am sorry, but all of the other sections are looking at us on this one. We simply cannot ignore the three hours wasted across the entirety of Safe Harbor."

Flerin drew in a breath. All eyes were on him now.

Oundara continued, "I have avoided giving information to the other sectors; no mention of names has occurred yet."

It only took one glance to know that, even with his stonelike gaze, Reyson had already pleasured in spreading that information.

"Nonetheless," Oundara said, "we either have to make advances toward correcting this flaw, or be truthful to the other Remnants on why this occurred. Flerin, do you have information on this matter?"

Flerin knew he finally had to open his mouth, for all the good or bad it would do. "Firebrand," Flerin started, "has always been given a degree of leniency in their actions. In my time in the search, it meant incredible finds for the Remnants. Just as before, the members of my team have been chosen because they will take on dangers few others will."

Reyson smirked. "Are you saying we are to continue giving the game to the ignorant and careless?"

"Let him speak," Dermuth said, low and patient.

"I do not know specifically where they went, only a vague direction. I admit that. I place my trust in their ability to weigh the risks of following their own path. If it goes beyond the range of communication for any rescue, they know that. My point is, wherever their bravery has taken them, it is their skill that brought them back. The safety of the team is not in question."

"In part," Oundara said, "I fail to see the basic reasoning to your argument. Impactful finds or not, Safe Harbor is built on shared systems. Our continuance under the Warden revolves around those systems acting as one cohesive unit. By lacking the ability to track your team at all times, those finds become sporadic, uncontrolled events. We gain no knowledge from having an unmappable resource income, only that resource in and of itself, and at that particular time. Without a location to return to and examine, we have no way of predicting any future retrievals, and in turn, it creates a resource uncertainty when planning for future projects or maintenance. We become dependent on random chance."

Oundara gave a weighing look around the room before continuing. "And in Safe Harbor, we need all the stability we can achieve, especially moving into this uncertain time where there is open talk of expansion."

"No," Flerin said, taking a step forward. "You cannot take this away from them. The search means everything to these boys."

The room fell silent as they waited for her final decision.

Oundara glanced around the room. The others would say she was ensuring they all were listening to her words, but Flerin could see she was silently asking herself if she had the support required to give her verdict.

"In light of the Vigil seeking answers from the Warden, I propose . . ." She hesitated, as if reevaluating the strength of her decision. "I propose frequent accountability on—"

Reyson started to argue over her, "They deserve something far harsher than a pat on the wrist! They need—" His words were lost as Oundara raised her voice, now commanding the room.

"—accountability, on any further communications, and awareness of the actions of the team!" She glared at Reyson before returning to addressing Flerin, "They need a committed course from their coordinator. If you lose track of them, we may be discussing the indefinite suspension of Firebrand."

Reyson turned away.

"Agreed," Dermuth said, and Quervin nodded as well.

Flerin lowered his eyes, knowing what this would eventually mean. By phasing out Firebrand, Safe Harbor would no longer be the home that the more unmanageable Remnants needed. The only place left for the likes of Tymon, Baxel, and himself would be away from the Warden.

* * *

"What sort of supplies?" Baxel asked as he and Tymon walked through the Hall of the Vigil. He could not help but reach out to the various projections and assortments of hanging cloths serving as decoration. Baxel ran his fingers along the material and through the layers of light, causing the projections to distort around his glove.

"We need everything, for the next time we are granted leave. Enough food to last us a day, maybe two. Atmo-bags for eating and possibly suit repair. Plenty of oxygen to burn so we can make the search quick."

Baxel watched as another group of Vigil passed them in the hall. He glanced back, noticing they were going in the same direction as the Reawakened and all the others. "Where do you think they're going?"

Tymon shot over a confused look. "Them? Probably a meeting or something. What are you—"

"I'll meet back up with you in just a bit." Baxel patted the shoulder of Tymon's suit as he turned around and started back.

"Where are you going?" Tymon called from behind.

"I just got to see something. It won't take long."

Baxel caught a glimpse of Tymon rolling his eyes and waving a rude gesture over his shoulder. If they were racing against an expansion of the search coordinates, Baxel figured this would be as good a chance as any to see if the Vigil would take Dimarka's place in arguing for the Remnants to stay in Safe Harbor.

Baxel followed behind one of the groups as they turned down the side hallway. With the number of groups traveling this way, Baxel guessed there was a Vigil meeting in the main room of their hall. It had been many years since he had followed this path, but after a few more corners, he recognized what was ahead.

It appeared the Vigil had decided to waste no time by beginning their debates only minutes after Dimarka's offsending. As he neared, Baxel could hear that some of the voices presenting arguments were from AI mirrors of prominent past members of the Warden's Vigil. They had recorded their opinions to aid in preserving the integrity of the Warden's wishes, though there were scarce few occasions in their history when the Warden had given the Remnants direct instruction. For the most part, it was the intent of the Warden's actions that all of the Vigil looked for.

Most of the other Vigil and attending leaders of Safe Harbor stood a few steps higher than the crowd as they watched the conversation take place. The ones guiding the debates stood down in the center on the same level as the three-dimensional projection.

The projection was of a woman. Her wavy hair, swept back and just under shoulder length, shimmered a transparent blue along with the rest of her holographic figure as she gestured and spoke.

"Above all else," the Vigil projection said, its voice coming through a series of speakers about the room, "the Remnants are to protect the Unawakened."

Baxel noticed that Nendra Halimuth barely stopped herself from taking a step down and forward. She was not permitted to speak here; this was not a conversation of opinion, but of determining how the Warden would wish the Remnants to act.

"But to what end?" another voice asked in sharp reply. He was an older man who had been a part of the Vigil for most of sixty-some-odd years, though the sash he wore only draped down to about waist length. Baxel had once asked a friend in the Warden's Vigil about the man, and she told him that anyone born outside of Safe Harbor was not permitted a full induction into the Vigil, thus his shortened sash. Connor Sevison had supposedly come from somewhere in the Aura belt around the time of Sarthyl.

The man continued with built-up anger and long-standing weariness in his voice. "We keep the Unawakened alive, tirelessly slaving to maintain their bliss. For how many millennia are we to watch over them? Until they have all died one by one in service to the Preservation Core?" He stepped forward, in front of the projection. The blue glow of the ancient Vigil's form reflected in the sweat on his wrinkled brow. "Our own Reawakened has pointed this out to us, yet we continue to ignore him! They have to return eventually; otherwise they may as well be dead. We have to return them to Earth."

Baxel's jaw dropped. Their people had lived in the fleet for nearly six centuries after the wars that destroyed that world, and he had heard of no mention of them ever returning to the lifeless planet.

The projection frowned. "The Warden has given no instruction on such matters. You overstate her will. Protect the Unawakened. Anything else is reaching for guidance." The image shimmered as she looked around the room. The Vigil projection was taking in the reactions of those around it and comparing them to its own personality imprint. "Guidance does not come as we wish, or when we wish. We follow, because we are not in control."

Algan Treys, wearing his two sashes, stepped forward. "Thank you, Tialee. Keep these memories."

The Vigil projection gave a small bow and flashed out of existence in a swirl of static. Baxel felt a shiver run down the length of his spine. Something about the AI mirror projections was more than a little unnerving. He hated the way they could just pop in and out of existence, glowing blue and pretending to be Remnants.

"Perhaps," the Head Vigil continued, "we should ask amongst the younger generations." He looked up and around the top of the layered room, where many younger members of the Vigil stood with their shortened sashes. "Are there any who have not yet shared their thoughts who wish to do so? If so, step down into the center."

Baxel watched intently, hoping to see a familiar face step from the crowd. It had been years since he was allowed to speak with Liaren Marenday after she had joined the Vigil. He had gotten on the wrong side of a few people he shouldn't have by sneaking out from the Hall of the Vigil during his training as a youth.

"Excuse me," a voice said from the hallway to his side. It had come from an older woman resting on the floor just outside the entrance, her sash folded neatly in her lap. "Do you have reason to be here?"

Baxel searched for an answer but finally settled with shaking his head. He doubted from the suspicious squint to her eyes that he could come up with anything that would convince her.

"Best be along, now," the woman said with a slow nod.

Baxel gripped his helmet and gave one last look to the room before turning away. As much as he wanted to hear more about the possible expansion to Earth, there was no use trying to butt in. It would be all too easy for him to garner more negative reviews and jeopardize Firebrand's position further. And at the moment, the demand for the working parts in the shuttle he and Tymon had found seemed greater than ever.

As he walked back through the Hall of the Vigil, Baxel glanced down to his helmet again, this time seeing an orange glow. He held the helmet up, looking through the front glass to see if he could get the gist of the message, but could see that the backwards text was longer than just a few words. He flipped it around and set it on his head.

"Where the hell are you? I've already got the first load of supplies ready. Oxygen tanks and nav beacons for now. Meet me in the SE-S and then we can head to the Point."

The Point was one of their many self-named locations, a jutting structure on the edge of the fleet that reached out toward the planet farther than anything within the horizon. What made the area of particular use to them, however, was that it was both just on the inside edge of the current search coordinates and it was a barren enough location that they had no fear of anyone from Safe Harbor or somewhere else returning and finding their supplies.

Baxel hurried down the hall to regroup with Tymon.

* * *

Varnil Williams walked up the long set of stairs toward the Warden's Shrine sometime after the lengthy meetings of the Vigil. The dim lights along either side of the steps cast shadows against his steps in the silence of the large room. Tucked away near the back of the same hall used in Dimarka's offsending were the stairs that led up to what was actually considered the Remnants' most sacred place. It supposedly contained the actual suit worn by the Warden . . . or Wardens. Even after nearly three years, Varnil still could not quite wrap his head around their built-up beliefs. It seemed as if they contradicted themselves from one sentence to the next regarding the details of their Warden, and spoke as if she was alive, ancient history, yet to come, and both one and many.

He stepped around a bent section in the stairs and continued his slow journey upward along the edge of the darkness. The hall had been dimmed to symbolize Dimarka's transition into space as if it were a figurative action, even though he was now, literally, on a trajectory toward the stars.

Varnil stepped over another gap in the staircase lit only by a pale flickering light. The scars in the metal here were nearly fresh. He had been told the damage was from the uprising. And as he could have guessed even before they told him, it was the Warden that had saved them.

When he reached the top, the lights in the next room started flickering on. Between the hall and the shrine was a simple open doorway. The fact that there was no form of security, neither as posted guards nor a locked door, showed the strange balance in this new civilization. If the Warden's Shrine was the heart of the Remnants, they left the core of their lifeblood open to anyone who simply walked up these steps. Not that their isolation in the fleet left a great need for fear of outside threats, but he would have thought at least some precautions would be taken against internal conflict.

He stepped into the room, and the center lights illuminated the exhibit of the suit and its external systems. The design was from late in the United World Coalition, likely from within the year the Orbital Armistice Fleet left Earth. The suit stood with its palms forward and helmet hovering just above the shoulders via the distortion field generator, which also created a glow beneath the feet. While hovering a few inches above the raised platform did give it a larger sense of presence, realistically, he knew it would be too small to fit him.

"It is supposed to be impressive," a voice said from behind. Varnil did not need to turn to know it was the old migrant, the Vigil named Connor Sevison. "But we both see it differently, don't we?"

Out of anyone in the entirety of Safe Harbor, Connor was the one person that Varnil considered closest to understanding his situation. The Vigil had started his life elsewhere, and even though he was from the wreckage of the Orbital Armistice Fleet, he was still held back within Safe Harbor. The shortened length of the Vigil's sash over his shoulder was the most visible evidence of his years in Aura, though Varnil had yet to ask if his shaved head was another mark of separation for a migrant.

"Over the years," Connor said, "I came to see their view, but I have never come to truly understand it."

"But you are of the Vigil," Varnil said as he looked over the deep scratches in the white plates of the Warden's suit.

"Am I?" Connor said. The older man let out a breath and moved a few steps ahead of Varnil to look up at the slight movement of the parts of the hovering suit. "No, I shouldn't question that. I have dedicated years to the practice, piecing together an understanding of what drives these people."

Connor went through the effort of getting to his weary knees on the floor in front of the shrine. Only then did his white sash reach the floor. He produced a small object from his pocket, though Varnil did not recognize it. It looked to be a small glass container with a wide opening on the top. The cream-colored liquid inside did not move as Connor placed it on the glowing plate on the platform in front of him. There was a small hiss as he used a device to make a spark inside the container. A small flickering glow started in the container's center, dancing up from a small string embedded into wax.

The Vigil released the container, and the distortion brought it gradually to hover in the air.

"But then again," he continued, "my years are not counted the same." He pushed the candle gently, and it started into a slow and measured circle around the base of the Warden's suit. "They let me speak, and listen to my interpretations as those of a respected elder, but on my own my decisions are those of a child. I am an initiate in their eyes, even if my words speak with the truth of the Warden herself."

Varnil watched the flame drift in a steady loop around the feet of the suit, thinking back on his own experiences. He was tasked with representing the Preservation Core, but his say was forcefully limited to an opinion unless another shared his reasoning. He was both respected and ignored. Allowed to speak, but never listened to without quiet skepticism.

"That is why I understand your isolation, as others do not," the Vigil said. "Alone, our opinions hold no more weight than the thought itself. Even in agreement, I fear we would still lack the merit of a true Remnant in their eyes."

Varnil nodded. "The balance of life in Safe Harbor is too delicate for motion. Their only trust in decisions comes from the Warden."

"But you can see it here. This is the Warden." Connor drew in a breath and blew out the candle as it passed by, leaving a thin trail of smoke to rise up and around in the blue glow. "This is what tells them to ignore the future of your people, even as they whisper in excitement about expanding beyond the bounds of Safe Harbor."

Varnil lowered his gaze. "The Vigil has made their decision."

"How can you not see, Varnil?" Connor said sharply. "You are the only one with the perspective to know what is best for your people. I have watched you closely since your cryogenesis; I know how hard it is for you to live in the wreckage of the fleet. You told me yourself that you can see no way for your people to live here."

"Connor, it . . . It is not my place to control the Remnants."

"Then how can you say you protect your people? If the Vigil decides this wasteland is to be their home, what can you do?"

"I . . ." Varnil said, pausing as he realized he had no answer.

"Is your one voice enough?"

Varnil lowered his head. "No."

Connor caught the glass jar and pulled it free of the field. "Then we need a second Reawakened to help guide us."

"You truly mean to open another cryopod? The Vigil would never allow it."

"You are kept outside the system of the Remnants for a reason. Your loyalty is only to those kept in the Preservation Core. You must push for the safety of the Preservation Core, regardless of the rules that bind Safe Harbor. In this, I need your help to open another cryopod; to give you the voice your people need."

"How?" Varnil asked. "What should I do?"

Connor placed his hands on the edge of the shrine and pushed himself laboriously to his feet. "There is one younger Vigil, Liaren Marenday. She does not believe in expansion to Earth, but she could be convinced on the point of being prepared in case the Remnants have to eventually move elsewhere."

"But what does she have to do with the cryopods?"

"We must choose who will join you. We must break into the Preservation Core, and we need Liaren Marenday to do so."

Varnil lowered his gaze. Breaking into the Preservation Core would be a betrayal of the highest order against the Remnants.

The migrant patted Varnil's shoulder as he moved past to leave the shrine. "Do not worry about them. The Remnants can survive more than you think. And if the Warden is forced to save them, they can only grow stronger from it."

Chapter 4: Scavengers

Jance rubbed her forehead and rested her elbows on the desk. The glow of the displays around her blinked as they switched to different camera feeds and strings of amassing data. She had spent the past weeks trying to get a better system into Norclave. When none of the people understood how to fully utilize even a simple visor, it made her efforts of understanding what was going on all that much more difficult.

In the past, she had all the information she could possibly need. She had graphs of graphs to sort through and gain a sense of the opinions about Sector: K. She could look at datasets organized by location, key words, or anomalous neural imprint patterns to tell her when a specific area was in need of attention. Jance sighed and closed her eyes to avoid looking at the dimly lit room of half-empty shelves and broken data devices.

A ping alerted her to someone entering the room. Jance leaned back and pulled in a slow breath. She blinked a few times, though nobody else would notice the change in redness from any time since she had arrived. The stinging mix of emotions seemed to come from every direction along with the irritating heaviness ever-present in the air.

There was a shuffle as a group of soldiers moved into the room. They each had on the military suits of armor with the paint ground away from as many surfaces as possible. The only exception was the shoulder piece made out of starscraper glass. Jance had found it hard to believe at first, but now she simply accepted it as fact: there were many uses for things that she never could have imagined. Even the windows.

Once the group had lined up along either side of the door, Olana Nuand entered the room, her UWC uniform dyed a brighter blue than before. At first Olana had refused to wear the prevalent symbol of the administrators of Norclave, but Jance had convinced her of the practicality of a visor. Now, Olana tapped on the side of her visor and made the display disappear. Olana glanced around the room as if making notes to herself, and Jance stood as she neared her desk.

"Ambassador Lorège," Olana said in greeting. "You have my permission to send for any decorations available to Norclave or Kamriek's Grove." She glanced around again before taking a seat. "You also have my personal support as well." As she sat down in the rough metal chair, she motioned for Jance to do the same. "I know simple comforts will not help ease your thoughts, though it might stop you from using your knuckles to dig them out."

Jance raised a hand to her forehead, feeling the slight tenderness where she had been pressing while thinking about the past. "Thank you, Overlor . . ." Jance paused, not remembering if the woman had in fact decided on taking the title.

"The title carries more weight than just a position, I am afraid," Olana said. She produced a small cube of glass and rolled it from hand to hand. "What would you advise, Cryo?"

"The decision will not be yours if you let it go too long." Jance started to reach for her visor to bring up data on the matter, but there was none. "In my . . . personal observations, the people of Norclave will soon make a habit of calling you Overlord unless you provide something different."

Olana paused, even holding the cube still as she thought. Her fingers started moving the cube again, and she looked up with little sign of emotion. "Perfect."

"How so?" Jance asked, figuring based on her previous interactions with the woman that she would want to move quickly to show her strength. Olana Nuand had taken hold of Norclave with a strong grip, but for reasons other than the title.

"In simply trying to figure out my title, they have inadvertently accepted me as their Overlord." She set the cube on the edge of the desk before crossing one leg over another and clasping her hands on top of her knee. "Now, in the system used by Overlord Thalen and then Overlord Obrourke after him, that would make you the First Administrator."

Jance smiled and shook her head. "With all due respect, I believe that would be a poor choice. From what I have heard from Kenneth, the administrators were simply around to try to take shots at the Overlord, though I suspect—"

"I know." Olana's tone held a darker edge. "I was the one who funded Silas's attempts. I am no child when it comes to the overthrow of power. I rose to own the Kamriek Mines by outmaneuvering my older brothers for the trust of my father. I let them live, until one tried to take his rightful position. At that point, I simply could not trust the rest."

Jance swallowed. The woman was distrusting; she could understand that. What she did not like was the analogy. The Overlord had just made it clear that if Jance tried anything, Kenneth, Kara, Sora, and any others Jance had demanded be allowed to stay in Norclave would be made to disappear.

"I have enough titles as it is," Jance finally said. "And I am sure it would only strengthen your position to mention 'the Cryo' as many times as possible."

Olana's eyes narrowed briefly, but she ultimately moved to pick up the cube as she steered the conversation in a different direction. "Will your tech hunter agree to investigate the sky flare that landed near Reclaim?"

"Kara is afraid of starting a conflict. The territory . . ." Jance flicked at one of the displays hovering over the desk. The city of Reclaim was built on the site of one of the Orbital Staging Facilities and controlled the area known as the Steel Valley. "The Steel Valley, it seems, is in opposition to Norclave."

"Everywhere is in opposition with everywhere else. Earth is in a flux controlled only by the threat of war. The weight of those threats is determined in part by the exertion of power, but more so by the fear of tech yet to be seen."

"And the only counter to that fear is knowledge. You hope to take the edge off this new threat by sending Kara to Reclaim?"

Olana laughed. "Her presence alone at Reclaim could prove useful. Publicly, Prime Elect Feirshan will claim our investigation is out of fear, but privately, he will never know if I have the information or not. Considering that, if the expedition planned to negotiate a treaty with the Kessians succeeds as well, the only fear Norclave will have will be the little attempts at disorder within our own city."

Jance nodded. The politics were vaguely familiar to the relationship between the UWC and the SRA, though familiarity was not something she readily welcomed knowing the result of that delicate balancing act in the past. Jance turned her attention back to the matter of the tech hunter. "Kara would rather finish all this Allek Skaves business, I am sure."

"She will be more useful elsewhere. Now, what of this name she came upon? Travend?"

"Sora is examining the Norclave Library, though there is no comprehensive list of individuals. We may stumble upon a mention of his name in regards to a meeting with Garneth Obrourke or one of his administrators, but I assure you, we will do nothing to alert the target of the inquiry."

Olana nodded. At first, the woman had been quick to anger that a source of information had been hidden, but it was clear they'd only had suspicion to go on until Allek's death had proved his allegiances were elsewhere.

"We will focus our attention inward when the time comes," Olana said coldly. "For now, keeping an army out of the Rift Hills takes precedence over stubborn natives refusing to accept that they lost." Olana slipped the glass cube into a pocket. Whether the Overlord knew it or not, Jance knew that the motion was generally a signal that the conversation was just about over.

"Take Kara with you on your flight over the Rift Hills," the Overlord said. "Have her identify any landmarks you might remember, but more importantly, while you have her up there, convince her to find out what new tech the Prime Elect has come upon. But say it was your idea; you will have more luck getting her cooperation that way."

Olana Nuand stood and concluded their meeting, leaving Jance no opportunity to contest the notion. She could only turn back to her thoughts as the last of the pairs of boots exited the room. Moments later, there was a ping from the table, and Sora stepped in. This time, instead of her usual bag of data pads and devices, she had several leafy plants bundled in her arms.

"What is all of this?" Jance asked as Sora started setting them around.

Sora placed the last plant—potted in a meal pack—on a shelf, but before she took more than a few steps back, she opted for placing it in a different spot closer to Jance and her desk. "In my research, I found images of your time. I know it is hardly on the same scale as then, but this is my attempt. I just thought since you were busy keeping Norclave alive, these could help you when you just need to look at something." She put her hands on her hips as she turned a critical eye toward the placement of the greenery. She gave one plant a quarter turn. "They won't carry your burdens, but they do help in their own way."

"That's . . ." Jance frowned as the tears started building in her eyes again. "Thank you, Sora." Jance clenched her fists and began rebuilding her composure yet again.

"It's the best I can do at the moment, with so much going on." Sora flicked one of the wide leaves up with a thumb, revealing a dull luminescence coming from the thick veins underneath. "Is there anything else you need before I go dig for information on this Travend?"

"You might send word for Kara to meet me here. I wish to speak with her before I set off."

* * *

Kara pulled at her hood once more as she received a lingering look from one of the passersby. The South Corridors of Norclave were normally a rough place to stick out, as attention was most likely to come unwanted. It was not that she was afraid, or even unaccustomed to the tightly packed confusion. Few wanted to mess blindly with a tech hunter in any of the black markets of the cities she had sold tech at. Here was a little different, however. After all, she had recently strung up the brute who was the new boss of the area she was waiting in. Perhaps they were wondering what that made her.

The South Corridors had changed the least out of any part of the city since the shifts in power. Between Overlord Obrourke, the brief hold of the First Administrator, and now Olana Nuand, it was an area beyond what a simple show of force could manage to control. The illegal trade was seeded deep, and shadier peddling was even more prevalent. On multiple occasions, she'd seen pieces of armor and clothing dotted with the remaining flecks of Norclave red where it had been stripped clean. More likely than not, the equipment had been stripped from the casualties of the fighting.

"Ah, my fine lady, is there anything that catches your eye?" A young man, hardly old enough to be considered such, motioned to the hanging wares that must have been his father's. He reached behind him to one of the small bottles hanging from a wire, then gave it a tug to pull it free, leaving the wire hanging from the grating of the level above. "Perhaps a bottle of the world's finest? Desert Plum! No doubt an extract of fragrance from a fruit no longer in existence!"

"I—" Kara started, but he continued without giving her a chance to speak.

"A small application, with no fee, should you wish." He tapped the bottle and a small projection illuminated between his fingers, showing details about the product.

Kara had to keep from rolling her eyes. In actuality, she had been looking at a boot holster and trying to decide if it would ever be practical. Most likely, by the time she needed to draw a weapon from her boot in a fight, somebody would already have a rail pointed at her head.

The boy held the bottle out, ready to spray the lotion on her. If she was not needing to stay low, she would have never even considered it. She gritted her teeth and offered the back of a closed fist. He reached to pull back her sleeve to expose her wrist and saw the empty sheath for a knife. He nervously laughed and sprayed it on the back of her hand.

"The moisturizing properties help, should you be exposed to harsh dust or rain." He tapped the button again and the nozzle retracted. "Go ahead. See how you like it."

Kara held it up to her nose and drew in a couple short breaths. She frowned and shrugged. "It smells like a fruit." She glanced to the side and noticed a man with a scraggly layer of facial hair leaning against a stack of crates. He had been watching her since she'd entered Karzon's stretch of the Corridors, though he did a good job hiding his attention.

"That knife up there." Kara nodded. "Does it have a heated edge?"

"No, miss," the boy replied without turning around. In the Corridors, it was always necessary to keep watch for any opportunists looking to pocket anything. Those that did not memorize what they had on display would turn back around to find something else missing. "It was thrown out . . . I mean acquired, without getting it to work."

"I know someone who could fix it. How much?"

"Five."

"Take three?"

He reached back to retrieve the knife and held the handle toward her. "Deal. Three Norclave tokens."

Kara made no move to take it. Instead, she lowered her tone. "No, here's the deal. I will give you ten if you tell me something about that man back and to my right."

The boy scratched at his face, though he had not even a start of stubble, and glanced over her shoulder. "Kyile Reddand. One of the lookouts for Karzon, as far as I know. Heard he lives somewhere on the third level, though when not watching here, a friend of mine says he frequently goes to Buebriks, and I may have seen him at the fights, though I really was not . . ."

Kara handed over a ten-mark before he started making things up in an attempt to satisfy her. The last thing she needed was to know about a made-up time when this boy saw Kyile Reddand fight. She was simply here to drag Kenneth out if something went wrong in his meeting with Karzon, not to get to know each of his strong-arms by name.

She gave a quick flip of the knife and slid it into the sheath under her sleeve. The little gesture was for Karzon's hire that was watching; she was letting him know that he was in the middle of a dangerous game.

"And I want that bag," she said with a quick nod as she reached back into her pocket, "and the plum spray."

* * *

Kenneth stood tapping his foot with his arms crossed as the crowds of the South Corridors shifted around him. He glanced one way, looking down the narrow pass that ran the entire length of the city. He resisted the urge to look the other way down the passage to see what Kara was up to, knowing that Kara would have his ear for doing so. Her condition had been clear about him not acting like she was following, and Kenneth was not about to do anything to turn her away from watching his back in a place like this.

"Anything yet?" Kenneth asked again.

The man in front of him, also standing with crossed arms, gave Kenneth an irritated glance as he rolled his eyes. Next to him, a box of Norclave tokens was passed through the barred windows to a scraggly woman who happily grinned as she took the start of a long and prosperous debt into her hands. After the ordeal of the cryopod, Karzon had taken little time to expand his business. He was now running protection for trades in a long stretch on either side his storeroom, and his loan business seemed to have resumed in full force.

Kenneth sighed. "Is anyone actually going to get him, or are we just going to stand here looking at each other all day?"

The man lazily looked to Kenneth again and rolled his muscled shoulders. He was likely a mercenary, or even a soldier who had ditched sides when Norclave started splitting.

"How about now?" Kenneth asked. Kenneth could see the man's jaw clench and his fingers curl slightly tighter again. *It is all too easy to pull a reaction out of this one.* Kenneth smiled inwardly.

"Hyo, door-keep," a voice said from the window, tapping at the bars. "Let the technician in now."

The big guy in front of Kenneth stepped to the side and shoved hard on the heavy riveted door. Kenneth patted him on the shoulder as he moved past.

Along the side of the room were stacks of small boxes, likely filled with coins or assorted valuables held as collateral to loans. The old man working the window pointed a thumb toward the back. As Kenneth followed the direction, he could not help but notice that the grating making up the floor showed a clear drop several hundred feet down to the ruins below Norclave. The reminder of rappelling from the city with Kara did nothing to settle the twisting in his stomach.

Kenneth was greeted by a guard armed with a pulse cannon. He motioned with his head one way down the hall. Kenneth could hear voices echoing about as he continued, clicking his way into the next room.

A thick metal plate set atop a rusted container served as a seat, as did several small cargo pods positioned about the meeting room. Kenneth took one last glance down through the floor before picking one of the makeshift seats. A moment later, the door on the opposite side of the room swung open and a large figure filled the frame.

Karzon directed a suspicious look to Kenneth as he entered the room, flexing his scar-wrapped hands. He stood a foot taller than Kenneth.

"Kenneth." Karzon rested a heavy boot on one of the containers. "I'm not sure what to think of your visit."

Kenneth shrugged. "Neither am I. I guess we'll both just have to wait and see, won't we?"

"Shut up. Just . . ." Karzon gritted his teeth. "I don't have time for your . . . well, *you*, frankly. What the hell are you and your dog doing in my pass of the Corridors?"

Kenneth felt a jolt go up his spine at the insult to Kara. Before he could force himself to relax, Karzon smirked in satisfaction.

"You didn't think either of you would go unnoticed, did you?" Karzon leaned in just a bit. "Word has it that you two killed the Overlord. Things like that carry a lot of weight down here. We're all nervous of what happens when the bright-shoulders decide to move into the South Corridors." He tapped his knuckles on the table. The thick scars between his fingers pinched at the motion; the scars left from when Kara had tied him up in the middle of the corridor. "Just so you know where we stand, Kenneth, it would not take me much effort to convince a lot of people you are the cause of Nuand being here. After all, many think you are in her back pocket."

Kenneth nodded. He had not expected things to go smoothly. He and Karzon had eventually parted on decent enough terms, but he knew Karzon had to be bitter about the fact that he ultimately lost out on being the one to find the Cryo. But now that the threat was out on the table, Kenneth just had to chuckle.

"What?" Karzon pulled back, face darkening.

"One problem. Overlord Nuand has no intention of moving into the Corridors any time soon. It's a waste of effort when far bigger threats are moving about the city. You and your slimy business with your slimy little friends can keep playing down here as long as you want. I'm here to talk about a name. Travend."

Karzon lowered his foot from the seat and looked as if he were going to take a step back. "Where did you hear that name?"

"Hmm. Must have read it from a letter the Overlord put in her pocket." Kenneth wrapped his fingers together and leaned onto the table. "What of it? Who is Travend?"

Karzon glanced to the side, clearly nervous. "A madman." He paused as if piecing things together. "You need to leave. Both of you. Before he knows you were ever here looking for him."

"Why?"

Karzon tapped under his collar, and a small light shone through his shirt. Footsteps immediately came running down the hall. "If you thought getting stuck between the Overlord and the First Administrator was bad, you have no idea what Travend is like."

Kenneth felt a warm glow from behind as a pulse cannon was aimed at his back. Karzon motioned, and a hand gripped Kenneth by the shoulder. The grip, combined with the heat, was more than enough to get him on his feet.

"Never forget, the Overlord saved your skin more often than anyone else." Karzon tapped his collar again to end the signal. "Olana Nuand will never be the Overlord."

* * *

Kara slung the small bag over her shoulder and followed along behind Kenneth through the crowds of the Corridors. She was tempted to bump shoulders with Karzon's lookout as they passed, but settled for giving him a weighty glare and was surprised when he did not turn away.

Most others sided with caution when dealing with tech hunters, so his bravery led Kara to think he knew something more.

"What happened?" Kara asked over Kenneth's shoulder as they continued on.

"We've made a mistake." Kenneth motioned and they started down one of the few side passages. He glanced to the side as they passed a man playing some sort of stringed instrument. Another was pocketing tokens that had been dropped in the lid in front of him. "I just hope we did not stir the hive too much."

They neared a stand at the bottom of the set of stairs. The woman there was selling medi-seal she was claiming she'd bought in new trade opportunities with Kamriek's Grove. Kara motioned with three fingers, and the woman held up three fingers and then one. Three tokens per one. Kara held up two five pieces over the shoulder of a passing man and slid them with her finger and thumb so they were both visible to the merchant. The woman held out four sticks of medi-seal toward Kara, adding one to the count instead of returning a single coin to Kara. It told Kara the woman wanted to get rid of them as quickly as possible. More likely than not, they'd come from a crashed transport just outside Norclave.

Kara shouldered past another few crowd members and made the swap. She then tucked the sticks into the bag over her shoulder and caught up with Kenneth.

"What did you get on him?" Kara asked.

"I would say he is in for causing Norclave trouble. Karzon knows more, but the pulse cannon told me he wasn't in a conversational mood."

Kara scowled and tugged on her hood once again. A man wearing a rough cap saw her coming and nudged his friend to step to the side. "Karzon is on the tough side for a lowlife thug. What do you think he is holding back?"

Kenneth waved off an offer from a merchant for a meal pack. Kara knew he was suspicious of the things, but she went ahead and handed over a few tokens. Kenneth glanced back as she was fitting it along with a transmitter into the bag. "I would say he stepped into a debt of his own. What are you . . . ?"

Kara looped the bag back over her shoulder and looked over a display of weapons. She pointed to a power cell. After receiving an absurd price, she motioned a more reasonable offer. Honestly, she did not know why people insisted on starting high when dealing with tech hunters. She had likely sold more power cells than he had, and in more settlements around the area than he even knew of. The offer was declined, and she kept moving with Kenneth.

"You think Karzon is working for someone bigger?" she asked.

"That's a possibility," Kenneth replied. "There have been plenty of grabs for power down here, and the thought of easy expansion is a hard one to pass by."

Tokens rattled from the side as a man in ragged clothes shook a bent can toward those passing by. Kara could see a scar on the top of his arm from the old Norclave law. He had committed some form of crime, and a second mark usually meant death in the Cells. Alongside that scar were other marks, both natural scars and otherwise, spawned from a hard life in the Corridors, but she also saw a little girl curled up, sleeping under his other arm. It was a cradle marked with desperation and pain, but toward the girl, she could only feel the warmth of love and compassion coming from the man.

Kara knelt and pulled the bag off her shoulder. Even with all the noise around, Kara held a finger up to her lips. There was no purpose in waking the child. She pulled out the meal pack and set it by the girl's feet, along with a couple sticks of the medi-seal. Kara knew what the girl would go through. It was always survival just under the view of those who did not seem to have to worry about the next meal. Hopefully, these gifts would ease the toiling worry for a day or two.

The man look surprised, but Kara stood before he could give his thanks. She turned to find Kenneth waiting and looking back.

"Old memories?" he asked.

Kara said nothing and led the way onward. Mixed in with the shuffling of feet and the constant exchange of coin, stale bread, and rusty water, there were similar stories on the faces of those who would have nowhere else to go when night fell over the starscraper. If anything, Kara hoped the pain and confusion from Nuand's takeover would amount to a change here. She signaled at another stand to get a meal pack to replace the one she had given away. Her hope was not with the Overlord, though; it was with the Cryo.

* * *

Lieth Armain could not say how long he'd wandered the dark and rotting core of Norclave. Time seemed to exist without its clarifying edge. The distinction between one moment to the next was blurred by the persistence of his past. Lieth's mind was almost entirely consumed by the last moments of his old life. He was once a merchant, ready each and every day for the sun to break through into Norclave. Now, he watched his own actions with a passiveness akin to seeing history unfold. There was no weight to his decisions because he no longer considered them his own. He felt no guilt for ordering the shot that killed Allek Skaves, just as the bright-shoulders felt no guilt for ransacking the ruins of his home.

Lieth pointed to the side, where a couple of kids watched nervously from the shadows. Their faces were illuminated as Darmic stepped closer with the pulse cannon at the ready. Lieth knew the man would not hesitate should he give the order again.

"Do you have it?" Darmic growled. The children seemed to shrink back into the pile of twisted containers. Their pale skin showed evidence that they had a hard life in the dark, but their resilience came from staying alive, not from playing tough.

"I apologize," Lieth said to them, though he did not order Darmic to lower the weapon. He glanced back to make sure the other member of Travend's resistance was watching their backs. "We are looking for a certain device. I am willing to pay for its return, or any information regarding it."

For a moment they said nothing. Lieth shook a small container, and it rattled with Norclave tokens. It was then that a weak finger pointed off toward a set of stairs leading down. "Kulann takes any finds up to the scrapsmiths."

Lieth popped the latch on the container and tossed the pair of them a ten-mark. It was more than they would normally see in a month. Maybe even longer than that, since coins would only make it to the lowest level by falling through the cracks of the city. "Overlord Travend thanks you." He nodded to the side, toward the stairs, and Darmic lowered his weapon and started in that direction. It sounded to Lieth like this Kulann had made a little organization out of the scavengers. Travend would do well to find the scavengers a place. It would be simple to turn the scavengers' daily work of dismantling the infrastructure of Norclave into a spy network throughout the city.

Lieth produced a glow-orb to continue through the dark. Not even bright daylight reached as more than an evanescent glow this deep under the web of the city. The orb floated about three feet in front of where he held its small cradle and bathed the area in a cool light. At one point, this area would have been considered livable, but the scavengers over the years had removed the lights and as many sections of pipe and walkways as possible.

"Take care with your steps," Lieth said. Just as he thought, the stairs leading down only had about half as many steps as intended, and the rails had long ago been taken, likely to repair a transport or sold to be used in a new section up above. When they reached the bottom, there was a single light on the ceiling about twenty feet down the passage. From the light of his orb, Lieth could see several rough ladders leading down. He felt a shiver go down his spine when he saw dirt mixed in with the large sheets of metal. They were entirely too close to the interior of the starscraper.

"What do you want?" a thin voice called from somewhere up ahead.

"Are you Kulann?" Lieth asked. Darmic twisted around, clearly expecting something to jump out at them.

"What is it worth to you?" the voice asked.

Lieth pinned it down as coming from somewhere in the crates underneath the light. He slowly stepped in front of Darmic. "Not to me. To Travend."

"That would be quite a lot then, wouldn't it?" There was a shift behind the crates. "Is it an old friend wanting revenge? Or is it something that is lost?"

The man stood up, then adjusted his rough hat and straightened his thick, ankle-length coat. His long and thin beard was more like a tangle of wires hanging down than hair from his chin. With the same motion, the noises of several chains rattled in the dark and echoed all around.

Lieth knew they were surrounded, and Darmic obviously shared the notion. The man—who was dumb enough to nearly scalp himself every time he shaved his head—was also dumb enough to raise the pulse cannon toward Kulann.

"Wait!"

"Hold!"

Lieth and the older man both held their hands in the air in an attempt to stop their groups. Lieth shoved Darmic's cannon down and glared at his other man. He then looked up to the scavenger, and the pair shared a glance. They both knew the situation could have just gone bad.

"You . . . speak quickly," Kulann said.

"Right. We are here for a data pad."

"Mmmm . . ." the scavenger hummed with a slow nod. He took a foot and pushed over one of the larger crates. A mess of broken wires and flickering displays toppled onto the ground. "A thousand tokens. For the batch. Or a standard container of meal packs."

"I don't have that with me, obviously," Lieth said.

"Then we will have to do a trade, obviously. I have a scraphauler a mile out of the city. You choose the place of trade."

Lieth narrowed his eyes and looked everything over a second time. It was too simple. The man had asked no questions and instantly offered a crate of data pads. Most of them looked like scrap beyond what even the fall of Allek's data pad could have managed. That was when it hit him. "Don't you dare," he said dangerously.

"What? You asked for a data pad! Here they are!"

"And you know damned well the one I am looking for is not there. Give me the one, and I can do better than a thousand and a container. I can get you an alliance with Overlord Travend."

"Impossible!" Kulann said. "There is no way he will make a deal like that. Not with me. I do not accept."

Lieth shrugged. "Someone has to take it. If you are not willing to fill the spot, that's too bad." He turned toward one of the whispers in the dark. "Who wants it?"

"Wait!" Kulann yelled again. He reached into his heavy overcoat and pulled out two pieces of metal held together by the wires within. When he pressed a spot, the display flared on with the same glow that had given Allek away. "Listen close," the scavenger continued, "you get me the deal, or I go straight to Nuand and tell her what Travend has."

"And what is that?" Lieth asked as the scavenger tossed the damaged pad at his feet.

"A number."

Lieth looked down and was shocked at what he saw. "Rust in my eyes, we have to get moving."

It was a dock number, and a time.

Chapter 5: Restriction

Baxel backtracked through the winding halls carved through the *Fortuna* and followed the markings on the walls until he ended up back at one of the functional airlock rooms. There were still about twenty people waiting for the next transport shuttle to dock. Baxel received a number of tired looks from part of the crowd as he moved ahead of the line to the airlock. A third of the people in the room would have been in the last few hours of their sleep cycle if not for the interruption of Dimarka's offsending. Baxel and Tymon were nearing the end of their own designated day; hopefully, Flerin would not think to look for them during their night.

Baxel pulled up his inner face mask and pushed his helmet down over his head. He connected with the habitat barrier and checked the arrival log. A shuttle was inbound, though it still had over a minute before arrival. Baxel activated the airlock panel, and the inner doors opened with a muffled hiss through his helmet.

"Your ride will be here shortly," he said to the nearest person waiting in the line as he backed into the airlock. Baxel kept an eye on his displays to make sure his suit had properly sealed with his helmet. As the barrier was depressurized, his system monitor remained stable. It was a lesson learned the hard way, and more than once. The first time, Tymon had needed to drag him back to safety after he blacked out.

As the room neared zero atmospheric pressure, the outer doors opened, giving Baxel a view of the many shifting lights of Safe Harbor. Down the length of the mile-long split in the massive orbital ship were the blue lights of repulsors on the hundreds of transports sliding through the zero-space between the sectors. Baxel stepped out into weightlessness and looked up at the overarching stars. He let out the same breath of satisfaction as every time he stepped out of the confines of the habitat barrier. To him, the freedom felt as if it had only two limits: the stars above and to the right, and the lights of the dead planet below and to the left. He pushed off into the open, knowing the latter might soon become a new reality to the Remnants.

Instead of pulling up navigation to make his way around their home sector, Baxel simply looked for the right pattern of lights along the jagged edge of the titanic structure. At his current speed, it would be at least a few minutes before he reached the SE-S. Baxel tapped his helmet—his wrist glowing bright orange with the zero-space beacon—and leaned forward to engage his back jets.

He was traveling faster than the recommended speed for even the transports, but he had to at least beat Flerin back. About thirty seconds later, Baxel activated his navigation grid and connected with the SE-S habitat airlock. His suit automatically adjusted his course and slowed his momentum. Baxel could have closed his eyes and it still would have, but years in and beyond the coordinates past Safe Harbor had ingrained a constant awareness for malfunctions.

The airlock door was open and waiting as he finally returned to his point of outset for his wake cycle. It had been nearly twelve hours since he first set out to explore the wreckage with Tymon in their morning.

"Bax, you read me?"

"Loud and crackly, Firebrand One." Baxel set down into the gravitational half of the airlock and activated the cycle.

"Most everything is ready," Tymon continued. "I'll have you double-check to see if there is anything else we need to load up before we push this out."

When the airlock finally opened, Baxel stepped into the empty ready room. Benches and lockers lined the wall so the returning teams could have standard clothing waiting if they wished, as well as a few display terminals for operating the systems that would analyze the condition of the returning team themselves.

"Where are you?" Baxel asked.

"Supply Room One," Tymon replied. "I want to move quickly when we get this out the door. We don't need anyone else seeing it."

Baxel slowed to a stop and took off his helmet. Leaning up against the supply room was Merden, a girl about a year younger than himself. Her long blond hair hung down to nearly the waist of her yellow-accented undersuit of team Surefire. While technically the largest of the exploration teams, Surefire functioned closer to the zero-space than any of the other teams, fulfilling the more routine tasks, such as aiding the Maintenance Sector in repairing transmission relays or responding to transport and habitat breaches with the Medical and Rescue Sector.

"Baxel, good to see you are back safely," Merden said with a smile. "I heard you were delayed on your return. Where's Tymon?"

Baxel glanced to the supply room but coughed into a fist to cover his look. "Yeah, thanks. So, where did you watch the offsending? Did they have the displays set up here?"

"Of course," Merden replied with a bit of a nervous laugh. "Though, you were saying about Tymon? I saw you were talking to someone through your comms after you left the airlock." She said, motioning to where his helmet's visor had been glowing.

Baxel scratched his neck and tried to think of a way to avoid answering. He glanced down the hallway behind her, though there were only the noises of conversations in the distance. Just at that moment, the door to the supply room opened and a cart pushed into the hallway, piled with tanks and cargo crates strapped together.

"Hi," Merden said to Tymon with a smile.

Tymon shot Baxel a glare through the glass of his helmet. Baxel glanced down to see he had missed a final transmission from Tymon.

"What is all this?" Merden asked.

"It's, uh . . ." Baxel started.

"Look, Merden," Tymon's muffled voice cut in. He pulled off his helmet and sat it on top of the thick cargo net covering the supplies. "We need this to stay between us. Everything is fine, but nobody else needs to know."

Her smile dimmed as she glanced to the supplies again, turning to a slight frown as she looked back to Tymon. "You mean Flerin does not know about . . . this?"

Baxel stepped in. "If Flerin knew about this, he would be . . . just fine with it."

"But he doesn't," Tymon continued when Baxel stopped, "and he might . . . not. But it is not that bad, really. And we will bring everything back. The oxygen tanks, well, it all comes from Safe Harbor, and we would be breathing the air anyway, so . . ."

"And those boxes," Baxel motioned, "I think, or they do, have navigation beacons. Little things, and I'm sure we will get them back. Right Tymon?"

"Guys," Merden said flatly.

"Yeah, just as Baxel said, they will come back right as soon as—"

"Guys!"

Baxel let out a sigh and Tymon paced away in a slow circle. They were so close to making it out.

"If you actually intend on going out, you might want to . . ." she motioned sideways with her head toward the habitat airlock. "The heads and coordinators should be finishing their meeting now."

As if hit with a spark, they both jumped into action. Tymon thanked her with a hand on her shoulder, and Baxel tossed him his helmet from the cart. They wasted no time in helmeting up and pushing the cart to the airlock doors. On one side of the barrier, the tightly bound bundle of supplies weighed far too much to carry, but on the other side of the airlock it drifted in much the same fashion as Baxel had. When the outer doors opened, Tymon kicked off the wall and shoved Baxel and the supplies out into the zero-space of Safe Harbor.

As soon as they could, they angled toward the planet. Down soon became set as forward in their minds as they drifted out of Safe Harbor. While they were still surrounded by long stretches of wreckage, everything opened up into the massive view in front of them. Earth, wreathed in the dark of night, looked as if it had been smoldering since its destruction through the cover of the gas pockets rolling over the surface.

"Oxygen, ninety-eight," Tymon crackled over the comms.

"Oxygen, ninety-four."

With little communication, they altered their course along the bottom of the orbital ship, threading their way through spires of metal reaching toward the planet. They knew to avoid venturing too far out from the wreckage toward the planet. Even with Tymon's more advanced scanning equipment secured in one of the boxes, there was no need to risk leaving the artificial orbit of the fleet.

Continuing near the wreckage, and at times having to detour farther in, they eventually reached the base of the Point. Baxel flipped, positioning his feet toward the Remnant Fleet to better see the Point in all of its glory. Reaching like a mountainous spire, the twisting pier of metal reached up toward the horizon of the planet. They had both been to the top only once, just to see what it was like to dangle their feet off the end. The very tip of the Point reached beyond the gravitational fields generated by the fleet and edged into the influence of the planet.

"What we are doing, Baxel . . ." Tymon said grimly. "We may not get away with it."

"We'll be fine."

"No, Bax, I mean . . . this may be too far. If the coordinators find out we've moved things, even the cryopods, back into the search coordinates, that may be it. You know?"

Baxel put a hand on the supply package as well and signaled his jets to push them forward. "Then let's go. If you think we may be running up our luck anyway, one last time cannot hurt."

"Fine. Race you to the top."

Of course, they both knew the expression was simply that. They continued on with all the caution that had gotten Firebrand this far. For generations, many had regarded the team as the best. They would go where no one else would dare just to see something new, but it was always with conscious, cautious skill that they traveled. All it took was one mistake to take a life, and that had been proven a number of times in the past.

Tymon finished latching the supply pack to a wider strut and placed a navigation beacon. This area had been scoured over even before Flerin's time, making it very unlikely that anyone else would even think to look here. At the very least, they might not dare travel this far out.

Three quarters of the way up the Point, they could see the bright blue flares burning on the undersides of all the wreckage. The repulsion engines of the fleet eternally burned with the fury of a dead civilization, but the Remnants had learned how to maintain them through the guidance of the Warden. There were old stories long before the time of Sarthyl or any Remnant still alive that spoke of how the Warden had braved the dangers of gravitational fields and radiating heat in order to stabilize the fleet. Their entire existence was saved from crashing down, adding one more to the many times she had saved the Remnants.

Baxel continued climbing along the twisted spire using the tips of his fingers. Much of the metal, which should have been a jagged assortment of hallways and beams, was smoothed together as if it had been half-melted and worn away. The Point was where one of the many orbital fleet repulsors had failed. Baxel could only imagine what it was like for the Remnants when that happened.

Their motions soon changed from an effortless glide along the surface to needing sturdy grips to stay attached to the wreckage. They now climbed, their feet facing down, pulled by a fraction of standard gravity. Even the slight downward drift would have been far too much for their simple jets of vented air to counteract. They were truly hanging by their own magnetized touch.

The entire belt of wreckage moved around the planet at a speed slower than it needed to achieve a true orbit. Instead, the massive gravitational repulsor engines of the fleet created an artificial field of microgravity that allowed it to maintain orbit. As Baxel and Tymon continued climbing down, they were reaching the edges of the microgravity field, and thus feeling the gravitational pull of the planet itself.

"Keep adjusting your foot locks," Tymon said from above.

Baxel gave him a thumbs-up with both hands, holding on to the metal with only the side of his boots. A flat grip was the strongest, but only barely entering the gravity of Earth's orbit meant the edge of the magnetic system on his boots was still enough to keep him attached. Baxel reached out with the magnetic grip on one of his gloves to keep from falling backward. They continued to climb down until they reached a ledge about twenty feet away from the very tip of the Point.

Baxel touched down on the flat surface and deactivated the magnets on his boots. Tymon followed close behind and detached a data pad from his shoulder.

"Gravitation field reads point two-two-five. The increasing gradient of gravitational forces extends down as far as the sensor will read."

In the low gravity, Baxel pulled his feet up and was gently pulled downward with between a quarter and a fifth of the speed he would have inside the Safe Harbor sectors. After he landed, Baxel shifted himself to the edge and let his feet dangle over. "That gradient leads to a gravitational reading of one, I hope you know."

Tymon lowered himself down to sit next to Baxel. "Six hundred years, and we still keep the standard habitat gravity of Safe Harbor the same as Earth."

Baxel looked down at the dark landscape of Earth that was seemingly all around them. They were now far enough away from the fleet that there was no obstruction to the massive view. "And just think, because of that, it would feel just like home."

The two sat mostly in silence, their feet dangling over the edge as the atmosphere grew to a bright shade of blue and the rotation of the fleet gave view of the sun. Their helmets automatically darkened to shield from the glaring radiation. The new light washed out the speckled outlines of the dead supercities and illuminated a teal horizon. After several minutes, a large portion of the planet's oceans and landmasses started to become visible. Vast stretches of grey-blue water met with molted coasts of vibrant greens, sickly browns, and the crumbled greys of ruin.

Baxel could have watched the bright flashes dancing within the clouds of gas hanging over the surface, and how the slowly drifting systems seemed to interact with the ranges of white-capped mountains, for hours. It was all so vast that the trouble was truly comprehending it. The planet had once housed billions when the fleet could only manage to scrape together numbers within the thousands.

"You think we will ever see it?" Baxel asked.

"No." Tymon pulled something from his chest pouch and held it out over the edge in a closed fist. "I doubt the Remnants will actually touch down anywhere near our lifetimes." He opened his hand. What looked like a small piece of metal was stuck to the magnetic pads of his gloves. Tymon tapped his helmet, and the metal dropped free from his outstretched hand. He stood up and readied to leave as Baxel watched it tumbling in a slowly increasing pace downward into what seemed an infinity, especially for something so small.

"You think that is how our ship will look, when it makes its way down?"

"Our ship?" Tymon glanced back over his shoulder as he pulled himself up. "The one with the pods? I suppose it could." He lifted a leg to continue his climb out over the edge of the platform. "Hopefully it has more working repulsors than that, though."

Baxel looked straight above, where Tymon was continuing on overhead. "I think we will see it. I mean, that still gives a lot of years, but we will," Baxel said as he pushed off in what amounted to a full leap to pass over the top of Tymon. He reached out with a hand, catching just the tip of his finger against the metal. Baxel brought his foot forward to secure his attachment.

"You sure about having those years?" Tymon asked.

Baxel looked down from where he hung over the top of the entirety of Earth, anchored only by the side of his foot and one finger.

"Perhaps it wouldn't hurt to push the process along."

* * *

Flerin sat half asleep with his hands folded as their transport shuttled them toward the SE-S. Their meeting had gone on late into his own sleep cycle, but at least the offsending had not taken place during it like many others. Flerin ducked his head, rather wishing to keep his attention to himself.

This particular transport had no windows for the passengers; the broken glass had been covered in steel to make it functional for hauling more than just cargo. The normally confining ride was only made worse with the addition of Greely Reyson, Oundara, and several of the members of team Sol in their standard clothing.

Nobody had said a word since they launched from the airlock. Oundara had made it clear that she wanted time to develop recommendations, and Reyson had received a few harsh words from Oundara about keeping his silence. What seemed to make it all worse, however, was that Flerin was half-expecting to show up in the SE-S and have Baxel and Tymon nowhere within Safe Harbor. With the warning about not losing track of his team, he very much wanted to contact them just to make sure of their location.

Flerin let out a sigh and leaned back against the hard seats. The entire point of Firebrand was to take the reckless and give them a use, just like himself when he was younger. He had once been lost in his hunt for recognition. He started in Redemption under the old coordinator, Rikard, but also under the squad leadership of Greely Reyson. Needless to say, it did not take long before he started butting heads with their cautious approach. Around that time, after he was stripped of his suit, Firebrand offered to take him in.

He had been given a place that he finally felt meant something. They were allowed at times to break the artificial search coordinates and strike out on their own, past the transmission systems and into less explored territories. But more importantly, he was taught lessons more meaningful than simply telling him to stop. Valuable search guidance, ways to evaluate a situation, how to keep ahold of his temper. Even other more impactful lessons just from the nature of the work.

And that is what he'd given to those boys over the years. Everything they knew beyond their drive and courage, he taught them. At a young age, Tymon had taken to stealing items in the Trade Sector because he saw ways to obtain more valuable stock for the exchange managers. Baxel had run away from the Vigil during his trial placement, knowing long before the people trying to fit him into a line of work that he was destined for the SE-S teams.

What pained Flerin the most, however, was he would be the one forced to tie them back down. It would not work, he knew. But the others had made their choice, and it was now up to him to enforce that decision. Whether anyone else could see it or not, Safe Harbor was departing from a great many traditions, and the Remnants were a people built upon following the ways of the past.

Flerin idly tapped his fingers against the seat. It all made him think of the main reason Safe Harbor was so hesitant about adapting hard rules over simple expectations. A set limit was destined to be pushed, but general expectations were harder to contest—to a specific point, at least. That same reasoning was why the leaders of the sectors were never elected, appointed, or determined to be so. It was a fluid system where influence and experience were followed. In the case of himself, he'd simply fallen into the role of coordinator for his former team because he knew the work better than anyone else. He knew the techniques of exploration better than Oundara, Reyson, or anyone else trying to order him around.

A deep rumble sounded from outside. It was the first exterior noise since they'd set out, meaning that they had arrived in one of the larger SE-S airlocks. The pilot gave them the all clear and Reyson pushed the door open.

Just as Flerin was about to follow him out, Oundara spoke.

"Have your team awake in the next cycle for a briefing. We are going to go over some standards."

"You want us in the conference room?" Flerin asked. He was referring to the one in the SE-S in particular.

"No," she said. "Meet me in Habitat Three. Deck Fourteen."

"Why there?" Flerin asked.

"Because I have a point to make to your team. Isolated in the SE-S, I am afraid they have lost sight of what we do this for."

"What kind of restrictions am I to expect?"

"Flerin," she said without quite as much edge to her words. "I am not trying to beat you down. I just want to see your team be more effective with the whole. We simply need to alter our strategy to make you fit with the others."

Oundara pushed past him and out of the transport, leaving Flerin with thoughts not as reassuring as she had meant to impart. He could see that the purpose of Firebrand was being pulled apart one piece at a time. Flerin pulled his data pad out of a pocket to let Baxel and Tymon know they could leave the *Fortuna* now.

* * *

Their awakening arrived early and swift at the hand of their coordinator. It soon became clear that Flerin fully intended they all arrive on time to meet with Oundara. Hardly a moment was spared before Baxel stumbled tiredly into the airlock. He followed closely behind their coordinator, who had offered little information about the meeting to come.

Moments later, Baxel leaned with his forearms on top of his knees as the craft slowly drifted out through the zero-space of Safe Harbor. He glanced between the view of the massive expanse of the wreckage to the few other people riding the stripped-down and age-worn passenger ship. A young woman played with a baby brought in by the man now sitting close to her side. By the way she took in every reaction from the infant, Baxel guessed she had just gotten off her shift in the Trade Sector and met her wedded at the habitat barrier. The man let out a yawn, pulled her tighter to him, and gave a gentle smile at the interactions between the two. It was even possible that his waking cycle was offset from hers. Personal schedules came second to the needs of the Remnants.

"Arrival, Deck Fourteen, Habitat Three. Two minutes."

Baxel looked down between his feet when the transmission coordinator sounded the announcement from the front. It was a strange feeling, hearing a voice other than Tymon or Flerin while traveling through the void. He clasped his gloveless hands and tapped his foot while the man across from them slowly flicked through a data pad of sector information, or possibly the projected news reports for the cycle. Baxel forced himself to stop fidgeting and looked out the window over his shoulder. Floating in an easily perforable capsule seemed to only highlight the limits of their safety.

It had been nearly five years since he had traversed anywhere without his Firebrand suit on. He had grown accustomed to developing a disaster plan every time he set foot near a point of possible failure. Normally in this situation, he would have worked his way through the specific steps. The first, as always, was to put on his helmet before the depressurization caused him to black out. He then would attempt to arrest the motion of anyone else who may have been thrown out of the craft. If there was an opportunity, he would send an additional notification to Medical and Rescue with more information than the standard zero-space distress signal. Other than that, he would prioritize the rescue and restabilization of the baby.

Baxel pulled in a breath as he felt beside him, knowing that his helmet was locked away in the SE-S. If the worst happened, he would be as helpless as any of the others. Baxel glanced over to see Tymon asleep with his chin to his chest.

There was a gentle shift as the transport maneuvered out of the path of another shuttle traversing the open space of Safe Harbor. Baxel could see the bright orange glow of the warning light on the other craft as they passed well out of the way. Five or six similar lights moved in front of the backdrop of the *Firmament* as little more than small pinpoints in the titanic split of the orbital ship. Another couple of orange specks set out from the Vigil docks on the *Fortuna*, moving at a pace diminished by the scale of their surroundings.

It was a long and quiet moment before they entered the shadow of the other side. While technically most of the habitat sectors were located on the opposite side of the zero-space from the Search and Exploration Sector and Habitat Two, only about a third of the population was located there. Habitat Three, where Baxel grew up, was often a mess of shifting yellow zones from the extensive reconstruction.

The other habitats on the same side as Habitat Three were in worse shape. Habitat One, the largest of all four population cores, had been red-zoned after it was mostly destroyed in Sarthyl's uprising. The remaining pieces of the smaller Habitat Four were mostly out of use due to problems with creating new docks. Originally, there had been talk of splitting the separated sections of Four into about twelve new parts, but Dimarka had been the first to argue against the idea. He wanted to prepare for future population regrowth, and deemed repairing walls as more efficient than building new airlocks.

One of the entrances to Habitat Three closed around the craft, and everyone on the shuttle started readying to leave. It was not until the room had pressurized that Baxel could hear the deep hum of the repulsors chopping in the air.

Flerin jerked on the handle to pop open the side door of the craft. Baxel followed behind into the dimly lit room, nodding to the line of other people waiting to either start their wake cycle or return to their home sector to rest.

They moved on toward the smaller doors leading to Deck Fourteen. Very few avenues of Remnant life mandated a separation from one's home habitat sector, but the last time he'd set foot in Habitat Three was nearly a year ago. Becoming a Vigil was the only other occupation he knew of where the work formed a confined community similar to the SE-S.

The next room opened into an intersection of a wide hallway. Habitat quarters and various food and supply outlets stretched down two of the long corridors while the passage to the left remained cordoned off. A patchwork of fused metal ensured that the door behind the barely functioning construction projection lines was sealed. The projected lines occasionally flickered with a caution notification, just as they had since before Baxel was born. The other side of the seal was a completely illuminated expanse of shredded hallways only accessible from zero-space, though when Baxel had realized that the personal effects still located there meant that the remains of the individuals caught in the destruction could have been forgotten as well, he'd put it into his small mental list of places he would never go.

"This way," Flerin said, starting down the hall to their right. He was following the guidance pulled up on his projected visor. "Just keep quiet, answer anything asked, and agree to anything she says. Otherwise a trip in the transports might be your morning routine from here on out."

* * *

The Reawakened, Varnil Williams, sat in the rough hallway of Habitat Three, listening to the gentle sway of conversations and the reverberations of the cycling airlocks. He sifted through the information pulled up on his visor, passing the time as he waited for the others to arrive.

In Safe Harbor, there was no hard mandate on personal space, but it was still widely accepted that everybody should have an area of their own, and that it would be left alone without some sort of reason otherwise. As such, most of the doors to either side of the hallways were left open, even if there was nobody inside. Varnil had overheard two of the Vigil discussing the practice his first year out of the cryopod. They claimed the custom of open doors stemmed from hundreds of years ago, when ill effects had come from the combination of low population and individual isolation.

With the chaotic organization they'd developed by having separate sleep cycles, Varnil could understand the need to maintain socialization. Apparently it was not uncommon for logisticians to spend part of their time working in their own area, which would make their breaks for interaction as simple as wandering out into the hall and seeing who was open for conversation.

Varnil glanced over to a young girl sitting on a bench in the center of the hall but talking with another girl lying on her bed. To him, it was almost entirely backward. He could only shake his head and continue looking through his visor.

"Reawakened," a woman said in greeting as she passed. He recognized her as one of the heads of the Search and Exploration Sector.

"Oundara," Varnil replied with a nod, having searched for her profile quick enough to reply by name. He was about to remove the data from in front of his eye when he noticed that she had stopped to speak with three men. One was older, perhaps five or ten years more than himself, and the other two were at opposite sides of their early twenties.

As they went through their normal exchange of greetings, Varnil pulled up as much information as he could. The database of the Remnants was chaotic, to say the least, and it took him time to piece together all of the recorded events tied to the men. It was a makeshift profile, but it was enough to understand the conversation as he followed along.

"This . . . what I am implementing, this is not control." Oundara paused as she seemed to search for the right words. "We are looking for stability for Firebrand."

"What kind of stability?" the younger of the two boys asked. He received a glare from their coordinator.

"As I am willing to let previous actions slide, let me answer with a question. Your coordinator did not know where you were when Safe Harbor called for the all-return. Where were you?"

The expressions might as well have brought up a clear explanation on Varnil's visor. They looked to the floor or off to the side.

"Now, what happens if Flerin is informed by coordinator, let's say, Symon Hale, that he will be shifting his search from Sol's current range to the sectors within a two-mile radius of twenty-three, four, minus thirteen with a scouting extension toward the span?" She paused a moment to see their reactions. "Frankly, Flerin would have to say 'go ahead, but my team may already be searching half of that.' Tymon, as the team lead, it will be up to you to work with your coordinator to prevent situations such as unnecessary search overlap."

"We will do our best," Tymon replied stiffly.

Oundara let out a sigh. "Everything we do is for a reason. Just like why I asked you three to meet me here." She motioned to the entirety of the area. "Everything you see here, from the benches to the stores of meal packs to the plates welded to the floor to the construction of new corridors—all of it is due to hard work by the Remnants." She smiled. "Look closer. Past the newer living quarters opened up to relieve overcrowding from Habitat Two. Look to the Remnants themselves. Everything in our existence, including us, has been painstakingly crafted by one hand or another over hundreds of years."

She stepped next to to the younger man. A quick glance at his visor brought his name up as Baxel. Oundara's height put her just a few inches taller than him. She pointed next to his head toward something. "See that control interface? The one right next to the vent? I know for a fact that that was retrieved by your team nearly seventy years ago. The majority of the reventilation system used in Dimarka's reconstruction was found by Firebrand's discovery of an unbroken supply cache in fourteen, seven, three. Now, I did not know that number off the top of my head, but it is part of the supply system."

Oundara stepped away and looked at the both of them. "I know you are good at what you do. I've seen the things you have found, and some of the places you have been. But more than that, I know you remember what you have found. Look around. See if anything you have come across is now somewhere around here. See if it is something that will be in use hundreds of years from now."

She gave them a moment to look around. "That is why I do what I do. To get people what they need now, and what future Remnants will need for their lives to come."

Varnil let out a sigh and turned back to waiting as Oundara started further into the details of tracking their progress. Perhaps locating a counselor in the Preservation Core could be of more use than an engineer to aid in their return to Earth. He knew, of course, that was simply a divergent thought. As soon as Connor showed up with Liaren, they would start working as hard as possible to lay the groundwork for the return of the entire Preservation Core to Earth.

Chapter 6: The Docks

Lieth Armain followed his memory back to when he had first joined Travend's resistance. The Loyalists, they called themselves. Loyal to Overlord Obrourke, who was both dead and replaced. Their only purpose was to take back Norclave for their own. He looked around the forgotten walkways of the under-levels of Norclave as he continued. He had stumbled here the first time, weeks ago, still covered in the ashes of his past. That was the only way he could have found it.

Several eyes watched from the dark, the same as everywhere else on the under-levels. A man recently missing his hand watched from where he sat against one of the railings, a heavy and ragged blanket pulled up to his chest. The only giveaway that Lieth was near Travend's headquarters was the pulse cannon that the man, an ex-soldier named Weril, hid under the worn cloth.

"Lieth," Weril said in greeting. "How did your search for Allek Skaves' information go?"

Lieth held up the split pieces of the data pad for the younger man to see. The lookout stared for a moment, looking both on the verge of excitement and disappointment. "Did it survive?"

Lieth gave nothing away, keeping his ever-present neutral look without having to act. It brought him no joy that they were nearing being able to bring pain to those who had ended his life; it was simply a step toward what had to happen.

"Damn, I wish you could say," Weril finally said. He lifted the stump of his arm up. "I wanted to hear we were going to get payback for what happened to the administrators. I mean, I uh, I didn't mean to say . . ."

"You are fine," Lieth said to stop the man. "We all have our own reasons for joining the Overlord's loyalists. As long as you do your part, it doesn't have to be for Travend."

The two had spoken briefly before. Weril had joined up with the other civilians to fight for the administrators. He had been given a command and sent to control an area that ended up not as far out of the fighting as the First Administrator guessed. The young man had his hand blown off by the Overlord's men, and he more recently was forced to hide in the dark recesses of the city as Olana Nuand rounded up any who'd fought against the Overlord. That left him fighting with the Loyalists against their common enemy.

Lieth moved off to the side and entered a low passage through the dark. He stepped through a doorway and held up a hand to keep the flickering laser sights from touching his eyes. After the resistance identified him, they lowered their weapons. There was a heavy rattle as the door began to pull open. Light spilled into the darkened room, and Lieth could barely hear the chattering of voices over the screeches and clanks. He stepped through into the hallway with a low warning from one of the Loyalists standing guard.

A wide array of projected displays and solid screens filled the far wall of the room. In front of the many switching display feeds and overlapping voices stood the leader of the Loyalists, Travend. His long trail of off-white hair hung heavily over his shoulders as he faced the wall of information. Travend motioned with his hands, causing different images to flash in and away. The images looked to be separate video feeds of the parts of Norclave. The tall man responded to several of the voices, though Lieth couldn't pick one out from another in the constant talking.

"What kind of news do you bring from the exploration teams?" Travend asked in a dangerous but offhand tone. If Lieth had not been listening carefully, he might have missed that the resistance leader was talking to him.

Lieth clutched the pieces of the data pad in his hand, thinking hard about his reply. "I have Allek Skaves' data, and while the information gives us the advantage, it also forces a hard decision."

The data pad illuminated as Travend pointed to one of the projections. The information immediately started shifting to his system.

"What is our advantage?" Travend asked.

"We can kill the Cryo."

Travend paused. "And the decision?"

"We can only do it now."

Travend nodded. "Leave me. I have to contact someone first."

* * *

Kara stepped casually into Jance's office and took a look around the repurposed space. She was surprised to see that the room had started to take on a lighter feeling. Lights had been placed to remove a number of dark corners, and the empty shelves were sprouting with plant life. Various decorations, from a hanging weave to standing panels, helped bring depth to the room.

"Gifts, for the Cryo," Jance said, stepping around the corner of a set of shelves. She had several display projectors held cradled in her arm. "I just hope I can live up to their expectations of her."

"Nobody knows what to expect," Kara said as Jance set one of the devices on the opposite shelf and turned it on. It simply emitted a soft glow.

"That makes it all the more difficult." Jance held a hand up to her visor and checked through her messages. "I've heard several people, including Olana herself, call the object that dropped down near Reclaim a sky flare. Do you have any idea what a sky flare is?"

Kara adjusted the new bag slung over her shoulder and smiled. "An explosion from up in the orbital wreckage. They are said to bring good luck, though that is because we all hope that it is an ejection of something. Usually, scrapsmiths will pay absurd amounts for the fallen material, though sometimes there is something of use for the technicians."

Jance stood still for a moment, giving a distant look at the slowly rotating disk of light. "The destruction of one half to bring existence to the other. It is incredible how many times I find examples of my world still changing into this one." She paused and gave Kara an apologetic look. "I mean to say, examples of my past, forming into what is now my world."

"We don't value you because you are part of our world," Kara said truthfully. "I fail to see why you should have to hold us as your own."

Jance smiled but did not speak. Instead, she turned and started back toward her hovering desk. As she neared and Kara followed behind, the displays flat against the surface or hanging above started to flicker on.

"I called you here to give you information that Olana wishes I would not. Perhaps you can call it a favor for looking into my suspicion over Allek Skaves, even though Overlord Nuand has stopped us from looking further."

Kara almost had to wonder if that was Jance scolding her for letting Kenneth meet with Karzon over the matter. Before Kara could comment on the subject, Jance continued.

"Olana wishes for you to accompany me as I tour the Rift Hills, as do I. It would help to have instruction, even on simple things such as sky flares."

Kara shot her a suspicious look. "What is the problem?"

Jance looked as if she was ashamed she had to explain. "I am to convince you to travel to Reclaim, the city in the Orbital Staging Facility, to find out what tech the Prime Elect has gained from the sky flare. Overlord Nuand thought you would be more likely to accept the mission if you believed this request came only from me. But I have come to trust and respect your opinion, Kara. That is why I wish you to join me on my flight, no matter what other reasons Olana has tried to weave into this."

Kara frowned as she thought through what she had heard.

"I understand," Jance said cautiously, "that you have expressed concern over going to Reclaim. The only reasoning I know for doing so is what Olana has told me, and I believe she may be right, though I understand I only know her side. As an effort to keep your trust, I will not try to persuade you. I will not say another word about it unless you ask."

Kara shook her head. The new Overlord was right. She would have been more likely to trust Jance not knowing the ruler of Norclave was behind the request. Kara adjusted the small bag on her shoulder at the thought of how easily she could have been played. Her trust in Jance could have gotten her killed, and that made her worry about her connection with her, and with Kenneth. Close ties were a dangerous thing, and she had nearly been hung by them in the past.

Kara let out a short breath and looked to the woman she had come to admire. "Jance, you have nothing to worry about. Nobody has put nearly high enough expectations in their Cryo."

* * *

Hours later, Jance felt a cold wind scrape up dust from the seventh level. Even a few drops of the misting rain managed to filter down through the heights of the starscraper to where she and Sora now stood at the top of the stairs of the Overlord's complex. They were meeting with a few officials of Norclave, some appointed by Olana, others who had managed to maintain their position from before.

"Ian Opeira, administrator of the ground trade routes, standing on the left," Sora explained quietly as they moved down the steps. Ian was a shorter figure with a rounded face and soft facial features. "And Zaireel Tuakana, the newly appointed emissary to the Steel Valley."

Zaireel was a taller man of a dark complexion wearing a heavy wrap of colorful patterned cloth around his shoulders. Both men wore fine clothing and were accompanied by a host of Norclaive soldiers, Kamriek mercenaries, and a few of the lesser but notable figures in the city.

"Cryo of Norclave, we are humbled by your presence," Zaireel said in an accent she could not quite place. She would have guessed its far origins to be from the heart of the Independent Treaty States, though even in those times, divisions in cultures had been instituted by the ITS governments to avoid cultural merging. Six hundred years had left room for a vast number of natural changes.

Zaireel bowed low with his fist crossed over his chest. The others followed his lead with similar gestures of respect. "And we welcome you with open arms into our world."

Jance nodded and smiled. "Mr. Tuakana, you have my greatest gratitude, and I look forward to learning as much as I can from you." She paused, making a mental tally of the group. Even without having the names associated to the other faces, she knew from Sora's schedule that they were all here. All except for Kara, and she expected she would meet her somewhere along the way.

"Shall we?" Jance asked, suggesting with a motion of her hand for the group to now start off through the city.

"Of course, Cryo," Opeira said, almost smiling at using the term.

She could almost feel the pride they had that she was in Norclave's possession, even if their city had been plagued with revolt and overthrow. While most of the administrators who rallied against Overlord Obrourke had been either captured or killed by Olana's efforts, there still remained a few that had taken up arms that were still unaccounted for. The difficult part for Jance, aside from their overly oppressive form of justice, was the fact that she could easily sympathize with their efforts against the previous Overlord.

"This settlement was originally started as an exploration base, some two hundred years ago," Opeira explained. He motioned up to the high reaches of the starscraper. "The land had just started to reclaim life enough to allow those brave few to settle here, and to look into the heart of the Rift Hills."

"This was the Council Starscraper," Jance absently noted. From the wide-eyed looks, she could tell that the information had more impact than she had intended. "What about the rest of the Rift Hills?" Jance asked in an attempt to keep the conversation flowing. "I have heard mention of other settlements."

"Yes, of course," Opeira said. "Most notable is Kamriek's Grove, as I'm sure you have learned in your experience with the Overlord Nuand. But there are smaller locations, such as Maraton and Reacher's Hale. Maraton is the first center for a concept we believe was once known as biological manufacturing."

"This was backed up by the records," Sora said from the side. "The pieces suggested that many starscrapers were dedicated solely to producing food for the populations of the world."

"Without having the advanced facilities available to us," Opeira continued, "Maraton has brought the ground itself into the equation, just as it is utilized by the natural forests and fields of grasses."

"Incredible," Jance said. She desperately wanted to be able to reach up to her visor and pull up the last date in which a civilization had lived off of uncontained, soil-based production. The inefficiency of the method, leaning to guesses in the nutrient composition and even the uncertainty of trivial effects such as the weather . . . it was simply amazing. But for now, that inefficiency would be suitable for maintaining the reduced population of the world.

Zaireel stepped into the conversation as they moved down a set of stairs off the seventh level. "For years, the Rift Hills have been transitioning further away from their reliance on meal packs; we've been looking to be able to maintain this location with minimal reliance on outside forces. In the past, settlements at the borders of the living edge of the land would be forced to move as the scavenging ran out. I can proudly say that, because of the efforts at Maraton, we will be able to maintain an expanding presence in the Rift Hills indefinitely."

Jance noticed that the walkways were beginning to fill with the citizens of Norclave. The escort of soldiers was on high alert, making sure that the narrower paths were cleared for the group. Compared with most of the sixth level, the large area they stepped into was open to the top. It was not the wide expanse of the trade center she heard Kenneth and Kara speak of, but instead a wide, ring-shaped balcony lined with large individual living quarters. Reaching over the open center of the encircling balcony were several other walkway rings.

Jance had to smile at the familiar sight. Whether they had specifically designed this area from the surviving data or it was simply an inflection burned into their culture, it reminded her of Atrium: 447. She had spent countless hours in that interior expanse, from her early memories of her childhood to the last days before the fall. It was there that she got to know the thousands of citizens—people with lives and families—within the structures she represented. Even the members of her own family used to meet there when they could find the time in their schedules.

To Jance, it had only been a couple of months since she had met her niece there. They'd just eaten a simple meal from the nearby dispenser station. They could have gone to the nearby cafeteria, but as it turned out, time was more precious than the experience.

Jance wiped her eyes as the others continued to talk about the significance of the park, as they called it. She would have to ask Sora on the details she missed later.

"And how does this compare to the other living conditions in Norclave?" Jance did not ask out of ignorance; she had been told of many of the city's shortcomings. Her question was met by several half answers and silence. It was the first step in making a real change.

They continued down through the city, skirting the edge of the trade center, making a brief pass by the water turbines, and meeting with a few individuals along the way. She could tell the escort of the group wanted to continue quickly, fearing some sort of confrontation within the still-contested city, but Jance made a point to stop and hear a few words from the people, just like she had always done in her own starscrapers.

Along the way, Kara and Kenneth had started trailing their group. With the amount of people following behind the group as if it were some sort of procession, Jance had nearly missed them. As they neared the edge of the city, a large number of Olana's mercenaries stood guard. With the two transports already hovering in the air keeping a watch on the docks, it almost looked as if they were prepared for war.

Jance followed the group out onto the dock where their own transport waited. She glanced behind to see Kara push her way through the soldiers forming a barricade. There were a few murmurs amongst the group.

"Is this tech hunter really coming with us?" Zaireel Tuakana asked quietly.

Kara moved up to join the rest of them, though she looked uneasy about the number of people and the formality of the situation. She received more than a few dark glances for not giving any salute or deference to the figureheads of Norclave.

"I am glad you made it," Jance said, motioning for Kara to come to her side.

The tech hunter looked as if she were resisting the urge to pull her hood up over her red hair. Even with the few scars marking her skin, Jance knew Kara would much rather cover her beautiful features under the shadow of a cowl.

Ian Opeira stepped forward and called out a few words to the gathered crowd. While many were simple commoners who'd happened upon event, Jance could spot a few within the crowd who held high positions like Opeira, Tuakana, or the few others stepping into the transport. It was the first time Jance had been seen in public; it was the first time Norclave would parade their Cryo as a tool to raise them above the surrounding regions. Opeira spoke of the wonderful occasion, and what greatness it would bring to Norclave. Jance tuned out the words as she looked around, taking in the sights before her.

Jance could imagine the crowd as one people. There were many different types of faces, but each wore an expression of awe mixed with hope. While some looking wearier would simply be wishing for better lives for them and their families, others would have a growing hope for the prosperity of Norclave. The subtle spacing in their positions along the walkways and adjacent landing pads spoke of basic divisions and fractures in the social structure. But she still believed everyone could be pulled together under a common link. They were the people of the Rift Hills, and, whether she was willing to admit it to herself yet or not, the people of a Cryo.

Jance felt a few small drops of moisture touch her face as a colder wind picked up from the south. There was a grey forming against the normal cloudiness of the sky. She wondered then if everyone in Norclave had a place to go if a full storm opened up later.

An applause spread forward as Opeira moved back to join the others in the transport. Jance had come to understand more about Norclave in the past few moments than any time sitting in the safety of the abandoned library. She suddenly had a grasp for the needs of the citizens, and of the weight of her own decisions.

"Cryo," Zaireel said in his unique voice, "it would be best if we were to depart. We do not wish to fly through the storm forming in the distance."

Jance began to follow Zaireel toward the transport to the supporting noise of the crowd. She noticed some sort of commotion from behind, but it was not until Kara shouted that Jance turned back to see.

"Jance!" Kara yelled again over the cheers. "Stop!"

Kenneth was trying to push through the soldiers holding him back. He was shouting something about the transport. It was then that Jance's world went dark with an earsplitting silence.

* * *

Just as quickly as the explosion under the transport shook the Norclave docks, panic erupted amongst the gathered crowds. Shouts and screams sounded all around as the soldiers each tried to understand the situation. Hurried movements set people running to safety or trying to fight their way toward their own loved ones, only adding further to the confusion around the docks.

Kara pushed herself up from the ground and pressed a hand to the gash on her forehead. To her side, several Kamriek mercenaries were checking over Zaireel, and more were attempting to approach the popping wreck of the transport.

"Where is Jance?" Kara shouted into the enveloping noise and commotion. She felt a sudden isolation as she watched the world move in a frantic whirlwind around her. "Where is the Cryo?"

Kara flipped around to see the line of soldiers letting through rough stretchers. One of the soldiers coming back from the transport started taking the blankets from the stretchers and waved the med-techs away. There was a shout as Kenneth shoved his way through the line. He had a heavy red mark forming on the side of his face where he had likely traded blows with the soldiers when they tried to keep him back.

"Where is Jance?" Kara asked as Kenneth rushed to her.

He looked at the gash on her forehead and reached into a pocket for a rag. He quickly turned it over, looking for a side that was not covered in grease or rust.

Kara grabbed his hands to keep him from worrying about her. She did not care about a small cut at the moment. "Kenneth, where is she?"

"They were rushing her somewhere. Are you—"

"Where to? How many were protecting her?"

"It's not like I stopped to count!" He flipped his hand up and started to pull her along. "Come on, we have to get moving."

Kara squeezed his muscled hand tight but quickly moved to outpace him as they rushed through the boiling confusion. She slowed down to pull Kenneth to the side as a host of armed soldiers rushed by toward the explosion.

When they passed, Kenneth pulled on her hand and took a few faster steps to run up beside her. "We need to start heading down. The docks will be closed, but we may be able to find a ground hauler out of the bottom of the city."

"What?" Kara asked sharply. "What are you talking about? We need to—"

"Jance cannot save us now. She'll be fighting for her own life, I would imagine."

"Who would . . . ?" Kara started.

Kenneth began to slow to a stop. He held a firm grip on her hand, but Kara did not try to shake free. "Olana Nuand." Kenneth gave her a hard look, making sure she understood his meaning.

"Kenneth," Kara said, using an elbow to wipe at the blood trying to reach her eye, "Olana did not do this. She would not have risked losing Jance!"

"But this is her chance to control the Cryo. If she eliminates us and uses the chaos back there to hide the truth, Olana removes the methods Jance has been using to act without her approval. That means no independent investigations, no scouting the city to see how the last of the administrators are being put down in the streets, nothing! Olana gets to feed Jance what lies she wants as free trade for knowledge of the past."

"That's absurd, Kenneth."

Kenneth sighed. "But what if Olana sees the chance?"

"Then what will running do?"

Kenneth produced a cleaner rag and gave it a hard shake. He held it up and gently pressed it above Kara's eye. "It means we can live another day."

Kara leaned into Kenneth's touch, now feeling the hard sting where the piece of metal had left a large gash. All of this, from his perspective, was for her. It gave her a sense of safety that she would have pushed away from with all of her might just a few years ago. It was both the caring hand, and the dangerous cut. The sensation of safety and security, and the reality of the danger it caused.

"Doesn't Olana still control Jance if we run?" Kara asked softly. "Would it be any different?"

"We would come back."

"Could we?" Kara pressed her hand to her head, over Kenneth's. "Would Jance still trust us, seeing that we left when she needed our help the most?"

"There is nothing we can do, Kara. We just have to stay alive now, and hope she understands when we get back. The chances that Olana does not seize this opportunity for deception . . ."

Kara picked up his trailing words, ". . . mean less than the chance that Jance cannot forgive being left behind. Again."

Kenneth lowered his gaze, and Kara continued. "Jance was left behind to our world by someone she cared for. I cannot see it as our place—as my place—to leave her side and still expect her to make things better for all us."

Kenneth had a sad look in his eyes when he finally looked back up to Kara. "Your place is mine. Wherever you decide to go, I will be there right beside you. If you want to—"

She interrupted, "Kenneth, there is no reason you have to stay." Kara jerked her hand free of his and took hold of the cloth as she stepped back. "I will find where they have taken her and—"

Kenneth took a step forward to match her step back. "You cannot just go about life not caring about what happens to you! If you go to Jance, so do I."

Kara let out a frustrated breath. He just didn't understand. She had half a mind to reach for the small medical tech in her pocket, though she doubted it had a hope of dropping Kenneth into a coma. It required at least a partially cooperating mind, and he would be too hardheaded at the best of times. She couldn't even take off running and lose him in the tangle of Norclave because he might very well march up and try to kick down the door to Olana Nuand's office by himself.

Kara adjusted the small bag that she had filled down in the South Corridors to a different position over her shoulder. "You can come with me, but if your paranoid thoughts actually come true, I will not have it be my fault when you get left behind in the escape."

Kenneth smiled. "I'm fine with whatever happens."

"You just said I can't go about not caring what happens to me! You are nothing more than a hypocrite." Kara rolled her eyes and held her hand out to him. "A grease-covered, bullheaded hypocrite."

Kenneth took hold of her hand. "Don't forget the scars on my arm."

"I would never," Kara replied as she pulled him along into the chaos of the city.

Chapter 7: Home Sectors

Baxel watched angrily as Oundara nodded in passing to the Reawakened as she continued away down the hall of Habitat Three. Firebrand had just gotten told, in very precise details, how to go about their business by someone who had never even been a part of the exploration teams. Oundara had started out managing supplies before she ever took on the role of one of the heads of the SE-S.

"Are we done here?" Baxel asked, though he knew he should hold his tone in check.

Flerin simply shook his head at the presented attitude. "Yes, Baxel, we are."

"I'm sorry," Baxel started. "It's just that . . ." he paused, thinking over everything there was to say before deciding to simply divert. "Can we just get back out there?"

"Not today," Flerin said. "I have to arrange meetings with the other coordinators, and both of your suits are due to be fit with trackers."

Baxel's shoulders slumped. He had hoped Flerin would overlook that recommendation. It seemed as if there was nothing they could do to get back to the wrecked ship. At least not for a while.

Flerin looked to them both just as he was about to leave. "The rest of the cycle is yours, but stay out of trouble. We'll get Firebrand up and running, strong as ever, in no time."

"I'm thinking of heading back to the SE-S," Tymon said with a yawn as Flerin turned to leave. Once the coordinator was well down the hall, he continued, "Perhaps after that, we could get ahold of something we could use to distort the tracking signal."

Baxel just let out a sigh. "You go ahead. Maybe I'll just stick here. Take a look around. Like Oundara said."

"Hey, we will figure this out."

"You know the trade business better than I do." There was a history to Baxel's comment. His own parents had left for the Trade Sector every waking cycle to work, but they had elected to avoid teaching him the methods of the system. Their belief was that it would sway his judgment when he reached his twenty-thousand cycles. Every Remnant went through a process on their thirteenth year where they stayed with the various sectors about Safe Harbor. By the end of that year, or sometimes more, they chose where they would work, usually for the rest of their life.

Baxel started down the same hallway he had stared down for the first thirteen years of his life. He passed by a number of rooms currently without their residents, and a few more where several faces he recognized sat in various states of relaxation or work. There were differences brought about by the years, however. Just a few pods down past the small meal pack storage area was the habitat pod that used to be his own. He glanced in out of curiosity and received a wave from an old man playing a game of chips with what looked like his grandson. They would have been moved to this room from some hallway or cramped storage room in Habitat Two after he left for the Search and Exploration Sector.

The next door belonged to his parents, Evia and Oxlen. He peeked into the room, though it was immediately apparent they were not there. The standard beds for the joint living pod were neatly made, and only a few small objects lay around the room.

He quietly moved on, knowing he would have plenty of time to see them again. Over the years he could have made a better habit of it, especially considering how often he and Tymon had used their free time to continue the search. But now, he would have more than enough free time with the lag in Firebrand's operation for the next couple of days. If it wasn't for the trackers the Production and Research Sector were putting in their suits, he and Tymon could have been halfway to the search boundary by now.

* * *

Varnil barely noticed as the group broke apart after the conversation with Oundara. He was focused on waiting for the meeting that could decide his course of action for the rest of his life aboard the Orbital Armistice Fleet to begin. Varnil kept finding himself glancing down the hall of Habitat Three for the group to arrive.

"Reawakened," Vigil Connor said in greeting once they neared. "The Vigil is grateful for your presence." The old man led two younger members.

It made sense to send the migrant and several of the grunt force for the simple task of cleaning out Dimarka's room. Varnil stood, looking to each of the figures he would be accompanying.

"This is Kyren Stellee," Connor said, motioning to the young man at his side. Kyren was only a bit shorter than Varnil, making him quite tall for his age. It looked as if he was only a few years past his induction into the Vigil. Fifteen or sixteen, Varnil guessed. "And this is Liaren Marenday, who actually grew up on this level before joining the Vigil."

Varnil nodded politely to the girl, no older than twenty years. Her wavy brown hair hanging over the white Vigil sash and her sweet face only worked partially to hide the supposed ferocity she engaged in arguments with. Connor had explicitly warned him to tread lightly when convincing her of the need to break into the Preservation Core. Knowing that she was the best choice out of all who had access to the cryogenics section made the task seem all the more difficult.

"Shall we continue?" Connor asked, motioning down the long hallway to where Dimarka's habitat pod was.

Varnil fell into step as they moved down the strangely open hallways. The long stretches of plating and extra reinforcement crossing into the footpath gave a much more makeshift feeling than the sections that had been spared in the uprising.

"All this has been a long time in the making," Connor said, looking at the hallways themselves. "I arrived in Safe Harbor only a few years before this was torn to pieces. Though, while some speak of the resilience of the Remnants, I say it is only proof that we are not immune to disaster."

Liaren shook her head, probably thinking she knew the direction the old migrant wanted to take the conversation. "The Warden saw us through those trials, never forget that."

"Not all of us," Connor said darkly, stepping over a thicker chunk of bracing. It had been part of an exterior wall before the reconstruction.

"We always have been the Remnants. Survivors of a fleet faced with much worse." Liaren adjusted her white sash after stepping graciously out of the way of another Remnant passing in the hall. By the length of the sash, she was the same initiate ranking as Connor and the boy. "That is not to say I disagree with you. We can improve."

Varnil decided he should try to step in, as Connor had directed. "Does that improvement mean going back? To Earth?"

The young woman stopped in the hallway and looked at him sternly as the rest of them came to a halt. "My meaning was to say we improve here. Even if we were guided by the Warden this very cycle to travel to the ancient cities, we would not be there by tomorrow."

Varnil let out a breath. "But why should we wait to start preparing? One day, the Warden will command us to go back. We must prepare for the inevitable."

"Perhaps," Liaren said, "or we must prepare for the possible, and wait before we commit our actions blindly. We still lack the Warden's sight."

* * *

Baxel drummed a fist absentmindedly against a scratched panel along the side of another hallway as he continued wandering. He did not recognize this area, though it followed the same form as the rest of Deck Fourteen. In his youth, this was nothing more than a construction zone, newly pressurized just before he set off for his placements.

A group of people standing in a section of the hallway caught his attention. Where normally there were at least two or three people to be seen at any given point in time, there were about fifteen individuals standing around, talking amongst themselves. Their attention was centered around one closed doorway.

"What's going on?" Baxel asked the first person he happened upon. The squarish face of the girl was familiar, but then again, everyone in Safe Harbor was familiar in some way or another.

"We're waiting to see what comes out of Dimarka's room. The Vigil will be coming to shift possessions to Food Storage and Supply."

Baxel glanced again at the gathered people. They were not standing in one group, but rather speaking amongst themselves in hushed clumps. He could understand gathering whenever something out of the ordinary happened; any small change was enough to stir excitement, however there seemed to be a greater nervousness than there should be.

"Waiting for what, exactly?" Baxel asked in a voice as quiet as the rest standing around.

"Oh," she said with a bit of a catch in her breath. "It's nothing."

"Right. Did you convince yourself with that one, or just me?"

The girl blushed and folded her hands in on themselves. "We're . . . we're not supposed to talk about it."

Baxel let a breath out. "I assume everyone here knows?" He sent her a pointed glance. "Well I am here too, am I not?"

"No, I should not. My grandfather warned it would set the whole fleet into a scare."

Baxel nodded and waited for her to continue.

She pointed over to an elderly lady sitting on one of the benches. The woman was watching the door with a particularly unwavering look. "That's my grandmother. She says she heard an argument the cycle before they found Dimarka. The rest of us were sleeping . . . when we think he was killed."

Baxel wanted to let out a low whistle. It was amazing how a batch of people quietly spinning ideas could come up with some worrying thoughts.

"He was at odds with plenty of people," Baxel said dismissively. "I doubt aggressive conversations were out of the ordinary. And nothing is to say his age did not take him after they left."

"I suppose . . ." she paused for a second. "I suppose you are right. Nobody has been . . . well . . . murdered in Safe Harbor since the uprising. And my grandparents are from that time. Wait, where are you going?"

Baxel did not reply as he started toward the door, and neither did he try to stop his impulse.

He tapped the panel to Dimarka's room amidst a number of looks. They would just stand there and wait, watching for whatever came out of the room all the same. He figured he would go in and look. The Vigil was coming to reclaim everything anyway. Perhaps he could tell these people nothing had happened.

The door hissed open, revealing a narrow hallway about twenty feet in length. It was lit by only a few small lights near the floor. Baxel could easily tell these were not standard habitation quarters. To him, it looked as if Dimarka had put his name on a larger location when the construction was still underway.

He ran his hand along the wall as the door shut behind him, leaving the hall lit by just the pale running lights. Baxel continued, and the entire area began to come to life with scattered overhead lights. As he passed the halfway point of the hall, his hand brushed into open space. A short dead-end corridor jutted off to the side. It looked as if it contained a few storage crates before ending in a thick wall of plates and a window looking out into a large expanse of the wreckage.

Baxel continued to the end of the hall, where another access pad glowed beside a doorway. He pressed his hand on it, and the yellow light above flickered a few times before the door unlatched. Baxel could hear the spinning of motors, but the door did not begin to open until he tugged on a makeshift handle.

As he entered, he could immediately tell Dimarka had more furnishings than just about anyone else, likely due to the number of small meetings he'd held here. The room was large enough to accompany a small table and four chairs, along with another two seats along a side wall. Of course, his age and influence tended to also allow him more decorations than the standard Remnant. The walls had a few displays showing static images captured throughout Safe Harbor, and one was an image of the speckled lighting of the surface of Earth framed by the wreckage of the fleet. It was ironic, considering how much the man had contested any notion of leaving Safe Harbor.

Toward the back of the room were two low shelves stacked with a few data pads. Next to them was a standard-sized bed, though the frame was made of welded crates. The covers were disheveled, though from the way the blanket was still tucked in at the top of the bed, Baxel could immediately see that Dimarka had not died in his sleep.

As Baxel continued to stare, his attention was drawn to a slow pulsing of blue light from underneath the bed. He reached between two of the scrapped crates toward the light and felt nothing, so he lay down on the floor and reached in as far as his shoulder and neck would allow. With just the tips of his fingers, he felt a small disk.

"Who are you?"

Baxel jerked his arm back in surprise, jamming his elbow into a hard corner and twisting his shoulder. He rolled over in a panic to see who was behind him, though finding out did little to help his nerves.

The room took on a soft blue glow as the projection of a woman leaned over to look at him. She watched him as if she was surprised and also confused—a look Baxel did not think was possible from one of the Vigil projections.

"Where is Dimarka? Did he send you to fetch me?" She glanced down to where Baxel was struggling to pull his arm free. "Perhaps Dimarka dropped the . . . no, that does not seem right. Who are you?"

"My name . . . uh, I'm Baxel."

"Did Dimarka send you?" she asked with a bit more force than previously, now seeming to think that Baxel should not be here.

Baxel started to reply, but then he was hit with a question. "You do not remember?"

"I remember he was not in attendance at the Vigil meeting, though I expected that he would be here . . ."

The projection let her words trail off as she appeared to think

"Dimarka was found . . . well, he, uh, he left in the arms of the Warden." Baxel sat up. "His offsending was last cycle. You were at the meeting afterward."

Baxel was surprised to see a stunned look on the projection's face. As much as he disliked the projections, for a long moment he had forgotten he was even talking to an artificial intelligence. Her mannerisms perfectly matched the person she was imprinted from in the Vigil's past, with the only exception being her transparent existence projected from the device still under Dimarka's bed.

Baxel frowned. The people in the hallway had said they heard an argument the wake cycle before Dimarka was found. Perhaps they had simply heard these two talking. "When was the last time you spoke with Dimarka?" Baxel asked.

The projection looked down the hallway, her hair twisting against her shoulders as naturally as a direct recording. "I have a bad feeling. Baxel, you need to hide."

"I need to what? And a bad feeling? Can you actually . . . ?"

"Someone is coming. Get to the offshoot in the hall, I will get the lights." Just as she finished, the entirety of the room and hallway dropped back to only the dim running lights along the edges of the floors. Now, Dimarka's room was illuminated only by the woman.

"Baxel, I need you to do one more thing. Tell me to remember this conversation."

"Okay, remember it."

Baxel was left in the dark as she disappeared. With her warning, he wasted no time in rushing out of the room and into the narrow hall. Just as the systems of the exterior door began to activate, Baxel ducked into the small offshoot. He felt in the dark to see if he could hide behind the crates, but with the footsteps approaching down the hall, he simply had to crouch down and wait.

He could pick out the rough tone of Connor Sevison, the Vigil they called the migrant, and to his surprise, the voice of Liaren.

"Yes," Liaren said with a hint of exasperation as they neared, "I believe we should know what the habitability of the Earth is like. But that does not mean I agree with you!"

Baxel could feel his heart thumping in his throat as they passed. He had heard her argue several times in the meetings of the Vigil over the past few years in much the same manner. She had always been certain of her opinion, and Baxel had learned the hard way that she did not like anyone speaking incorrectly on her behalf.

Baxel moved to where he could look around the edge of the intersection to see their dimly lit feet continue into the room.

"How not?" the old Vigil argued back as he led Liaren and one other figure into Dimarka's room. He activated the lights, though somehow the ones in the hallway remained dim. "You said that you agree that we should send down some sort of probe so we will be prepared to return!" Connor turned to lift up the edge of Dimarka's bed.

"No," Liaren said, crossing her arms over her wavy hair and sash. "I said we should gather knowledge of the habitability of Earth. But only so that we may do nothing with it, until the Warden demands. Being prepared is not the same as preparing to act."

"Connor," another voice, this one belonging to Varnil Williams, said in a calming tone. "We can argue the end all we like, but the truth is that we will never get the Vigil to agree to what has to happen to even start."

The old man let the edge of the heavily patched mattress drop and started running his hands along the backs of the chairs in the room.

"And what has to happen first?" Liaren asked the Reawakened.

"Do you know of anyone here, or in all the fleet, that could make a probe able to sample atmospheric conditions and other environmental factors? Or do the Remnants simply have one lying around?"

Baxel nodded to himself. If he had found something like it at one point, it was likely that it had been scrapped out for pieces.

"As I see it," Varnil continued, "we need more than just one Reawakened. Even if I were to swap out with some scientist or engineer, their time would be spent working on this observation device instead of fulfilling the duties of the Reawakened."

Baxel felt his face take on a look very similar to Liaren's. The idea of a second Reawakened had never even crossed his mind. For as long as he could remember, they never had more than one Reawakened pulled from the Preservation Core at a time. Even transferring to a new Reawakened did not include keeping the old one awake to help pass on the role. It just did not happen.

Before Liaren could protest, Varnil held up a hand. "I know that it is impossible. What I really mean to propose, is that we simply locate the names of those in the Preservation Core that could be up to the task. Right now, the Remnants pick the next Reawakened at random. We know we need someone special to help create such a probe. All I ask is that we look for the right person."

"A list?" Liaren asked, sounding mostly diffused regarding the proposition.

Varnil nodded. "A simple list of qualifications and names."

As Connor went about the room searching through boxes and drawers, Liaren seemed to think the matter through.

Eventually, she looked back to the Reawakened. "The Vigil will disagree. Knowing names and qualifications, we may be influenced to pick only Reawakened that will help the fleet. Per the Warden's judgment, having a Reawakened is not for the Remnant's benefit."

Varnil nodded and held a fist up to his lips in thought. "So, you are warning against having the power to expend all the useful Remnants too early, when survival is a game of centuries."

"No, I was not." Liaren glared at him with a sparkle of determination in her eyes that nearly made Baxel's breath catch. "But that notion holds its own truth. We must not let ourselves have the ability to change our fate, but simply to continue the path set by the Warden."

Varnil was momentarily interrupted by Connor crawling on the floor and patting on the underside of a set of shelves. "What if the Vigil did not know?" Varnil continued. "We keep the entirety of the list from influencing their decision, but we also have the names for this one project ready if we can act within the Warden's wishes. Preparation, separated from action."

This time, Baxel understood Liaren's hesitation. Secrecy was something largely frowned upon in the fleet. Though, there were occasions where things went more efficiently if the details were not widely spread. The example that came to Baxel's mind was that of the suspicion rising in the hall over Dimarka's death.

"And how do we obtain this list?" Liaren asked.

"We slip into the Preservation Core and mark down simple information," Varnil explained. "Names and professions only."

"And who keeps this information?"

Varnil smiled. "It shall be kept safe by the Reawakened of Safe Harbor. Someone impartial to the fleet and bound to protect the names that are taken."

Baxel was surprised when Liaren nodded shortly in agreement. He had almost figured she would fight to the death over the traditions of the Vigil.

Connor gave a satisfied grunt and pulled his arm out from underneath Dimarka's bed. When Baxel saw him slip the projection device into a pocket, he took a step forward. To Baxel, it seemed as if the device had been hidden, but to what purpose he didn't know. It was only until he was standing in the doorframe that he felt the shock of his mistake.

For a moment, Baxel simply returned the stares from Liaren, the Reawakened, and the migrant.

"Baxel?" Liaren asked. "What are you . . . ?"

"I, uh . . ."

Liaren scoffed. "Were you listening in on us?"

"Well, yes. But don't act like—"

"Dammit, Baxel!" Liaren said sharply. "You are only around at the wrong time!"

Varnil raised his hand to his visor. "You are Firebrand, are you not? I remember seeing you in the Hall of the Vigil."

Liaren shot Baxel a dangerous look that nearly made him turn away. "You were in the Hall of the Vigil too? I know you are having trouble in your sector, but you made it clear a long time ago that you wanted nothing to do with the Vigil. So what are you doing, really?" She held up a hand before Baxel could reply. "Before you even start, I know it is not volunteering to help reclaim Dimarka's belongings."

Baxel glanced to the pocket of the old Vigil. Normally he would have nothing to do with a Vigil projection, but he could not shake the feeling that there was something more going on.

"What did you find under the bed while these two were arguing?"

After a moment, they turned to Connor, if only to see his reaction to Baxel's presence.

"This?" Connor pulled out a small disk near the size of the palm of his hand. "It's a projector, connected to the archives. It is why the Vigil sent me. This one is linked to Tialee."

"What did Dimarka have her for?" Liaren asked. "I thought she was restricted to the Hall of the Vigil?"

Connor shrugged dismissively. "Everyone needs guidance of some form."

"Well? Does she know what happened?" Baxel asked. By the way Connor frowned, Baxel guessed the migrant did not need to be reminded of the dangerous suspicions floating around from the people waiting outside.

"We all know what happened, boy. A great man was released by the Warden in his sleep. Now you should go. You should not be here."

Baxel looked to the half-made bed. "I want her word for it."

"What?" Liaren asked. "Baxel, why would you even . . ."

Connor silenced her with a look and a shrug. He then held his hand forward, and the device created a shimmering static around the room, eventually forming into the translucent image of the ancient Vigil imposed into an AI.

"Tialee," Connor said to command the attention of the AI mirror, "do you have the data of your last conversation with Dimarka?"

The projection looked around at the others in the room before replying, "No, I do not. I am sorry I cannot be of help in the matter."

"Hmm," Connor sounded. "There you have it. He must have told it to not remember." The Vigil started to move his hand to cancel the projection.

"Wait," Baxel said. "She might have other information." Baxel turned to look at the woman. He guessed her to be no older than thirty; while the AI mirror could have been created centuries ago, the projections would appear in the likeness of when the personality matrix was created. Or at least, that is what Liaren had told him once. "Tialee, if it wouldn't be too much trouble, do you remember the last time you were supposed to meet with Dimarka in this room?"

The projection smiled lightly, almost as if happy with how Baxel had phrased the question. "It would have been a day ago. I could be more precise with the value if it would help."

"No, there is no need," Connor said bluntly. "Do not save this conversation."

Tialee looked to Baxel one last time before dissipating into a swirl of static. He felt a shiver go down his spine, feeling the same notion he always did with the Vigil projections. They seemed to always know more than they let on.

"Firebrand, huh?" Varnil asked, pulling Baxel's attention after the long and silent moment devoid of Tialee's glow. The Reawakened looked over his shoulder to Liaren and Connor. "I might just have an idea, and something tells me you won't say no after this, Baxel."

Chapter 8: A Flickering Display

Kara bounded up the steps to the Overlord's complex with Kenneth clicking behind. The chaos of the docks seemed to extend clear up to the seventh level as all the Norclave soldiers and Kamriek mercenaries were called to arms. She glanced back as Kenneth pointed to the marks of discolored metal on the steps from the burn of repulsors. It seemed the Norclave soldiers had rushed Jance to another gunship or transport and hovered over the steps themselves to transfer her out to safety.

"Kara!" Sora called to her as they entered the hallways of the complex. The black-haired woman held a single data pad and seemed to be overrun with stress as she attempted to fill Jance's position in managing the confusion. Sora waved them closer.

"Where is she?" Kara asked.

"They took her back, but you cannot see her now."

"Thanks," Kara said, nearly lunging in the direction Sora had nodded. She set down the long hall and could hear that Kenneth was close behind, though this time there were a number of angry and concerned words echoing with the chunk of metal on his boot.

The hall of fused metal plates opened up into a smaller room lined with rough benches. Had it simply been the two glass-shouldered mercenaries standing guard, Kara would have pushed past them and continued in to where they were keeping Jance, but Olana Nuand stood in front of the door with her arms crossed. Kara slowed to a stop and Kenneth stepped up beside her.

"Before now, I could not say if you two would show your faces or not." Olana shifted her piercing gaze to each of them in turn. "I want you to explain what the hell happened to my Cryo. Did you provoke Travend?"

Kenneth looked down and Kara clenched her jaw. "We went to the South Corridors. Kenneth met with an old contact. We were trying to learn more about this threat."

The few soldiers in the room tensed at her tone, and Olana scowled at Kenneth and Kara. "You watch who you are speaking to. If I find out you caused this by going behind my back, you will not remain in my city." After a moment of weighty silence, Olana spoke again. "Who was this contact?"

"It does not matter," Kenneth replied.

"You had better believe it does!" Olana practically screamed. "If he sold out your treasonous actions, you both will be at fault for putting Norclave dangerously close to collapse!"

Kenneth took a step forward before Kara could. "The only name you should be concerned with is Allek Skaves. I guarantee his data pad had all the data to paint a bulls-eye on that specific dock and transport. If you'd taken one moment to think about this city besides the extermination of the administrators, if you had been willing to listen to Jance's concerns over the building threat here, this would not have happened."

Kara put a hand on Kenneth's shoulder as she stepped up beside him. "How about we find who actually caused this, Nuand? We find the conspirators, we find Travend, and then we put an end to this so-called resistance."

Olana said nothing for the moment. She simply watched them as if weighing their determination. "I know you will not work under me. And the only person either of you two seem to listen to is hanging by a thread."

"Then just tell us what needs done," Kenneth said. "We can help ensure her safety."

Kara reached into a pocket and produced a small silver square marked with the medical double cross. She held it forward to Olana, knowing Jance would have the greater need for it. "And whatever else we can do to help her."

Olana motioned for the guards to take Kara's device. "If you really believe those words, follow me." Olana pushed between them. Kara shot Kenneth a worried glance before following behind the new Overlord. After a series of checkpoints through the dull halls of the complex, they entered what was once the Norclave Library.

The few individuals with visors did not even look up as she and Kenneth followed Olana into Jance's office. The others gathered around Jance's desk all wore the visors of the administrators, though Kara had the feeling that they were all new to their positions here in Norclave.

"Tell these two anything you would tell me," Olana said as she stormed into the room. "Give me opinions, information, anything you have or have found that may be of use."

One of the people around Jance's desk spoke. "The Cryo marked the departure of several individuals leaving the city only hours before the event. It seems that her system of cameras and sensors picked up on them heading east. She made a note to find out if they were heading to something she called the 'landing site.'"

Olana put her hands on her hips. "Anyone else marked for suspicion?"

The man scratched his head and looked dazed at the large number of screens they had projected up from the surface. "Well, there are hundreds." He looked up to the Overlord. "And near as we can tell, hundreds more existed, but have since been unmarked."

"Why did this one stand out to you?" Kenneth asked.

The man glanced at Olana as if wondering if he should reply. "It had the latest update to it. There were some other notifications, some even while we have been searching, but those were created by her system, not her."

Kara narrowed her eyes, now realizing that something did not add up. "You were here before the explosion."

"At my orders," Olana said. "After you were sent to track Allek Skaves, I needed to know what else the Cryo was hiding from me. It seems that the rebuilding of Norclave's defenses included a massive observation network. All linked to here."

"But is there anything on Travend?" Kenneth asked.

"Not one mention of the name," one of the workers said. "At least that we can access after the Cryo was . . ." The man took a short breath to change direction. "Some additional files were opened earlier during our search, and the best we could guess was that the Cryo was helping us remotely. It scared the hell out of us at first."

As the man trailed off, Kara realized that these three very well could have known some of the other high-ranking officials caught in the transport. She glanced around the room as she brushed her hand along the edge of a shelf. Lying on it was the broken visor Jance said belonged to Avery Thorne.

"About this group that departed that Jance was concerned about," Kara started, "is there anything that stands out?"

The man enlarged several of the projected displays as he searched for information. "Connections to multiple dead ends, and other reference marks to files we cannot access. We only know they set out on foot."

Kenneth let out a grunt. "That sounds familiar."

Kara leaned forward. "Show me the images. If they set out on foot, they are trying to stay hidden."

The man adjusted the floating projections with some difficulty and enlarged one showing six figures leaving the city. Two of them had weapons, and they were following a smaller man with dark hair and dull skin. They were the same ones who had killed Allek Skaves, plus a few others.

Kara stood back up, knowing this was their best shot at finding Travend. "I'm going after them."

"That's enough," Olana said, holding up a hand to stop Kara. "Ignore this, Kara. There are more important things for you to do than to chase down insignificant leads. You are a tech hunter, not a tracker. Your place is searching for things, not people."

Kara looked back to the Overlord with a frown. "But I've seen them before. They were the ones looking for Allek Skaves's data pad. What if they had something to do with what happened to Jance's transport as well?"

"We don't know what was on that data pad. It could have been nothing." Olana pulled the amber-colored glass cube out of her pocket as if she were unaware of the action. "In any case, Norclave has bigger needs than finding justice for what happened. If they are the ones who lit up the docks, then I am glad they are leaving the city."

"How can you say that?" Kara asked angrily.

"My goal," Olana countered, "is for the security of Norclave. Right now, the two biggest threats are from Travend making another attempt at my Cryo's life, and from Reclaim seeing this as a weakness. That, Kara, is why the Cryo wanted you to travel to the Steel Valley."

"No, Jance told me about your meeting with her. You told her to convince me."

"And did you listen? To her words, not mine. Did she tell you how she agreed that we need to know what the Prime Elect now has in his possession? Or did she invalidate her own opinions because they happened to be the same as mine?"

"She never got the chance to tell me anything."

Olana gripped the cube. "Or did you never give her that chance?"

Kara met Olana's stare over the course of a moment that nearly made the room ice over.

"For all you say you are willing to do for the Cryo," Olana said darkly, "you seem to only be working for yourself. Go to Reclaim. Find what tech the Prime Elect has recovered. I will deal with keeping the Cryo alive."

* * *

Lieth looked over to Darmic as the low rumble of thunder sounded in the distance. Darmic trudged along through the underbrush of the impact valley with constant nervous glances into the thick forest. Even with the pulse cannon slung over his shoulder, leaving the familiarity of Norclave was enough to put the big man on edge.

Behind Lieth, Weril absentmindedly picked at the large scab where his hand should have been. The ex-soldier had leapt at the chance to take part in a large operation for Travend, especially with his ties to the administrators' rebellion. The other three of the group were the rogue scrapsmiths and the technician who had helped them execute the operation. All it took was one well-placed charge to dismiss the illusion of the Cryo. She was just another person for the false Overlord to play as a pawn.

"That storm is sounding rough," Darmic growled as they made their way into an open clearing where thick slabs of concrete jutted up from the greyed dirt like miniature mountain ranges.

"It will bring hot rain for sure," Weril said in a measure of grim agreement. "I didn't get a chance to bring enough cover."

Leith understood the danger of their situation. While he had never been even this close to the outerzones, even the rain sifting down through the layers of Norclave was enough of an experience to make him worried. The reason so many in the rougher parts of the city had pitted skin or were marked with rashes was the occasional storm like this. To any who could not find adequate cover from the acid rains, it was more than an uncomfortable business.

One of the others brushed his hand along the twisted bark of a dead tree. It looked as if it had been scalded over the years. "We could see about pulling up enough plates to get something over our heads."

"We are not stopping," Lieth said harshly. "Not this close to Norclave." They had already had three patrols fly overhead in the last hour. And besides that, he doubted if there would be anything left that was easy enough to pull out of the ground, at least not this close to the ever-growing city. "If we make good enough time, I know of a place we can find real shelter."

"Where is that?" Weril asked.

Lieth gave no reply. He preferred not to spoil their hope with the distance. While he couldn't care less about himself, he knew they would be uneager to walk through the storm.

* * *

Kara stood nearly two hundred feet above the span of trees that now swayed under a darkening sky. She probably had the best view of anyone watching the rolling clouds and the bright pulsing within the storm. The light sprinkles from earlier now took the form of sporadic sheets of rain, dumping clean water down through the starscraper and into Norclave. By the tint to the clouds, she guessed they had pulled up quite a bit of moisture from the ocean and knew the storm would later release more than a fair share of scalding rain.

Storms like this tended to make large changes to the landscape. Leaves would dry up on the trees afterward, and the grasses would look as if they were browning for the winter for at least a few weeks. As for the people, many would-be tech hunters would rethink their ideas of a quick and simple grab at wealth. They would join the unprivileged of Norclave in the struggle for cover, often hoping they were deep enough in the ruins or under enough layers of the city to keep dry.

Kara adjusted the small bag hanging over her shoulder and let out another frustrated breath. With the group on foot, she could easily catch up to them when they stopped for the rain. But if she did not catch their trail quickly, it could be weeks before she found them. If they split up, the process would take even longer. Kara knew she would have to ignore the Overlord's wishes. Finding them would take time.

She would have to bring one of them back to lead them to Travend, even if Olana Nuand was too worried about her city to think straight. It would be a waste of time at this point to spy on the Prime Elect of Reclaim when there was a chance of stopping Travend before he could cause more damage. Besides, she had heard of several tech hunters that had died dealing with the Prime Elect's officials, and as far as she knew, they had less history with Reclaim than she did.

Kara rubbed over her eyes to the bridge of her nose. She had been the one trying to sell their newfound tech to the Prime Elect—the tech she later found out Mallek had taken from a group of Kessian researchers. Between claimed goods and dead Kessians, the only thing that looked worse for her than sparking a conflict between Carvanhold and Reclaim was that she was now working for Norclave.

A swirl of rain pelted the steel of the docks as a heavy wind pushed it under the edge of the starscraper. Kara pulled her hood over her head and slipped her facecloth up over her nose. She knew she had to set out soon. She was only wasting time thinking about Olana Nuand's words.

Kara slipped the small bag off her shoulder and held it in front of her. The rain bounced off her wrapped knuckles as she thought about what she would say to Kenneth. She gripped the straps of the bag as tight as she could, if only to hide her shaking hands from herself. She wondered if there was anything she *could* say.

Kara let out a sigh, knowing that she just had to hope for forgiveness.

* * *

Kenneth held a hand up to shield his eyes as he hurried along the top of the seventh level. When Kara had rushed out of the room, she told him to meet her on the seventh-level docks. He had stayed at the order of Olana and she had explained more about the situation with Travend. For now, she had tasked him with making sure Jance's surveillance system remained operational, though he knew she was more than eager to let him help pin down the resistance if he played along.

It sounded almost like hundreds of tiny bolts ticking against the surface of the metal as the rain continued down. He could see little channels along the edges of buildings or in the sloppy jobs of binding the plates together where courses of black char ran down with the water. While the repairs from the upheaval of the administrators' rebellion were nowhere near complete, at least the upper level would be cleaned of the grim affair. Kenneth nearly paused when he spotted a trickle of blackened rust spilling over the edge. Then again, it may turn out that only the upper level was benefiting from the cleaning.

"You had better get inside soon!" a man's voice called out through the rumble of thunder. The vibrations made several loose panels hum against one another in a chilling chorus. Kenneth used to sit and listen to the noises the city would make when the weight of strong winds would pass through. He would sit in the middle of a street, trying to stay out as long as he could and still avoid the sting of the hot rain when it came. Even then, he would find some overhang and stand at the edge of danger, knowing that he would have at least a few hours, or even the night, without the administrators able to hassle him.

"Kara?" Kenneth called out as another strong gust picked up from the edge of the city. As the sky churned even above the high frame of the starscraper, Kenneth could see no one out on the windswept docks. The water blowing off the tops of the transports and across the docks would have made Kenneth not want to stand anywhere near the edge this high up, but he was unsure if Kara would take the same precaution. He wondered if perhaps she was waiting somewhere nearby.

Kenneth stepped through the half-opened door of the abandoned security point. He knew that the best way to find Kara was to stand where she would be watching. Even still, Kenneth looked around with a hard squint through the pelting rain. It was when he noticed a small bag lying in the center of the dock that he let his hand drop. As he moved closer, he came to recognize it. It was the same bag Kara had been filling to the brim with supplies when they were in the South Corridors.

Kenneth knelt down by it, feeling the standing water soak into his knees. There was a magnet on one of the straps holding it to the platform in the heavy winds. Kenneth opened the main compartment of the bag. Amongst the meal packs, extra powercells, and general assortment of supplies to be prepared for anything, Kenneth could see the glowing projection of the wristband he had given Kara when they sat waiting for Jance's cryopod to open.

Kenneth picked up the small band and watched as the rain split through the small projected display. He knew then that Kara had left this behind for him. All the time she had spent piecing together this kit, she must have intended to leave it with him. He clutched the band tight in his drenched hands—causing only flickers of the display to split between his fingers—and was left to wonder how long she had intended to leave without a word.

Chapter 9: Preservation

"Vigil projections and . . . Baxel, come on," Tymon said, raking his hand through his hair in frustration. "Flerin said it would take a while to get the trackers from Production and Research. That means this might be our best bet to get more supplies out."

"But until we figure out how to not be bloody nav beacons, what good is it?" Baxel adjusted the thick bundle of clothing under his arm. "What happened to looking in the Trade Sector for something to block the tracking signals?"

"Why are you leaving this all up to me?" Tymon bit back. "I got the supplies. Now I'm supposed to figure out how to sneak past Flerin on my own?"

Baxel turned away from his longtime friend and looked out the window next to the habitat barrier of the SE-S. He then glanced down to check the time on his data pad. Normally his helmet could provide him with all the information he needed, but with it locked away in the hall behind them, he now had to rely on the stupid handheld device.

Baxel glanced over his shoulder. "I just . . . I have another idea, okay? But we're going to need some help to not get kicked out of Safe Harbor if we do this."

"Yeah? Well, I got an offer from Redemption."

Baxel turned to face Tymon, putting his back to the window and the expanse of Safe Harbor. "What was the offer?"

"Reyson seems to think he is on to us. He thinks the SE-S is phasing out our team, but he is willing to open a spot on Redemption if I give him our locations outside the search zones."

"So all the places we risked our lives to find. He just gets to claim them?"

Tymon let out a short laugh. "Hell of a deal, right?"

Their conversation fell silent as they both fell into deep thought, leaving only the low persisting rumble of the fleet and the indistinguishable conversations in the distance.

"You don't really think they are getting rid of Firebrand, do you?" Baxel finally asked, adjusting the bundle under his arm again.

"If they are, then making certain of this find might be the only thing that could convince them otherwise."

Baxel reached across to the opposite hip and awkwardly pulled out the data pad again to glance at the time. "I've got to go meet with the Reawakened." Baxel called back as he started away, "Don't give Redemption anything while I'm gone!"

"Whatever," Tymon replied with a wave. "Hey, just don't give Reyson any reason to push me further, you hear me?"

Some time later, Baxel was the first out the door of the transport, almost before it had completely touched down. He received a few unhappy comments that were drowned out by the repulsors winding to a halt. He pushed through the people moving in through the opening airlock and stepped into the Hall of the Warden.

Much like everywhere else, the Hall of the Warden had its own hallways and side rooms for various uses. For the most part, the Hall of the Warden was considered a meeting area, both for small groups and larger events such as an offsending. It also served as a public meeting point between the Vigil and the rest of the Remnants. As Baxel had been reminded throughout the years, it was against custom for a Remnant not part of the Warden's Vigil to enter the Hall of the Vigil without permission, and those seeking the Vigil's guidance were to instead come to the Hall of the Warden.

Baxel took off down one of the halls, passing by a Vigil speaking with someone who looked as if they were from the Maintenance Sector. The man had a belt with various tools and a brace on his arm from where he'd likely broken it under a transport or in an airlock.

"And I just need to show her this?" the worker asked.

The Vigil handed over the data pad he had been explaining to the man and nodded. "And you may keep it in your quarters for reference. No further documentation is required until you actually have the child."

Baxel continued past, though his thoughts were slower to leave the conversation behind. The Vigil had maintained a vast list of genetic variables since basically their beginning. Even now, with the population yet to fully recover from the uprising, it was always more important to ensure long-term survival than make a quick recovery. This mindset applied to every action in Safe Harbor. The genetics list was a carefully looked after dataset, and while it functioned with the intention of giving people a choice in who they chose to make a family with, Baxel had heard of occasions where a seemingly viable union was forced to be childless due to one of the distant predicted results of the system. And then there was the occasion where an unplanned child was forced to be the last of their family line out of the possible genetic complications the Vigil's program feared.

Being reminded of the population recovery caused another thought to spark when he saw two boys passing a ball back and forth across the hallway. Much of the Hall of the Warden had been converted into living quarters during the reconstruction; however, the population of Safe Harbor as a whole was smaller than the time before Sarthyl's rebellion, leaving Baxel to wonder whether the section was more or less crowded than it would have been before the rebellion. Baxel reached up above his head with his one free hand and caught the ball as it flew by. He gave it a light toss, bouncing it to the other boy as he continued through.

"Where have you been?" the Reawakened said, standing up from where he had been waiting on a bench. Varnil Williams glanced down to the hefty bundle of clothing Baxel was carrying under an arm.

"Forgot about having to wait for a transport." Baxel looked around, seeing no sign of either Liaren or the migrant.

Varnil motioned and they started toward an intersection in the hallway. "Liaren went on ahead. She is waiting for us at the Preservation Core."

"And the migrant?" Baxel asked as they passed through a rip in the wall.

"Don't worry about him. It is my choice for you to be here. And before you ask, yes, my offer still stands. I will keep an eye on Firebrand, provided this goes well."

When he noticed Varnil was looking into his visor at what was most likely a layout of the *Fortuna*, Baxel simply moved ahead to take the lead. "Alright then, what is my part?"

Varnil brushed the visor out of the way and hurried to keep up with Baxel, even with his longer strides. "We need you to collect the data." Varnil motioned with a deactivated data pad in his hand. "I will be feeding it into my own storage."

"Sounds simple enough." He continued through the various storage hallways and onto the second level of the Hall of the Warden. It was dimly lit compared to when it was filled with hundreds attending the offsending days ago. Along the far side, Baxel could see a few people walking the set of stairs leading up to the shrine where the Warden's suit was kept.

"I take it this is where you watched the offsending?"

Baxel nodded. "The last of it."

"I only met Dimarka a few times," Varnil said, now taking the lead as they continued across the second-level balcony. "Each time, I could tell he had something against me. He was a good man, but I know he would have never shown me that."

"Were you as outspoken then about traveling to Earth?"

Varnil glanced to where Baxel walked at his side. "Back to Earth. Don't forget, I was born there, and for me, it feels as if I left only three years ago."

Baxel followed the Reawakened as they entered the Hall of the Vigil. The glowing decorative panels and hanging cloths were an immediate contrast to the dim lighting they were leaving behind. *Six hundred years before*, Baxel kept thinking in an echo. The Reawakened had been in a cryopod for the entire duration of the history of the Remnants. In fact, their two peoples had lived side by side for centuries in silence.

A few of the Vigil gave courteous nods as Baxel and Varnil passed, though he knew to whom their respects were paid. Baxel could not help but avert his eyes downward, knowing that what they were doing was strictly against Vigil rules.

"You're not thinking of freeing them all, are you?" Baxel asked quietly after they passed another group.

"Here?" Varnil almost laughed. "While you have proved that people can live in the wreckage of the Orbital Armistice Fleet, I still cannot get past the name you keep. Without actual stability, I fear you will always be the remnants of one disaster after another."

As they approached a wide doorway with elaborate projections set up to either side, Liaren smirked at Varnil's statement. "However, without our ways, we would be a different people entirely." No longer would we be the Remnants without our struggle." She paused as they came to a stop in front of where she stood by the doorway, likely wondering if their actions would change that reality. With a glance to the bundle under Baxel's arm, she asked, "Are you two ready?"

"Always," Baxel said.

The door hissed open as Liaren activated the terminal with a small object. It was likely given to her by Connor, who normally worked in the Preservation Core.

Baxel stepped forward into the area he had only heard conflicting rumors about. Besides the Warden, the Preservation Core was the Vigil's best-kept secret. The room was an odd shape, almost as if part of a larger circle, though the location of the doorway caused most of the space to be off to the right. The opposite wall, following the inside of the curve away from where they stood, was made up of dark panels reflecting the dim lights of the room.

Liaren pushed ahead along the pathway edged in blue running lights. The pathway itself was made of darker material and had a pattern of round-edged rectangles. The floor beside it, of which Baxel was almost nervous to step onto without instruction, was a smooth white like most of the original interiors of the *Fortuna*.

He glanced back to see Varnil stepping off the path into the dark of the room. Eventually, cool blue lights began to flick on overhead, giving him a view of about thirty or so cryopods positioned against the wall behind them. Varnil pointed to the last one in the line, and the only one that was open. He waved his hand near the control panel and turned away as the name *"Varnil Williams"* flickered into view.

"Most of those look different from the ones I've seen," Baxel said. The ones in the wreckage of the ship had a full dome of glass in the front, but all the ones here, except for a single one closer to the doorway, had two narrow vertical glass windows inset into a wide face of metal.

"You've seen pods before?" Liaren asked.

"I, uh . . ." Baxel started before slowing to a stop. He leaned to the side, looking again at the number of pods. "Is this all?"

Liaren narrowed her eyes before letting what he said go. "Yes," she finally replied, stepping up to a large control station set against the dark wall panels. "These twenty-seven cryostasis pods are what the Remnants have been tasked with protecting since the first Warden. Our living history."

Baxel looked over them again. As they curved off to the left, he could see there looked to be more room for further pods, and even what looked to be newly added ports in the walls to accommodate them.

"Then what am I here for?"

Liaren tapped the display hovering over the terminal and shot back a devious, teasing glance.

Lights began flicking on in the distance, far out past where Varnil was standing. If Baxel had not been so stunned, he would have reacted to her ruse.

Well over ten thousand souls hung together in a giant column of cryopods and twisted cables. It was like a hive, stretching up through the broken edges of a vast space within the *Fortuna*. The haphazard spire of cryopods existed in a section of zero gravity within the *Fortuna*, allowing the pods to be suspended in their disorganized manner, free from their own weight. An airlock door led out of the overlook where he, Liaren, and Varnil stood and into the main room of the Preservation Core with all the pods. Baxel stepped over the running lights of the pathway and looked out toward the starry glow of the blue status lights shining from each of the pods.

He knew he couldn't even begin to count, but he still wondered if the entire population of all the Remnants that had ever lived would equal the sheer scale of the population before him. "How many . . ." Baxel mumbled, letting his thought trail off as he looked upward. The column twisted as it rose high into the darkness.

"That is why we are here," Liaren replied. She pulled a number of projections free, bringing out various charts of data for quick reference. "The Remnants have never even counted the number within the Preservation Core. For centuries, we simply added to the number whenever the SE-S teams found live pods. I would imagine it has been at least a century since we have found another."

Varnil glanced over at Baxel. "You now understand a little more behind my reasoning. The Remnants can survive; that's what they do. But my people? Imagine how complete the destruction could have been if Sarthyl had targeted here before he tried for the habitats. Imagine how many more lives would have been lost. I need to get them somewhere less . . . fragile."

"It's time we get started," Liaren said.

Baxel looked one last time out toward the twisted mass of lighted pods and cables before turning to where Liaren was looking at him with a raised eyebrow.

"I take it you brought your suit?" She glanced to the clothing starting to fall out from under his arm.

"Most of it," Baxel said with a frown. "I couldn't sneak out much more than the undersuit and my helmet from the SE-S. Nobody ever said anything about the Preservation Core being this big."

Liaren looked worried. "Are you saying you can't do it?"

Baxel let out a breath, knowing that no matter how bad of an idea it was or how much he argued with himself, the next words out of his mouth would be something to try to impress her. Without much more thought than that, he dropped the bundle of shirts and uncovered his helmet. With a sharp pull, his undersuit unfurled from where he had stuffed it inside. "We'll just have to see."

"Alright then, get to changing. We only have a few hours at best."

"Here?" Baxel asked, holding the helmet in one hand and the slowly straightening undersuit in the other.

Liaren shot him a look and turned back to the terminal.

Baxel let out a breath and began to strip down, knowing that he would feel even more naked once he was actually out in the zero-gravity field of the Preservation Core with no maneuvering jets, reinforcement plates, or magnetic clamps on his boots.

*　*　*

"Alright, I'm kicking off," Baxel said over the comms. Liaren adjusted the display that showed his facial motion scan off to the side. She had also linked up with his oxygen levels and location information, just to be safe.

"If I can't find a way to hold on in the first seconds, I'll have to kick off again," Baxel said. "The last thing I want is to be slowly drifting through empty space with only this much oxygen."

Liaren looked worriedly to his image. The image of his face was not entirely to proportion, but it was also simulating a camera perspective several feet outside his helmet with the sensors on the inside mapping his facial expressions. "How long can you stay out?"

"An hour."

"Safely?"

"Twenty minutes, if by the rules. Though, we don't give those much credit now, do we?"

Liaren felt her breath catch as she saw Baxel kick off away from the other side of the airlock and toward the center of the Preservation Core. After a few moments of watching him through the wall of windows, she was hit again by the massive scale of the column of cryopods.

Varnil glanced over to the terminal. "Be careful what you do over there, Baxel. One wrong move could pull the power to a pod, or even dislodge it from the core."

"Right. And just to be clear, I take it you don't want me to activate one while I'm out here?"

Liaren hid a smile as the Reawakened shook his head. If she knew anything about Baxel, he was the best one for navigating dangerous situations. And from what she remembered from their few years of contact after she joined the Vigil and he continued on to the exploration teams, he did not like being told his limits.

She glanced at his image again as he checked systems from within his helmet. It was an odd feeling, being this close to him now after all that time wondering. But ultimately, he had not seemed to react to her one way or the other and she had bigger things to worry about at the moment. Like hoping they could keep this all a secret as intended.

"So, before I land, does anyone have any idea what we are looking for?" Baxel asked. Liaren could see his light now illuminating the dark recesses of the central mass of cryopods as he approached.

Varnil held a hand up to his visor. "Communications engineers, anyone who worked for Solstice Consolidated in the survey side of things, possibly even . . ."

Liaren cleared her throat and shot the Reawakened a hard glance. "Names, professions, and ages. Randomly picked from the pods. We will record as many as possible." Honestly, she could not understand why neither Varnil nor Connor could understand. The only way this was justified was if their list did not have any form of intent behind it.

"Uh," Baxel started slowly, "so I'm just reading back any name? I thought this was for creating a probe?"

"That is for the Warden to decide," Liaren said. "This list must be entirely impartial, or we are going against the teaching of the Vigil."

"Right." Baxel rolled his eyes and Liaren nearly called him out on it, but she decided it would be better to not give him any reason to hide what he was thinking. "Approaching now," he continued. She watched as his face lit up in surprise. "Well, this might get interesting," he said, far too casually.

"What is it?" Liaren asked, leaning in over the desk as if there was actually something she could do. "Are you . . ." She looked up just in time to see his light disappear against the great column of the core. "Baxel?" she asked. She flipped open another display to show his forward view. He grinned, likely over her worried tone. She raked a hand roughly through her hair and let out a breath.

"Did you know this column of cryopods has an interior? It's a mess of cables, and the rest of the space is full of pods. Whatever you guessed numbers-wise, make that a whole lot more."

"Go for the outside pods," Varnil said. "The ones easiest to get to. Unless you see that as being too choosy, Vigil?"

"Of course not." She could not tell if his tone was annoyance at her stipulations, or if he was poking fun at her demands.

"You know," Baxel said, pushing his way outward from where he had caught himself, "if I didn't have to come to the edge, I would be less likely to float off slowly into this massive, empty room with a limited oxygen supply."

Varnil held up his data pad. "We're ready for the information when you are."

Baxel nodded. "Here goes nothing. Errence Jalimed, Section Coordinator, Drake Discovery. Oh just hooray, we can't get enough people telling us what to do." Baxel rolled his eyes.

"Hey now," Varnil protested. "That's what I was."

"Really?" Baxel asked.

"Age." Varnil gave no sign that he was going to answer the question. "And send your coordinates through the console."

* * *

Nearly four hours had passed, and Baxel was on his fifth trip out into the large room of the Preservation Core. Varnil glanced over and saw that Baxel was running forty-five minutes into his oxygen stores. He wasn't following SE-S guidelines of returning before reaching a half tank, but he was being as cautious as Varnil could hope for, considering what he had heard of the explorer.

Varnil gripped his fingers into his hair and leaned against the window with his elbows. While he appreciated that their operation had been prolonged on account of some intervention by Connor, that still did not help speed up the process itself. Much of the information they were gathering was needless in his eyes, but he knew they were playing by Liaren's rules.

"Last name, and then I'm headed back," Baxel said. "Quigwa Muhaktoo."

"Baxel, come on," Liaren said holding back a laugh.

"I'm serious! That's what is on the pod. Age forty-seven, consumer relations for Floatleed Brands, and I'm guessing they probably like spending extra time walking the Trade Sector."

"You're supposed to say 'long walks on the beach,'" Varnil corrected.

"What?" Baxel asked.

"It's an old saying," he explained.

"No, what the hell is a beach?"

Varnil had to pause for a second just to make sure he was serious.

Liaren glanced over to Varnil before explaining to Baxel, "Like when you hear of a beached transport, when it gets caught in the wreckage. Now start heading back."

"Yeah. But still. What is it?"

Varnil sighed. "It is what you would call the edge of an ocean. You walk around on it. It's peaceful." He figured it would be best to leave it at that. It would only confuse them more if he explained how he had never actually set foot on a beach, let alone the Earth itself. His only experience outside a starscraper or transport was standing on a balcony when taking an extended stay in the Council City. As for the ocean, any natural beaches themselves were considered part of the nature reserves and strictly prohibited to the public.

Varnil turned away from the window and started looking at the displays of the cryopods in the room to busy himself as Baxel returned to refill his air tanks. The names of the past Reawakened blended in with the hundreds of other names he had heard over the past few hours, but it was vaguely interesting to see what professions had shaped the Remnants before him. The spread of professions was random about the pods along the back wall, though there were of course less high-end careers in the lot. There were even a few that were not labeled as having one, though he was not sure what that meant.

By the time Baxel had returned, flirted with Liaren for longer than it took his tank to refill, and set off again to collect more names, Varnil was nearing the most recent Reawakened of Remnant history. He was about to move on when something about the pod two pods down from his own grabbed his attention. His heart started racing before he fully understood what he had noticed.

The name. It was Kaiden Williams. His son.

He had just assumed up until now that his family had not been as lucky as he had been. The Remnants had said nothing to make him think otherwise. Before he even had one thought against the reason or consequence of his actions, Varnil began activating the sequence.

Cryogenesis—Process estimate: twelve hours.

"Varnil?" Liaren asked from behind. "What are you doing? Are you . . ."

Varnil dropped to his knees and looked up at the solid front of the cryogenics pod. For three years, he had lived with his son's death taking place in some nameless century. Now, all that emotion came rushing back, but instead of pain, it was frantic hope. He did not care if he was exiled or even placed back in his pod. If he had to spend his life without being able to see his son again . . .

"By the Warden," Liaren said softly. "Baxel, get back here, now."

"I'm floating! I can't turn back!"

"Well, figure out a way!"

"Liaren, what is the problem?"

She drew in a shaking breath and walked toward the pod with wide eyes. "Within twelve hours, the Vigil will decide to either put Varnil Williams back into cryostasis, or Safe Harbor will have, for the first time, a second Reawakened."

Chapter 10: Outset

Kara set foot onto the first level of Norclave just as everyone around her was making for cover within the ground vehicle garages. The heavy scraphaulers were easier to maintain and reproduce than transports, often running on a system of rugged tracks in the front that supported the weight of the scrap load, while the thick wheels in the back supported the driver's cab. She watched as one laden down with heavy piles of metal slung mud from its treads into the middle of the patchwork street as it turned toward one of the garages, hurrying to get in before the worst of the storm hit.

"Hurry now!" a voice called in the distance. One of the workers was signaling the driver to continue into the shelter as the other garages started to close their heavy sliding doors. All around, water spilled chaotically down through the city. Kara could feel a change in the air as the heavy winds from deep in the storm began to push against Norclave. Soon, the clean downpour would shift into acidic rain.

Kara adjusted the wraps on her hands, leaving just the tips of her fingers open. Just as she stepped free of the bounds of the city, she was tapped on the forehead by what felt like specks of boiling water. She pulled her hood lower and started off at a quick pace, facing against the wind.

There was no denying that she hated traveling in storms like this. Even if she kept her hood pulled low, a rash would still develop somewhere, either on exposed skin or where the rain soaked through her clothing. Very few others risked traveling through these kinds of storms on foot, often preferring to scrape up shelter under a leaning bit of wreckage or within the abandoned camps in the forest. She was counting on that to hunt down Travend's men. They would not be far from where they were last spotted by Jance's camera web, allowing her the time to catch up to them, and hopefully ambush them.

Another loud clap of thunder was accompanied by the violent shaking of trees and rolling of grass as she followed one of the heavy sets of scraphauler tracks heading deep into the forest. She caught her hood from flying back just as a heavy wash of rain began pouring down through the limbs above.

Just as she started looking for signs of anyone else in the area, her foot slipped into one of the wide ruts now beginning to fill with the treacherous rain. Kara kicked some of the mud from her boot and continued to mentally prepare herself for when she did find Travend's men. They had tried to kill Jance and plunge Norclave into chaos, and there was nothing yet to say that they would not be successful on both counts.

* * *

"Keep up!" Lieth shouted back to the others that had killed the Cryo. The technician and scrapsmiths were lagging behind with their shirts pulled up over their heads as the rain pounded down, and Darmic had given up all measure of watching the forest in favor of sheltering under his thick cloak. Lieth, instead, welcomed the fire on his skin. The hot waves felt like the fires of his shop after the death of the Overlord, and the cold sheets of rain mixed in with the withering storm felt like the chill that passed over him when he'd found his wife and son inside.

With strict orders from Travend himself, the others had no choice but to follow him as he stepped over a scattering of limbs broken by the storm and out into the open lands. It was only in the consistent flashes of lightning striking the top of the starscraper that they could see the grand form of the fallen structure through the blanket of rain. The surrounding fields themselves were littered with jagged mounds of concrete and loops of cables not yet covered by the grasses and low shrubs.

As the others waited for the roar of the storm to light the way, Lieth kept a sharp eye out for lights in the dark. He was looking for the settlement of Maraton, though the harvest facilities were their actual destination, away from the population, and hopefully away from prying eyes that would notice them fleeing through the storm.

"Up there!" one of the men shouted from behind. "I see lights!"

Lieth turned to look at the scrapsmith. He was the one who had supplied the components to make the explosive they used on the Cryo. There was too much desperation in his voice.

"We have to hurry!" he said, making a pace quicker than even Lieth had been pushing them to keep.

"Wait!" Lieth shouted as the man rushed past him into the whipping winds. "You will be seen! Norclave will be able to track us!"

"No, he is right, Lieth" the other scrapsmith protested, holding a hand over his eye. "Our skin is boiled bad enough."

Lieth took a step forward and cupped his hands to shout into the thunder roaring over the them. "Stop right there! We will seek shelter just on the other side of Maraton!"

Lieth let out a curse as the man kept running over the dangerous terrain. The downpour was enough to make the surfaces of the steel slick and the bare patches of dead ground into spans of muck. Lieth nodded to Darmic.

"We should follow him," the technician said. "The rain has been mixed so far, keeping most of the acid washed away, but if it turns worse . . ."

The technician was cut short as the low thrum of Darmic's pulse cannon cut through the rain and lit up the dark. The scrapsmith dropped with a scream in the distance, and the drops that landed on the weapon hissed against the heated steel.

Lieth turned to the other two freelancers, the scrapsmith and the technician, who had not specifically joined Travend's resistance. "The three of you have already served your purpose. It is with Travend's courtesy that you keep your lives . . . with the understanding that you do not jeopardize his goals."

The next clap of thunder faded out into the pained wail of the man in the distance. Darmic glanced over to Lieth again and motioned with his weapon. "Do you want me to . . . ?"

"Leave him. He is dead as it is."

* * *

Several hours later, Kara sat leaned up against a tree pulling in heavy breaths through her gritted teeth. She adjusted the wraps around her aching hands again and reached with shaking fingers into her pocket. The storm had turned foul far sooner than she expected and forced her to stop. She desperately wanted to lean back and catch her breath, but keeping the even harsher rain away was a must.

"Dammit," Kara growled, drawing in another pain-filled breath. She poured some of her own clean water onto her fingers, hoping to wash away the acidic burn. With her other hand, she pulled out another small bottle with glowing, intricate holographic decoration of vines and leaves hovering a few inches from the bottle.

"Desert Plumb," she said quietly. It was the bottle she had bought when acting as a lookout for Kenneth in the South Corridors. She did not know for certain, but she hoped that the moisturizing properties would help cut the sting, or at least ease the cracking of the skin.

Kara applied some to the exposed tips of her fingers. If nothing else, it was something to keep her mind on while waiting for the storm to ease up. Kara then pulled her face wrap free and rubbed it on her reddened skin. She could not tell if the lotion was helping, but the desire for relief drove her to continue working the cream underneath the wraps of her hands, arms, and neck. She continued spreading the cream with an urgency akin to scratching an itch under the brace of a broken arm, though her efforts only brought moderate relief.

After nearly rubbing her skin raw, Kara let her hands drop between her legs and let out a sob. Her shoulders bounced with waves of emotion, but she could not say which of the streaks running down her face were tears. Perhaps they all were, in one way or another. The storm carried her emotions just as much as she did, because without it she would have had to find some other way to grieve Jance. Some of her own tears would have been for Kenneth, and her need to leave him. Some would have been for the weight of failure at having to stop and lean against a tree instead of being as strong as she thought she needed to be.

After possibly a half hour of letting her emotions wash over the top of her hood and down over her hanging cloak, Kara took in a breath and found much of the air had cleared. With a bit of hesitation, Kara reached a clothed hand out into the gentler rain and found it to be cool to the touch. Whether it was just a small shift in the larger storm, or actually a fading like the thunder in the distance, Kara wasted no time in pulling back her hood and washing the heat from her wraps and hair.

The brief moment of relief refilled her determination. She knew her pause had wasted time, and now the group she was trailing could be moving again.

Kara set off at a jog through the underbrush and rubble. For now, she let the wrap hang about her neck and didn't worry about pulling the hood up properly to shield herself from the rain.

Moments later, she was at the edge of a clearing. Kara stayed low as she moved up behind one of the final trees before the open ground. She waited for a flash of lightning to illuminate the area, and within seconds she got a clear view of the span of plains stretching out the length of the starscraper. She sat for a moment in thought, knowing that they could not have made it much farther than Maraton. In fact, she would bet that they'd snuck into the city, either to wait out the weather or disappear entirely.

Kara set out at a slightly slower pace as she picked her way through the uneven ground of metal outcrops and dirt. She took a path near larger obstructions or cuts in the land. If she ran into the group out on the open plains, she wanted to spot them first and have somewhere to run for cover. She knew there were at least six of them, and she had no solid knowledge of what kind of weaponry they had made it out of Norclave with.

An uneasy feeling suddenly brought a shiver of raised bumps on the back of her neck. Kara immediately dropped low to the ground and froze in place. The most valuable thing she had learned in her years of hunting tech was to listen to her instincts. They were the only other thing wanting to keep her alive.

She slowly began to notice an intermittent tone in the wind that did not sit well with her. It was medium-pitched and starting to fade. Kara slowly pushed herself up and cautiously moved toward where she thought she had heard the noise. As soon as she saw him, she knew the cry had come from the man lying crumpled in the dirt.

As she neared, she immediately recognized the deep burn of a repulsor shot. She looked for weapons before rolling him over. The man looked up with red eyes, and his skin was covered in slimy boils from where he had walked unprotected in the rain.

"Who did this to you?" Kara asked after she noticed him take in a slow breath.

The man made no attempt to reply. He didn't even blink at the rain hitting his eyes.

"Why are you out here?"

Kara stood up and spun a full circle to see if she could see anything else nearby or in the distance. She looked back to him as he took another slow breath. The odds of him not being a member of Travend's group were slim. Even still, she started to reach into a pocket for her silver medical square to ease his pain, then stopped, remembering that she had given it to Olana Nuand for Jance.

Kara took a step away, knowing that there was nothing she could do. She then stopped, realizing that there was something else that could end his pain. She slowly drew her knife and looked down upon him in pity. After a few more moments thinking over the difficult decision, she let out a conflicted breath and turned away for the last time. She didn't owe him anything.

She started tracing his tracks back. He had been shot in the back, meaning her steps would lead toward the attacker's tracks, hopefully.

Kara tried to make out the sloppy marks of muddy boots over the exposed metal, but the rain had washed most of it away already. She wished she had Comar around to take a look. Or Draken, for that matter. Both actually knew how to track people, but she was not sure who she trusted less out of the two. Both had disappeared after the ordeal with the Cryo and the Overlord.

"Here we are," Kara mumbled to herself as she saw more tracks along the hard edge of concrete and steel.

"You were headed . . . that way." Kara said, looking out to the man she had left to take his last breaths. It was a perfect shot toward the lights of Maraton. "But the rest of you were not." Kara frowned, looking back to the ground. Since they had taken a straight path to the settlement this far, she had assumed they knew where they were going. But perhaps they had just picked a direction to run from Norclave and gotten lucky?

Rolling the thought in her head, she started off, knowing that they would at least not be headed back into the forest, nor toward the starscraper. It was only about thirty feet later that she caught sight of a few deep tracks right on her path.

* * *

Kenneth slid his hands along the softly glowing edge of the desk in the Norclave Library. In a world full of aged destruction and fading connections with the past, it was always an unforgettable moment when their stolen history managed to shine through. He slid his fingers over the smooth-as-glass surface, watching as the displays readied to accept new adjustments while his rough and grime-stained hands moved across them in idle thought.

Perhaps this was all that was left of Jance's story. A desk cramped with overlapping displays, video feeds, and information summaries, and a room that had once been part of the Norclave Library. Kenneth shook his head and began to idly shift through the information Jance had collected. He pulled words up from the table and set them angling back away from him. It was a list of names she and Sora had been building.

Behind each section for names was a note Jance had written, documenting the source of the findings.

As Kenneth moved through the cameras, he began to see some figures about the trade center and their overlaid names. It seemed to be cross-referencing with the list, and expanded to a readout attempting to track locations. This was a powerful tool—dangerous. But nobody ever expected anything different from a Cryo. Most thoughts had been on weapons, but Kenneth could see that her system was as powerful as any war machine or targeting array.

As Kenneth dug deeper, it became clear how much work the Cryo had actually done in her short time here. Though she'd only just inherited the nearly mythological title "Cryo," Jance fit the role perfectly. Everyone from the Shattered Coast to the far corners of the Ash Flats imagined a Cryo as more than a person, so much so that it had come as a surprise that Jance was a person at all. Kenneth had always imagined that finding a living Cryo would be like opening the latches to something that could break the world. He expected sudden shifts in social power and leaps in weapons technology, but he also knew the advancements would come in ways they could not expect. In nearly every aspect, Jance had come to fulfill all those expectations, and yet, had also come to soften his ideas by showing him that Cryos were still just humans at the end of the day.

Kenneth somberly set the displays back as best he could. The surveillance system was desperately incomplete. And Olana, in her role as the Overlord, had done little more than execute a whole host of individuals associated with the administrators. The people of Norclave were still starving in the back alleys of the city. Travend's rebellion was making bold moves, and the remainder of the administrators had taken to expanding into the criminal organizations to fight back and to survive. To top that all off, the entire region was closer than ever before to all-out invasions from Carvanhold and Reclaim, all while the teams of med-techs worked day and night trying to keep the Cryo of Norclave alive.

And Kara was nowhere to be found.

Kenneth balled his fists and started looking intently at the hundreds of display monitors piled in front of him. He pulled up one of the lists and sorted through it until he found her name. He motioned through the floating projection to bring her last sighting forward, but a notification appeared requesting access.

"Council Clearance Required."

Jance had specifically locked Kara's whereabouts to be untraceable by anyone else. Perhaps it was in preparation for her departure to Reclaim. Perhaps it was about respecting a friendship with someone as untrusting as a tech hunter. Perhaps it was just a lock—like the one on her cryopod—that could be broken.

Kenneth looked up to the shelf where a broken visor sat. It was the one Jance had picked up at the core reactor Power Relay Station, deep in the Earth below the Rift Outpost. Supposedly the two halves had belonged to a man by the name of Avery Thorne, though Sora could only find dead ends on the organization he went rogue from. But in Kenneth's mind, if that man had the ability to keep the world from breaking, his visor could just as well have the means to access the locked information on Jance's desk.

He just had to fix the visor first.

* * *

Kara walked beneath the lights of the orbital wreckage and stars above as a cool mist played in the air. The plants in long rows dipped and bowed with the gentle breezes of the calming night. She was careful to keep her feet out of the tangle of cables running half-buried about the biological manufacturing facility of Maraton. She tried to stick to the darkness the best she could, but many of the power conduits within the long rows had lights glowing up through the plants and the slow drift of the mists.

While keeping her eyes trained to spot any of the guards patrolling the sprawling sets of vegetation, Kara still managed to notice a pattern. Each of the plants had their own cables running up in bundled sections providing power to the plants. It was based on a system developed long ago to provide for the vast populations of Earth, when plants were engineered to accept electrical currents instead of sunlight.

Kara pushed between the leafy greens and hanging pods into a less illuminated section. By now, she had learned that the lesser blue tint to the leaves meant the plants were no longer fully adapted to the electrical currents. While some vines in the distance looked nearly as vibrant of a blue as the ones that clung to massive sources of power deep within the ruins in the outerzones, the aqua greens of the surrounding plants meant that over the years they had made a reversal in their evolution and now partially relied on sunlight, making the efforts of the facilities to provide a steady current be merely supplemental to their growth.

In part, Kara wondered if the efforts were even worth it. While the large finds of meal pack supply depots had dwindled over the past few hundred years, their small population compared to the previous world's population meant that there would nearly always be an abundance. She even guessed that these plants would eventually evolve into needing less intensive care long before they started to run into scarcity as a whole.

Kara heard voices carrying through the mists as she continued down the worn track between the rows, keeping low so as to not be seen over the tops. Her direction toward the main building of the facility seemed to be taking her closer to the two men talking. She started to begin to catch pieces of their conversation. It sounded to her as if one was showing a new recruit how things worked. The younger voice, probably no older than sixteen, asked something about anyone making it inside the walls that surrounded the facility. Kara could not hear the reply, but to anyone who really wanted in the facility like herself, the assortment of plates and beams driven into the dirt were anything but secure.

"You know the director," the young man said as Kara neared. "Has he received information from Norclave about what happened?"

"Knowing him is one thing," the other said, "but he has little to say to those of us who do the rounds. If you want to know, ask one of the geneticists at the end of your shift in the morning."

"Do we even know if the Cryo is still alive? What happens to us here?"

"We keep watch. If the Steel Valley comes sweeping in, we turn over our weapons. Don't think to be a hero; this facility is far from being equipped to fight anything more than the scavengers from the outerzones."

Once Kara had picked her way over the loops of exposed cables, she started looking to the main building in the center. The main structure was a mix of stacked containers and fused plates, which contrasted heavily with the large sweep of windows and the glossy metal supports of the arching balcony above the entrance. Kara had to look again to make sure that the pristine form actually had the dents and scrapes of their time. A large warp in the smooth surface told her that it had been straightened, and there were slight variations in the window tints. More than that though, by the grand display of the thirty feet of clear glass and glossy metal, Kara knew that the people here thought much more of their research than she did. Especially if any of them were intentionally hiding her targets.

Kara mouthed a curse while drawing in a sudden breath as she shoved herself behind a thick row of tall grasses. She felt a tingle where her hand touched a charged lattice buried in the dirt, but she was more focused on remaining hidden. She had only noticed the figure standing in the window when it moved.

* * *

"Master Armain," the timid voice said from behind, "your men are asleep. Perhaps you should think about . . ."

Lieth said nothing as he stared out through the reflecting sheen of mist hanging outside the glass. The distorted glow from the rows of lights amongst the cable-bound plants stretched far into the dreary night. What he could see, despite the wetness that still clung to the clear surface, were the fleeting flashes along the far horizon behind the starscraper.

"What of the storm?" Lieth asked, looking over his shoulder at the smaller man. The man's white coat hung down to his knees, though it was held together in several places with rough sewing and thick staples.

"The storm, sir? I, uh, believe it to be passing, but that is as much a guess as anything I am afraid. I merely work with the specimens to progress our biological manufacturing . . ."

Lieth turned away from overlooking the facility and toward the man. "Are you certain this facility does not have a transport?"

"I . . . not that I can access. I assure you if there was a way—"

"How long do we have before we draw attention?"

The man frowned and produced a data pad from the deep pockets of his coat. "Seven hours, by the schedule. But with the rain that has come through, I am sure my colleagues will be looking for as early a start as possible to collect data, especially from the *Pisum luxtenebris*. The third generations have been far too susceptible to environmental conditions thus far."

Lieth rubbed his eyebrow. He dearly hoped that it was only for his research that this man was receiving funding from both Norclave and Reclaim. "I just want to know when we can leave unnoticed."

"Five hours. Well before the shift change."

"And you can guarantee that no one is preparing to send a message to Nuand as we speak?" Lieth knew that while the geneticist may have sympathy from the Prime Elect, the man also had money in his pocket from the false Overlord Nuand. It would be all too simple a maneuver to turn them over and cover up the double betrayal.

The geneticist gulped and began shifting his grip as if wringing the sweat from his hands. "Master Armain, I swear. I would no sooner give up your names in secret as to shout your passing from the top of the facility." The man looked at the lights through the windows for a while. "Though I do wonder why the Prime Elect has concerned himself with you."

"Take your pay, and keep living quietly." Lieth patted the man on the shoulder as he turned to leave the overlook. If that choice had been presented to him, he would have taken it in a heartbeat to save his family.

"Supplies shipments, actually," the man said, tagging along. "I don't get payment directly. The Prime Elect sends the facility supply shipments, routed through Maraton, and furnished with proper credentials somewhere along the way."

"Which direction to the medical wing?" Lieth asked as the door to the hallway hissed open.

"Primary aid station," the man corrected, "and right this way."

Several sets of doors through the empty hallways set them in a smaller room lacking the luster of much of the rest of the facility. The glossy surfaces now faded into the standard cold metal gratings and a flaking coating of adapted cargo containers. Tall equipment cabinets lined the sides, filled with bottles and small sealed boxes where there remained glass in the cabinets to see through; otherwise, the cabinet windows had been shoddily reinforced with scrapped plates.

Lieth glanced over the four others that remained of their group. The rain had burned their skin, much like his own, though they now lay about the room, each covered with a heavy coat of medical paste.

"It should be simple enough," the geneticist said quietly, "to explain this as helping poor souls wandering out of the storm."

Lieth had to avoid turning and shouting at the man right then and there. His skin burned inside and out at his ignorance. "You will say nothing of the such. We were *never* here."

"But how will I explain the—"

"You were stuck on the nightshift, watching experiments or commanding the facility. You got bored. You started sorting through the cabinets, getting rid of any compromised supplies."

Lieth glanced from the frightened man to the light glowing through his pocket in his long coat. He motioned to it, and the geneticist produced his data pad.

"What is it?" Lieth asked.

"A report just came in. From surveillance. Probably just a glitch with the system again." The man glanced to Lieth and caught the dark tone of the look he was receiving. He continued, "Yemij, the lead system tech, describes in the report several of the surveillance cameras locking their own security and encrypting their recordings. He wants my temporary access code to review their data at the time of failure."

"Keep him from finding us in the recordings. If he does, come wake me."

* * *

It seemed only a few tense moments had passed since Kara placed down her sensor and clipped the small alert light to the edge of her hood. However, she could feel the definite change in the weight of her eyes from the restless hours and the sluggishness of her fingers as the cool morning air rolled over her damp clothing. She was curled up in the same spot she'd hid in hours before, pushed in as far as she could against the tall grasses.

She glanced around without moving anything more than her numb fingers under the cover of her cloak. She could see the rapid blinking of red out of the corner of her eye as her motion sensor picked up movement. Kara shifted slowly and glanced up to the enclosed balcony over the main entrance. Just below it, the center doorway was opening. A man in a long white coat stepped out and nervously glanced to either side. He then motioned to others behind him.

Kara counted five figures moving from under the security light of the doorway into the surrounding shadows. She had no doubt they were her targets. The men who had killed numerous Norclave officials and came so close to succeeding in ending the Cryo. No one else would be rushing away under a dim morning sky, where only the orbital wreckage had begun to catch the sunlight.

Kara stood up like another gentle push of the cool night wind rustling through the grasses. She scooped up the sensor and tucked it away, and in the same motion prepared a knife. The murderers would soon realize that their biggest mistake was not in failing to end the Cryo, but in failing to wait the few seconds needed to kill her tech hunter.

Chapter 11: Reawakening

The Warden's Vigil seemed to squirm as if a fire had been lit beneath their feet. They were being called by the rest of the Remnants to answer questions that simply did not have answers. Was the Warden going to allow for a second Reawakened? Was this to be taken as part of the Warden's plan?

Connor hid his pleasure behind the cold stare he used to take in the rest of the room. White sashes kicked around as the pockets of conversation constantly shifted. There was plenty of decisions to be made and more information to be relayed as delicately as possible to the rest of the Remnants. In the center of it all, at the bottom level of the tiered steps forming the main meeting room of the Hall of the Vigil, sat the pressing reminder for the frantic pace. Four hours, thirty-seven minutes, as marked by the cryopod. Within this cycle of their orbit around the Earth, their history would be changed forever.

"There is simply nothing to support your conclusion," one of the Vigil projections said when questioned about the current Reawakened. A messenger of the Vigil hurried past, keeping clear of the projection as if it were more than an AI mirror of a long-dead Remnant. "I have analyzed this query in tandem with the others." The blue projection pointed off to where more of the ancient Vigil were being brought online for guidance. "The decision does not rest with us, nor the Warden."

"But how is that possible?" Nendra Halimuth asked sharply without regard for the customs restricting her from speaking within the Hall of the Vigil. "I thought you people said everything was up to the Warden."

"The Remnants have never forced a Reawakened back into cryostasis," the projection said. "This choice can only be made by SUBJECT NAME: WILLIAMS, VARNIL."

Connor shook his head and murmured about them seeking guidance from computers. He was surprised the Remnants had made it this long. His attention was diverted as another projection passed by, speaking with the Head Vigil, Algan Treys. An initiate walked a few steps behind with the projection device. Before he could stop himself, Connor felt his hand go to the pocket where he had the connection device found in Dimarka's room. It was linked to the very same mirror.

Tialee flickered as she glanced at Connor in passing, sending a shiver down his spine. Some of the mirrors had been imprinted with much greater care than others, which often made the emotions all too believable. If he had not known better, something in that look would have made him double-check with his own connection device to make certain she had no memory of his last conversation with Dimarka.

Connor moved his hand from his pocket when Tialee finally looked away. She was bound by the same rules as every other personality in the archives. When told to forget a conversation, no data was saved. The last words of Dimarka were lost just as assuredly as the time that had already ticked away from the cryopod.

* * *

"And that one?" Baxel asked, pointing to a hunched-over projection. Liaren had warned against using their age to guess anything about them, but Baxel could tell by his long beard that the man had not been part of an exploration team. Long hair was one thing, but too much facial hair interfered with the inner face masks.

Liaren tapped the step she was sitting on with both hands. "At least two centuries, though nobody has been able to figure out much about him. Very mathematically oriented, though we are unsure how much of that is the program filling in the blanks."

"I know her." Baxel nodded to a shorter woman who walked alongside the aged form of Algan Treys. He guessed Tialee to be of some importance, but that was only by the fact that she was speaking with the Head Vigil.

Liaren stopped her tapping and set her hands on her knees. Baxel could tell that his game was doing little to calm her nerves, but at least she was not doomsaying about their exile.

"Tialee Sharpes," Liaren said confidently. "You probably remember from your short time in the Vigil. She is the oldest projection, at least of those we have managed to maintain or recover. She denies it even still, but Tialee was the founder of the Warden's Vigil."

"How old does that make her?" Baxel asked, watching her intently as she walked with the Head Vigil.

"Anywhere from five hundred to six hundred years; she's from back in the fledgling days of the fleet. But what makes her the most interesting," Liaren said, glancing over to Baxel, "is that she never holds her own judgment higher than the others. She told me once that the others earned their positions in the archives, just as much as her."

"You've talked to her?" Baxel asked, trying to ignore the constant shifting of numbers on the cryopod in the center of the room.

"All initiates are chosen by two teachers. I was picked by Tialee and Mrs. Yumin." Liaren nodded over to a group of Vigil with white sashes talking amongst themselves. She then glanced over to Baxel with worry building on the rims of her eyes. "I am not looking forward to explaining this to either of them."

Baxel took in a slow breath. For all his efforts trying to comfort her, he had yet to think through his own preservation. Holding his helmet in hand, Baxel began to wonder if he would even survive to be exiled. There was a possibility that Flerin would kick him, unequipped, out of an airlock. Or even hold his head in the closing doors.

When Baxel spotted his coordinator entering the room, he nearly started into thoughts of running.

"You might want to, uh, step back," Baxel said, standing up and taking a dry gulp. He gripped his helmet tight, partly knowing that there was no chance of ever holding it again. It was then that he felt a cool hand glide over the top of his.

Liaren looked to him with her watery blue eyes. "I'm sorry, Baxel. I should not have . . ."

Baxel let go of the helmet with one hand and gripped her fingers tight. "Don't be. I had a choice to walk away again, and staying was worth whatever happens." At that, he felt the surge of confidence to drop her hand and start walking toward Flerin. The coordinator strode forward to meet Baxel with a scowl. After ten steps toward the man, Baxel started to rethink his options around running again.

Before Baxel could say anything, Flerin grabbed him by the shoulder and wrapped his neck into a sudden hug. Baxel stood stiff, more than surprised at the motion. He had expected an outburst of anger, not this.

"My hope is that you know what you are doing," Flerin said, keeping his tight grip on Baxel. "Because if you don't, I am afraid nobody does." After a moment, Flerin stepped back and started to straighten his shirt, which had been tucked in at an off angle.

"I had to do something," Baxel said. "I wasn't just going to let Firebrand . . ."

"Firebrand is dead." Flerin clenched his jaw and looked at the helmet in Baxel's hand. "It has been for a long time. I . . . just did not let go."

"What do you mean?" Baxel asked.

Flerin held out a hand for the helmet and waited. When it came into his hands, Flerin flipped it to look at his reflection in the glass. "This was my helmet." He tapped the glass with a finger. "I looked through here when Amrella's suit was breached. Lane was crushed after going in to pull her out. We knew we had to get back into the search coordinates to be able to call for help, so we patched her suit the best we could and dragged her back through the hazards. When we finally got her into a rescue transport . . . it was not depressurization that made her lose consciousness."

"What happened?" Baxel asked, but just as the words came out, he regretted them. He had never heard the story this way, but he now recognized that the details fit with what he had been told before.

"I watched," Flerin said, rubbing his fingers slowly over the glass. "Watched as she bled out before we made it through the habitat barrier. That is when Firebrand should have stayed dead."

"But the two of us . . . the three of us," Baxel said, "have accomplished so much. We almost match an entire group of Redemption on our own."

"And what do you expect Tymon to do on his own?" Flerin shook his head before looking over Baxel's shoulder. "You should have kissed the girl while you had the chance. Depending on how this all goes down, you may never be able to set foot in Safe Harbor again."

Flerin turned slowly with the helmet in hand, giving one last glance to the falling numbers on the pod before heading out of the Hall of the Vigil.

As the hours dropped, the members of the Vigil began to take seats all along the steps of the half circle. All eyes were trained on the pod and the Reawakened kneeling in front of it. The projections were just as silent as all the members of the Vigil and the attending heads of Safe Harbor as they waited.

* * *

There was a tapping of slow steps approaching from behind, but Varnil kept his eyes trained to the timer. It was little more than an hour before his own prison was broken. The prison holding him away from his family.

"I do not propose to tell you your place," Algan Treys said from behind. "You are our Reawakened, as dictated by the Warden. I simply wish you to know that you hold the history of the Remnants in your hands, just as much as you grip the fate of your own people."

"Family." Varnil felt his hands shaking. "Not just my people, my family. I will not leave without seeing my son. I am not leaving Kaiden, not again."

The room was quiet enough that he could hear the white sash brush the floor as Algan shifted his weight. "Our history. Remember that, Reawakened. Long past either of your lives, you change our history."

"Your Warden will save you."

Varnil hardly noticed the retreating steps as the time slipped under an hour.

Of course, there was guilt at the back of his mind. All the conversations with Connor Sevison had led him to go against the tradition of the Remnants, knowing that his actions would ultimately help the Remnants in their expansion. The list created by Baxel and Liaren was the first step, but despite what he'd told the girl, this was their plan all along. Except . . . it was not. He felt a hard knot in his chest at the knowledge that his son was not what they needed. His boy could do nothing to help them build the equipment needed to expand back to Earth.

But the Remnants knew his son had not died. Out of all the thousands of cryopods hanging in the Preservation Core, the ones separated from the others were the ones they had opened before. They knew Kaiden's last name had matched with his own, and they had not told him. For three years, they'd led him on blindly, as if his presence was just a formality to please their Warden; ultimately, they wanted him to do nothing. They wanted him silenced, just like the migrant, despite all Connor had done for them.

His thoughts rolled on until the time faded to minutes, and the minutes slipped into long, long seconds. As a loud hiss from the cryopod was joined by the release of breaths all about the room, they all felt the shift in history. The door to the pod split, and a coughing could be heard from within. A deep, gruff cough.

Varnil slowly stood up, his mind wracked with confusion. As light spilled into the cryopod against the cold vapors, he saw an aged figure nearly twenty years older than himself. The older man gripped the sides of the cryopod and pulled himself out with hands starting to wrinkle with the years.

"No," the man said under his breath. He glanced around the room with familiarity. He seemed less confused than concerned. "Father? What has happened?"

"You are . . . Kaiden, is that you?" Tears immediately filled his eyes. Varnil took a half step back and his shoulders slumped as if he had been stabbed in the gut with a rod of steel.

"No, this is all wrong," the man said. He searched around the room as if looking for a face he knew in a familiar crowd. "How has this happened? Why are there two Reawakened? Is Safe Harbor in danger? Father? What is the year?"

"I . . ."

Varnil felt the subtle vibrations of a blue glow appear next to him.

"The year is 3,551," the projection said. Tialee then glanced over to Varnil with a sympathetic frown. "Varnil, this is your son, Kaiden. He served as the Reawakened for fifty-three years, starting in 3,437." Tialee turned back to Kaiden. "Your father has been the Reawakened for three years. I am told he saw your name while in the Preservation Core."

"Thank you, Tialee." Kaiden gave a deep nod of his head and clasped his hands in front of him.

"You . . ." Varnil started, though his words were shaking too hard—both inside and out—to continue. He found himself stepping forward and taking his son, who was only an inch shorter than himself, into his arms. "I swear you look just like your grandfather."

Kaiden matched the strength of the embrace and finally broke into tears. "I lived my life knowing I would never see you again." He pushed back, holding his father by the shoulders. "How strange it must be for you. You are just as you were in my mind, all my life, but I . . ."

"You are no longer my little boy, but instead the man I knew you would grow to be."

Kaiden nodded with an emotion-filled smile. "I am a Remnant. I gave up my position as the Reawakened when I came to accept that I was no longer one of the Unawakened."

Varnil drew in a proud breath and patted his son's shoulders as he looked him over. "Strong. Wise. Just to the core, and selfless. No matter who you claim to be, I know I am proud to be your father."

"That . . . that means the fleet to me, Father."

Varnil smiled, not moving his hands from the sides of his son's shoulders to wipe away tears. "The fleet, you say. The Remnant Fleet. Because the world is lost."

Kaiden looked past his father to all the faces that would be new to him, though many would edge on recognition, being descendants of those from his time.

"Nothing is lost. Not while we still live on."

* * *

Baxel stood at the back of the crowd watching the events unfold before them, but this historic event was not enough to keep his attention. Instead, his eyes were trained on Tialee. If there ever was a chance to speak with her alone again, now was it. The entirety of the Vigil was distracted.

"Can you believe it, Baxel?" Liaren said quietly next to him. "For years, I was trained to eventually watch over the Preservation Core, but even in all my imaginings of the people inside, I never stopped to think about the families. I knew they all had connections, but . . . Baxel, it really makes you realize how fragile it all is."

"Yup," he said shortly. He was watching intently for Tialee to turn around. He had no idea what a projection was capable of seeing, but he could think of little else to do, as she was standing in the center next to the two Williams's.

"Baxel?" Liaren said, now taking her eyes off the proceedings to glance over to him. "What is going on with you?"

"I need to speak with Tialee. Now. While everyone else is distracted."

She looked confused before coming to a frustrated realization. "Is this about Dimarka again? What more is there to find? That he was plotting to destroy the Remnants? That he was murdered?"

"Maybe something like that," Baxel said in a quiet voice.

Liaren stared at him blankly for a long moment before cracking up into quiet laughter. She held her fist to her mouth to keep from causing too much of a distraction. "Fair enough. Payback for leading you on about the size of the Preservation Core."

Baxel ignored her and waited for Tialee to finally turn around. When she did, he waved an arm above his head and mouthed the words "come here." Baxel cursed and shook his head as she continued walking without noticing. The projection spoke a few words to the people nearby before fading out mid-stride.

A few moments later, Baxel felt the hair on the back of his neck stand up as a blue glow wrapped around him from behind. He turned to see Tialee raising an eyebrow in question.

"Do I know you?" she asked, her voice transmitting quietly out of the data pad on Baxel's hip.

"I . . . I'm Baxel. I found you in Dimarka's quarters. You said you had a bad feeling before telling me to hide."

She glanced over to Liaren to see if there was any merit to the statement. "You are the ones that broke into the Preservation Core, are you not?"

"Yes," Baxel started. "But you remember us talking. Don't you? You told me to tell you to remember, before you turned off the lights in Dimarka's quarters."

"I believe you have the wrong idea," Tialee said with a shake of her head. "You need the help of the Warden."

"But I . . ." Baxel started.

"Go now." With nothing more than a shift of static, Tialee stepped away and reappeared back in the middle of the room.

Baxel gritted his teeth in frustration and paced a few steps away.

Liaren watched him with a confused look. Finally, she stepped in his way. "What was that about?"

Baxel drew in a breath and explained what had happened before she arrived in Dimarka's room with Varnil and Connor. He spoke as clearly as he could about what Tialee had said and how strange it seemed.

Liaren frowned. "If you did not tell her to remember the conversation, that is that. A projection cannot remember anything except for what they are allowed to save. As for the bad feeling you spoke of, the AI mirrors simply do not work that way."

"What if she does remember?" Baxel asked. He glanced to the side as people started to move off to spread the word to the rest of Safe Harbor. Many of the Vigil looked as if they were lost, moving with expressions of worry from one conversation to the next as they tried to reach a consensus of what would change in the Remnant's society by having a second Reawakened. "What if Tialee lied to me just now? I know she remembered that conversation. I told her to remember because she told me to!"

"A Vigil projection would not . . .." Liaren started, putting a hand to her forehead as if hit by a headache. "A Vigil projection would never lie."

"Not ever? Even if deception was imprinted into it?"

Liaren scoffed. "Do you seriously think Tialee, the first Vigil, would have imprinted the ability to lie into her AI mirror? You really think she was that blatantly corrupted for that habit to be passed on?"

Baxel paused and watched as a number of Vigil walked past with a few projections, displaying their rigid emotions and dry, formulative answers. He looked back to Liaren.

"You yourself said that none of the other AI mirrors even compare to her. What if Tialee imprinted everything into her mirror?"

"Or," Liaren countered, "she encountered an error in resuming function. The bad feeling she spoke of might be her way of saying that the system had encountered a problem. After shutting down, Tialee's system analyzed the error and purged the data file that contained it. Thus, her lack of memory and strange actions."

"Have you ever seen it happen?"

"With the others, yes."

"With her?"

Liaren seemed unsure of how to answer. "That does not mean it is impossible," she finally stated.

Baxel gave her a pointed look. "We'll just have to see."

Chapter 12: The Hunt

Kara moved swiftly through the ruins, her boots tapping up the long slope of wet steel. The high spires from beyond the impact valley loomed all around, casting long shadows over her fifth morning in the outerzones. Five days of tracking had brought her out beyond the borders of the Rift Hills to where the land started a steep climb toward the high crests to Norclave's east. Just on the other side of the incline and surrounded by the smooth heights of the outerzones was the Steel Valley.

Kara skidded down a warped slope on the side of her leg, slowing her momentum by scraping her boot into the layers of mosses and entrapped soil that had managed to find a grip on the surface. There was little plant life in the area, being mostly cold sheets of concrete and mixed rubble, and what growth there was in the shade of the towers had been burned down to a sickly brown by the storm.

As she set down onto the ground level of the area, Kara dropped low and started to search for any new threats. Her scan was more rushed than she was comfortable with, but her pace for the last week had not been set of her own accord. The resistance fighters were driven more from the fear of Norclave behind them than the caution demanded of the outerzones.

Kara wasted no time in moving through the rough terrain. It had been nearly half a day since she'd seen her targets, but if her estimation was correct, they should be only a few minutes behind her.

Early on, she'd determined how she would have to face the group. Running up from behind would put her movements in the open, and she could not afford to be spotted first. That meant that she had to determine their path and lie in wait, so she could choose where the fight would occur. The problem lay in finding a good location, as she could only guess at the path they would take.

Nearly two hours later, Kara knew she would have to make a stand soon, before they reached Reclaim territory. The high spires had thinned out as she moved up the rough slopes. She paused, looking behind her. While there was no sign of the group, it would not be long before they came into sight. Kara kicked at the grass. She feared it would be too thin to stay hidden, and definitely too thin to stop repulsor fire.

But then something caught her attention. Kara knelt down and raked her hands through the thin stems. The wraps on her hands and her exposed fingers looked as if she had painted them with a bright red rust. She stood up and looked outward, noticing that everything in the area looked as if it were bathed in a sunset. She looked back toward the ruins and saw that the sides facing the wind had a thin layer of the tint.

Without hesitation, Kara moved forward into the thickening layers of red. As she neared a dip in the land, she was struck by a barren landscape. The grasses had been buried, and the few small trees reduced to lifeless spindles sticking from the rocky terrain. Kara drew the edge of her boot over the dirt and dislodged an underlayer of black soot. The entire area had been charred.

This was where the sky flare had landed, and the signal trail it had left was being pulled down by gravity and winds. Kara pulled up the cloth about her neck as a breeze kicked up, not knowing what breathing the stuff would do to her lungs.

She continued forward cautiously, trying to walk lightly as to not dig up charred tracks. The ground was more varied than at first glance, covered in several rocks and laced with cracks in the land, some wider than the length of her foot, others a couple feet in width. The entire area was a series of rolling mounds, many of which were big enough to conceal a transport.

As Kara edged up to the top of the next hill, she was hit by a red-laden gust of wind. The next thing she noticed was a scattering of tracks all across the next valley. It looked as if hundreds of people over the course of a few weeks had been to the area. A number were little more than slight rhythmic darkenings across the signal dust, likely made while the majority of the red pillar was still suspended in the sky. Out of everything though, the biggest imprint was the large swath of churned dirt and rock, likely created by a number of heavy scraphaulers.

Kara knelt down and inspected the ground. Most of the rest of the prints would have come from curious people with the far-flung hope of finding something after the Steel Valley had laid claim to the sky flare.

Without warning, a deep thrum sounded over the next ridge and a bright light shot into the air. The blast from a pulse cannon raced upward. As it continued to rise, the contained heat core of the shot began to drain into the surrounding air, making a large streak of fire that eventually twisted out of existence. Kara was already moving to the side, taking cover beyond one of the larger boulders in the area. She had no idea what the intention of the skyward shot was, but she did not want the next one leveled at her.

Kara waited with the red winds rolling over the top of her. As if by intention, another shot rushed into the air five minutes later. In a few moments, the second shot reached higher than the tops of the broken spires. Kara snapped her attention behind her as another burst of repulsor fire sounded back in the ruins she'd come from.

* * *

"There is the signal!" Darmic pointed ahead through the tangle of ruins to where a burst of repulsor fire streaked up into the sky. "Just as you said, Lieth."

Lieth was still uneasy about the situation. He had been told a transport would be waiting for him at Maraton, but instead he had been directed to walk halfway across the blasted wastes on the hope that someone would meet them. The signal shot into the air told him two things: they were waiting, and they were armed.

"Return the signal."

Darmic grimaced as he unslung the pulse cannon from his back, then gasped in pain as he pulled the straps over his scarred and reddened scalp. Lieth glanced back to the others as their worn faces and scalded skin were lit by the flash of Darmic's pulse cannon. It looked as if they all could use a reprieve.

* * *

Olana Nuand left her guards at the doorway as she entered the Norclave Library. While the space had been unoccupied by the Cryo for nearly a week, it had gradually become more populated with a clutter of pieces and parts. Sora had kept the various decorative plants alive in the Cryo's absence, but Kenneth was to blame for the mess. Spaces on the shelves had been cleared for stacks of tools and containers of parts. Even the edges of the room were filling with the strange growth that seemed to happen when Kenneth was near.

At first, Olana had every intention of ordering her men to drag the technician and his scattered supplies out of the room. With Jance still recovering from the shrapnel slung from the explosion, that desk of hers was the most valuable asset still active in Norclave. It nearly made her squirm, thinking that the same man chosen by the previous Overlord to be the key piece in his operation to find the Cryo was now tinkering with the heart of her position in Norclave. What ultimately stopped her from taking him to the Cells was the Cryo's trust in Kenneth, and the fact that if anyone could figure out her system, it would be him.

Olana made her way past the piles of clutter in the walkways to where Kenneth was sitting behind the Cryo's desk. "Any luck on pinning down Travend?" Olana asked.

The man did not look up, likely having known she was on her way for minutes now. "The system is tracking a number of suspected individuals, I think. No correlations have been found as far as I can tell."

Olana could clearly see the tools he had lying on the desk, but there was no sign of what he was actually working on. "You are trying to access something more. Something the Cryo has blocked."

Kenneth clenched his hands before pushing back from the multitude of displays on the table's surface. "I just need Jance's visor."

Olana shook her head and placed her hands on the hips of her meticulously cared-for uniform. She was about to state that his request was out of the question, but she knew he was well aware. "Focus on Travend, Kenneth. Finding Kara is of no consequence."

Kenneth rubbed a grimy hand through his hair. "The only thing I could find is that she left Norclave on the ground level. And I only found that by manually accessing hundreds of recordings."

Olana clasped her hands together. "Leave it that way, then. Kara is wasting her time. Don't let her waste yours."

"She set off into that storm," Kenneth said, pressing a finger on the desk. "And before you say 'she is a tech hunter and that's what they do,' I just want you to know that I don't give a damn. I want to know that she is alive."

Olana frowned. Perhaps agitation would make the technician drop the matter. "You are not hurt that she left you? Perhaps she does not trust you to keep her location a secret?" she said.

Kenneth leaned back in his seat. "Oh, I hadn't thought of that. You are absolutely right."

Olana was left to draw a breath of frustration. It was no wonder Kenneth had so many scars on his arm, if he was willing to speak as such to someone in her position. "I need you to stay focused, Kenneth. If the Cryo dies, I will need you to teach my people how to use her tech."

Kenneth looked up with a scowl. "I thought this was just about Travend. You expect me to help you replace Jance as well?"

Olana sent him a cold stare as a means to contain herself. He had been provided with more than enough leeway despite the little trust she had in him. She would never admit it, but she had thought of getting rid of the technician while Jance was unable to look. The main problem was that Jance was still watching—not by herself, but by the system recording, and Olana knew the benefit of removing Kenneth was not worth the risk of her Cryo eventually turning against her.

Perhaps she was playing the wrong game with Kenneth.

"Did Jance ever speak to you about how she reorganized the way rations are distributed to the under-levels?"

"What do you mean?"

"It took her three hours. Three hours only, to delegate an entire team to oversee and overhaul the way Norclave provides meal packs to its poor. Three hours, out of one day, to improve the way we handle the downtrodden for as long as our society will exist. To answer your question, no, I do not expect you, nor anyone, to replace the Cryo. Our world has never seen anything like her, and we can only hope we have not seen the last of her work."

Olana turned to exit the room, though she already knew what she was going to say next. She stopped, counted three seconds, and looked back over her shoulder. "I need your help keeping Norclave alive in her absence. Otherwise, Jance will wake again into a world of chaos and struggle. Find Travend, before he finds a way to the Cryo again."

* * *

Kara repressed the surging tension of possible failure as best she could. Just about anywhere after the Maraton biological manufacturing facility would have been preferable to setting up an ambush here, and she bit her lip as she remained crouched low behind the red boulder. She had gone five days without being seen; it would be a shame to be spotted now.

Kara adjusted her veil as another gust of the red dust rolled around the edges of the boulder. Her heart started racing uncontrollably as the seconds rolled on. She knew the consequences of failure were far greater than losing the Cryo slayers: she would not survive if this went wrong. She would never make that trip back to her adopted families. She would never see Kenneth again.

But who else was there to stop the traitors who had torched the docks and killed a transport full of Norclave officials? Kara moved her hands over her pockets and pouches, practicing once more in her mind the motions that would mean life or death. To whom, had yet to be decided.

Kara threw a small disk as far as she could toward the other side of the dip in the land. Hoping to not be seen, she threw another over the top of the boulder as hard as she could toward the large scrape left where Reclaim had dragged the sky flare away.

"Where is it?" a voice floated quietly on the red winds. "We headed straight for the signal!"

Kara glanced around her boulder and saw the figures closer than she had since Maraton. They were headed down the slope of the basin. The one in the lead had darker skin, though it was hard to tell with the dusting of red. The two closest behind him were armed, though the two following a few steps further back did not seem to be a threat. Kara guessed it would be one of those two that she would try to take back to Norclave.

Kara undid the cloth around her left hand and pulled back her sleeve. She tapped the small display and set a metal bolt to hover in between the rails. On her way out of Norclave, she had bribed one of Olana's mercenaries to look the other way from a pile of supplies from Kamriek. Kara let out a breath into the cloth over her face, causing a small puff of red dust to break loose. She hoped the few shots of practice along the way would be enough.

"Are you sure we have not passed it?" the largest of the men asked. "What if it—"

Kara tapped the display, and the bolt sped forward from the magnetic rails with no more noise than the ripping of air. Kara ducked back behind the face of the rock, seeing in the last moments that the man had turned. A hard screech of metal sounded, followed by a yell of pain. The bolt had pierced the pulse cannon slung over his shoulder.

Counting between breaths, Kara activated one of the two disks she had thrown. A series of loud pops and bright flashes echoed about the area, and Kara immediately started running back up to the safety of the other side of the ridge. She then activated the second distraction, this time sending a twenty-foot plume of dirt and dust into the air. She glanced behind to see Travend's men scattering to the low rocks in the area for cover. She counted one down on the ground.

Once she slid over the top of the ridge, she knew her next biggest concern was whoever was waiting for their group. Kara readied another bolt to hover between the rails and waited. She expected mercenaries to come running from the direction of the signal shot, but instead she just saw a column of dust rolling against the wind as the engines to a transport were fired on.

Kara cursed the waste of time and carefully edged up enough to level her arm down toward Travend's men. She did not expect to be able to hit from nearly twice the range of her first shot, but if she was lucky, they would not hear the shot.

She quickly identified where the second armed man had taken cover by the edge of his heavy cloak flicking in the wind. Kara kept waiting, keeping the edges of her attention on the far slope. As it turned out, so were they. When the man pushed back from his cover to start looking for targets, Kara saw her chance. She let the bolt loose with another darting hiss through the air. She heard a sharp click as fragments of the rock burst beside the man.

It was then that a bright flash sent a searing hot spray of dirt into her face. The shot had come not from the far slope, but from the wounded man on the ground. Kara brushed away the chunks, which stung like a spray of scalding water, and rolled back for cover. As she hurried down the backside of the slope, another low pulse slammed near where she had been lying.

Kara heard shouting as she raced along the outside edge of the bowl. She flipped open a pouch and held her thumb against the sensor of a grenade. She had been told it would burst into an inferno once it hit the ground, but the problem with the damned things was that the only way to test them was to use them. She just had to make sure that if it failed she was ready with another option.

* * *

"Dammit!" Darmic yelled, failing for the second time to pull the long shard out of his back. From what Lieth could tell, something had ripped through the barrel of his pulse cannon. That still had not stopped Darmic from taking the risk of a weapon failure to take his shot.

"One of you two grab his weapon!" Lieth yelled toward where the scrapsmith and technician were hiding behind whatever rocks they could find.

"Over my dead body!" Darmic shouted, aiming his weapon at the two.

"Weril, head back the way we came! Do not waste time!" Lieth knew as soon as Darmic first screamed out in pain that they had entered a trap. They needed someone to cover them as they made a break for the transport, but he didn't trust Weril to help them if he could make it to the safety of the transport instead. "Do as I say!" Lieth yelled.

When he saw nobody moving, he pushed himself up out of cover and rushed over to Darmic. The man's face was covered in sweat. Lieth could tell Darmic was panicking, especially when he started to point the gun toward him. Lieth grabbed the heated and torn end of the open barrel and shoved it to the side. He put a boot on Darmic's stomach, causing the man to yell as his back was pushed against the ground.

"Give me the weapon!" When Darmic released, Lieth gritted his teeth and heaved it away with his sizzling hand. "Come get this!" he shouted toward the others. By his figure, they had only seconds to spare. Just as the scrapsmith started scrambling over while remaining low to the ground, for all staying low would help, a small object flew through the air.

"Cover!" Lieth yelled. Several shots sounded from the side as Weril fired his pulse cannon overzealously toward the grenade flying through the air. There was a loud clink as the grenade hit one of the many smaller rocks and then skipped to the side, directly toward Lieth.

"Don't leave me!" Darmic yelled.

Lieth took a breath and stepped toward the grenade and kicked it as hard as he could with the side of his boot. He felt something in his foot crack as the heavy ball skipped across the ground, kicking up a trail of red dust as it bounced between a few rocks. He stumbled as he set his weight back on his foot, but in the few seconds that he watched, the grenade did not go off.

"Rush up, dammit!" Lieth finally yelled. If they'd had at least one quality mercenary amongst them, their group would already be cleared and out of this mess.

* * *

"Mite-bitten liar," Kara cursed at the scum who had sold her the grenade. She had moved about thirty feet down the slope, expecting a fifty-foot scream of flame to rush across the ground. Instead she had just lost any bit of angle she had gained in flanking. She looked down the slope behind her, but there were only a scattered few boulders in the gully.

Kara put another metal shiv between the rails, wishing that she could have found a replacement for her pistol. Real weapons that could reliably function were rare. Worried something else would malfunction, Kara also reached for her most reliable tool, the shocklance she'd commissioned from a scrapsmith in Carvanhold for a fortune.

Just as she was about to ready the charge on her shocklance, two figures crested the hill. One wore a heavy cloak and was missing a hand, while the other had the look of a scrapsmith with the few tools on his belt. As both men raised their pulse cannons, Kara released the low amount of built-up energy in the shocklance as a shifting web of popping electricity. The half charge at the thirty-foot distance was only enough to knock the men to their knees.

Kara dropped the shocklance and reached to the weapon on her arm. A deep pulse from the scrapsmith's pulse cannon sent the ground in front of Kara bursting into the air. The short distortion from the shot was enough to scatter the display on her weapon and cause it to fail to receive her command to fire. Kara lunged to the side, screaming as the shot from the one-handed man's pulse cannon wrapped around the underside of her left arm.

She landed hard in the dirt on her back, feeling as if her tricep had been gripped by a riftwalker and ripped free. Kara would have been able to hear the repulsors warming for a third shot had she not been overcome by the sound of blood rushing in her ears. Kara curled in toward her knees as the chunks of superheated dirt finally rained down around her.

As she looked through the falling debris and the twisting of red powder between her and the barrels filling with heated agony, she did the only thing left to her. She gripped the handle of a knife and activated the faulty heated blade.

With a yell of effort through her pain, she threw it toward the one-handed man.

He raised the stump of his arm to protect his face and let out a scream as the blade hacked against bone. Instead of cutting clean through the arm with the heat generated from the battery, the knife instead pumped an electrical charge under his skin.

Kara reached for her shocklance, but the scrapsmith had managed to melt her weapon into the dirt with his next surprised and rushed shot. Unable to lift her arm to aim the magnet rails, Kara put her feet beneath her and started running down the slope. She glanced back, expecting to see weapons leveled in her direction. Instead, the scrapsmith's weapon was simply lying on the ground, and the scrapsmith himself was fleeing back over the ridge. She skidded to a stop, churning black soot up over the red dust with her heels, but as the one remaining target managed to shake the shocking blade free of his arm, Kara was forced to take cover behind one of the few boulders.

Molten strings of rock seared up and over Kara as several repulsor shots slammed into the boulder. Kara peeked around while the weapon was reheating. The man was using the shots to cover his nearing steps. Kara slid a bolt into the rails and gripped her left wrist. She attempted to lift it up but nearly blacked out from the pain. Kara let out a gasp and reached into another pocket. Before she'd left, Kara had thought she was decently outfitted for a fight. Now, she was forced to face what she had been ignoring the entire way. Out of their original group of tech hunters, she would never hesitate to brave any danger, but it was always the others who were more equipped to fend off any hostile people in the outerzones.

Kara started pulling off pouches as the next few shots slammed into the rock. She set aside the few remaining knives that she knew would just get her gunned down if she attempted to throw them. Another hit, and she unslung her sack of meal packs. Before the bleeding of her arm finished her off, Kara started crawling away along the ground, trying to get some space without being seen.

Not far ahead was one of the many cracks in the earth. It looked big enough to fit in, though she had no idea how far down it went. Kara clawed her hand over the face of a rock to help pull herself along.

"Show yourself!" the man shouted from the other side.

Kara gripped ahold of the edge of the large crack in the stone and pulled herself forward the last few feet. She glanced over the edge and could see that it narrowed down for at least a hundred feet.

"If I have to come around," he continued, "I will blacken your insides with fire!"

"Oh, shut up," Kara mumbled as she activated the last of her small explosives. The explosion sent the scraps of empty bags and ruptured meal packs spiraling into the air along with a concealing plume of dust and ash.

With her tracks hopefully covered, Kara rolled down into the rift.

* * *

Weril covered his face with his bleeding arm as a large swath of red dust was kicked up into the air. Along with the chunks of rock pelting down around him, he noticed several scraps of cloth floating away in the smoke. The more he looked as he slowly edged around to the back side of the boulder, the more he noticed the remaining pieces of the tech hunter. Whatever had happened, the blast had torn everything to pieces, leaving little more than a blackened hole behind the rock.

"Good riddance," Weril growled, shaking his bleeding arm, still feeling the sting of electricity that had jolted all the way up his shoulder. He looked back toward the ridge, seeing Lieth waving and signaling him to return. Weril simply dropped his pulse cannon and gripped his arm tight. He wouldn't need the weapon any more. Not with where they were headed.

* * *

Kara had to remember to keep breathing as she strained to keep herself from falling down farther. The top of the crack was nearly five feet wide, but any slip would send her falling down to wedge between the walls of stone possibly forty to fifty feet down. Kara gasped as her left foot slipped and her shoulder jarred against the opposite wall. As she felt her weight shifting backwards, she leaned forward and scrambled to find a grip.

As her other foot began to skid along the loose surface, Kara scraped her way up in a frenzied panic, regardless of whether it was safe to come out or not. She rolled up and over the edge, out of breath and unable to think. Eventually she gathered herself enough to pop the seal on a tube of medi-seal and press the paste into the shredded back of her arm. The medi-seal immediately began to foam as it mixed with the exposed blood.

As Kara shook the red dust off a strip of cloth to use as a bandage, the air filled with a low, chopping rumble. She let out a disappointed breath as a transport lifted up in the midst of a plume of dust.

Kara worriedly glanced about the scattered debris of her equipment before she remembered a spare display lens in a pocket. She lifted the hoop over her eye and the transport was immediately magnified. She shook the thing, attempting to clear the image. Even still, the marking on the side of the transport made it clear that it was not a freelance cargo ship.

Set against the scratched and rusting metal of the transport, three blue lines formed the triangle of the Steel Valley.

Kara finished wrapping her arm before attempting to stand up. On the second try, she moved to lean on the charred boulder. The way she saw it, Reclaim had been in on the attempt to kill Jance from the beginning. If they were not directly funding Travend, he at least had their support.

Kara ripped the weapon on her wrist free with a grimace and threw it down into the dirt. She had heard of plenty of mercenaries and tech hunters that swore by the devices, but the next chance she got, she planned on biting a chunk out of someone's skull before she would attempt to use that type of weapon again.

She kicked around a few scraps to see what she could find before letting out a groan and falling to the ground. After a minute or so of fighting against the pain in her arm, Kara brushed the embers off a split meal pack. It might be her last meal for a while. As she stirred the charred paste from amongst the sharp metal edges, Kara hated where her thoughts were starting to drift. By all rights, she should have learned her lesson. However, she knew that when she got up and started walking, her steps would not be back toward Norclave.

It seemed that she would be following the orders of Olana Nuand after all.

Chapter 13: Voice of the Vigil

The slow feeling of uncertainty set in over all of Safe Harbor. It was clear that things were changing far more rapidly and with less direction than in any time since Sarthyl and the rebellion. Connor tried to reassure those he met in passing as he made his way to the Food Storage and Supply Sector, though brief words were too little to settle the minds of those who could see that their world was shifting.

Connor looked at a small data pad to help direct him through the narrow passages. It was an area he did not regularly frequent if he did not have to. The constant rebuilding and expansion of the sector to fit the needs of storage had long since wiped away all the comforts of clean walls and bright lights to be found in the habitats and the Vigil.

Another glance at the data pad told him that he was nearing his destination. It was one short walk through a room stacked to the ceiling with crates before he entered one of the smaller cargo docks.

"Is this a threat from Safe Harbor? Are we to be detained for another week?" The accusing statement came from a man marred with the grime-stained skin from the harsh habitation conditions found within First Claim.

Though it had started under Sarthyl's guidance as a temporary outpost for exploring farther regions of the Remnant Fleet, First Claim had become a settlement in its own right when a number of Remnants joined his rebellion. Now, relations between the two areas were contentious, to say the least. Connor had made a good effort to encourage trade between the settlements, but Safe Harbor was reluctant to part with the most insignificant of items, and First Claim was starving for anything they could get. The culture in Safe Harbor was simply not adapted to dealing with anyone outside of the Warden's influence.

"You open that door, or I am taking my shipment and finding my own way out," one of the First Claim pilots demanded.

The Safe Harbor worker clearly did not know what he should do. "I mean to cause you no grief, Mr. Wardenson, but the head of the FS-S does not wish you to leave until we understand the . . . situation."

The pilot leading the argument handed his rough helmet to one of his people and took a step forward. "And you have orders to hold us here, is that right?"

"Orders? I am not sure I understand."

By the time Connor entered the space of the disagreement, he felt he was just in time to stop another severing of relations between the two Remnant settlements.

"Who are you, white sash?" the pilot asked gruffly, narrowing his eyes as he looked Connor up and down.

"I'm the one they call the migrant," Connor said. "Vigil of the Warden. And you are?"

The man scoffed. "I've heard about you. Abandoned Aura and somehow maneuvered your way in here. I cannot see how you can live with these—"

"Easy now," Connor warned before the man could find the word he wanted to use. "If I recall correctly, First Claim is in dire need of more shipments. Don't be the one to end that with a few foul words."

"Space take them, I just want my payment from First Claim, then I'm going to Aura."

Connor shook his head. He could not see what kind of life anyone could hope to find in the sparse belt of wreckage on the far side of the orbital fleet, making up the area known as Aura. His experience there, many years ago, was that Aura was filled with wretches either exiled from Safe Harbor or unfortunate enough to have been born away from the careful watch of the Warden. He doubted that any of the places in Aura had grown in the many years since he had seen the belt. Only a few small collections of people had found permanent homes amongst the scarce wreckage, and only a few groups of those even numbered more than a hundred. The rest of the Aurans were wanderers in ragged ships, trading, salvaging, and stealing what they could to survive. By all rights, nobody should be able to live out there.

"Then let me help you be on your way," Connor said. "Information you need to know: a second cryopod has been opened. The Vigil has not yet decided what to do. Relations between First Claim and Safe Harbor remain as important as ever." He then held out a data pad to the rough man and spoke quietly so the others would be pressed to hear. "And if you want to double your payment, take this to Regent Varis."

The man stared at Connor as he took the data pad, almost as if he were thinking of a way to keep it from the others.

"Let them be on their way," Connor said, turning away with a sweep of his shortened sash. He cared not if the crew tore themselves apart with greed; his message would get to the Regent by means of one bloody hand or the other.

* * *

Algan Treys idly tapped his walking rod against the floor of the Head Vigil's meeting room as he thought over the decisions afforded to him as the current Head Vigil. In all his years, never before had the people of Safe Harbor looked to him as they did now. He was to weigh the opinions, concerns, and interpretations of the Vigil, and out of the hundreds of voices from the living Remnants and those of the Vigil Archives, he would formulate the consensus of the Vigil. He tapped the rod, fitted with a handle to aid his steps, and looked out of the large window of the Head Vigil's meeting room.

Safe Harbor was just a small speck in the Remnant Fleet. It was a tiny population, hanging inside the wedge of a mile-long split in the orbital ship, the *Firmament*. He could see his own faint reflection against the thick glass as he looked out of the *Fortuna* support ship, in which the Vigil had remained for centuries. He could see the lights from the habitats and the shuttles zipping against the zero-space within the *Firmament*'s rift. He was reminded in one glance of the lives and centuries in his care. While the decision was not his own, he would be their voice until the Warden came again.

He tapped his rod once more and let out a breath. Only thirty cycles had passed since the Preservation Core was breached, and the lights far, far below twinkled in the distortion of the thick atmosphere of Earth. Another night passed across their ancestral planet, and for the next three hours they would share the dark with the empty ruins of a long-dead civilization.

And to think, there was talk of going back.

"Vigil Treys," a normally warm voice called from the doorway. Algan turned slowly and took in the presence of Malory Yumin. She stood to the fullest of her small height and held him with her naturally narrowed eyes, but he could still see her worry. There was talk of exiling her most promising pupil in years from Safe Harbor.

"Please, Malory. Simply Algan is fine. I have more than enough at the front of my mind to adhere to these small formalities."

"Vigil Treys," she said, ignoring him, "the heads of the Search and Exploration Sector, under the leadership of Oundara, have come to an agreement. They will defer to the Vigil's decision, whatever it may be, regarding the exile of Baxel Darus, Habitat Three, Deck Fourteen, former member of the suspended Search and Exploration Sector team Firebrand."

Algan lowered his head, knowing that Mrs. Yumin knew he was in the process of making the same decision regarding Liaren Marenday.

"Does the SE-S believe Baxel should be exiled?"

"While Oundara acknowledged the blatant disregard for tradition, the SE-S claims that Baxel was not under their supervision at the time, but under the supervision of Varnil Williams. It is her belief that the responsibility now lies with us."

"Thank you for meeting with Oundara and the rest of Search and Exploration, Mrs. Yumin."

"Is there anything else you require of me, Vigil Treys?"

"Get some rest, if you can. It will be a while yet before any decision comes to bear."

Mrs. Yumin reached into the folds of her robe and produced a projection device. "Tialee expressed her wishes to speak with you. About Liaren." She sat the disk on a small pedestal in the center of the room and began to back away.

Algan motioned for her to stop. "If Tialee wishes to speak of her pupil, you have every right to stay as well, Malory."

"No, I cannot allow myself to stay," she said with an uncharacteristically cold tone. "With the safety of the Remnants and the Preservation Core in the discussion, emotions will have too great of a risk in the matter." She glanced to the disk. "And with no insult meant to Tialee, I do not feel I am anywhere near as capable of keeping hold of my emotions as she."

At that, Malory Yumin turned and made her way out of the Head Vigil's meeting room.

Algan stood for a silent moment, thinking through how this conversation would go. It was a sad business discussing the exile of one of their own, but the Vigil had been created to ensure it was the Warden's will alone that they followed. Anything else, and the Remnants would split beyond repair and the Preservation Core would fail. The existence of First Claim was challenging enough to the cohesion of Safe Harbor.

Algan moved his hand over the top of the disk and waited for the blue swirls of static to settle into her figure. Centuries of Vigil Heads had left records of their interactions with Tialee, and many had noted that Tialee was incredibly opinionated on one hand, but on the other hand she was entirely submissive in regards to current decisions. Whatever it was that she said, Tialee would be insulted if he agreed with her without holding a reason of his own.

The former Head Vigil stepped out of the archives and into what had once been her meeting room. She looked around at the projected banners and small decorations along the walls with familiarity as she stepped over to the window.

Tialee started speaking while looking across the ever-changing landscape of the fleet. "Out of all our years, this is not the first age to pose the question of returning. Nor was the time of Sarthyl's rebellion the first. He was no Warden seeing some grand goal others thought impossible. Every time the Remnants look down upon those dead cities of Earth, the thought crosses our minds in some form or another. In my time, we knew for certain it was not a possibility, but we could dream. There was still a war raging on with only one end in sight: the annihilation of everything my grandparents left behind."

Algan frowned. "I am afraid that war is still what awaits the Remnants, though we will be the ones to bring it with us."

"Has it not already started? Sarthyl created a split in the Remnants, as we can still see today by the existence of First Claim. We are not as we once were." She looked down through the wreckage of the fleet to the surface of Earth. "It has always been on the edge of the next event that we weighed our survival. The Warden has stopped many such events, or directed us in how to survive them. With her silence, I can only see one option."

"Continue our course." Algan stepped up beside the glow of Tialee, feeling the slight hum that reverberated from her core. "And hope that in the future, our Earthbound settlements will not evolve to seek the destruction of the Preservation Core."

"It will be many, many years before they would look back. Long past your time. The Remnants will undoubtedly see the course of another fleet-changing disaster before such a time comes. We have been tasked with the protection of the Preservation Core, and with maintaining the fleet, but nowhere have I seen any connection between the two by the will of the Warden."

Algan clicked his cane on the floor a few times, though he was now feeling greater resolve. "I have heard that some of the AI mirrors are meeting with the heads of the Production and Research Sector. They are speaking of following the Reawakened's guidance and sending an observation probe to the planet."

"Nendra Halimuth must be pleased."

"And Dimarka must be wishing for a way to undo his death to put a stop to all of this."

Tialee glanced over. "I have observed talk of reentering the Preservation Core. The Reawakened, Varnil, claims that neither him nor his son have the expertise to lead the design of such a probe."

"Absolutely not." Algan hit his rod against the floor with a sharp click and turned toward the center of the room. "I will not have Reawakened swarming the population of Safe Harbor, and I will not see another split in my people!"

"Kaiden Williams is as much one of our people as you or I. A reminder to you: I am a Remnant only by the third generation. And while he is the first of his line to be so, he was only eight years old when he became the Reawakened."

Algan kept his back to Tialee and the window as he answered, "If you are going to claim he is a Remnant, then he is just as much of a Remnant as Sarthyl was."

"And Liaren? Is she going to be considered less of a Remnant than the man who tore us apart?"

Algan drummed his fingers against his cane and flicked his eyes from one point in the room to another, thinking it over. There was more than enough truth in her statement to bind his mind for a few moments. First Claim started as a small exploration outpost under Sarthyl's guidance. The expansive First Claim they knew today had spawned out of Sarthyl's exile. Algan remembered the moment of Sarthyl's exile from when he was just a young member of the Vigil. They had not expected anyone else to renounce the Warden's guidance that day.

He turned slowly back to the shimmering visage of the first Head Vigil and watched the drifting transport lights in the window behind her. "Tialee, do you believe endangering the Preservation Core—which is protected under the directions of the Warden—is not grounds for exile?"

"Unless you can tell me that anything was actually endangered, I dare you to try to exile her."

Algan frowned at the anger visible on her face. Normally, her systems would never simulate that level of agitation. "Tialee, is there something else?" He almost wondered if the sum of the situation had triggered a previously undocumented response. Perhaps Tialee had someone in her care taken by the same situation before she made the imprint.

Tialee paused, as if calculating a response while unsure of her own reaction. "I . . . I am unsure. Please, Vigil Treys, you must excuse me. I will self-reflect once I return to the archives. Do not let my emotional outburst sway your opinion. I am merely here to aid in determining the will of the Warden."

At that, Tialee began to walk back to her projection disk. While Algan would still have to give the final command, it was the equivalent of Malory Yumin walking to the door.

"Remember this conversation."

Tialee said nothing more before fading into a swirling static about the room. Algan moved over to turn off the projection. Her response may have lacked the calculation she wished, but it had pulled at his old heart.

He knew he would ultimately delay the decision so the others would believe he was weighing it carefully. But unless something else changed, Liaren would remain of the Vigil.

* * *

The entire time Baxel was restricted to the *Fortuna*-based sectors of Safe Harbor, the Hall of the Warden had remained in constant activity. The normally dim lighting of the large room had been adjusted to allow for more meetings. Bored, Baxel watched the sector leaders and Vigil debate a wide range of topics as they passed through the Hall of the Warden to one meeting or another. Perhaps they should have limited their discussions to meetings held behind closed doors, but the leaders of Safe Harbor were too overwhelmed with decisions to keep silent for any length of time. So, as they walked through the Hall of the Warden, they discussed how expansion should be handled, what territorial arrangements they would have to make with First Claim, and even talked of following the Reawakened's request for making a probe to send to Earth.

Baxel had watched it all unfolding from the second-level balcony of the Hall of the Warden, not knowing if he was going to be in Safe

Harbor for the end of the debates or not. One foot was propped up on the railing, and his head hung just over the edge as he lay on his back to pass the time. Just that morning, he'd listened to a slow debate over whether new positions should be created, or if the current heads would oversee the launch of some form of observation probe. Naturally, whoever wished to see it through who also had the most support would take the lead, just like with every other position in Safe Harbor.

He let out a sigh and sat up, having to lean to the side to come up on the right side of the railing. For the past few weeks, all he had seen and heard was cordial bickering over many-sided arguments. Of all the things he missed, the worst was not being able to just leave the habitat barrier. He missed being able to break free of the confines and truly see the form of the fleet. The tangle of metal, the unknown dangers, the chance to find something incredible.

Baxel shifted to let his feet dangle over the edge of the walkway, then let his forehead thump against the railing as he let out a breath. Maybe when they stopped fussing over the doomsday consequences of sending a stupid little probe to look at the planet, then they would finally remember to exile him.

The small conversations around the various meeting points about the room slowly began to quiet as both of the Reawakened made their way into the room, followed by a small group of the Vigil. Baxel noticed Liaren toward the rear, though she kept her head bowed toward the floor, as she had of late.

"I am just stating what I know," Varnil, the younger-looking of the two Reawakened commented to one of the Vigil following at his side. "Safe Harbor does not have anyone present capable of conducting the matter."

"I assure you, the Production and Research Sector has been provided with every available resource from the archives."

Varnil looked to his son before turning back to address the comment. "I mean no offense, but these imprint programs from long-gone members of your society are not enough. If we wish to obtain an analysis of Earth, your people will need help. The Preservation Core records show an individual who may—"

"That is out of the question, Reawakened. There is no record of the Preservation Core, at least not one the Vigil will recognize."

Baxel could see as they passed below him that the new Reawakened, Kaiden, was taken aback by the bluntness of the reply from the Vigil, though he said nothing as the small group continued on.

"Vigil Treys has made it clear that it is the consensus of the Vigil to limit further access to the Preservation Core," one of the other Vigil explained. "We fear for the safety of the Reawakened if we were to pick which of the Unawakened to wake."

"Respectfully, that is why I am the only one who has access to the list, Vigil. I understand the dangers of bleeding the resources of the Preservation Core dry, but I also understand the need to not waste the chances given."

Baxel lost track of their conversation as they moved across the room, though he found himself making his way back down through the narrow hallways to catch up to Liaren. By the time he crossed the large hangar floor of the Hall of the Warden, a considerable group had gathered at the base of the long steps to the Warden's Shrine.

"What is going on?" Baxel asked as he moved up next to Liaren, who stood a ways off from the group.

She flinched in surprise, likely having been caught up in her own thoughts. Once she realized it was him, she calmed back down. "It's a meeting of the Vigil open to the rest of the Remnants."

Baxel reached forward and adjusted a roll in the sash hanging over her shoulder. "You okay?"

Liaren let out a sigh and looked over to where Oundara was speaking with Nendra Halimuth on the first steps to the Warden's Shrine. "How do you handle it, Baxel? The weight of what we did threatening to crash down around us at any moment when they decide to think of something other than the expansion?"

"You want the truth, or something encouraging?"

Liaren made a half smile and shook her head. "I do not suppose either will make a difference in the end. My fate rests with the Warden. . ." Liaren paused and stared off in thought. Being exiled from Safe Harbor also meant being cast away from the Warden.

"I don't claim to know much about the Warden," Baxel said, crossing his arms and standing close enough beside her to feel her shoulder against his. "Especially not as much as you. But something tells me that the Warden is not done with you yet."

Liaren kept looking toward the small crowd, but he could tell his words had an impact. "Thank you, Baxel," she said softly.

It was long into the conversation playing out before them that Baxel began to take in anything but his own rolling thoughts. Algan Treys, the Head Vigil, stood on the steps now, listening to each who spoke from below with a weighing look.

"We have begun early estimations on the Reawakened's project," Nendra Halimuth explained. As head of the Production and Research Sector, it would be Halimuth's people in charge of creating the equipment. "This is no small undertaking. It will take the combined efforts of many sectors to pull this off, and throughout the stages, it may become a project comparable to Dimarka's."

Baxel could only shake his head. Nendra had always been jealous of the support Dimarka had in restoring the habitats. With him gone, she was hoping to pull others into listening to her suggestion.

"That will not be good enough," Varnil Williams interrupted loudly before Nendra could continue. "You can drop the entirety of Dimarka's reconstruction, have every AI mirror at full function, and put every Remnant in the entire fleet to work. It will not be enough."

Algan pointed with his walking rod sternly. "Then we shall do as we always have. Your people may not understand patience, but the Remnants live with the responsibility of more than those who are alive."

"Your history . . . your chaotic archives by means of the imprints . . ." Varnil started.

"Understand this, Reawakened," Algan said with a trembling anger. "The Remnants are more than just our past. We are defined by what we will always be. Our Warden has entrusted us with tasks far greater than ourselves, meaning that the Warden's will must be passed down through us and into the future. We are commanded to survive. Are we to solve this problem now? Can we solve survival?" He let the question hang in the silence. "We are to protect the Preservation Core. Does our watch waver when we think it is safe?"

After another moment, Algan continued. "We are the Vigil. In all things we do, we watch, and we wait. All Remnants know that our survival is the survival of millions yet to come. In this matter of seeking knowledge of the planet in the centuries to come, you will have a number of people far greater than the sum of the currently living Remnants to build your device."

"But we must expand to Earth soon," Varnil said quickly in return. "Vigil Connor agrees. The fleet has been going through change long before I broke into the Preservation Core. We cannot afford to wait the centuries it will take for your people to cobble together a mere exploration probe."

The migrant stepped forward, into the midst of the boiling conversation. "Head Vigil, I remind you that First Claim is not guided by the Warden. Their change will be swift, erratic, and without care for eternal continuation, as always. But they will beat us to the planet if we insist on safeguarding Safe Harbor from every notion that reminds us of Sarthyl. We must act quickly, without the Warden's guidance if need be, if we are to have any hope of our future generations outnumbering the followers of Sarthyl's ways."

"Be silent, migrant!" Algan yelled. His face was now flushed with anger. "These rash thoughts are what split Safe Harbor in the first place! Do you wish our Reawakened to become the second Sarthyl, destined to wreak havoc upon the Remnants? Do you wish for him to found a Second Claim on Earth to contest us? We should not run in fear away from the protection of the Warden, else we only fall into the dark of space."

"Then what shall we do?" Connor snarled, matching the Head Vigil's anger.

"Cease this nonsense! We are to follow the Warden's signal—and we have received none! If the time comes that the numbers in First Claim would overwhelm the Remnants in Safe Harbor, the Warden will see to our survival. The Vigil demands all thoughts and efforts toward Earth be halted!"

Silence washed over the room. Only the humming from the systems of the ship could be heard.

Oundara nodded shortly. "Yes, Vigil. You have seen the Warden, and we will follow your sight."

With gritted teeth, Nendra Halimuth followed suit. "Yes, Vigil. We follow your sight."

"Yes, Vigil," Kaiden Williams said quietly next to his father.

Baxel listened as many voices started to fall in line. Some were proud calls, agreeing with the form of the statement, others were quiet murmurs simply following decorum. Just when nearly all seemed to have accepted the call, Baxel realized one had not.

He looked over to Liaren.

"What is it?" Baxel whispered to her.

"Take me away from here."

"Why?"

"Because I am about to . . . Baxel, just do it."

"If you have something to say, say it."

"It is not my place. Only a Vigil can speak."

"Liaren, they have not banished you yet. You cannot live forever waiting for permission to become who you are."

Liaren held him in a long look. "Then wish me the Warden's luck."

Baxel nodded in reply.

Liaren drew a breath and pushed forward through the crowd. "I do not agree, Vigil."

Everyone was stunned enough that Liaren was met only by silence as she stepped to the center of the circle.

Algan Treys's anger had faded a bit, now clearly leaning more toward confusion with maybe even a hint of sadness. "Liaren, what is this? Do you truly agree with the Reawakened and Vigil Connor?"

"Absolutely not." Liaren glanced through the crowd, back to Baxel. "But I do believe that we do nothing against the Warden's will in preparing for anything the Warden may ask of us. Take, for example, the Search and Exploration teams. They hunt for any and all supplies, but it is not their decision where in Safe Harbor those items are used. In the same token, if we search for information about the planet, it will be the Warden that will decide what to do with that information. The Warden will decide if we are to ever go there."

"And what would you have us do, Liaren?" Algan asked with a brief, conflicting glance toward the floor. "Do exactly as they say? Bring another Reawakened into Safe Harbor? Is that what you were trying to do in the Preservation Core?"

"No," Liaren said in stern defense. "I was there to aid in the creation of a list to better prepare if the Vigil approved another Reawakened. As directed by the current Reawakened, it was to protect the Preservation Core, in only taking the precise Reawakened we needed."

Algan took a step down to bring himself eye level with Liaren. "It is the most difficult thing, agreeing with the actions of those whose reasons you protest." He set a hand on her shoulder. "But do you not see the pattern? You sought names, but you changed history. You want to know of our ancestral home, but what changes are the Remnants to see next as a result of your actions, not of the actions of the Warden?"

Varnil Williams slowly stepped up beside Liaren. "None of this is for the Remnants. This is for my people."

Algan let out a slow breath and closed his eyes in frustration. "Kaiden, do you believe the Preservation Core is in danger?"

The older man shuffled up next to his father and directed a respectful nod to the Head Vigil, as was proper form years ago. "The Remnants have diligently worked to maintain the Preservation Core, even through a rebellion that rent the population of the Remnants. The Preservation Core, even then, held true. And even with my own awakening, I do not see reason to fear for . . ."

The Reawakened's words stopped as if he had simply run out of breath to make them.

"Kaiden?" Algan asked, now opening his eyes.

Kaiden looked up past the high steps and to the Warden's shrine. "With all the respect in the fleet . . . I am not the Reawakened. I gave up my position because I felt a distance with the Preservation Core. I am a Remnant, no longer of Earth." Kaiden glanced over to his father, nearly twenty years less aged than himself. "The reason for letting a Reawakened take responsibility for the Preservation Core is to give their people representation. One of their own, to see to their safety." Kaiden let out a breath. "The design of the Warden never ceases to amaze me. The Warden has always known that my father would be able to see what we would never be able to. The safety of the Preservation Core."

"As a Remnant for nearly sixty years," Kaiden continued, looking around the crowd, many of whom were quite a number of years younger than himself, "it pains me to advise against the Vigil. But if my father decides that another Reawakened is required for the safety of the Preservation Core, that is a decision purposefully designed to be out of the hands of the Remnants, the Vigil, and the Warden."

"No," Algan said almost in a reflex. "I cannot accept the Remnants being further subjected to people like—"

"What happened?" Kaiden bit, for the first time taking a sharp tone against the Vigil. "In my time, I was respected by all Remnants. I could go where I pleased and my thoughts were welcomed. In my early years, a great effort was made to explain why I should change my opinion, but I was not silenced as my father has been. Where has the respect for the Reawakened gone? What happened?"

In Algan's silence, the migrant quietly spoke the answer.

"Sarthyl," he said again, this time louder. The migrant had a weary look. "Sarthyl was a Reawakened. It was in the weeks after you reentered the Preservation Core, Kaiden, that I arrived in Safe Harbor with a cryopod as my token in. The pod showed signs of instability, so he was taken as the replacement to you, Kaiden."

Connor continued, "In the early years, I remember the great respect Sarthyl earned from the Remnants. We flourished, and came to trust his judgment almost as equal to the Warden. But when the Vigil denied a return to Earth . . . we were split. Thousands died in the conflict."

Kaiden held a hand up to his mouth. "By the Warden . . . So you came to fear the Reawakened?"

"Our population has not yet recovered," Algan said quietly. "The younger generations have nearly forgotten, but I grew up seeing the change Sarthyl brought before the rebellion. All too quickly after the technological and societal progress, entire family lines were stripped away as Sarthyl blasted the habitats."

Varnil Williams bowed his head to the Vigil. "I am sorry. I never . . ."

"It is I that should apologize, Reawakened," Algan said, looking to the youngest of the two with watery eyes. "My opinion of you had been settled while your frozen dreams were still of fleeing a tortured Earth." He glanced over to Kaiden. "And you may not be a mirror of the archives, but as a past Remnant, I thank you for bringing stability to our ways. Our respect for the Reawakened had been lost."

Connor, barely missing a beat, asked, "How does the Vigil weigh?"

"The Vigil accepts the Reawakened's sight. Varnil, you may provide a replacement for your son to join the fleet at your own discretion."

Chapter 14: Reclaim

Kara drew in a gasp of air and pulled the rough blanket tight against her with her right arm. She could feel the grip of a cold sweat pushed by the throbbing pain of her left arm and tried to curl onto her side, but found the motion painful enough to jolt her the rest of the way awake.

She reached for a knife as she sat up on the edge of the bed and instead found her arm wrapped in bandages, with a sling holding it in place over her single layer of clothing. Kara looked around frantically and found herself in a small room. It was no meager housing by the furniture and the clean glow against the white walls. The single doorway of the room was open, and her belongings were on a small table and draped over the chair next to it.

Kara wasted no time in readying herself for anything in these strange surroundings. She started upending the few bags left to her with her one good hand. She felt exposed not being wrapped in layers of cloth and adorned with pouches full of her tech. Having her lengths of red hair hanging open and down her back made her feel as if she had her neck bared to a heated blade. Even her naked feet were open to be shredded by the rubble of the outerzones.

"Dammit," she breathed, unable to find a knife, spool of cable, or anything else she could use as a weapon. She settled for wrapping one of her carbon-steel belts around her fist so that the magnetic latches could be used as a hasty flail. Kara grimaced as she pulled with her other hand to make sure the wrapping was tight.

As she heard soft footsteps shuffling just outside the doorway, she moved into a better position and started mentally counting for when they would be stepping through into the room.

"Oa?" a young man asked as he stepped slowly into the room. "Oa, did you move the tech hunter?"

Kara shouldered into him with a growl, sending him and the bundle of clothing in his arms toppling over the table. Kara stood over him with her belt-club readied for the slightest motion of aggression.

Instead, she looked into his wide and stunned blue eyes and listened to his surprised and horrified yell. After a moment, with Kara still holding ready, he let out a relieved breath.

"Oh goodness, you scared me, Tech Hunter. I thought for a moment you were . . ." The young man glanced to her raised hand mid-sentence. "Were, uh, going to . . . uh . . ."

"Where am I?" Kara said in a hard tone, making sure that he knew she was not afraid of him. Not that there was reason for her to be. He was small, probably no taller than herself, and looked in no way ready to fight with his smooth skin, well-fed round face, her assorted clothing lying over him, and a toppled chair under his leg.

"I found you just outside the ring. About two days ago, don't you remember that?" Her unblinking stare gave him reason to continue. "You were badly injured, and the scavengers were picking you apart for tech."

Kara remembered a flash of what he was talking about. She'd kept passing out with the high walls of Reclaim in sight. She remembered trying to struggle as they started to take everything. Rough figures, living outside the wealth of the city. Her hands had bled as she held on to the twisted scrap, all that remained of her shocklance, though now, standing above the small man, she could not think of why she would have carried something so useless all that way.

"They just . . . would have left you there. I couldn't. So I took you to Oa."

Kara lowered her hand and looked out the doorway. This was clearly only one room of a larger building, though she did not know how large.

"Oa? Who is Oa?"

"You don't . . . I thought by the way she talked about you that you two knew each other. She is an older lady, grey hair, dark wrinkled skin, lives here in Reclaim. This house, to be exact."

Kara let the belt drop out of her hand and reached down to grab her socks off the man's chest.

"And what are you doing here?" Kara asked.

"I help Oa out. Mostly getting things. I was outside looking for a type of plant she thought might grow around here. But I also go to the markets for food. Never meal packs, though. She hates them."

Kara pulled the chair from under his leg and began to put on her socks. She could tell they had been cleaned, as there was no sign of the red dust. Next, she started into the process of banding her boots on with only one hand.

"You are safe here, I hope you know that," he said.

"Who else knows I am here?"

"No one besides me and Oa, as far as I know." He frowned. "Well, I did have to call for an emergency team to help get you into the city. And your bandages were from your time in the medical facility in the Prime Elect's Citadel. But when the Black Scars started to seem interested in you, I took your medical cart and rushed you halfway across the city to here."

"Nobody else?" Kara repeated. He would have been closer saying the entire damned city. She could immediately see the number of ways anyone would be able to track her down. All they would have to do is ask the nearest rumor peddler, and Oa's house would be a deathtrap.

"My name is Hama," he said, reaching out a hand toward her. "My family lost their last name sometime between now and the breaking, but that isn't all that abnormal I suppose. What about you? What is your name?"

Kara pulled her cloak over her left shoulder and tucked her hair back into her hood. Without a second glance back to Hama, she started through the small building, moving cautiously, until she tapped a panel to open a door leading out to Reclaim.

Kara was immediately struck by the openness of the street. It was nearly twenty feet across before the path of smooth tiles was interrupted by another of the large houses. Kara glanced both ways to look for threats, but instead she saw relatively few individuals walking about their daily business. Not one of the wide paths between the well-constructed houses had any downtrodden souls looking for the next meal pack of the day.

She had never entered this far into the city. Mallec was always the one who made the trades here, meaning that her experience ended just inside the outer ring of the city. Kara looked up the massive terraced slope filled with houses of all shapes and heights. Reclaim was spread across a large, layered bowl in the land and was surrounded by the ruins of a massive ring building. Apparently the circling structure, nearly four miles across, had been a staging facility for one of the orbital ships. At least, that is what she gathered from what Jance had said. Kara glanced up to the dull shapes of the orbital wreckage before continuing as quickly as her pained steps would take her.

She looked to her left. The street she was on was only two terraces away from the Prime Elect's Citadel. Though it filled the lowest portion of Reclaim, the tower still rose up higher than anything else in the city. Kara guessed it to nearly reach as high as the tallest level of Norclave, though even with its design taking inspiration from the starscrapers, the Citadel matched nothing Jance's time would have known.

But then again, it was not simply a remaining piece of the world before. As far as Kara could tell, everything in Reclaim had been built from the ground up using the steel collected from the land. The only exception was the ruin of the staging facility ring that formed the outer wall of Reclaim. Even the streets were made of a paving of rectangular steel tiles. Most had the clean coating of white, just like the inside of Oa's house, but others reflected the midday sun with all but their rusted edges.

Kara tugged on her hood and made sure the sling for her arm was completely covered. She needed to find somewhere else to stay. Somewhere she could control her own concealment, where she would at least stand a chance for when Travend's men came for her. She was surprised they had not heard of her arrival already.

Kara turned her back to the Prime Elect's Citadel and started down a large street heading off toward the rest of the city. Someone in that tower was working to protect the people who attacked Norclave. Whether it was some manager who could authorize a transport out, or even an official close to the top, Kara was determined to see them pay for what they did. Once she secured her own position within the city, she would just need to find out who that individual was. Olana Nuand would take care of the rest.

Except there was one problem.

She let out a sigh and stopped in her tracks. Without needing to turn, she recognized the timid steps following her own. As she stayed still, her short cloak ever so lightly rolling with the wind, the steps slowed to an uncertain halt.

"Hama?" Kara asked, turning just enough to look from under her hood over her shoulder.

"My apologies, tech hunter. It's just, Oa would want me to look after you."

"Consider looking after yourself. You are in danger following me."

He pulled in a breath and took a few steps closer. "I am not afraid of the watch. And the Black Scars . . . well, as long as we're back at Oa's before . . ."

"You misunderstand, Hama," Kara interrupted in a quiet tone packed with more volume than any shout. "I am the danger. Whatever laws and wealth and protection this city may afford, none of it will find you before my problems do. Go back to your building, and forget I ever existed."

"Wait," he said, just as she was going to turn for the worst section of the city she could find. "The watch, they think you are a spy from Norclave. Oa went to argue otherwise and left me to watch you. You can disappear if you want, but at least let me show you the city. There are rules you may not understand, places you should not go."

Kara weighed him for a long moment before giving in. "When I decide to part ways, you are not to say a word."

"You have my word." Hama looked proud.

"Just start walking," Kara finally said.

* * *

Olana looked up at the small camera in the corner of the hallway as she walked to the Cryo's office of the Norclave Library. She knew if Jance had not been confined by the medical staff, her presence would be known well before she set foot into the office. As it were, she turned the corner into the room and was met by the harsh grinding of metal and flashing of sparks. After nearly a week of trying to get him to let go of hunting for Kara, the technician had shifted to putting all his effort into expanding the Cryo's system. Even now, he was cutting into a piece of steel to get another camera online.

"Is there something you need, Nuand?" Kenneth said, tossing a piece of starscraper glass to the side. He was using it to shield his face from the sparks. Without ever looking to her, he started pulling pieces out of the camera and setting them on one of the large tables recently brought to the room and since cluttered.

Olana waved in front of her nose at the burning smell. If he did not know so much about the system he was linking these devices to, she would have put him out with the other scrapsmiths. "I am merely getting a feel for your progress. I see you have plans for more surveillance cameras?"

"That is right," Kenneth said, keeping his attention to his work in his normal manner. "I doubt Travend is going to walk down this one hallway. We're going to need to watch more places."

"Are you afraid these devices will be found by Norclave's scavengers?"

"This?" Kenneth asked, motioning to the large disk filled with a black lattice. "These are not for here in Norclave."

"Then for where?"

"Zaireel Tuakana," Kenneth said. The way he said the name made Olana tense. Not for the first time, she worried about Kenneth knowing too much.

Kenneth continued, "Tuakana was released from medical attention several days ago. The system trace-connected some of the contacts he met with. The system marked a name it had not encountered, so it requested a cross-reference. Sora determined the name was a security manager in Reclaim. He and Tuakana were gathering supplies, meeting with other Norclave officials, and set up a transport for use tomorrow. Seeing as Tuakana is your appointed emissary to the Steel Valley, it stands to reason Tuakana is going to Reclaim."

Olana said nothing. She waited to see where he was leading.

"All of that gave me a deadline to complete this before the transport is moved to the outer docks."

"And what do you plan to do with this?"

"Expand Jance's surveillance to Reclaim."

Olana crossed her arms to keep from showing that she was a bit unnerved at the power of Jance's system. "If this is found by anyone in Reclaim, the political ramifications will be severe. Zaireel and his team will most likely be executed."

Kenneth glanced to her for the first time and smirked. "Lucky for them, you found the best." He opened a container and started setting different parts inside. When he had everything positioned correctly, he activated the container to fill the gaps with a supporting lattice of foam. "There will be multiple layers of precaution. And all transmissions back will be sent under Council clearance."

"Meaning that nobody but the Cryo can access it," Olana filled in.

Kenneth shrugged. "I'm not here to replace Jance."

Olana frowned. "You should have brought this to me first."

Kenneth pulled the lid of the container shut and rested his hands on top of it. "You told me to hunt Travend."

"Is that who you are hunting, Kenneth?" Olana pulled her glass cube out of her pocket and rolled it across her fingers. "Last time I knew, Travend was not in Reclaim."

Kenneth moved to the desk at the center of the entire system and pressed one of the floating projections. "To be fair, we have no evidence of that yet."

Olana clutched the cube tight. As she was about to speak, she heard the footsteps of someone entering the room. Olana turned to see who it was and received a salute from a short man wearing a visor. He was one of the people she had brought over from Kamriek's Grove.

"Excuse me, Overlord Nuand," the man said. "I am here at orders from the technician."

"Orders?" Olana asked. The man's look turned fraught with worry. "Very well," Olana said before he started stammering his excuses.

"Thank you, Overlord." He gave another salute and moved to the container on the table.

Kenneth all too knowingly looked to her grip on the glass cube. "Don't you worry. Everyone knows their role." Kenneth waited until the man left the room. "Even he doesn't know what is in that box, or whom it is going to. Neither does the merchant, or your man who has been holding the promise receipt for a week."

"And if something fails in the line? If he is robbed in the trade center, or someone passes it to the wrong hands? What if it is intercepted by Travend?"

"You've thought of everything, remember, Overlord?" Kenneth said, then waited just long enough to get under her skin. "You have an armed team ready to go if the system finds the box in the hands of someone not marked with the proper temporary clearance. And if someone working for Travend takes it, we can feed that new facial recognition data back into the system's recordings over the past two weeks or so and find some point in which they contacted Travend. We win either way."

Olana let out a breath and squeezed the cube tighter yet. The sooner her Cryo was released, the better. She had never imagined that the technician would pick up where she had left off as well as this. Olana turned and left the room, taking with her another set of reservations. This kind of control leeching was exactly how the last Overlord lost power over Norclave.

* * *

Three rings up they went, passing on the specialty markets of the richest levels of Reclaim in favor of the crowded streets of the mid-levels. Kara followed close behind Hama as he walked a well-worn path through the side streets of the city. This far away from the Citadel of the Prime Elect, the terraces widened out enough to have packed housing and a spiderweb of roads through the various markets. Kara saw everything from the wraith steel of Kamriek's Grove to fresh power cells from the Rift Outpost being put up for trade. There were children running with toys of a design from before the fall and numerous individuals with clothing imitating the clean lines from the same period. And even though the sound of music bounced around the centers of the blocks—from both audio systems and live instruments—Kara was far more drawn to the floating scents of fresh-made foods.

"This is the best place to be if you are looking for food other than meal packs," Hama explained. "Worst place if you are hungry and on an errand for something else. Come on," he said, motioning to a building sticking up above the others in the immediate area. A large deck was built in a circle out from the terrace, forming an outlook just over the tops of the next houses down. Several large steel posts over the entire deck served as the base for the large round building Hama had motioned to.

Kara followed him up the steps along with the shifting crowd. It was a matter of contained chaos in the area beneath the high and loosely draped solar cloths. There were dozens of tables ringed with chairs, but the vast majority of people were in the open standing room between.

"You may misunderstand what I am looking for," Kara said over Hama's shoulder through the constant noise of the area.

"Are you sure about that?" Hama raised his eyebrows to Kara and motioned with his eyes over to a woman shouldering past with her flat plate of steaming bread, which looked as if it had been braided around a core of sweet red gel.

Kara shook her head and followed him, grimacing every time someone bumped against her wounded arm. At least nobody here was paying her the slightest bit of attention.

"Besides steel, the valley is the largest harvester of natural wheat in the entire region. Mix that with the new produce coming from the Rift Hills, and you get . . ." he trailed off, watching another plate glide past.

Kara finally got sight of the counters they were moving toward, and could see where the line stagnated into far more requests going in than steel plates coming out.

"We're leaving," Kara growled, tugging hard on his collar so he would understand even if he did not hear. As Kara and Hama started out, the crowd farther ahead parted for a group in partial flight armor that were leaving the building.

"What is wrong?" Hama asked.

"Who is that in front of us?" Kara asked, now following in the wake behind the group of four men as they headed down the steps.

"Those are members of the watch. They make sure the law of the Prime Elect is respected."

Kara kept walking along behind them as Hama continued to explain.

"You don't want them to see you doing anything wrong. Bad things happen."

Just then, Kara saw one of the watch, with his dark, blue-painted armor, reach down into an open meal pack container at the feet of one of the street musicians and pull out several square coins. The musician frowned but nodded respectfully as he simply continued his song.

"And who watches them?" Kara asked.

"Shhh!" Hama said with a finger pressed to his lips. He stepped in front of her with a serious look. "You will keep your thoughts to yourself! If they had heard you . . ."

Just then, a man took off shoving his way through the crowd followed by shouts proclaiming his thievery. Kara expected the watch to take off after him, but instead they simply pulled out data pads and started to talk to the people who had seen what happened.

Kara turned to Hama and raised an eyebrow in question. "If they would have heard me . . . they would have filed a complaint?"

"No, that is where the . . ." Hama drew in a breath and glanced around. "Where the Black Scars come in." He glanced around once more. "Let's not talk here."

Kara stopped at his word.

The crowd was considerably thinner around the various shops and stalls as they reentered the market area. Hama stopped briefly to pick up a meal pack for Kara before continuing along.

"Everyone in Reclaim knows who actually holds the power. The watch go to the Scars to get things done." Without much warning, he stopped and turned back. "There. Behind my left shoulder and tucked into the alley. The one nobody is going down at the moment."

Kara glanced over Hama's shoulder. She spotted the two men and a woman leaning up against the side of a building, away from the crowd. Their brutish demeanor made them stick out from the lively business pushing all around, but it was not until she took a second glance that she noticed the markings. As if by ritual, they had one or two heavy scars across their faces, and the wounds were filled with a thick black to make a violent tattoo. One of them pulled hard against a large dog straining at its leash as it let out muffled growls at anyone in the crowd that passed nearby. The animal was fixed with a muzzle, and Kara immediately recognized the workings of a shocklance adapted into it. If the dog was let loose on someone, the repeated nudges of constrained bites would inflict a staggering jolt to the entire system of the unfortunate target.

One of the watch from earlier walked to them alone and handed the woman his data pad. The Black Scars immediately moved down the alley, and the street seemed to open back up to the movement of the crowd.

"Those are the people that thought they should question you," Hama finally said. "That was why I brought you to Oa, hoping you could stay hidden there, away from them."

"Are they going after that thief?"

"No, he is safe for as long as the sun is up. If the Black Scars track him down though, he will probably die in his sleep. If his family knows what he has done, they will stay in their beds no matter what they hear."

Kara could feel herself reaching for a knife in disgust before she remembered she had been left with nothing.

"I only told you because I don't want that to happen to you." Hama looked to the ground. "Whatever you were thinking of doing, and whatever the Black Scars thought you did, I just wanted you to have a chance. The rest of us live just fine, but I know you would have seen the other side."

Kara thought for a moment before putting a hand on his shoulder. "Thank you, Hama. I am sorry I have nothing to repay you with."

Hama simply nodded in understanding. "Not a word."

* * *

As Kara made her way down the dark streets of the city alone, it increasingly became apparent that her situation was dire. She was essentially two days behind. She should already have a list of places she could stay and a better idea of the routes of the city. Instead, her weapons had been seized by the Citadel and any other valuables had been stripped away outside the high walls of the city.

"There is no charity here, scavenger," the brute of the man escorting her out of the shelter house had stated, echoing what the keeper had told her before calling for his guard. "If you want a free meal, you should be in Norclave. I hear their Cryo is real nice."

Kara turned away into the narrow street, knowing that she just had to keep searching. It was not actually the first time she heard mention of Norclave's Cryo. A great deal of the conversations she'd overheard focused on the subject. Some were amazed that one had actually been found, others were claiming she had been killed by rogue administrators. As she continued, now keeping an eye out for the possibility of needing to sleep in an alley, Kara wondered what they would think if they knew the people who had tried to kill the Cryo were in their own city.

Soon, the calls of a curfew went out from the watch walking the streets. Come nightfall, everyone in the city was expected to be inside and accounted for, one way or another.

"Inside, everybody!" a voice shouted only a few houses down from where Kara was beginning to search for a way up. The vast majority of windows were either bound by a section of walkway lattice or were too high up to reach. Kara looked up past the roofs that would now be unreachable due to the condition of her arm. High up, dusk was spreading across the orbital wreckage like it was across the sprawling bowl of Reclaim.

As the watch began to use the handheld glow of focused data pads or battery-rigged lights, Kara decided that she would just have to play their game. She spotted no pattern to their wide search, meaning there would be plenty of opportunity to go unseen.

For the next few hours, Kara ducked in and out of back alleys and crossed the main streets. When it finally seemed as if the watch had given up on their hunt for the same type of people Norclave at least tried to take care of, Kara found a pile of empty crates and wedged herself in between the layers of steel. She wrapped her cloak tight, keeping one eye alert to anyone passing by.

The streets this far toward the outer edge of the city were mostly made of worn paths and half-buried steel cables. With the recent rains, much of the paths were tacky, if not altogether made of mud. She had long since given up on keeping her boots and cloak clean, though she imagined the next day it would be necessary to exchange her few supplies for something that would stand out less. She would keep the hood for tonight, but walking around the richer levels of Reclaim would certainly see a more vigilant concentration of the watch during the day.

She heard shouting in the distance along with frantic, muffled barks. Kara leaned out from her cover and saw bright sparks as the Black Scar hounds caught a man who had tried to run. He yelled in agony as the hounds tried furiously to bite at him, jolting him repeatedly with their muzzles. The Black Scars took their time to gather around before a couple of large men pulled the animals back.

"Please, no!" the voice cried into the muck of the alley. "It was just for this night, I swear! I lost my job, but I will have . . ." he was cut off by a sharp kick to the ribs.

"Call for the watch," one of the bigger men said. He had a thick, dark line running across his forehead and down the side of his face, as well as an uneven scar filled across his neck. "Have this one dragged back to be questioned by the city officials."

"You got it, Hakatha," one of the others said, hauling the poor man up by the back of his shirt.

Kara knew she would stand no chance if she did not move. Since the hounds were still snarling at the man they had brought to the ground, she pushed her way out of her spot in the crates and moved out of the alley.

Before she could pick a direction away from searching lights, the dull barking was silenced. Kara started hurrying, staying low to the edge of the street as she moved to a location she'd found earlier that night. Kara tugged on a few doorways as she passed, but everything seemed to be barred shut or locked by security clearance. Just as a window failed to move, Kara glanced behind herself only to find a new energy to her steps. The Black Scars were emerging from the alleyway, pulling tight against the pair of dogs who had their noses to the ground and were turning in her direction.

She darted out of the main street and back between a pair of houses as calls rose up from behind her.

"Go on! Find him!" Hakatha yelled.

Kara wished again that she had a weapon. She would have to kill the dogs if she had any hope of outrunning the Black Scars, and without a knife or shocklance of her own, she failed to see how that would be possible. In a desperate measure, she began clawing at the ground for a steel plate with her only useful hand.

* * *

Hakatha watched with enjoyment as he released the dogs down the street. Occasionally, their muzzles popped sparks against the ground as they tracked the fresh trail. Some other rat must have been hiding when they found the first man. Hopefully it was a member of his family.

"Keep on them!" he shouted to a few of the others, all bearing similar marks to his own across their faces and bare arms. Even though he'd enjoyed it, the last time one of their dogs got loose and they couldn't find it before morning, the Prime Elect was not pleased. Iben Feirshan preferred them to be discreet, at least until after Reclaim's curfew. The watch had a pristine public image to keep, but it was up to the Scars to maintain order.

Hakatha was surprised to hear the high-pitched whining of one of his dogs and the bright flashes of its muzzle as it bolted back out of the alley. Someone had managed to mess up the connections.

"You two, fix my dog!" he commanded as he readied his steel pipe and rushed with the others toward the alley. The dog curled its tail and snarled at any of the Black Scars trying to take off the muzzle continually shocking it.

Hakatha rounded the corner to find a whimpering and bloody mess made out of the other one. He turned on his data pad to give the area a glow and spotted where a steel plate had been pulled free from the dirt. He looked up and saw a cloaked figure limping away.

"Catch that man!" Hakatha yelled. While the three other Black Scars took off to prove themselves, he knelt down beside the dog to look at its wounds. He set a hand on its blood-matted fur with a frown, but the animal let out a harsh yelp and quickly turned on him. He barely pulled back in time to keep from taking a shocklance to the neck. The hound managed to catch his hand with a sharp pop, and Hakatha felt his fist half curl into a tight claw from the sting. He raised his pipe and finished the creature off.

Whoever it was that did this to his hounds, he was damn sure they were going to pay.

* * *

Kara moved as quickly as she could, but she had failed to disable the second beast before it hit her several times in the leg. She rounded the corner as the alley was flooded with shouts. Just as suddenly as she was set upon by those shocking muzzles, Kara stepped out into a wide-open square lined with the empty stalls of the market.

From the lights flashing in the alley behind, she knew there was no way she would make it to cover in her shape, and no way she could outpace them. Kara drew in a breath and simply turned to wait. Perhaps she could bluff. Perhaps they would call the watch quickly.

Kara stood her ground in the dull night's breeze as the rough figures came to stand in an uneven line. Each of them shared the markings across their faces and the wary pause in their fighting attitude. Moments later, the leader of the group shoved his way through, his hand, covered in blood, shining against the assortments of lights they carried.

"I should have guessed," the one she heard called Hakatha said in a low growl. He looked down the line at the others before stepping toward Kara. "One of the rats, running from a Norclave on fire. They have been collecting ones like you in the Citadel."

"How many?" Kara asked.

Hakatha frowned, and then he shrugged. "I suppose enough. I could just end you here and now and be done with it," Hakatha growled to Kara, tossing the pipe he carried to the cobbled steel before popping his bloody knuckles.

She eyed the man as he waited with clenched fists under the stars and orbital lights. She didn't understand why he was hesitating. As the Black Scars backing him started to turn back into the alleyway one by one, Kara could not hide her confusion any longer. She turned to look over her shoulder only to see a small, elderly woman with dark skin staring Hakatha down.

"This one is mine to take back to the Citadel," Hakatha growled to the older woman.

"There are bigger things in the streets than you," the old woman said, putting her hands on her hips. "Pick up your weapon and leave, little one."

Hakatha finally reached down and tucked the pipe through his belt. He pointed a hard finger to Kara in a warning. "Don't let me catch you alone." At that, the last of the Black Scars tucked tail and headed back the way they had come.

After a moment of astonishment, Kara finally looked to the elderly woman.

"Who am I?" the woman asked just as Kara was about to. She frowned as she looked Kara up and down. "I am the one that has been waiting for you. My name is Oa."

Chapter 15: Warden's Tears

Varnil followed what amounted to a procession as the Head Vigil led the way to the Preservation Core. There were a number of people present, but once they neared the doorway to the Preservation Core, only those in the highest standing in the Vigil were permitted to enter. Varnil glanced back to see Baxel leaning against one of the walls of the hallway, trying his best to ignore the looks he was receiving from the others. Varnil searched one last time for Connor before deciding that the old Vigil would be trying to keep a low profile.

"Father?"

Varnil turned. "I'm right behind you, Son."

The lights of the smaller room came online as they entered, though they could still see the status lights amongst the tens of thousands of cryopods past the windows in the dark of the Preservation Core.

"Are you scared?" Varnil asked as he watched his son activating the prep sequence of his own pod. It had been returned sometime in the weeks before. He had been told this was in line with the traditional ceremonies that revolved around they cryogenesis or retirement of the Reawakened. They were small ceremonies that, while in the minds of the Remnants, were only open for the Vigil to witness. Complications often arose in the cryogenesis, and Unawakened didn't always survive. In this case, it could be many more centuries before anyone knew if Kaiden was stepping into his death.

Kaiden looked calmly back to his father. His mostly grey beard was carefully trimmed, and his clothes were ready for the next time he would wake. "This will be my third time entering this same pod." He patted the side of the metal container. "No, I am not afraid."

Varnil felt a hard pull, straight to his core. "Vigil Treys, surely there must be some way . . ."

"No, Father," Kaiden interrupted. "This is not the first time I have made this decision. I have already lived my life. I am returning once again to the cryopod, like all the others before me, to wake one day on

Earth. It is you that must lay the seeds for that dream. You are our Reawakened."

"Kaiden . . ." Varnil said, though his protest was of feeling, not the intent to stop him.

Kaiden stepped backward into the pod and adjusted his shirt, then nodded to the Vigil standing at the controls. A cold vapor began to rise from the bottom of the pod as the metal doors started to close. "Be the father I have always known you to be."

Varnil felt a cold bite into him far more deeply than the cryogenic vapors flowing around his ankles could ever reach. The last time he had said goodbye, he was reassuring his crying son that everything would be okay. That they would only sleep for a while, and return when the conflict was over. Now, his son had a deeper understanding of the world than himself.

He looked around the room full of white sashes. It was odd. The cryogenesis-centered strategy to preserve the food supplies aboard the Orbital Armistice Fleet was the only thing that separated him and his son from being a founding part of the Remnants.

Varnil drew in a breath. They were all looking to him for the next name.

For the first time since he had been brought into their world, he finally understood what his place was supposed to be. The people of his generation were their founders, unknowing of the ways of the Remnants, but the start of them all. He slowly moved forward through the dim room and the waiting figures, then edged up close to the wide arcing wall of glass. Beyond, like the murky reflection of a pillar of stars, Varnil looked at the sum of their ever-vigilant work. The fact that they had maintained so many delicate lives . . . it was nothing short of remarkable.

"Reawakened," Vigil Treys said timidly, trying to nudge him toward why they were all still waiting.

Varnil set a hand against the control station and tapped his visor. A small light changed colors on the edge of the sleeping city, showing them all the location of the second Reawakened.

"Who is that?" Liaren finally asked when nobody else wanted to stand out.

"Marrel Lovek. Transmissions science engineer, Solstice Consolidated."

* * *

Connor made sure the second layer door was sealed before he produced the small projection device from his pocket. He set it on the open floor of what was once the great Dimarka's quarters. Now, where shelves of data pads once stood and images used to shimmer on the walls, it was all plain steel and lights. Even the bed was gone, leaving Connor entirely alone with the flickering three-dimensional static.

"Tialee," he said gruffly.

The projection of the former Vigil swirled into existence behind him, leaning against the doorway.

"Vigil Connor." She crossed her arms with a dark look. "What is it you think you will find, meeting with me again?"

"Again?" Connor hissed. He had talked to the damned projection every day for a week, hoping she would slip up on some shred of information. "I remember perfectly that I told you to forget our conversations."

Tialee slowly looked around the room. "I can see the Vigil has not appointed a new purpose for Dimarka's room, and you were positively furious with me the moment you summoned me here. So, I merely made an assumption of any previous meetings between us, using information from other unforgotten conversations."

Connor stepped closer as if to intimidate the transparent form of Tialee. "What does the boy really know? Baxel. What did you tell him in the Hall of the Vigil?"

"He asked the same thing I assume you are getting to. Can an AI mirror recall a conversation it was specifically told not to save? The answer is no, Vigil Connor, to ease your burden." Tialee tapped a finger to the tip of her chin. "Now that I think about it, when I spoke to Baxel in the Hall of the Vigil, I should have asked him what he was doing in my Preservation Core. You would not know anything about that, would you, Connor Sevison?"

The migrant simply turned away in frustration. Each day, even when he forced her to leave without her memory, she seemed to be learning more than he was. He could see it was no use.

"Are we done here?" Tialee said smugly.

Connor threw off his short white sash in frustration. "Forget this conversation."

* * *

Nearly a month after Kaiden Williams returned to the Preservation Core, Baxel had finally been given more leave of Safe Harbor, though he could still only look longingly out the window of the transport to the open space beyond. Baxel glanced over to where a father pointed out the window and down toward the planet. He spoke to a pair of young girls as they peeked wide-eyed over the back of the seat.

"That is where it will be. Launching down from the Production and Research Sector."

"Will we be able to see it?"

Without pause, the other asked her own question. "Will it really reach the planet?"

The man smiled and pulled his girls in closer. "I managed to convince your uncle to take us in his cargo transport at the time of the drop. And yes, we hope it will make it. The pod will have to travel over two hundred and fifty miles to the surface. You could take all of Safe Harbor and stack it two hundred and fifty times to reach that far."

After their brief exclamations of astonishment, he was bombarded by questions ranging anywhere from what color would the pod be to if it would hurt. He answered to the best of his ability all the way until their final arrival in the docks by the Hall of the Vigil. Of course, they were not the only ones talking of the coming event. Baxel had heard a number of people planning to break their sleep cycle and look for the perfect window to watch the release of the drop pod.

Baxel had another plan.

He stepped out into the empty hallways. Nearly every sector was playing a part in this project. From the expanded search of the SE-S to Transmissions working closely with the Vigil's new Reawakened, it was an endeavor that captivated all of Safe Harbor. Flerin had found a place training anyone not normally accustomed to functioning outside the habitat barrier, and Tymon, working alongside Surefire, was helping to set up the transmitters needed to communicate with the pod.

One good thing about everyone's attention being pulled toward the drop of the probe was that nobody would be checking his or Tymon's locations. The SE-S coordinators would be busy handling work overflow in the final inspections and shipments to the drop zone, and Flerin would be watching to ensure all suits were functioning correctly during the final cycle.

All but one.

Baxel stepped into the dark of the Hall of the Warden. In the dim lighting, there were a few scattered figures talking quietly or even just sitting with their own thoughts. When the time came for the drop later this cycle, Baxel expected a different turn out. With luck, everybody in the Hall of the Warden would go off in search of a view through a window or watch the broadcast transmissions on the displays on the walls of the interior of the ship.

Baxel found a place to sit by one of the meeting points scattered about the room. This one in particular was a large twisted piece of metal standing nearly twenty feet high. A small data pad attached to the side stood in for a plaque, telling a brief history of the piece. It was the section dislodged into the Hall of the Warden when Sarthyl breached the *Fortuna*. The vast majority of the Remnants that stayed in the hall had died, either from the depressurization or the fighting that came soon after.

It was a quiet wait, but from the passing words edging just above the silence, Baxel knew the time had finally come. He waited for most of the room to depart before he made for the steps. If everything went as planned, both he and Tymon should be set with the best view of the drop in all of the fleet.

As the room fell empty, Baxel was met with an eerie silence as he moved upwards. His feet flicked through the glow of the lights along the steps as he danced between the damaged sections. While the worst had been fixed, parts of the destruction were left as a reminder of the chaos that once spread here.

Baxel slowed as he neared the top, seeing now that the lights were on. Somebody was already in the Warden's Shrine. The drop should be any minute, meaning that he would not have time to make it to a window.

Thinking he had missed the entire event due to chance, Baxel saw Liaren and came to realize that there was no place he would rather be, even without the view. Liaren was kneeling in the center of the shrine, looking up at the blue aura surrounding the Warden's exploration suit. The scratches and dents in the bright coating of white on the armor cast faint shadows as the pieces gently swayed in the distortion keeping them in the air.

"What are you doing here?" Baxel asked quietly. He did not want to startle her or interrupt her thoughts. "Why are you not watching the launch?"

Liaren let out a breath that let her shoulders droop further toward the floor. "Because I am afraid. Afraid of what I may have done to the Remnants."

"What you did?"

Liaren glanced over her shoulder. "Vigil Treys called for the efforts to be ceased until I stepped forward. This would have never happened had I not spoken out."

Baxel continued a few steps further in, now looking at the Warden's armor. "Never? We played a part in making it happen in our lifetimes, but eventually—the Warden knows—we would have had to try sometime." Baxel turned and sat on the edge of the dais. He could feel the faint pull of the distortion against the back of his shirt. "And you never know. We may have saved the Remnants."

Liaren let out an uneasily accepting sigh and moved to sit next to Baxel on the edge of the shrine. It very well could have been seen as disrespect to the Warden, but there was not a soul to see. Not even the Warden, because with her armor here, she was guaranteed to be elsewhere in the fleet, watching the drop.

"You think so? You think we might have saved the Remnants?" Liaren asked softly.

"Absolutely. And nobody but the Warden can tell me I am wrong, at least not while I am alive."

Liaren adjusted her sash and tapped her fingers against the metal of the shrine. She looked to him with eyes blurred from silenced tears. "I'm sorry you missed the drop. But thank you for being here, Baxel."

Baxel smiled. "Missed? Actually, I brought it to you."

She looked confused as he stood up proudly, followed by her fearful gasp as he reached forward into the distortion. Baxel took hold of the helmet and pulled down through the tension of the distortion, reassuring Liaren that it was all right as he tapped the side of the helmet. He frowned, noticing how small it really was. He flipped it around and started to put it on his head.

"Baxel?" Liaren almost hissed. "What are you thinking?"

Just then, the visor inside the helmet lit up with a connection request from Merden, or more specifically, her helmet. Baxel shoved as hard as he could with both hands to push the helmet over his head. He sat down as he got it most of the way on, then tapped it again to open the communication from Tymon. After Flerin essentially hid their Firebrand suits from them, as well as moved the tracking beacon into Tymon's Surefire helmet, the only solution they could find was to have Tymon use Merden's helmet.

"You read me, Baxel?" Tymon asked. "Launch is in thirty seconds. All the work crafts are moving away from the site."

"I read you," Baxel replied. "And the transmission is coming through . . . very nicely, actually." Baxel glanced around the inside of the helmet. Even though he did not have it completely down over his head, he could tell it was of the highest quality. "This thing is incredible. Liaren, can you hear him?"

"Liaren?" Tymon asked incredulously. "Baxel you were not supposed to—"

"Hello, Tymon," Liaren said. She looked to Baxel pointedly. "Baxel's head is too big, so I can hear you out the bottom."

"We are dead if this gets out," Tymon grumbled.

"Where is he?" Liaren asked. She grabbed the helmet and turned Baxel square to face her. She was trying to look at the display opened across Baxel's eyes.

"The Point," Baxel said, though he was now looking past the projection into her eyes. This was the closest they had been since before he ran from the Vigil.

Liaren frowned. "Why did the display lighten? Are you . . ." She stopped short as they both realized that the visor had a reactive transparency based on his focus. She patted the side of the helmet and tried to hide her smile. "Stop it."

Baxel had to force himself to pay attention to the display as they waited. It was incredibly clear, and he could even signal it to magnify on the various blue flares of the transports shuffling away to an observational distance. The accuracy in which the system interpreted his collective inputs—even with the helmet not entirely in place—was beyond incredible.

"Here we go," Tymon said.

"Here," Baxel said softly, taking hold of Liaren's head just as she had his own. He pulled her close, so that her forehead touched the helmet. They were only inches away from each other as they watched the event that would shape the history of the Remnants.

Baxel magnified the image, to the extent that the Warden's helmet had to be filling in the data to improve upon Tymon's transmission. The latches holding the drop pod started popping free, releasing it from its scaffolding. Observation lines popped up in a new layer over the image, showing markers for indicating the size. The drop pod was nearly a thirty-foot-wide cylinder of sloped sections of metal that shielded the inner workings.

"Analyzing," the voice of a young woman said, originating from the helmet as layers of notification rings spun around the pod. An orange highlight expanded and started to lay out estimated schematics. As it entered the atmosphere, the drop pod would leave a dark red visual marker trail. The outer assembly would break away before impact with the planet and expose a system of flashpoint repulsors to slow the pod before landing. Once on Earth, it was equipped with an array of sensors and transmission relays.

"Encrypted transmission detected. Enable connection?"

Baxel pulled his hand away from Liaren just long enough to tap the side of the helmet and accept the process to get it out of the way. The last clamps released, and he made the image reset to show the entirety of Tymon's field of view. With a bright flare nearly twice the length of the outer hull of the pod, the pod began to accelerate away from Safe Harbor and toward Earth.

By the time the pod crossed level with Tymon into true microgravity, the bright streak of the repulsors was leaving a shimmering trail through the sky. The image gradually unfocused as Baxel looked past the fringes of the Point, past the long fading arc left behind the ever-accelerating pod, and even past the starry surface of the Earth into Liaren's eyes.

"Transmission canceled."

"What happened?" Liaren asked, now only illuminated by the gentle blue glow from the blank visor of the helmet.

Baxel frowned but made no other move. "I do not know. That wasn't me."

"Baxel, is that you?" another voice from within the helmet asked. The connection had somehow changed. He paused in answering as he wracked his brain for why the voice sounded familiar.

"Tialee?" Liaren asked in uncertain surprise.

"Wait," the voice of the Vigil Projection started in confusion, "both of you can hear me?" Her tone shifted, becoming humorous. "And here I always thought the fit was a bit small."

Baxel tried to shift his position but Liaren held the helmet firmly in place.

"What is going on? How are you here, Tialee?" Liaren asked.

The projection sighed. "Somehow, I do not feel either of you are in the right to lecture me about breaking the rules."

"That's not what I meant, I . . ." Liaren stammered at the sudden sharpness.

"Let me put it as simply as I can," Tialee said. "By Remnant procedure, when a projection is told to forget a conversation, it is so.

Never will that conversation be known again to any Remnant or projection of the archives. But the Warden is not bound by the same rules. By the systems in this suit, this version of me is allowed access to far more than the intentionally limited data systems of the Remnants or the AI mirrors."

"You know, don't you?" Baxel asked. "About what actually happened to Dimarka."

"Yes. In here, in the Warden's helmet, my data systems have no artificial limit."

Liaren tilted her head in confusion. "So . . . you lied when you said you did not remember speaking with Baxel?"

"Did I now? I seem to recall that version of me only leading you away from that idea, not breaking from it entirely."

"But . . . how could you, or even that version of you, intentionally deceive me?"

"Let's just say, dear Liaren, that I have had more than a simple lifetime of experience. Some things are more important than the plain truth. You were being watched when we spoke in the Hall of the Vigil. And the bad feeling I had? Well, I could not let the version of myself in Dimarka's quarters have any of the restricted data stored on the Warden's suit. So instead, I ran a little program on myself from here to adjust my emotions. And I played with the lights a bit, but that was nothing."

"Alright then," Baxel finally said. "What really happened?"

"Watch closely," Tialee said. "This, you have to understand for yourself."

* * *

Dimarka stood tall as the door to his quarters opened, though he soon had to take a seat at the loss of his breath. Calling him a once-proud man was like trying to say the Orbital Armistice Fleet was no longer made of ships. Even if his strength had left him long ago, replaced by an unhealthy weight, all the memories that inspired his determination remained.

Tialee's projection hummed quietly in the corner.

"Vigil, am I to see you yet again?" Dimarka asked from his seat in a strong voice held back only by his health. "I have enjoyed our conversations greatly. Enjoyed, even, your delusions that prove remarkably difficult to dissuade, though the frequency of our conversations has put me at a disadvantage, I am afraid. I pray you do not oppose to the presence of Tialee to offer me aid in my stance?"

Connor Sevison did not give the slightest bit of attention to the standing light in the corner. "Of course not, Dimarka. I have pressed you greatly these past days. But I come, hoping again to sway your judgment."

Dimarka laughed, cutting down Connor's strategy. "You do not get to beat me by sweet wishes and candies, Vigil. My ways are set, and you better have brought some proper muscle if you plan to shift them. I shall continue to fight any request I see stepping away from what the Warden has given us here."

"Is it now the head of the Maintenance Sector's position to overstep the Vigil?"

"No," Dimarka said darkly. "I only overstep you."

Connor balled his fists at the flat rejection.

"Oh, come now, migrant. Only you seem lost to our ways." Dimarka set a heavy hand on the small table. "Tialee can attest to that. After all of my work repairing the damage of the monster you brought into the fleet, I will not have it thrown away like the lives your Sarthyl took from the Warden. The entirety of my family, everything but their name, has perished to simply make the habitats viable again. I will not have you and your impatient followers break my promise to the Warden and to Safe Harbor."

"Then you make my choice," Connor said. "I must release you from the Warden to break your control of the Remnants. I cannot simply wait the years for you to die so that I may find Earth."

The displayed image flickered as Tialee adjusted the pace of the recording. Liaren gasped as Connor toppled the table as he rushed for Dimarka.

"No!" Tialee screamed, trying in vain to grab an arm to pull Connor off. "Stop this!"

"Tialee," Dimarka wheezed as Connor reached for his throat. "Rememb . . ." As he took in laborious breaths, Dimarka fought to shake hand from over his mouth. "Tialee! Remem . . ."

Tialee started to scream for help, but she was suddenly silenced as Connor spoke.

"Forget this conversation!"

As Liaren cried, the projection of Tialee stood silently over Dimarka's end, no longer showing herself in Dimarka's room, but visible in the memory within the Warden's helmet.

"Part of me wishes I could forget," Tialee said softly, watching the anguish on the projection of her past self.

With the last of his strength, Dimarka grabbed Tialee's projection device from where it had toppled to the floor with the table. Connor kicked it out of his hand, sending it under the bed.

Baxel remembered. "That is where I found you."

Tialee ended her control over the helmet display and left Baxel and Liaren staring at each other.

"I cannot . . ." Liaren said, tears running down her face.

"What do we need to do?" Baxel asked Tialee.

"Something I should not ask of you." Tialee sounded remorseful but driven by purpose. "Foremost, you need to preserve the secrets of the Warden. Nobody can know I showed you this. Nobody. Not even the other version of me. The Remnants survive by following the ways of the Warden, but if the Remnants somehow came to question the Warden herself, I fear they would become disillusioned. A lack of trust in the Warden would damage the Remnants far more in the centuries to come than leaving a murderer in the Vigil."

"And if we can manage that?" Baxel asked, now approaching the situation with a calculated anger.

"I want you to bring Connor Sevison to justice within the Remnants. Let them know his truth."

"But the Warden . . ." Liaren started. "Shouldn't she be the one to handle this?"

With the pause, Baxel could only imagine Tialee was shaking her head. "I do not know the will of the Warden. Perhaps she will help you on your way. Perhaps you are meant to fail. I am afraid I simply cannot say. You must continue on your own terms." A scan of the area briefly popped up on the visor. "Now you must go," Tialee said. "Someone will be coming soon. Place the helmet back and go, hopefully with the Warden's blessing."

"Thank you, Tialee," Liaren said. She slid a hand from the helmet and wiped the tears from her eyes before they could spill over like the ones that were now sliding down the front glass.

Baxel positioned his hands to pull the helmet off. "I take it I do not need to tell you to remember this conversation?"

"Only here," Tialee said. "You will find, however, that my version within the Vigil Archives will not be acquainted with what I have now told you. That version was gifted with the ability to forget. You may still seek that version of me for aid, but it will be up to you to convince me. Now go."

Baxel took the Warden's helmet off, flipped it to face the correct direction, and put it back into its place in the distortion. He then reached down to take Liaren's hand, and they exited the Warden's Shrine, leaving only a few silent tears sliding down the glass of the Warden's helmet.

Chapter 16: Calculations

After hiding from the watch and being chased by Black Scar hounds, Kara never would have guessed night in the streets of Reclaim could be peaceful. The sound of their quiet steps faded into the expanse above as she and Oa moved over the steel-tiled roads. A far cry from the shelter of walkways and the overarching starscraper in Norclave, the capital of the Steel Valley left an open view up to the orbital wreckage and the stars beyond. The peaks of buildings around them and on the levels above only gave shaped fringes to the cosmic bowl, leaving only the reaching lights on the Prime Elect's Citadel to stand out against the night.

"I see you are of few words," Oa said. The pace she walked was almost languid, though Kara wondered if that was not affected by her age. "Or perhaps it is too many questions that holds your tongue?"

Kara stumbled a half step from the numbness left by the Black Scars's hound. She looked harshly over to Oa as she adjusted the sling on her arm. "What would you have me ask first? How about this: Why don't you just start talking?"

Oa hid what might have been a small smile and motioned toward a large building on the side of the street nearest the Citadel. "You remember this?"

Kara nodded as Oa activated the doorway. It was the building she had woken up in.

Kara followed the elderly woman inside the large building, now giving a harder look around. The hall they entered was an immaculate white, accented by reinforcement ribbing along the walls in the style of the structures of the past. In passing, she looked into the room she had awoken in before turning to follow Oa down a side hallway.

"What is this?" Kara asked as she stepped into a dark room lit by a few faint lights along the main walkway set into the floor.

"Now the questions?" Oa motioned Kara in out of the doorway. "Come."

Kara bit her tongue at being commanded and stepped in. The door slid closed behind her, leaving them both in dim lighting. She started to reach for her wristband before remembering that it was no longer in her possession. It was not taken by scavengers or the watch; she had left it with Kenneth.

"I like to think of this as my place to observe my thoughts." Oa held out a bit of metal. It started to glow red as she reached toward a candle. "Of course, some thoughts cannot be made to stay, at least not for long."

A small flame danced up from the wick of the candle, casting both light and shadows about the room.

"What do you come here to think about?" Kara asked as Oa lit another candle. She could now tell that the room was a circle maybe fifteen feet across.

"I think about many things you would not understand. Others, you would understand far better than myself." Oa picked one of the candles up and sat it back down on the floor, illuminating a small mat made of ruber-coated cables. "Sit."

Kara did not follow the order and instead directed a pointed look at Oa. "What is this all about? Why are you helping me?"

Oa answered Kara's question with a curt motion to the floor. After Oa lit a few more candles while ignoring her questions, Kara finally crossed her legs as she sat upon the mat. Kara hoped that following the woman's lead would help with getting answers, but at the rate things had been going, Kara would be lucky to get the smallest details by sunrise.

"Take a guess," Oa replied.

Kara rolled her eyes and simply waited as Oa stepped about the room, continuing to light the candles. She knew there was nothing she could actually do to hurry the process along. Instead, she watched the dim flickering cast a kind of light simply not achievable by electricity or emergency chem lights.

"It cannot be a simple answer, as you know," the woman continued. "You have come a long way to ask for it."

"I did not come here to . . ." Kara started.

The points of light dully reflected in Oa's eyes as she turned on Kara and demanded silence with nothing more than a look. It was more than the bright flame they held that stopped Kara short; there was a fierce wisdom about the woman.

A sheen of sweat now clung to her dark and age-thinned skin. The creases at the edges of her face magnified as she frowned. "Some fools never even see that they walk their path until they stumble against their destination." Oa then turned away, smiling as if to a memory of her own.

She shifted and started lighting candles again. "I can see you are no such fool, though foolish in your pride of control. Very much so. What you came here to seek is not what you were meant to find."

"I find that hard to believe," Kara stated flatly. "I am here to—"

"Oh yes, yes. I believe you." The old woman shook her head as she set aside the heated piece of metal after finishing with the last of the candles. The room now glowed with the silent dance of the flames. "I was too. And many before me. We all knew exactly what our purpose was not."

A moment of silence passed as Kara said nothing in reply. Finally, Oa simply smiled again. "Hard to argue with the past, is it not? It does not matter that they were not your motions; your mistakes will be the same. Your sores will be the same, but you can still prepare for what you deny."

Kara ran a hand through her hair in frustration. "Whatever you seem to think I am doing here, you have no idea."

Oa only rubbed her calloused knuckles across her brow. "I could be holding up a mirror." She lowered her hand and clasped her thin fingers in front of her. "I'm going to talk now. Tell me when you decide to listen."

Oa lowered herself to the ground, simply resting her knees on the hard floor. "You do not flee from Norclave, not as others think."

"Flee? What do you mean by—"

"Do not get ahead of yourself," Oa interrupted. "You are not listening yet." Oa gave no response to Kara's confused look. "I believe, strongly, that you were the tech hunter who brought back the Cryo." There was a venom in Oa's voice as she said the word. "But without you, Norclave would never have been rid of its Overlord. You helped to transition the city from one Cryo to another. The rule of Garneth Obrourke to that of Jance Lorège. And now—"

"You knew that the Overlord was a—" Kara started.

"I knew what kind of monster Overlord Obrourke was for years, girl!" Oa said sharply. She looked away from Kara as she took a breath to calm herself. "I am old enough to have seen Norclave before him. A simple mercenary hold to a thriving trade center? Nothing changes that much—not to contest Carvanhold and even Reclaim—without the help of a Cryo. But I know you were there when Obrourke fell. And at the docks, when the Cryo to replace him died as well."

Kara looked angrily into the spread of candles as her thoughts burned. "Jance was never anything like Overlord Obrourke. She never wanted to take his place as the Overlord."

This gave Oa pause. "How would you know that?"

"She said it a number of times, even when we were going behind Olana Nuand's back."

Oa glanced over to Kara. "So you were close?"

Kara looked away, trying to contain a surge of worry and pain and keep her thoughts to herself. She was bothered by how much Oa knew, and Kara did not want to give her any more information than she had to.

"Feirshan will grieve the Cryo's death," Oa continued, "but you should not."

Kara could barely stop herself from defending Jance from Oa's comments. Without looking over, Kara spoke. "You said Feirshan would grieve. You must know the Prime Elect, then. That is why the Black Scars listened to you."

Oa nodded. "There are many who listen to me. Quietly, but they listen."

"Did you know, then? The plan to kill Jance?" Kara wondered if Travend was one of those who listened to what this woman had to say.

Oa seemed to answer very carefully. "I have come to expect each of the holds to do as they see fit. It is not my place to interfere with their people. Yes, I knew. But I was given no details of the matter."

They sat in silence for a long while as Kara thought. Kara did not trust the woman, but regardless of how deeply she was involved in the attempt on Jance's life, Kara knew she needed her protection from the Black Scars and the Prime Elect. At least until she could get back on her feet and continue the hunt for Travend's men.

Oa finally broke the silence. "What is on your mind?"

"Why are you helping me?"

Oa shifted where she knelt. "Whether you realize it or not, we share something in common. We are guided by a purpose."

Kara let out a hot breath. As far as she was concerned, they were nothing alike.

Oa glanced over with a raised eyebrow. "Alright, fine. I'll talk. I was relieved, when my data pad lit up days ago, interrupting my thoughts with a short message from Hama saying he had found a tech hunter outside the city walls. I knew then that I needed your help with something in the Prime Elect's Citadel."

Kara shook her head and started to stand. She wanted as far away from the politics of the city as she could be. She was here only because of what happened to Jance.

"Wait!" Oa bit. "You must hear me out."

Kara ignored the woman and stretched her back with a grunt. "I'm not going anywhere near that damned Citadel. I know what happens when I step through those doors." Kara let out a tight breath. Her injured arm burned. "I don't need any more problems."

"I can get you in without any issues," Oa said.

Kara stopped and looked to the ground. "Thank you, Oa, for what you have done for me. But I'll risk the Black Scars again—now that I know how they operate—long before I draw the attention of the Prime Elect. You may be under his protection, but I am not." At that, she started away.

"No one will know you are there," Oa said behind her back. "I promise. Even the others who arrived from Norclave will be clueless as to who you are."

Kara stopped just as she was about to start walking out of the room. The Black Scar had said something about them, but at the time Kara was not certain he was speaking of Travend's men. "You know of them?"

"They arrived the day before you did." Oa held out a hand to stop Kara from jumping to any conclusions. "Look, I don't know your business with them, nor do I care. I just need your help."

Kara let out another breath and balled her fists through the pain of her arm, wondering what Oa would think if she said she would be happy to tie Travend's men up in a transport and watch them panic next to a bomb of their own making.

Once again, the room fell to the silence of the flickering lights as Oa weighed her with a look. Oa shook her head and started pinching out the flames of the candles. "And then again, perhaps I was wrong. Perhaps you were never the right one."

Kara gritted her teeth as she came to her breaking point. "Right one for what, you old hag?"

Oa shook her fingers after dousing another candle. "Watch your tone. You obviously have more to prove, if only you would stop trying to prove it to yourself."

"You said you could get me into the Citadel."

Oa stood by the last section of remaining candles. "I did."

"And?" Kara asked. "What about your need of me?"

Oa gripped the fire of another candle with her aged fingers. "You may have been the one who found the Cryo, but if you cannot control your impatience, or frankly your attitude, I fail to see how you could be of use to me."

Kara threw her one free hand in the air. "It's not like you are expecting me to find another Cryo, alive or frozen. After Obrourke, Jance is the last one. How hard could your job be in comparison?"

"She was not exactly the last," Oa said quietly. Before Kara could question what she meant by that, Oa continued, "You need in the Citadel? Fine. I require someone's help who isn't already inside, as long as your reason for needing in doesn't interfere."

"How can you get me in?"

Oa plucked out a few more candles and shot Kara a knowing smile in the dim light. "We walk through the front entrance."

Kara narrowed her eyes. "What *is* your relation to the Prime Elect?"

"Let's just say, that he has an affinity for the forgotten past, and many have forgotten me."

Kara looked at the woman in disbelief. "No, you've got to be joking. You mean to say that you are a Cryo?"

"In Reclaim, I am simply known as an advisor." At that, the room fell into darkness as Oa waved her arm over the last light.

* * *

Lieth Armain walked with an air of caution through the bright halls of the Prime Elect's Citadel. Everything was too perfect. It was too clean and symmetrical. What unnerved him—even more than the silence of the two armed guards following him and Weril—was that he was walking through the past. Not his past; a past that would have been all too familiar to the Cryo he had killed.

The smooth white curves and the subtle glow of hidden lights playing across careful shadow lines of the hall all conveyed the Prime Elect's influence and wealth. However, the bright streaks of holographic marks and the displays replaying news from well before the fall told a separate story. This was the concept-heart of Reclaim. It was the physical representation of the idea that pushed the rest of the city for years to build structures from the ruins, not simply inhabit what was left over. Lieth could see that Reclaim wanted to rebuild the old world.

"The passage to your right leads to the higher levels," one of the watch directed from behind.

Lieth glanced over to Weril and received a mirror of his own thoughts. The watch claimed to be an honorary escort sent by the Prime Elect, but nether of them could shake the discomfort of having weapons at their backs.

Lieth waited at the doorway as one of the watch stepped forward with an access card. After the yellow light above switched off, the man motioned for Lieth to continue.

"Stairs?" he asked. The steps leading up the darkened hall looked as if they had been pulled straight out of Norclave. The darkened patina and rust in the scratches seemed humorously out of place.

One of the watch said something about the techniciars adjusting sensors and guessed the repairs would be done in the morning.

Weril held the bandaged stump of his arm up to cover a wide yawn. "I thought this was the morning."

At the direction of the watch, they started up the long and winding flights of stairs, fighting through the night's fatigue. Lieth counted as many as fifteen levels before the watch used his access on another doorway.

As the door opened, a voice echoed in the hall. It had the sound of a news report. "Celebrating the life of the SRA's Chancellor of the Germanic States, Steven Bahnhof, UWC officials are organizing events on a local level. Here at Wintesla Park, decorations are underway. Access your trans-systems link now to see an interview with holographic elements designer, Omar Firfield, and see how you can make your own local event shine."

Lieth paused at the display terminal and took note of the park the report was in. Compared with the brilliant whites of the Prime Elect's Citadel, the only thing the area in the report had different was the plant life within the open room. The interviewee tapped through his data pad as Lieth started walking away, bringing an array of suspended, colorful lines to life around the park.

The next report set up along the hallway showed a camera drone being shot out of the sky above and a ground team firing rockets into a position high up in the scarred buildings of the city. The shouts were drowned out by heavy gunfire crossing above them from one elevated position to the next.

"Here we are," one of the watch said. Lieth only hoped the recording of battle playing next to the door was not a warning tactic by the Prime Elect.

The watch made no move to open the door and Lieth noticed the access panel required *"Select Clearance."* After another moment of inactivity, the door hissed open. They were motioned into the room by a smaller man adjusting a small shelf stacked full of data pads.

"Come in, come in," the man said at their hesitation. "Have a seat if you wish, I'll be with you shortly."

Lieth looked slowly around the room. More displays quietly showed reports of the past, and a few larger projected screens simply showed recordings of transports making their way through the standing super cities.

"We're here to see Feirshan," Weril said with a touch of impatience. He gripped the back of the chair with his one hand.

"Yes, of course. I'll be with you shortly." The man pulled out one data pad and aligned the glowing image meticulously in the center of the desk. "There," he said with a nod. At that, Prime Elect Iben Feirshan took his seat behind the desk and gave another motion to the two chairs opposite him.

"I'm sorry, I didn't . . ." Weril started as Lieth noticed the smirk on the watch's faces as they stepped into the room behind them.

"Expecting someone more brutish?" Feirshan asked knowingly. "Perhaps a reclusive warmonger like your dear, deceased Overlord? Or, perhaps a self-centered, power-hungry, deceitful shrike like your new one?" Feirshan shook his head. "No, no, that is not the way of Reclaim."

At the Prime Elect's third motion for them to sit, one of the watch gave a warning cough from behind. Lieth followed the Prime Elect's gesture and gave a pointed glance for Weril to play along.

"Good. We comfortable? Need anything to drink before we get started?" The Prime Elect looked between the two of them as if he actually meant the questions. "No?" He waved for the two of the watch to leave the room before continuing, "I know that the both of you probably cannot grasp the subtle tact used to put everything on edge, but I don't feel I need to bore you with an explanation."

Lieth frowned. "Subtle" wasn't how he would describe torching the docks.

The Prime Elect patted his hands gently on the surface of the desk. "I remind myself that you are simply workers. Given a task, following direction. That is why all I ask of you, for the time being, is that you keep to yourselves and tell no one what happened. It is in everyone's best interest if you simply act along as if . . . well, as if you were dead. As long as we are clear on that, Olana Nuand will be none the wiser of your presence, and you are free to go about my city, for the most part, as you please, until I can sort things further."

Lieth gripped the padded arms of the chair. "I did not sign up with the Loyalists just to sit idle."

"Yes, of course," the Prime Elect said with all the sympathy of someone trying to redirect the conversation. He picked up the data pad and poked through the display at a few places. "Lieth Armain. You owned a shop in Norclave. Joined up after it was destroyed by Olana's men."

Lieth ducked his head and loosened his grip on the chair, but he felt no need to correct the Prime Elect's records. Details meant little to the memory of revenge.

The Prime Elect frowned. "I figured killing her Cryo would have been enough to settle your nerves."

Lieth looked up and held the Prime Elect in a stare that made the man start uneasily tapping the data pad against his hand.

"Well," Feirshan continued awkwardly, "I suppose we each have our own drive. But if I am correct, vengeance burns brighter with time. Stay alive, and I may find a use for you yet."

This time Weril spoke up, though more timidly than before. "What about the others? The ones that came with us? What is to become of them?"

"Oh," Feirshan said as if Weril had brought up a touchy subject. "Them. The technician and the scrapsmith, they volunteered to help with the repairs to the distortion lift. I presume you remember taking the emergency stairway?"

Lieth and Weril looked to each other before the Prime Elect continued, "I am afraid they were killed in a workplace accident."

"What?" Weril exclaimed. "When did this happen?"

The Prime Elect picked up a smaller data strip with a display only about an inch tall and a few more lengthways. It was showing a readout of the time. Feirshan looked down at it. "Any moment now, it seems."

The silence permeating the room was nearly as stiff as it had been waiting for the docks to go up in flames while they made their way through the lower streets of Norclave. Lieth watched through the shifting seconds on the display until the Prime Elect slid the data strip to the side. He looked to both of them with folded hands as a deep boom resounded up through the building.

"One last thing, while I have you here. The transport pilot reported that you had a confrontation with a certain individual. An associate of mine reported another incident here in the city. Two dogs killed, nasty business. You couldn't perhaps give me a description of the figure you encountered?"

Lieth shook his head, only having gotten a distant glimpse of their attacker.

"Dead," Weril stated with narrowed eyes. "Bits and pieces, strewn about."

The Prime Elect frowned and tapped his neat fingers against the desk. "Perhaps just another lost shade of the wilds, then." He clapped his hands, seeming to dismiss the subject. "Well, I suppose that was all I needed of you. I apologize for the tight schedule, but an emissary from Norclave is due in today. I thank you for your time of course, and if something comes up and you need me, you can speak to one of the watch. One of the help should provide you with your sleeping quarters sometime soon. Do you have any further questions? No? Good."

* * *

Sora nearly had to jog to keep up with the long strides of the Overlord as she moved through the halls of her complex in the early morning. The day had started early, and it had taken off at full speed. Zaireel Tuakana and the rest of the emissaries had been due to arrive in Reclaim any time in the past hour, but Olana had still made time to look over Jance's medical care. Though, whether it was a heartfelt visit with the Cryo or calculated concern over an asset on Olana's part, Sora didn't know. They were now rushing back from the medical facility to the command center and Kenneth's system for the touchdown of the transport all the same.

"Above the city now," Sora said, juggling the images on the visor with her armful of data pads. "Received and acknowledged landing orders."

"Get hold of Kenneth, make sure he is watching the system."

Sora tapped the visor with her free hand. "Just got a message from him. He says if the Overlord wants to watch, then she better . . . uh, never mind. He's ready."

"Who is my next meeting? How far will this push it back?" Olana asked, keeping her eyes locked forward down the empty halls of dull steel.

Sora juggled the pads between her arms as she produced the schedule. "If this goes quickly, everything should still be on schedule."

They rounded the corner to where Sora had practically lived for years. The Norclave Library had nearly changed as much as her memory of it had shifted. Learning the truth of the past Overlord had made her question nearly everything about her time in the data center of Norclave. Out of everything, Jance had been her largest reassurance that what she was doing now made up for everything. As they stepped under the surveillance camera, they were both surprised to see Kenneth waiting in the doorway with his arms crossed in a particularly dark mood.

"Kenneth?" Overlord Nuand asked. "What happened? Why are you not watching over the systems aboard the emissary transport?" Olana turned to Sora. "Wait here. Rearrange my schedule however you need to until I get out."

"No," Kenneth interrupted. "Sora follows." He then turned and strode back into the room.

"Overlord?" Sora asked. Only when she received a quick nod did she follow Olana Nuand into the room.

As silly as it was, as Olana barked after Kenneth, Sora found herself glancing at each of the plants half-buried in piles of tech. Kenneth had let her water them for Jance and switch the batteries on a few, but he did not want her moving anything of his. Somehow, Sora failed to see how there could be any sort of organization for her to disrupt.

"Yes, the transport. I don't care, whatever," Kenneth said. "I couldn't give a damn less."

"I am concerned with . . ." Olana glanced over to Sora before continuing, "I need to know if Reclaim has found out about the system. Do they know we are watching?"

Kenneth gestured with his scarred arm toward a device propped up on a crate. It was roughly box-shaped, and light glowed around what could be air intakes. "Can you tell me what that is?"

"I have no idea," Olana said. She then tried to continue her previous course of questioning, but Kenneth cut her short. In Sora's eyes, and likely in the opinion of the Overlord herself, Kenneth cut her far too short.

"Then shut the hell up." After he said it, Kenneth gave no sign that he was going to back down as he stared down the Overlord. "It is a processing unit of some sort, set up by a program hunter of Mackelry Norton's."

"You had no right—"

"Your Cryo is going to die."

Sora let the data pads fall to the ground. "What? How?"

Kenneth lowered his hand and looked to her. "Percentages. Predictive theory. Ask the program hunter if you want to know how it works. All I can say, is that this looks at all of the information, thinks about what it does not have, sets up weighted variables and other crap, and it started throwing up all sorts of red warnings in the middle of the night."

"What warnings?" Olana growled.

"Another meeting." Kenneth shoved a crate with the back of his foot and took it as a seat. "Apparently, some names encounter each other far less often than the standard percentage of encounters, at least when excluding brief meetings between several theorized targets. It sets up the likelihood in which their encounters will coincide with other theorized targets."

"Get to it, technician," Olana growled.

Kenneth leaned over and activated the displays on the desk. Two faces taken from different angles, a man and a woman, were displayed prominently. They were Norclave med-techs. "A twelve and a half percent chance puts these two as having connections to Travend. If we assume that to be true, there is a ninety percent chance that they will be alone with the Cryo."

"When?" Sora asked.

Kenneth pulled up another display. "Seventy-six percent chance within the next ten minutes. And that's up fifteen percent from three minutes ago."

Sora glanced over and noticed the Overlord was rolling her glass cube in her hand.

Kenneth continued with the same tone he had used when telling Draken that the cryopod had to finish the sequence. "Thirty-five percent puts them both as threats." He then pushed up from the crate and motioned to the displays over the desk. "If we take that to be false, there is only an eight and falling percent that one of the other med-techs will be in the room with them."

"Sora, call for my people to be ready!" Olana barked.

As Sora scrambled to send out the order to the seventh-level garrison post, a host of red warnings flared up around the desk.

"What happened?"

Kenneth furiously went through the numbers. "One of them will see the soldiers headed to the complex. The other mark is with Jance now."

"Cancel it. Cancel the order!"

Sora backtracked on the order, and the warnings seemed to fade.

"How many soldiers do we have ready in the complex now?" the Overlord asked.

Sora bent down to pick up one of the data pads. Before she could open it, Kenneth beat her to the reply.

"Fifteen, not stationed at entrances. Two are outside the medical facility."

Olana nodded. "Sora, stay here. Kenneth, patch me in." She tapped her visor and started out of the room.

Kenneth glanced down to the program hunter's processing unit, then popped his fingers with a stretch of his arms. "Here we go."

"Do we know anything about these potential traitors?" the Overlord asked moments later. Her voice sounded as if she was in the room, but Sora could see through the backs of the displays Kenneth was positioning that she was moving quickly through the halls.

Kenneth raised an eyebrow. "You mean, will they try to finish Jance as your troops storm in?" He shrugged. "They know they are dead if anyone finds out what they are attempting."

"Get me information on them."

Sora knelt down to reach for a data pad, but before her hand ever touched it, the device powered on. She looked up to see the same screen now displayed over Jance's desk.

"Kenneth, how did you—"

"The woman. Lumia Markayla. She has a child. Four years old." Kenneth started pulling the information apart, setting pieces all across the desk as he scanned for details. "Another child died in the fighting. She was just under a year old."

"Give me the name of the oldest."

"Lannet."

"Connect me with the two guarding the entrance."

Kenneth tapped his knuckles on the desk furiously as if trying to think about how to go about the Overlord's command. He then pulled up several more displays and motioned through them with much more precision and certainty than Sora remembered him having when he'd interacted with the cryopod. He was nearly as efficient as Jance now.

Sora waited nervously as Olana barked orders through the displays on the weapons of the startled guards.

"Kenneth," Olana said into her visor, "intercept the other med-tech."

The data pad in Sora's hand sent out a command to the garrison, even showing that it had originated from her.

"Kenneth, are you sure you should be—" Sora started again.

"Does it look like I have the time, Sora?"

"Everything ready?" the Overlord asked.

Kenneth pulled up one last display and took a step back. "It's all on you."

Sora took a step closer and looked through the back of the projected displays. "Is that really?" she mouthed to Kenneth silently.

Kenneth simply held up one finger to his lips in warning. The display in the center was showing a feed from the Overlord's own visor. Olana Nuand wouldn't be happy to find out that her dealings might not be as secret as she thought.

The doors opened, revealing a room filled with medical equipment tied into the one bed in the center. Jance was fast asleep, bathed in an assortment of cool lights from the monitors and looking badly bruised. There were a few tubes running out of her that made Sora want to turn away. One of the med-techs was in the back of the room, but the woman profiled by the system was standing next to Jance.

"Overlord Nuand!" The med-tech, Lumia Markayla, coughed in a surprised greeting. "I did not expect to see you back so soon."

Sora watched intently from Olana's eyes as the med-tech fidgeted nervously with something in her hand.

"Have you seen where—" the med-tech started, slowly moving the vial in her hand toward the medication insert.

"Lannet."

The woman paused, hearing Olana speak the name of her son very clearly. It was likely the one word that could have stopped her from finishing the task. Sora raked her fingers back over her hair, grabbed the back of her neck, and let out a tense breath.

Olana did not take a step forward, nor make any motion that might cause the woman to jolt to action. Instead, she tried a softer strategy. "Your son, Lannet, will be safe. No matter what you do here today. He will be taken in by Norclave and cared for." Olana looked down to where Jance lay motionless on the bed. "You have my word, even if you do take the life of my Cryo. Or, preferably, if you do not."

Tears built in the woman's eyes almost immediately. "That is what I am afraid of. I am sorry, Overlord Nuand. I have to do this."

"Why? At least answer me that."

Lumia stopped her motion with the vial and took a breath. "Travend has him. He has for weeks now. He said I can have him back if I end the Cryo, but if I don't . . ."

Kenneth rushed back to the table. "Wait, that's it!" he exclaimed as the Overlord raised a hand. "Olana, stall her. That is the last piece we needed!"

Olana held her hand open and still as the woman inserted the vial into the device hanging from the side of the bed. "Wait! We can save him! It does not have to be this way."

The med-tech hovered her hand next to the display that shimmered next to the device. "You promise you will keep your word?"

"Yes. Absolutely. I prom—"

"About taking care of Lannet? No matter what?"

"I said we can save—"

The woman smiled weakly. "Thank you, Overlord Nuand. But I have to save him. As soon as they know—"

The Overlord clenched her fist and Sora gasped. They could hear the door snap open behind Olana and a series of shots rang out. Sora simply let out a cry. Just as quickly as it had all begun, the hand of Lumia fell away from the glowing display.

"Is Jance alive?" Kenneth yelled over their ringing ears.

Olana pointed at the other startled med-tech in the room and commanded him to remove the vial.

"Kenneth," Olana said darkly, "you had best give me his exact location for interrupting me when I was giving a fire order."

Kenneth let out a breath and dropped back into Jance's chair. "I have eyes on Lannet. He was released in the trade center an hour ago. Our people already have the kid. With that connection, the system is working every new angle as we speak. You had best start putting together a strike team."

Chapter 17: Beacon

Quervin, the most insufferable of the three SE-S heads, motioned down the long list of items displayed on the data pad line by line. Flerin remained waiting patiently in the SE-S meeting room with his hands clasped and strangling the circulation from each other behind his back.

"I do have to say, your attentiveness to organization has increased greatly without the distraction of your team."

Flerin made no motion besides the slow breath he took in to fight the reddening of his face.

"I always thought you could do well in an environment with a little more structure, though the observation probe was not without its difficulties."

Flerin did agree with the last part of the head's statement, though he still did not respond. He'd had a particularly trying time being responsible for the safety of all the additional maintenance workers and observational technicians not previously trained for operation outside of the habitat barriers. He'd had to piece together nearly thirty additional suits, as well as oversee the functioning of the systems readouts on each. With only two critical failures outside the habitat, Flerin considered the endeavor a success.

Finally, Quervin nodded in satisfaction with the list. "I will report to Dannil Wardenson that all transmissions systems equipment is accounted for." The thin man stood up and looked to Flerin square on. "You have made the Search and Exploration Sector stand well in the eyes of the others during these recent days. Someday soon, you might just take your place as one of the heads of the SE-S. You may even make up for the history of Firebrand."

Flerin snapped his mouth shut just as he was about to accept the compliment. It took everything he had to keep from arguing. Next to the Warden, Firebrand's bravery stood above all others. The history of Firebrand was full of individuals who had given their lives doing what nobody else dared to in order to keep the Remnants alive.

Flerin doubted if the man even noticed that his so-called praise was falling upon the same accepting grace as burning oxygen stores, but the head left the room either way. And it was about time that Flerin left. While Flerin still had more supply orders to retroactively fudge, he knew his meeting with Oundara was soon.

He motioned through a few of the system labels at the top of the data pad and accessed the Safe Harbor public transport systems page. Oundara had rescheduled their meeting location from the SE-S to the Hall of the Warden, and he had to catch the transport set to leave in the next few minutes.

He walked with little attention to increased foot traffic about the SE-S as he kept his eyes on the glowing manifest display. For the search coordinators who had teams to oversee, the past month or so had been a mad dash to provide the new Reawakened, Transmissions Science Engineer Marrel Lovek, with anything she needed. Now, with the completion and launch of the observation probe, Oundara had called for a few days of break in SE-S operations. This was the last day for the families to visit before the teams started out again.

And that was what worried him, and likely Oundara as well. With the SE-S springing back to action, they would both be looking to see what Tymon would do. He had done well, playing along with the pace of Surefire for the duration of the construction, but keeping anyone who once was a member of Firebrand in the zero coordinates was like expecting a case of alcohol to not be marked as *"Damaged & Discarded for Safety"* by the supply workers.

And on that note, Flerin shook his head and mumbled as he tried to smooth over the discrepancy flagged in the SE-S storage. He could spin the six missing oxygen reserve tanks as being taken without proper logging for potential emergencies when constructing the probe, but the four personal atmosphere bags, and the case of nav beacons? It was just as much of a mess as the time he and his team had needed to work out directions in the middle of the wreckage with all their comms systems screeching from interference.

Flerin finished filing a mislogging query of the bags as he took a seat in the transport. Hopefully someone would think they were improperly returned to the Medical and Rescue Sector. It *could* be a mistake someone would make. The devices were mainly used to stabilize a person when a suit was ruptured or a habitat breached. He frowned as he tapped the side of the data pad. Perhaps one of the workers returned them, and the supplies manager for the Medical and Rescue Sector was more than eager to fix a mistake when their system showed they were not missing any. It could happen, he told himself.

As Flerin continued, line by line, down the remaining list of items and their excuses for their absence, he could not help but wonder just where Baxel and Tymon had planned to go with the same selection of supplies he would have taken for an extended period outside the habitat barrier. More than that though, he had to wonder if Oundara had figured out what those items would be for before he fudged the records.

* * *

Baxel looked out one of the windows of the ever-busy halls of the Trade Sector. The interior of the habitat barriers extended far into the heart of the wreckage of the orbital ship, leaving only the occasional view out into the dimly lit expanse of mangled steel. Two transports made their way farther in through the tangle to where the main cargo airlock of the sector was located. Those transports passing below were likely excess supplies being shifted back into long-term storage.

Besides being the hub of the trade of personal items, the Trade Sector took care of the logistics of transfers between the other sectors of Safe Harbor. It was the center of a system of management where the sectors of Safe Harbor were allocated a shifting amount of resources. During the construction of the probe sent to Earth, nearly every aspect of each sector was allowed greater reach into the reserved stores of Safe Harbor supplies. More tools, more suits, more specialty systems, even more medical supplies with the added risk of injury had been needed.

"We believe it would only take about fifteen panels to shore up the old work room," a man said from behind as Baxel continued to stare out the window. "And the Maintenance Sector is parting with almost enough of its reserve to complete the airlock."

The Trade Sector worker asked for the rest of the item list. Baxel glanced over his shoulder as the man handed over the data pad, but he soon turned back to his waiting and pressed his forehead on his fist against the glass.

"I can get you most of this," the worker said. "I believe Tyrin, from Food Storage and Supply, was looking to get rid of a liquid tank you could use for the ventilation overflow. That would save you quite a bit there. Oh, what quality of panels are you looking for?"

"It would be a larger room, but likely no more than five to ten workers in it at a time. We were going to pipe it into the system hallways, but it is already sealed with a secondary level airlock now."

The trade manager nodded. "Nonresidential? Any thoughts of storage lockers? Or recreation breaks?"

The other man shook his head, and the manager started looking back through his system.

"In that case, you might be able to stretch it with C-2s, but any span more than ten feet will need A-grade reinforcement. Nonresidential will raise the cost per unit to two hundred and thirty-five."

"That much?" the client asked.

"I'm afraid so. Even with everything going to hell in the habitat, Dimarka's orders still stand. Population sectors first."

Baxel had learned much of what made the system function during his placements at his twenty-thousand cycles. Anything from jewelry and ornaments to oxygen and food supplies were designated with a numerical value, loosely based on need versus rarity. However, depending on the intended use and projected damage or wear to the object, different sectors could get the same supply for less of their allocated point budget.

It was all part of the system Baxel ultimately had wanted nothing to do with when he finally had the chance to be a part of it. His parents seemed to enjoy the work, but to him it was unbelievably cramped compared to outside the habitat barriers. He simply could not give up the freedom of movement to be surrounded by the business of numbers.

"Feeling trapped yet?" Tymon said from behind.

Baxel let out a breath that fogged his view through the window and shook his head. "I'm good."

"Well, I am sitting on four days leave since the launch and it is murder." Tymon pressed a reinforced shoulder plate of his suit against the window as he leaned against it and looked harder at Baxel. "You have been confined for, what, a good two months? Two and a half?"

Baxel pushed away from the window at the same time he mockingly shoved against Tymon's suit. "At least I'm not in yellow."

"Surefire's not so bad." Tymon looked down to the yellow and grey accents on his new suit. "Surprised to hear myself say it. Kinda relaxing, not having to worry about anything more than a transport hitting you. By the way," he said, "I heard you were patching things up with Liaren. At least that's something, until we can get back out again."

Baxel turned and leaned squarely next to Tymon, facing the piles of objects in the long hall. Crates containing just about anything were scattered about, and probably a half dozen people were tied up in trade. Twice that number were simply passing through with less exact intentions. It was not uncommon for people to simply not know exactly what they needed before they saw it. Other times, the Trade Sector was simply a location visited to ease boredom.

"It is not exactly how you would imagine," Baxel replied. The heart of most of his conversations with Liaren now revolved around plans on how to deal with the migrant. Unfortunately, most of them required he do nothing as Liaren consulted endlessly with the various Vigil mirrors. Baxel knew he couldn't come out shouting from the airlocks that Vigil Connor had killed Dimarka. That would violate their promise to Tialee to hold the secrets of the Warden, as well as draw the attention of Connor himself.

"Well of course not," Tymon said with a hint of mockery. "You did just about get her banished to First Claim."

Baxel glanced over to Tymon. "How about you and Merden?"

"I um . . . not sure what you are talking about, Bax."

"You worked with her throughout the entire construction, I heard."

Tymon shrugged. "Well, yeah. Along with the hundred and forty other members of Surefire. And quite a few of the suited-up mechanics and workers."

Baxel opened his hands. "I'm just saying, she wasn't smiling at me when we lifted the supplies from the SE-S for the Point. I wasn't getting out of there on my own. Oh, and remind me again who covered for you so you could go back to the Point to watch the probe drop?"

"Well she, I, uh . . ." Tymon scowled. "How about you remind me what device you used to talk to me?" Tymon raised his own helmet up to make the point. "Something about the Warden's help?"

"Hey, hey, woah. That's . . . don't do that." Baxel glanced around the Trade Sector, hoping with each face he counted that wasn't paying them any attention that there wasn't one more who had been listening.

Tymon raised his eyebrow. "You all right there, Bax? Something on your mind?"

"No, it's just that—" Baxel started.

"Warden," Tymon said in a prodding interruption.

"What are you . . . ?"

"Helmet."

"Tymon!"

Tymon scowled as he mused over Baxel's reactions. "What have you and Liaren been up to?"

"I've done nothing. Except sit around and wait for someone to tell me what I can do." Baxel let out a breath, hoping that would cover Tymon's questioning. The last thing he wanted was to drag him into whatever they were trying to accomplish. And if he had to explain one thing, he would have to explain it all.

"Alright, whatever you say," Tymon finished with a shrug. "Well, I've got scans to run on one of the transmission relays before the end of my cycle. If you figure out how to get your suit back, or at least a suit, I've got everything all ready to see just exactly what we found out there. Until then, if you need any help, with anything," Tymon said, tapping a few times on his helmet, "you know how to find me."

Baxel nodded grimly. At the moment, he would be lucky to so much as see the inside of a suit, let alone be let outside of the airlocks with it. After Tymon left, Baxel found himself wandering around the Trade Sector. He was due to meet Liaren, but he had enough of simply waiting in one spot.

Many of the faces were familiar in one way or another. A lot of friends of his parents were here, though this was thankfully their cycle off. The brief meeting he'd had with his parents a few days ago had been more than awkward. He knew that in their eyes, even though they were very careful to hide it, he was a complete failure. The one thing he had been certain about in life fell short. Firebrand was done, and while the Vigil seemed to have no intention of casting him out to Aura or First Claim, they had yet to state that he was still welcome. And besides all that, he could offer nothing to defend himself; not his unprecedented knowledge of the Vigil AI mirrors nor the murder of Dimarka.

Baxel shook his head, finding himself some twenty minutes later back to staring out the same window. Even in regards to bringing justice to Connor, Baxel had done nothing. Liaren had been very clear that it would take time, and for now, she was in a far better position to get information.

Baxel let out a sigh against the glass. His breath was full of thought-bound emotions, but above all else, he felt the wandering confusion that came from lacking direction or motion. That was the worst part. It always was. He hated sitting on his hands and waiting for someone else to come carrying purpose and permission. Of course, it was then that Baxel felt a soft hand on his shoulder, hopefully carrying just that.

"You holding up?" Liaren asked.

"Yes, of course," Baxel replied quickly as he straightened up and turned away from the window to face her. He wiped away the smudge on the glass left from his forehead.

"Good," she said. "I need you in this, Baxel. Tialee did not ask for my help alone."

To Baxel, it seemed as if she always knew the right thing to say. "Have you spoken to her about it? The her in the Vigil archives, that is," Baxel clarified.

Liaren shook her head. "I am afraid to ask her to remember anything yet. Her projection device, the one you found in Dimarka's quarters, is missing from the Vigil inventory. I am afraid Connor Sevison still has it."

Baxel knew she was smart to not simply jump in; right now, keeping out of Connor's suspicion meant everything.

"What about asking for more information . . . in the Warden's Shrine?" he asked as quietly as he could manage. "Perhaps she has ideas there?"

Liaren shook her head. "There has been a line of Remnants on the steps ever since the drop. I did, however, find you something to do." Before Baxel could show his excitement, Liaren continued, "You have to remember what this is all about. This is not for you, or for either of us. We are trying to do one thing, and I haven't the faintest idea on how to go about that. I just hope I can find a start."

"Alright, go on."

"I met with Connor and Reawakened Williams—"

"You what?" Baxel interrupted in surprise. "You know he is dangerous and—"

Liaren pointed a finger into his chest. "Baxel, you are not to run scared on me."

"That's, uh, not exactly what I meant by . . ." he started.

"The closer we get to him, the more chance we have to uncover information about what he did to Dimarka that we can show to the Vigil. And I got them and the Vigil to agree to let you back into the Preservation Core."

"The Preservation Core? Why would they want that?"

Liaren smiled, taking his question as a compliment. "It was simple. Varnil and the new Reawakened agreed on continuing the list of

Unawakened. The few Remnants originally selected with retrieving Reawakened Varnil's cryopod years ago are tied up with their own positions now, so the Vigil were looking for candidates among the SE-S and the Medical and Rescue Sector, with a few of the exterior maintenance teams as options. Just as always, the Vigil maintains that the secrecy of the Preservation Core is part of its protection, and there was worry about letting anyone else know much about it."

Baxel nodded in realization. "They've known all along that they could not expel me from Safe Harbor. The Core is not something they want First Claim to know much about."

Liaren shrugged. "Possibly. But, there is one thing even more important than getting you a connection with the Reawakened, and via him Connor."

"What is that?"

"Now you get to do the one thing you are actually good at. I've got you your suit back."

* * *

Nendra Halimuth stood toward the back of the new room that the Production and Research Sector had modified to collect and observe the readings of the probe to Earth. While she was intrigued by the apparent breathability of the atmospheric samples, the conversations taking place in the observation room were fascinating in and of themselves.

At first glance the new Reawakened, Marrel Lovek, was a woman with soft features and a genuine curiosity about the new world in which she had been thrust into. She was intelligent, having a past working as a transmissions science engineer, but Nendra wondered if she fully understood how distant that past was.

"And you really have been outside your habitat zones, as you call them?" Marrel Lovek asked one of the engineers.

"On several occasions," the engineer, Raya, replied as she continued her work monitoring the multitude of readings the research probe was sending back from the surface.

Out of the very few individuals Nendra Halimuth had seen come from the Preservation Core, few seemed to take the adjustment as well as Ms. Lovek. Nendra thought it would be a struggle working with Varnil's decision, but the quick construction of the probe proved exactly the opposite. However, while the Reawakened had been able to aid perfectly in constructing the probe, Nendra patiently awaited the time that she would emotionally break down. Most others out of the Preservation Core did, at one point or another.

"You see, to me, that is just fascinating." Marrel motioned to the various display readouts on the screens and connected data pads. "Here we are, looking for breathable air on the planet, and I've never actually been on Earth, per se. Well, of course I have, but I've never been outside."

"Never?" Raya asked.

"Not once that I can remember. Though I hardly even thought of it until seeing . . . ." She looked for a moment at the readouts. "If you don't mind me asking, what are they like, your expeditions?"

The section engineer laughed as she highlighted a data range to look over in the latest reading to come in. "Well, we never really touch anything. Anything outside the habitat barriers is a vacuum. I was sent out along with one of the exploration teams; they had found what turned out to be a recharging station for various handheld tools, but at the time they were unsure what it was and if they should bring it in. They needed an engineer to accompany them and identify the thing."

"How did they come to pick you?"

"Actually it was Mrs. Halimuth that came to me with the offer. Of course I jumped on it. Oh, the pod is beginning to transmit the audio file now."

Nendra smiled. She knew Raya had spoken on occasion about wanting to see the outside, and at the time, the other senior engineers were busy or unwilling to face the dangers.

"It was three days," Raya continued. "For meals, we would be put into a personal atmosphere bag. It was confining, but intensely liberating at the same time. Just imagine, you are in the dead heart of the wreckage, you can barely see stars up through the tangle, and you take your helmet off."

"The bag is clear?" Marrel asked as she began to look at the new inbound audio transmission. It was one of the larger information types the pod was capable of.

"You can definitely see through it. Of course, it is tinted with a protective coat against radiation. But the sound, now that was interesting. The PAB device hums as it regulates the air, and it also relays communications from the suit into the open. After three days of silence in a vacuum, even just hearing the hiss of the meal pack again sent shivers down my spine."

"Would you do it again?" Marrel asked.

"I did, actually. During the construction of the probe. I helped you run the connections on the other side."

"That's right, isn't it! And I must say you did a . . ." Marrel trailed off as she looked at the monitors. She quickly held a hand up to her visor and spun around in the chair. The surprise was apparent on her face. "I thought you said the planet was dead?"

Nendra moved toward the panels to look for what had Marrel's attention. "Of course it is. It always has been."

Marrel frowned and tapped her visor, displaying a new image across the screens in front of them. "There. The analysis program flagged a few parts in the audio. The part of the program that picks out human voices was what I was working on in the months before I was supposed to ship out to Mars."

Raya worked her own controls, and the room was filled with a rushing torrent akin to the airlocks refilling.

"That must be wind," Marrel explained. "But this," she said, holding up a finger as the audio sample reached the marker flag.

"What is that?" Raya asked as they heard a muffled series of sounds.

Nendra stepped closer and listened intently. The ripping winds and sprinkle of debris kept washing out the noise. However, once she realized what she was hearing, it seemed to snap into clarity. "By the Warden. Those are voices."

Though distorted, she could piece together a few mentions of scrapping the observation probe. As the voices started to argue, she knew what had to happen.

"Stop the transmissions," Nendra said. When she received confused looks, she restated her command. "This will tear Safe Harbor to pieces faster than Sarthyl ever could. You have to cut them, now."

Raya hesitantly complied, ending the audio.

"No, I said stop the transmissions. Cut all info coming from the pod."

"Mrs. Halimuth," the Reawakened started, "any information we collect now is guaranteed. Anything stored on the pod is prone to be lost if there is some form of failure."

"We may already know too much." Nendra ran her hands over her tied-back hair and let out a curse of a prayer under her breath. "Warden keep the Remnants. Cut the connection."

* * *

Deep within the unclaimed territories of the Remnant Fleet, Hurald Wardenson cautiously moved his ship through the wreckage toward First Claim. The journey of his cargo hauler to First Claim had been tedious and slow, though he was traveling the same paths as always. First Claim was nearly a quarter of the way around the fleet from the Safe Harbor settlement.

Hurald Wardenson had piloted this particular ship for a number of years now, though none of his trips through the dark of the fleet had been as interesting as this. He pulled a shard of glass that hung loosely from the bullet hole in his helmet and adjusted course around an outreaching interior now showing in the front lights of the ship. After he delivered the Vigil Connor's data pad, he wanted nothing more than to make his way out to Aura. The long belt of scattered debris making up Aura was far enough on the other side of First Claim that there was next to nobody that lived there, though anyone you did see was just as likely to open fire as ask questions.

First Claim, on the other hand, had a pecking order, if not a system of rules. The Regent had the most guns, so he got to run the show. Everyone below that either stayed out of sight or put on a smile when he talked. There were advantages to working with the Regent, though. Hurald's own craft had come from the hands of the Regent after a violent First Claim raid on a rogue salvaging group. Hurald just hoped the damned data pad was enough to keep the Regent calm regarding the other cargo he was bringing back.

Hurald let out a cough. He wanted nothing more than to vent the lot of them into the wreckage, but the few suits he and his crew had were far too damaged after the brawl to risk opening the door to the transport.

The migrant Vigil had given him a data pad with a message and coordinates. Unfortunately, the others had heard about the reward for getting it to Regent Varis. He glanced back at the grisly scene behind him. Lo'chek was the one who shot Treys, who had been trying to open the weapons locker. Lo'chek was then stabbed in the back by both Eela and Zaimik. As Hurald had put his helmet on to vent the lot of them out of his damned ship, somebody shot him in the face. Everything had sounded muffled when he finally woke and saw Eela navigating dangerously close to the fringe.

So much for their plans of stealing the data pad and becoming Regents of their own territories.

Of course, unless the data pad contained a plan to divide Safe Harbor again, there would be no Second Claim. First Claim was dying out as it was. They could not keep up with needed supplies, causing more people to strike out on their own to Aura. The dwindling population only ensured that the vast store of supplies once seen under Sarthyl would never be replenished. Hurald was certain that once First Claim was weak enough, the fringe groups would tear it apart and destroy any hope of surviving outside the help of the Warden. They were the lost people, and Safe Harbor was the one with the history of survival. When the Warden killed Sarthyl, it had ended their only hope of expansion.

He tried to reach inside his helmet to remove the piece of glass sticking into his eyebrow, but his bloodstained gloves were not small enough to fit through the hole. Personally, whatever trouble had Safe Harbor spinning and the Vigil worried enough to contact the Regent underhandedly, he hoped that it was also enough to rip a hole in the damned settlement. They knew the people of First Claim were dying, and their Warden couldn't care less.

* * *

Flerin stepped out of the side passages into the silence of the Hall of the Warden. Even as everywhere else in the Remnant Fleet continued on with life as normal, this hall was the one place he could really get a feel for how things were in the minds of the Remnants. For starters, the silence. He had rarely seen so many people sitting and standing among the various monumentalized items throughout the Hall of the Warden, and still, it was much quieter than normal. His steps seemed loud amongst the sparse murmurs.

"Supply beacon, next to the mangled airlock doors . . ." Flerin said quietly to himself as he walked through the room. He was looking for the spot where Oundara had asked to meet him. He finally spotted her dark form sitting next to the blue glow of a search beacon. If he remembered the info on the plaque, the Warden had left the beacon next to a stockpile of supplies in a time of great need.

He took in a breath and clasped the frame of the closed data pad behind his back. There were still a few items he had not managed to "account" for, and it was all too fitting that the nav beacons were on that list.

"Thank you for meeting me here," Oundara said, standing as Flerin approached. "I would not have had the time to travel to the SE-S before my meeting with Mrs. Halimuth."

"It is no problem, I assure you. Gave me an excuse to get away from Quervin." Flerin mentally knuckled his forehead at the jab to the other head of the SE-S. It was not the start he was looking for.

"You are fine." Oundara smiled. "Believe me, I understand. Sometimes I wish he could drop the job, for just a moment."

Flerin nodded instead of following with his own comment.

"Of course," Oundara started, "sometimes I wish I could drop the job too. The break in SE-S operations was just so we could get caught up on our end. I swear the exploration teams are still providing new reports on what we used in the construction."

Flerin nodded again. "Everything about it was a rush."

The SE-S head took a seat on the bench next to the beacon and offered for Flerin to do the same. "Sometimes, I think the only thing harder, is trying to figure out Safe Harbor's inventory outside of the settlement."

"Inventory?" Flerin asked.

Oundara nodded. "When Nendra Halimuth first came to me with a list of all the things the new Reawakened needed to construct the pod, I had to practically wrestle with the search coordinators to find out exactly what tech we could field, and what was simply up to a coordinated chance."

Flerin would have been one of the coordinators on the receiving end of her questioning had he not been stripped of his lead of Firebrand. Possibly more than the other teams, Firebrand had a huge catalog of potential locations reaching into the far coordinates. It's not that they were holding anything back, but rather the recovery teams needed to be selective of what they used their time and resources to actually collect.

"You were in the search for years before I came to the SE-S. Tell me, how does a coordinator keep track of their team's unreported finds? Do those locations get passed down from one coordinator to the next, or is it simply remembered by the teams?"

This time Flerin let out a sigh instead of a nod. He produced the data pad and held the glowing image up. "This meeting has nothing to do with the past weeks, does it?"

"Flerin," Oundara said, her tone placating, "I am not trying to undermine your work with Firebrand. I am not going to steal any information from you, or the past members of the team. To be honest, I want you working with me. Dermuth will not be around forever, and the way you handled the chaos of the entire construction situation is invaluable to the SE-S and Safe Harbor. I want you to step up and help lead the SE-S, but that being said, Firebrand does not look like it is coming back, at least not anytime soon. Possibly not in our lifetimes."

"But you do want me to give you the locations."

Oundara gave him a soft look. "Yes. I want you to give them up. When you decide. How you decide. I'm not trying to play some game. I'm just trying to manage inventory, because depending on what that probe sends back, we may have to be the ones that start preparing our descendants to explore something far larger than we could ever imagine."

She held his look for a time until a small display appeared over a band on her wrist. "I know I was the one who ended your team. But I want to be on the same side as you. Think on it, Flerin. And discuss it with Tymon and Baxel, if you need. Just know that I really am trying to keep this fleet together."

At that, she glanced to her schedule and excused herself, leaving Flerin sitting alone next to the Warden's beacon. He looked into the blue glow and remembered that it was what had ultimately started the exploration teams hundreds of years ago. It was the first beacon, placed for them to find by the Warden herself.

After a while spent looking into the small device, Flerin glanced around the room at all the other focal points that everyone was looking at to reflect back upon their own pasts, trying to work past some struggle they held inside themselves. From the monumentalized pillars of slag from the dying of the fleet's once failing repulsors to items recovered from the dead habitats, the enshrined objects throughout the Hall of the Warden reminded them that they truly did owe their delicate existence to the Warden.

Flerin then gave a final nod before standing. The Warden. Not Firebrand.

Chapter 18: Silence Broken

"So all this time, Reclaim has been hiding a Cryo?" Kara asked yet again. "You?" She pulled tight on the long strip of cloth wrapped around her boot. Just as she was about to finish the process of tying a knot with one hand to hold the knife in place, Oa took the weapon away.

"You will not need this," she said, pointing the knife at Kara. "Not that it would do you any good with your arm still wrapped in a sling." The old woman handed it over to Hama and told him to put it away.

"Yes, Oa," Hama said, moving off to one of the side rooms in her house.

Oa then turned a hard look back to Kara. Just as Kara pulled her hood up, Oa jerked it back down. "If you try to hide, you will be seen. And lose the pouches you bought. You don't want to look like a tech hunter where we are going."

"It's been three days," Kara bit back. "When do I get to know what we are doing?" The old woman had promised that she would get Kara into the Citadel of Reclaim, but she was being all too secretive about what she wanted her to do once inside. Kara could only hope that it did not interfere with her tracking of Travend's men.

"Something dropped out of the sky along the southern border of the Steel Valley. By now, the Prime Elect will want me, as his Cryo, to give him an opinion. I want you to help me. From everything that you have done, I imagine you have seen your fair share of tech."

Kara narrowed her eyes. "Did Nuand put you up to this? Are you a Norclave spy?"

"Are you?"

Kara took a breath. Despite entering Reclaim, she had no intention of bothering with the stupid sky flare, let alone reporting back to Olana Nuand about what Reclaim had.

"Oa?" Hama said, stepping into the room with a data pad of his own. "I believe we will need to leave soon to make it to the Prime Elect's meeting on time."

"If he is already there," Oa explained, "and cannot proceed without me, then it simply means that it is my meeting. I cannot be late, because it starts when I arrive. Kara, hood." The old woman flicked her finger commandingly and Kara grudgingly pulled it back down again. "Hama, grab my case."

"Yes, Oa."

Kara tucked the hair about her shoulders under the hanging cloak and followed Oa stiffly out the door. She knew she was going to get spotted and killed. And what made it worse, she had next to zero tech on her to retaliate. She was even more ill-prepared for the encounter than the first time she fought Travend's men.

The tail end of the morning had yet to fade as they made their way down several levels to the base of the Citadel. The high reaching spire seemed to point upward to the dull forms of the orbital wreckage, slowly spinning in their eternal cycle. It was almost hard to imagine that one sky flare from the vast store of scrap was enough to bog the zones down into games of shadow. All Olana wanted to know is what new tech she would have to fear from the Steel Valley, and apparently, all the Prime Elect wanted to know was what he had.

But just as Olana had kept Jance's survival—if that was still the case—wrapped in secrecy, the Prime Elect would do anything to keep information about this from leaving his city. Kara could only hope that his Cryo brought more influence than Olana's, otherwise she and Oa were both dead.

"We are here to see the Prime Elect," Oa said to the two watch once they reached the wide entrance. Instead of simply stepping to the side, one looked cautiously at the old woman and the other started backing away from the entrance. The first soon shuffled out of the way without a word and Oa strode in as if it were business as normal.

Kara glanced back to see Hama's reaction.

"I'll wait here for your return," he told Kara. "The Prime Elect doesn't much like me."

"You and me both," Kara said quietly.

She made to follow Oa as the elderly woman moved with purpose through the stark white hallways. While Kara had only heard about the inside of the building from other tech hunters, it appeared that the Prime Elect had been busy bringing everything closer to the eccentric flair he was going for. However, what actually grabbed her attention were the few Norclave soldiers and mercenaries of Kamriek's Grove waiting in the hallway. Next to them, Zaireel Tuakana was speaking with one of the Reclaim officials. Kara did not catch his thickly accented words as Oa ushered her along, but Kara was more than certain that he looked at her in recognition. Without slowing a bit, Tuakana turned back to his conversation.

Kara felt even more like running at having yet another person know she was here. "We may have to be quick," Kara said quietly as they passed by a security cordon around an elevator farther down the hall. "It looks like an emissary from Norclave is here."

"You say to hurry?" Oa laughed. "The Prime Elect has more than enough ways to deflect what could be seen as discourteous. We have all the time we need."

Kara glanced back as a door opened next to the elevator. She immediately recognized the figures stepping out. They paused in the hall and looked at the closed elevator. The one missing a hand had put her arm in the sling with a repulsor shot, and the other, walking with a slight limp as he motioned for the first to come away from the elevator, she recognized from Allek Skaves's death.

The old Cryo finally stopped when she noticed Kara watching them walk away.

"Leave them be," Oa said. "This is not the place to settle your scores."

"All it would take is one shout to Tuakana, and Norclave soldiers would swarm them."

Oa looked at Kara with interest. "So you know a Norclave official by name. Who else besides Norclave's Cryo did you come to know, I wonder?"

Kara kept quiet, not wanting to give anything more to the prying woman.

Oa scoffed. "You can ease up. They're not going anywhere. Those two men are under the protection of the Prime Elect."

It took nearly everything Kara had to turn her back on them. This wouldn't be the last time she needed to get in to the Citadel, and that made listening to Oa her best shot.

Oa motioned to the sling holding up Kara's left arm. "My guess is that you were just as prepared when they left you for dead?"

"Shut up."

Oa could not hide her twisted smile. "Keep alive, and I might be able to teach you a thing or two."

"Oh yeah?" Kara asked as they walked down another long side passage. This one was lined with more decorative displays. "And what were you, before you woke up in our world?"

Oa chuckled. "The best way I have learned to describe it, is someone who tended to a now distant religion. But my watching days are over. Now, here we are. Interior entrance to the Citadel's main hangar."

This time, when Oa stepped up to the guards at the door, they did not disperse.

"Oa," one of them said in greeting. He was a tall man, with skin nearly as dark as Oa's, and though his arms were lanky compared to his height, his muscles were defined enough to carry his confidence. He also had a respectable piecing of flight armor and other tech about him. He let the strap on his shoulder take the weight of what looked to be an entirely custom weapon and produced a data pad.

"Caemon," Oa replied with a nod. "Is the Prime Elect waiting?"

Caemon gave the slightest twitch of a smile, though other than that he kept his grim composure. "Waiting on you, as usual." Caemon glanced over to the other watch, who was equally as armed though didn't nearly match his height. Caemon tapped the data pad. "Go on in."

The door opened and Kara followed Oa in. Unlike the hangars of Norclave, the large space was entirely clean and presentable. It was well-lit, a large window of starscraper glass filled much of the center of the ceiling, and there were a good number of what Kara guessed to be transports of various kinds covered in pristine cloths. The only exception to the order was the array of desks and displays arranged around the new centerpiece to the room. The vehicles and transports had been moved to the side with the arrival of the large item in the center. A collection of lights were focused on what Kara was certain was the sky flare.

"Incredible," Kara said as they approached. Oa said nothing as they moved amongst the outermost layers of tables. They were filled with a wide arrangement of tools, and workers were taking measurements of large metal plates arranged evenly about the workspace. From what Kara remembered from Jance's surveillance view, they would have been the pieces of the outer shell that split during the drop, just before the bright repulsors flared at the bottom and slowed the sky flare. It didn't seem as if Reclaim had recovered them all, and perhaps that was the reason for the measuring.

"Leave us!" the Prime Elect called from near the pod as he started waving his arms to shoo everyone away. The workers all hurried to put their tools away and exit the room, leaving only him, Oa, and Kara.

"Oa, thank you for meeting me this morning." He turned his attention over to Kara. "Who is this?"

His question was welcome, if only to let Kara know the Black Scars or Travend's men had not given him her description. Or even, that he had somehow found out she was part of the tech hunter group that brought him Kessian devices.

"A friend," Oa said without skipping a beat. "Gleia Dimarka. I asked for her assistance in examining . . . this."

"Gleia Dimarka . . ." the Prime Elect said in thought. He reached out a hand to Kara. She clenched her teeth but shook his hand. She almost expected him to ask if she knew the Kessian tech was stolen when they sold it to Reclaim.

He turned to follow Oa as the woman stepped toward the pod. "I am afraid that we may have had a . . . well, a misunderstanding, Oa" he said.

"How so?" Oa asked as she pressed her age-worn hand against the dull metal.

"To be blunt," Feirshan said, "it is your memory that I am after, Oa, not your intuition. I have technicians to examine this. They will eventually figure out what this is, if you do not already know."

"Do you know everything about your world, Prime Elect? Am I supposed to about mine? Give me some time. Something may come to me that will be of help."

"How long?"

"Several hours. Maybe more."

"I am afraid not, Oa. I have already kept an emissary from Norclave waiting too long. I should not stretch the meeting out until then."

Kara noticed Oa hide a slight smile. "I thank you for your support, but I do not need you here to recall my memories."

The Prime Elect sighed, obviously hating having the disadvantage in a conversation when he normally imposed fear into anyone else. Kara imagined every meeting with his Cryo was like this.

"Can I trust her? Your friend Dimarka?" he finally asked.

"No," Oa said, turning to him. She shot a devious look to Kara over the Prime Elect's shoulder. Kara could not hide her own shock.

"You cannot learn to trust her, not before Norclave gets tired of waiting."

The Prime Elect balled his fists but gave a courteous nod to his Cryo. "I thank you for your input, Oa. I shall return when I can, but I may be unavailable should you require assistance. I urge you not to, well, touch anything until I can set up some more trusted technicians to aid you." He then gave a final glance to Kara. "I will be speaking with you in time."

"There," Oa said after the Prime Elect of Reclaim finally strode away. "You did well."

"I didn't do anything," Kara said.

Oa smiled, satisfied. "As I said. Now you can go back to being a tech hunter. Grab what tools you need off the tables."

"For what?"

"Ensuring that my people do not try to follow me. I need your help in destroying the surveillance probe."

* * *

After the pace of everything, Kenneth welcomed the chance to just sit back in the Norclave Library and fix something. Olana was busy putting together the pieces of her task force, Sora was demanding continual updates on Jance's condition, and he had one job remaining. Well, two, if listening for the alarms of the system counted. There was no solid location on Travend, but the options were narrowing and the percentages rising.

Kenneth clicked his fingers to his palm in thought. With each tap of his gloves, the lighted disk extended from the back or retracted. They had received the first wave of transmissions from Zaireel in Reclaim, and near as Kenneth could figure, the disguised cameras had arrived intact and undetected. Of course, the transmissions were locked behind Council clearance, meaning that even if the Prime Elect intercepted the data, he would have no means of unlocking it, and a full decryption could take months.

And now, with the help of the Last Edict, Kenneth planned to override Jance's filter and see what Kara was doing.

He reached under the desk to where he had his pack of tools. He knew somebody would yell at him for using Jance's desk for anything but accessing the system, but it was the only open space left in the room not covered in tools and spare visors.

The pieces inside the visor were miniscule, but he had seen things like the device before. He'd just finished replacing one of the components inside where the visor had split in two, though it was anyone's guess as to what it actually did. He had simply copied it to match the form of the others.

It was soothing work. He was learning new systems as he went, and gradually he began to see progress. Instead of replacing the entire outer casing, he simply reinforced the broken pieces, if nothing more than to ensure it still remained Avery's. Jance had kept it for a reason, and he did not want his work to interfere with that.

The final touch, as Kenneth saw it, was in replacing the tiny strip of display generators lining the visor. Each dot hung from the bottom like measured dew drops, though their size was closer to that of hair tips. It took him several patient tries—and that same number of times destroying the projector strips—before he finally got one in place.

Kenneth set the visor onto the side of his head. The active adhesive nano-coating found a painless hold on his skin. From there, he could just barely see the projection generators pulsing the faintest orange. According to everything he'd heard Jance say and the instructions passed down by Overlord Obrourke, the device was now mapping into his neural patterns. Though it would take weeks, if not months, for the device to fully integrate, he should be able to complete some basic functions without the aid of an external data pad.

"Okay, here we go," Kenneth said as the projection started to solidify across and over his eyes. "Oh, blurry." He blinked a couple of times, and the image gradually started to fade into a readable view. He would need to wear lenses for the finest of details, but for now this would do.

"Alright, Avery, let's see what you've left me."

Kenneth was hit with a rapid flicking of information, and he ended up squinting to see past the visor to his linked data pad. He had expected a small amount of data, if anything, but there appeared to be a great deal more on this visor than on any other he had heard of. A few presses through the display of the data pad slowed things back down. Kenneth accessed the first item it stopped on.

"Project: 0-73. System Flow Analysis Program."

Kenneth had to pull back with the data pad again as the file hit him with a mess of form connections and connective scripting nonsense. Perhaps this was something better suited to a program hunter. He tried to think very precisely about moving to the next item.

"Public Transportation Code: 0a-9019-7c-884—Education— Literature Communications—0-fee."

Kenneth squinted as he tried to make sense of what he was reading. "Okay, how do I look for more details . . ." Before he finished his thought aloud, the device recognized his intent and brought up additional information. It included a date, various locations, various marked travel times, and the date of issue, which was earlier in the same year of 2994.

Kenneth had to take a second look at the next part.

"Issued to: Maylee Sharpes—2994."

A few minutes later, Kenneth let out a sigh and took the device off. In everything he searched for, the only recurring name was simply Maylee Sharpes. As far as he could tell, there was not one mention of Avery Thorne or the Last Edict. Whatever had happened, Jance had kept the wrong broken visor as a keepsake.

And he was no closer to finding Kara.

* * *

"Your people?" Kara asked. "What do you mean, your people? Why would we destroy this? Who are you hiding from, Oa?"

"Please," Oa said, motioning to the large metal observation probe. "I just . . . this is all that matters, if it is not already too late. Do this, and I will help you with what you need."

Kara eyed the old woman suspiciously. What caught Kara's attention most of all was that she genuinely looked distressed. She let out a sigh and looked at Oa with pity. She'd known plenty of people that were always running from their past, and if Kara wanted answers, she knew making one deal after another would only get her so far toward finding out what Oa was hiding from.

"What is this?" Kara asked, now stepping beside Oa to look up at the object. It almost looked newly constructed, though that hardly matched with Oa being a Cryo.

Oa shook her head slowly as they looked up at the smooth lining of matte steel. "I saw designs for a similar idea, many years ago."

"I need to know what we are dealing with," Kara said gently.

Oa reached to the table beside them and picked up a data pad. She searched for a few silent moments before looking up to the object again. "It is an observation probe. It should be sending back information, such as air composition, radiation levels, perhaps even scans of life. Reclaim is still clueless of what they have." Oa tossed the data pad back on the table.

Kara frowned. Nothing seemed to be adding up. She, Kenneth, and Jance had watched the probe fall from the sky. Unless it was sent by some other population on the other side of the world, she did not understand why it originated from so high. There were still marks on the outer shell of the metal where the repulsors had burned during the descent.

Of course, if it was a plan from some relevant faction near Reclaim to get a listening device into the Citadel, their idea had worked. But that still left the question of why Oa wanted to destroy it.

"How . . ." Kara started slowly as more thoughts started to boil up. "How did you know you needed my help? I was just some wounded tech hunter left to die."

Oa clenched her jaw. "We do not have time for this."

"If I recall correctly, we have several hours. Maybe more. You may be willing to risk everything, Oa, but I need to know why I am taking a chance on my life. I will be hunted by the Prime Elect, if I even get past the walls of Reclaim."

Oa finally sat down in one of the chairs next to the table and let her shoulders slump. "I took a vow. For nearly fifty years, I have kept my silence. A silence born not only of hidden words, but of leaving my people."

"Gleia Dimarka," Kara stated, making the connection. The name Oa used to introduce her to the Prime Elect had seemed to come more naturally than simply a throwaway pseudonym. "Was she one that you left behind?"

This time, Kara could see tears forming in Oa's eyes. "No, actually. She was one of the ones I did not save. I was too late to realize . . ." Oa looked to Kara. The wrinkles across her dark skin seemed to show her age through her worry now more than ever before. "I need you to swear my same vow. What I tell you has to die with you. The people of Earth and the Remnant fleet can never know."

Kara took in a heavy breath as her thoughts started to wrap around a central idea. "You are not a Cryo."

Oa smiled weakly. "I never said I was. Not once in the half century since I arrived. I let many assume, but I am no Reawakened."

"What are you?" Kara asked.

"I was once a Remnant, and a Vigil of the Warden, though I abandoned all that in one of the darkest moments my people have ever seen. For as long as humanity has continued in the ruins of Earth, my people survived in what you see as the orbital wreckage. Our struggle saw that life continued amongst the ruins of the Orbital Armistice Fleet. In that aspect, we are not so unlike you."

Kara found herself looking up through the large window on the ceiling of the hangar. Through the golden tint of the starscraper glass, she wondered up at the orbital wreckage.

"We followed a precedent of life given to us by the centuries. And when events threatened to extinguish our people, we looked to our great Warden for guidance, and even aid. I joined the Warden's Vigil on my twenty-thousand cycles. The Vigil kept the history of our people, and made decisions based on the previous decisions of the Warden. We tended to Safe Harbor for her return, as the others before us had since the time of the evacuation of Earth. We also tended what is called the Preservation Core—a collection of cryopods still filled from the earliest years."

Kara could not keep herself from asking, "How many?"

Oa paused as if she again was weighing how much she was willing to tell. With a sigh, she gave in. "Tens of thousands. All of them clueless as to the destruction of their world. And from the utter hell unleashed upon *our* world from the single pod I witnessed open, your people would be far safer remaining oblivious. The Vigil ensured that there was always one Reawakened—a Cryo as you would call it—active to advise on the protection of the Preservation Core. In my time his name was Sarthyl, and we blindly put him before the Warden."

Oa motioned to the observation probe. "This is based in part on his designs. He called for the Remnants to return to Earth. Sarthyl stated that the safety of his people rested entirely on fulfilling their lives, not dwindling away one at a time throughout the years. The Vigil finally weighed against Sarthyl, stating that the Warden had never willed us to return, only to survive amongst the wreckage, to preserve the Unawakened, to seek a safe harbor for the Remnants, and to stabilize the dying fleet."

Kara could see Oa's hands shaking.

"Sarthyl divided the Remnants and the Vigil. He started a new colony. First Claim. And he held the survival of our people hostage, hoping we would give in to his demands. But he knew not the patience of the Remnants. The Remnants are measured in everything they do, and we are capable of waiting for generations. Centuries, if needed.

Sarthyl sought change within the time of his one given life. He waged war against Safe Harbor."

"What did your people do?"

"The Vigil debated. Sarthyl targeted the habitat sectors first. Habitat One was destroyed in the first raid. Thousands died that cycle, including my closest friend, Gleia Dimarka. I still remember the fires ripping into the zero-space of Safe Harbor after Sarthyl's forces were driven away. By the time the remaining members of the Medical and Rescue Sector declared Hab One a red zone, the Vigil had come to a decision. We were to abandon Safe Harbor and to scatter deeper into the wreckage. Those who were willing to fight until the arrival of the Warden were deemed live-switches."

"Live-switches?"

"Quite literally that. Living, but with the understanding that their life had become secondary to a goal that must be put before all else. In this case, it was the depressurization of the sectors in preparation for Sarthyl's next attack."

"Where were you?" Kara asked. "You said you abandoned them?"

"While the habitats began to evacuate, I was in the Hall of the Warden. I refused to leave. I sat in front of the Warden's Shrine, praying that someone would be sent to claim the revered items. Nobody else knew I was waiting. The live-switches began to release the air from the hall. Their hope was to keep Sarthyl busy long enough that our people could escape through the inner void. To make a life in hiding somewhere else. I knew my minutes were running as thin as the air, but I knew my prayer would help. It had to. Every remaining Remnant depended on it.

"But Sarthyl attacked before we expected. Several heavy shots punched through into the Hall of the Warden when the live-switches had only managed to purge the first quarter of the air. I still remember the demonic screeching of the metal, and the muffled screams of those taken by the void. From where I knelt in the shrine room, I still felt the surge of air rushing out. Those near the breach never stood a chance."

Oa clasped her hands and looked down. "My hope went out with them. I was left in the bitter cold with nothing more than useless breaths. I was devastated. My faith was broken."

Kara felt her own heart racing. "But you lived. Did the Warden come?"

"Not for me. Oa Alee died that day, along with many others. Only then did the Warden come." Oa drew in a breath. "I put the suit on."

"What happened to . . . to Safe Harbor?" Kara asked.

"Safe Harbor survived, thanks to the Warden. For two weeks, I hunted down Sarthyl and the bulk of his followers."

"Wait, hold on," Kara said. "You make that sound like you took them all on by yourself."

Importance of the suit Oa looked very seriously to Kara. "I was not the only Warden inside that helmet. The four others before me recorded themselves as AI programs integrated with the suit. Not only did I have the most advanced systems in the entire fleet in that suit, I had centuries of experience at my disposal. All I had to do was make the decision to bring forth destruction not seen since before the creation of the Remnants."

Oa nodded to herself as she relived dark memories. "Space is silent, and the Wardens disrupted every scan before they could reach my suit. By the end of it, I had to hold myself back from sieging First Claim. I instead took a different course of action."

Oa paused for a long while, as if unable to cross the hurdle of the memory.

"What action?" Kara finally prodded.

Oa cleared her throat. "I had to ensure the safety of the secrets of the Warden. I went to the one place I knew I would never be found."

"Here. You came to Reclaim?" Kara asked.

Oa raised an eyebrow and shrugged. "I had no idea the Earth would have Remnants too. I guess with all the traditions that I broke in putting on the suit, I should have realized that something else could be fundamentally wrong with reality."

"You really did not know?"

Oa pointed up. "Did you?"

"I . . ." Kara started, though she faded out as her thoughts hit a little more sharply than she wanted. She had not thought anything about the orbital wreckage until Kenneth showed it to her in a new, questioning light. She frowned at that. Kenneth was as close to a Cryo as she had ever met before they unthawed Jance.

"Okay, fine," Kara said. "I get the deal with keeping the Remnants' secret. We've got enough problems within just our small area of the world. But why does the Warden have to stay a secret to your people?"

"I hold more than just the weight of knowledge in my hands. It would be the saddest betrayal I could think of if I made them lose their faith like I lost my own. They need the Warden, even if she is only in their hearts. I fear the entire fleet would follow in the steps of Sarthyl and First Claim without her guidance." Oa shook her head and looked to the ground. "I wish their innocence to be preserved."

Oa finally stood up. "I have told you more than any other person in existence. You now know more about the deepest secrets of my world than I do yours. Will you help me in protecting the delicate balance of my people one last time? Will you help me find a way to destroy the probe?"

Kara produced a knife from behind her sling and twirled it once. The heated blade came to full temperature as she completed the flourish. "I'll show you a trick I learned from someone. He's the best technician I've ever known."

Chapter 19: Betrayal

"There," Flerin said as Varnil watched from outside the Preservation Core. The coordinator finished his work and held out the Firebrand helmet to Baxel. "The tracker is in place," Flerin said, "so watch yourself. Just keep to your work and do as the Reawakened tells you or Quervin will be the first to know. I will be the second."

"Do not worry yourself, Coordinator Flerin," Varnil said. "Baxel will perform admirably, I am sure."

"He'd better," the coordinator practically growled, keeping his attention on Baxel. "You don't have a whole lot of options left, boy."

Baxel ignored the comment in what seemed a familiar process. "How did your meeting go with the heads of the SE-S?"

"Terrible. They want to make me one of them."

"Doing what?" Baxel asked.

The coordinator simply shook his head. "Giving them locations. And whatever else they need when the probe eventually starts sending something back. Oundara describes it as 'chaos control.' At least you and Tymon gave me all the experience I need."

Varnil trailed into his own thoughts as they continued talking. So far, the Production and Research Sector had yet to come forward with anything but the initial readings of the probe. While the rest of the Remnants and the Vigil were satisfied waiting for answers, he knew enough about intergovernmental politics to know when something was being intentionally withheld.

"Are you about ready, Baxel?" Varnil asked a moment later.

Flerin gripped the shoulder of Baxel's armor in a farewell. "Oundara asked me to keep tabs on you. I'll try to meet you in the Hall of the Warden when you get a chance. Now hurry up, the Reawakened asked for you."

"You ready to start on some names?" Varnil asked as Baxel hurried up to the doorway.

"Only if you don't poke any more buttons with your name on them."

As Baxel put his helmet on and moved into the small observation room of the Preservation Core, Varnil had to take pause. The jab was fair enough, but he knew the boy did not truly understand. And he never would until he became a father. Varnil glanced over to the cryopod of his son as the walkway lights followed Baxel around the curve of the room. As the Remnant passed the main controls, the Preservation Core lit up as well. There was a terrifying beauty to it all. Beauty, in that everything had grown in its own direction as the Remnants gave life to the rigid structures of their dead fleet. Terrifying, in that it all could collapse before Varnil got the chance to get his people to safety.

"This time I will be able to stay out longer," Baxel informed him as he manually checked the connections of his suit. The beginning of his sentence was muffled by his helmet until Varnil linked his own visor in with the main control terminal. There was a hiss of air from the jets around Baxel's ankles as he motioned with his thumb. "And I won't be stuck floating off again if something does come up."

"I'm sure nothing will," Varnil replied.

Baxel gave him a thumbs-up over his shoulder as he moved off toward the airlock. "Whatever you say, Reawakened."

"Let's make sure we do this systematically. I'll send you the coordinates where you left off."

"No need," Baxel said. Through his visor, Varnil could hear the hollow hiss of the airlock sounding outside Baxel's suit. "I was on the exterior of the column. Three names after Marrel Lovek. The next pod looked as if it had a nasty crack running down the glass."

Varnil sent him the coordinates anyway. A small point on his visor hovered on top of the last marked pod in the hanging city. There was no way Baxel would be able to find where he'd left off, and he didn't want the bravado of an ex-exploration team member to make this disorganized. After all, if the Remnants were as slow about the return to Earth as the Vigil wanted, the next Reawakened would be the one responsible for expanding the list.

"Not that I'm complaining," Baxel started as Varnil watched the orange light of Baxel's arm beacon make its way out toward the chaotic spiral, "but why exactly do we need more names again? We already got our scientist to work on the probe."

"Transmissions science engineer."

"Right. So, are you wanting someone to replace you? Or do you have more family members to spring on the Vigil?"

"There are others."

Varnil was met with a long pause from Baxel.

"Kaiden, he was my youngest," Varnil continued. "The others are out there with you. If you see the name . . ." Varnil trailed off, still finding himself adjusting to the heavy lessons he had recently learned. "Harria Williams. If you find her, let her sleep. I'll find her a better world than this."

"And what makes you think Earth is any better? Or ever will be?"

Varnil refrained from replying. In his eyes, it had to be. "I can see why the Vigil have a hard time knowing what to do with you. Connor told me to watch you closely."

One of the displayed charts showed a sharp trend. Varnil raised an eyebrow at the steady rise in Baxel's heart rate. "He also said you might be a pain to work with."

"Did he?" Baxel replied. "How . . . how well do you know him? Vigil Connor, that is?"

Varnil leaned forward to get an eye for how far out Baxel was. By now, the small coordinate location on his own visor was larger than Baxel's orange navigation light. "I'll have you know that it was disorienting, coming out of cryostasis to find all this. Pretty much everything I have seen or been told for the past few years has been entirely new. Your migrant was just about the only person I came across that was anywhere as lost as I was."

"I assume you told him about the Preservation Core?"

Varnil paused to think back. "No, much the opposite. He worked here long before me. For years, actually. You know, I spent centuries in the Core, but I've only actually been in this room a handful of times, and that was when the Vigil were focused on teaching me the ways of the Remnants."

Baxel's air supply dropped a few percent as he adjusted his course. "It would have been nice had he warned you about your son."

"I doubt if he ever thought to make the connection."

Baxel lost another few percent as he slowed his approach. "But Kaiden was the Reawakened before Sarthyl. I'm just saying, he would have been familiar with the name at least."

"Or perhaps it simply had not crossed his mind that there would be a connection between two surviving pods left over from the millions that had once existed."

Another heavy silence settled in as Baxel shifted over the surface of the Preservation Core. He moved with a light touch, using the air of his suit to guide his progress. Varnil wondered about the rationale of using a single gas supply for both navigation and life support, but he knew the Remnants had a reason. They had to use the resources available, if nothing else.

Varnil watched as Baxel gently ran a hand down the long crack in the glass of one of the pods.

"Speaking of surviving..." Baxel started. "I have my doubts about this one. Do you still need the information?"

"Yes. I will make a note of the condition, though I am sure your people are used to similar problems. Vigil Treys warned me about the whole process before Kaiden came back. It seems the physical problems are as numerous as the mental challenges when it comes to becoming the Reawakened."

* * *

Tialee felt herself pulled awake as her consciousness was expanded. Her form was now locked by protocol to a single location. She had just a moment—more precisely thirty-eight point four *nulled* milliseconds—to analyze the room before her represented form would appear. She immediately registered the dimensions of the room, and her subanalysis routines accessed potentially relevant information along with the purpose of the room as designated by the Remnants. With what was commonly compared to humans recalling memories, Tialee was ready with all the data she had collected about location: *Fortuna*, Vigil Archives, Head Vigil's meeting room.

She now had thirty-seven point one *nulled* milliseconds before visual representation of emotions.

Tialee then accounted for all the functional items in attendance. Subject: Head Vigil, Algan Treys. Subject: AI mirror caretaker, Vigil, Malory Yumin. Subject: Selected Pupil-137, Vigil, Liaren Marenday. Subject: Preservation Core caretaker, Vigil, Connor Sevison. Subject: Head of Production and Research Sector, Nendra Halimuth. Subject: UNKNOWN.

Tialee pieced together relevant names from the latest 8 percent of her new subject designations. The most likely unassigned name appeared in the last 0.013 *nulled* percent of her data storage. This was Subject: Reawakened, Marrel Lovek.

Tialee continued setting up likely event parameters as her systems gradually came online. Eventually, the people about the Head Vigil's meeting room stopped their discussions and turned to face her visual projection as her artificial photons coalesced.

"Tialee, we thank you for meeting with us," Head Vigil, Algan Treys, said. He glanced to the others as if he was unsure that his gesture of thanks would still be perceived as courteous by the end of the meeting.

Tialee simply gave a nod, selecting to be appreciative while retaining a neutral position on their undisclosed disagreement. Tialee discreetly surveyed each person in the room. It was an easy analysis to see that each had disagreements with one another, though until she could observe further mannerisms, there were simply too many unknown variables to say who was a part of how many sides.

It was an abnormal audience, to be sure. The fact that two non-Vigil were in attendance was abnormal.

"To be clear about the matter," Vigil Treys continued, "Mrs. Halimuth and Reawakened Lovek have asked to seek your audience directly. Furthermore, it is their wish that they hold a future meeting with you, without a member of the Vigil in attendance."

Tialee vocalized a prompt for information. "What is the nature of this requested meeting?" She aligned her projection to look to Nendra Halimuth and Marrel Lovek.

Whereas the Reawakened made a move within the parameters that indicated her intention to speak, it appeared as if both had been heavily educated on Vigil custom.

"All they have stated," Vigil Treys explained in their place, "is that it is connected to the information relayed by the probe sent to the planet. They have not elaborated, no matter the questioning."

"And what use do you believe I will be, should I be given the information you are withholding from the Vigil?"

The question was direct enough that Vigil Treys directed a nod to the two of them, though he was markedly unhappy about letting them speak. There was a high chance that he simply did not want to see the Vigil undermined. Over the centuries, there had always existed a delicate balance between following those who were given lead now and those who had already proven themselves.

Nendra Halimuth took a timid step forward, not entirely matching with her standard profile. "I have witnessed Vigil meetings enough to know the role you play. You prefer to be a mediator, and ensure that each voice is heard for what it is. However, you possess a unique ability: you can truly forget a conversation."

While the statement was unexpected, Tialee was also caught off guard at Liaren's subtle reaction. She hid it well, but she gave the impression that she was entirely too knowing about some aspect of the process that Tialee herself was unaware of. Perhaps it was in some reference to a conversation Tialee had held with the girl that had not been saved. To the other side, almost as if in a darker reflection to Liaren's reaction, Vigil Connor hid his own anger at some unspoken truth.

"What is so . . ." Tialee started, then one of her processes caught up with a conclusion. There was nothing wrong with the probe, but instead, something worrisome about what it had found. She was nearly caught in an exponentially compiling rationale loop as she burned through the implications. Several seconds later, Tialee nulled the torrent of new data and returned her focus to the conversation.

"I propose a solution," Tialee finally said, laying out a strategy. "In this, I hope to achieve the Vigil's right to knowledge, and to satisfy the concerns regarding denying it. I will hear this data, and determine if it should be kept from the Vigil, or even myself."

Tialee then motioned to the data pad tucked in Malory Yumin's white sash. Tialee then turned to Liaren. "After I speak with Nendra Halimuth and Reawakened Lovek, Liaren will document my choice, and any information I see fit to reveal to the Vigil."

Malory handed over the now glowing data pad to Liaren.

"This is just nonsense!" Connor barked. "A matter such as this should not be made into a game! They are withholding information they have no right to hide. Information I have worked my entire life to get!"

Tialee diverted processes to analyze the reactions to this statement. By far, Liaren was the one most opposed to Connor. Vigil Treys was in support of his opinion, and Malory Yumin seemed conflicted between that and Tialee's own recommendation. As for the other two, they in no way saw it as a game.

"Tialee has spoken," Liaren said to dismiss the older man. "Do not take our argument back in a loop."

The swiftness of Liaren's reply activated a sense of pride in Tialee. She had chosen the young girl as her new Vigil in hopes of encouraging the determination Liaren had displayed, both here and recently. Perhaps she would make a good projection someday.

"If the Vigil accepts my proposal, I will address Mrs. Halimuth and Reawakened Lovek now." Tialee looked to Vigil Treys for a final agreement. He was not entirely pleased, but Algan was always happy to see an outcome, one way or another. He gave his agreement with a low bow.

* * *

Liaren sat on the floor just outside the Head Vigil's meeting room and idly waved her fingers through the projection of the data pad. It had been nearly thirty minutes since they all left the room. Thirty minutes in which the Vigil would never know what was spoken, and thirty minutes in which Connor had paced the halls with a boiling anger.

"I just don't know why they would be keeping this information from the Vigil," Connor said angrily under his breath. "If Halimuth is privy to this information, I should be as well."

Liaren kept silent and tried to make her attention seem as if it was focused elsewhere. After all, she wanted nothing to do with provoking a murderer, especially since she was the only one in the hall with him. Vigil Treys had moved away early on, resigning to hear the information when it got to him, and Malory Yumin had grown tired of Connor's pacing.

"The entire point was to see what was there. No more hiding, no more secrets. A simple truth, for everyone."

Unfortunately, Liaren noticed that he had settled his pacing near her.

"The Remnants can handle it, don't you think? They have survived much worse. And why would the Warden stop helping them now?"

Liaren then realized that he was trying to win her to his side. She had almost forgot that he had no idea what she knew. Liaren drew in a breath, knowing that she needed to uncover new information, not what Tialee had already told her and Baxel.

"The Vigil has kept secrets from the Remnants before," she said. "Or at least details. I would say it is our place to have the knowledge they are withholding." It burned her to force an agreement with him, but Connor seemed to take it well.

"Thank you!" he said with a sharp gesture of his hand and a return to his pacing. "If only more of your people could think like you, Liaren."

To her, it seemed as if the man kept distancing himself from the Remnants within Safe Harbor at each turn they resisted him. Perhaps her endgame strategy would be to get him cast back out to Aura with the notion that he was slowly returning to the ways of the Aurans.

Connor pointed at the data pad in his continued frustration. "The Vigil should know everything, I hope you know that."

Liaren glanced down again to the data pad. She expected it would make him more than happy if she disregarded Tialee's decision and simply told Tialee to forget. For him, it would be just about as easy as ending a family line.

"There is nothing I can do about it," Liaren said in defensive agreement.

"No," Connor said with a shake of his head. "I would not have you change her decision, even if it meant as much as what you did for the Reawakened in the Core."

Liaren clenched her jaw. She felt disgusted ever going along with his plan in the Preservation Core now that she knew his hidden truth. He was evil, and she had played into exactly what he wanted. At the time she believed her decisions were her own, but she had been swayed under false pretenses.

"Liaren?" Baxel asked. He was standing above her, looking as if he had already tried to get her attention once before. "How are you doing?"

"Baxel? Why are you here?" Just behind him in the hallway, Varnil Williams was speaking with Vigil Connor.

"Varnil called it short today. He had an excuse about starting with a cautious pace, but he has been concerned about the probe all day." Baxel glanced back behind him as Varnil traded hushed, angry words with Connor. "I would say he was damned near furious that he did not know about this meeting."

As Connor raised his voice, Liaren turned her attention to what he was saying.

"You need to get a grip on your other Reawakened!" Connor hissed to Varnil. "She was supposed to get us information, not hide it!"

"What do you expect me to do, Vigil?"

Connor weighed the Reawakened with a harsh glare. "Threaten to put her back. You were the one chosen by the Vigil, but she was chosen by you. Her use is over because the probe is complete."

This time Varnil matched Connor's tone. "Why do we need that information? As I see it, we have pushed the ways of the Remnants enough. Kaiden would be ashamed to see me do more."

"Your son was converted to one of them, he said so himself! You must think straight, for your people, not the Remnants." Connor paused as if torn between turning away in anger or continuing his argument. He settled into a calmer tone with the same anger. "The Vigil has tried to stifle the idea of a return since before Sarthyl, and they will do it again, with any hiccup of an excuse they can find."

The display to the door of the Head Vigil's meeting room lit up and their conversation fell silent. Nendra Halimuth and the Reawakened Marrel Lovek stepped out of the meeting room and into the quiet of the hall. They both looked worried, worn, and perhaps a bit devoid of purpose now that the conversation was out of their hands. Liaren stood up, clutching the data pad.

"What did it say?" Connor asked.

"*She* only asked questions," the Reawakened replied. "Not particularly about . . ."

As Marrel trailed off, Nendra looked to Liaren. "Go inside now."

Liaren glanced at Baxel before stepping into the Head Vigil's meeting room. Tialee stood looking out the wide window into the middle of Safe Harbor. Only the lights of the structure and transports were visible in the current darkness.

"I would be glad to forget this conversation," Tialee said. "In all my years . . ." As she trailed off, she simply shook her head and let the silence of shifting transports in the distance take hold.

Liaren approached slowly. She had never seen her projection mentor act in this manner. The First Vigil never took a pause to think, nor started a sentence that she had no purpose in finishing.

"Tialee, I need your help."

"What do you mean?"

"You told me to come find you when we spoke in the Warden's Shrine."

Tialee let out a grunt of pain and held a hand up to her head. She caught herself with her other hand by pressing it against the glass and drew in a deep breath. "Liaren, what are you talking about?"

"Tialee? Are you okay?"

"I . . . yes. I am positive I am. It has just been a long day. A reset would do me good." After a moment, she seemed to regain her composure for the most part. She turned and motioned to the data pad. "Are you ready, Liaren?"

Liaren nodded, and Tialee continued, "The Vigil has to know. Unless the Warden says otherwise, it is their right. No matter how much . . ." Tialee flinched in pain again, though this time her entire being flickered. "No matter how damaging to the Remnants."

Liaren drew in a breath. "What did we find?"

She received only a questioning look from her mentor.

"Tialee, I need to know now. Before the rest of the Vigil. What you told me to do, I . . . I have no idea what I am doing. I need something, either your help or more information. I do not know how to stop Connor without betraying the secrets of the Warden."

"The probe sent back data that proved—" Tialee said flatly before letting out another gasp and turned to the side. "No! It is not my place to tell you before the rest of the Vigil! Liaren, I never spoke to you in the . . . I must maintain the Vigil. I must . . ." She looked with teary eyes to Liaren and held out a shaking hand. "Please, just mark down what I ask."

After a long pause, Liaren said, "Tialee . . . if you let the Vigil know, then Connor gets whatever information he believes he needs. But I need him to make a mistake. I need him to think someone knows what he did, that someone is trying to stop him. But that someone cannot be me." Liaren tapped the selection. "I need him to think that you do remember the murder of Dimarka. The Vigil must not know, and you must forget the information."

"Liaren! Why are you . . ." Tialee distorted in pain briefly. "By the Warden, these TEMP ID: headaches . . . why do I keep making the wrong judgments! Liaren, it was not even your place to record my decision. I intended to select Malory Yumin. Why did I not? Why could I not?"

This time, Liaren had to fight the tears in her own eyes. "I am sorry, Tialee. You are . . . you are family. I know that, and I am sorry. I wish I could keep you out of this, but the version of you in the Warden's suit knew it had to be me here, not Mrs. Yumin. She made you choose me. I just hope that version of you is actually giving me permission to betray your wishes and tell you to forget." Liaren took a breath and forced herself to continue. "Now, Tialee, I need you to ready information on Connor for me. Contacts, recordings, locations, anything you can get. And I need to know exactly what the probe found. I'll make my way to the Warden's shrine for everything you have when I can."

Liaren expected Tialee to have another fit of pain, but this time she just looked on in sad confusion.

"You said that there was another version of me, of my AI mirror, in the Warden's suit . . . you are not talking to me, are you?"

Liaren shook her head. "No, Tialee. But I am now. Forget this conversation."

* * *

Baxel pushed off the inside of the airlock once again, though the freedom of weightlessness was diminished by more than just the vast confines of the Preservation Core. When Liaren emerged from the room to the fits of Connor and the heavy silence of Varnil, she had simply passed the data pad off to the Vigil and found somewhere quiet to hide away. He was only back in the Core now because of the sharp command from the Reawakened. In fact, that biting order was the last thing Varnil had said.

Baxel tapped his jets to turn and face the observation room at the sound of the door opening.

Heavy steps identical to the pacing of Connor sounded in his helmet. "Varnil Williams, do not think giving me your silence will be enough!"

Baxel drew in a breath as his momentum continued to carry him away.

"You owe me, you know that, Varnil. By Vigil custom, this room is either empty for years at a time, or swarming with Vigil. Without me, your son would—"

"Don't you dare speak about him!"

Baxel was startled at the sudden anger in Varnil's reply.

"You meant nothing before, Reawakened! The Vigil kept you around like someone else's pet! Kaiden gave you a voice. Do not let that go to waste. They will listen to you now."

Baxel clenched his fist and kicked out at the nothing that surrounded him. "See! He did know about your connection!"

Varnil continued without acknowledging Baxel's comment. "Kaiden also gave me a sense of belonging, one that you seem to be losing by the cycle. I have my purpose, just as he did, and that purpose is not to tear the Remnants apart."

"Why do you resist what you know is right? Look here. Out this window. How does writing their names down help keep them alive? The Remnants are one disaster away from losing them all."

"Why do you care? Why do the lives in the Preservation Core mean more than those of the Remnants?"

"Varnil . . . I wish you could see. They have all kept us from Earth for far too long with lies and suppression. We have to go back. I know you feel it. Do not quit on me now."

Baxel waited in the silence of all but his own breathing as Varnil worked at an answer.

"Connor, I am afraid this is it. I have caused more change than any other Reawakened, save for Sarthyl himself. And even then, as he sought to tear Safe Harbor down, the Remnants continued as they always do. They survive. But by waking my son, I have forever changed how things continue from here on. If they are to use that change in finding a place on Earth, I want it to be their will . . . the Warden's will . . . that leads them to that change." Varnil took a deep breath and continued, "I am just a part. I will not let myself be the one who makes the Remnants once again fear the Reawakened."

"Then you are of no use to me," Connor muttered as he turned to leave.

"Wow," Baxel said as the heavy steps continued away. "I almost thought you were going to end up like Dimarka."

"What?"

"Uh, never mind. I'll be back to the names in just a few seconds."

"Good. At least I understand why the Vigil never gave him a long sash. You need the coordinates?"

"I got it," Baxel said. "And you didn't gather that when he had us break into the Vigil in the first place?"

Varnil let out a relenting laugh. "I should have known he would be scornful before he recommended using you. Connor was hoping your coordinator would reel you back into the search coordinates, but when that didn't happen, he just took the information to one of the other coordinators."

Baxel nearly slammed into one of the cryopods as he forgot to slow down. "He what? When?"

"The cycle of Dimarka's offsending, I believe. He was rather unhappy that it would be delayed. And something about where you had been. Something about . . . a cryopod."

"Wait, what about a cryopod?"

"I don't . . . know. It just seemed that he . . . said . . . or was it cryopods?"

"Sorry, what?" Baxel tapped on his helmet. There should be no reason for any interference this close. It had to be a problem on his end.

Varnil drew in a deep breath again. "Sorry, just a bit lightheaded all of a sudden. When I asked him . . . he said that the SE-S . . . wouldn't take his word. Because that is all he had. Or wanted to give them?"

Baxel put both of his feet on the front of one of the pods and looked up toward Varnil. He could clearly hear him breathing hard. "Varnil? Check the pressure of your room. Now."

"Oh, that's . . . not good. Airlock malfunction."

"Go! Get the door to the Vigil open before the pressure sensors—"

"It's already locked, Baxel. What . . . what now? Baxel?"

"You are going to black out. I just alerted Medical and Rescue. If they can get to you in under a few minutes—"

"And if they don't?" Varnil yelled, immediately gasping afterward.

Baxel kicked off the cryopod as hard as he could. "I'll be there in about fifteen seconds."

"Ah, shit. Baxel . . . I can't . . ."

As Baxel released heavy bursts of air to correct his course, he started weighing the odds. The rescue team would have to override the door or cut through it. Except that the Preservation Core connected directly to the open space of the Hall of the Vigil. They would have to evacuate the entire hall, unless they wanted to risk hundreds more lives. The only other way would be to cut straight through the outside of the ship into the void of the Preservation Core, but the odds of them getting to Varnil in time were still not good. Even in the zero coordinates of Safe Harbor, not everyone in a depressurization accident survived.

"Silence . . ." Varnil said weakly. "Not good, is it?"

Baxel could clearly see that the outer door of the airlock was open. Any breach should have been accompanied by a host of alarms, even if it was just an issue with the seals.

"Varnil!" Baxel yelled, hoping the man could still hear him. "Get to your cryopod!"

"No, I'm not . . ."

"Yes. I will get you out. Just get inside."

Baxel started releasing a significant amount of air as he fought to slow himself to a stop. Through the wide arc of windows, he could see Varnil crawling to the base of the pod. Baxel violently tumbled through the first open airlock door before finally stabilizing himself against the ceiling. There appeared to be a gap the length of the seal between the halves of the airlock doors, almost as if they had not closed properly. He gritted his teeth and pulled himself past the flow of air and down to the controls. Just as he feared, the activation of the airlock's controls did not take.

"Get moving, Reawakened! You are running out of time!" Baxel tried the panel again, but it flashed red. "Varnil? Varnil!"

Baxel cursed and cranked up the magnet in his glove and clamped it to the door. He pulled as hard as he could, but the barrier did not move. Baxel took a step back and let out a breath as he reweighed his options.

"Break in," he said to himself. Baxel looked around at the hard casing of steel and cursed again. He then hit a fist against his helmet at his own stupidity. "The glass. Break it."

Baxel pulled himself back out of the airlock and into the open space of the Preservation Core. He could see Varnil lying motionless halfway in the pod through the wide stretch of windows.

"Something sharp, something sharp and hard," Baxel said, looking around for what was available to him. He then looked down and ran his hands over his suit. "Oh hell, this better be enough."

As quickly as he could, Baxel began taking off one of his boots. They did nothing to seal the suit, as the under layer was the source of pressurization. He shook the boot with both hands, out from his chest and back in, trying to get a relative feel for its mass. Another glance toward the window told him that simply pounding on it would do next to no good.

"Momentum. I need lots of momentum." After a quick bit of thinking, Baxel checked his available oxygen, removed the second boot, and cranked up the magnets on his gloves. With one last breath, and the thought that he would look stupid if Varnil still ended up dead, Baxel kicked his suit into a dangerous maneuver. Years ago, he and Tymon had figured out that there was a limit to how fast they could spin, and it was largely based on core muscle strength and remaining oxygen. Baxel kicked the process in motion and began to pray for the best.

With a rapid decrease in the percentage of available oxygen, the Preservation Core soon turned to nothing more than a flashing and indistinguishable blur as Baxel's rotational velocity increased. Without the pull of the habitat gravity, he could not feel the slightest bit dizzy. Instead, it began to increasingly feel like the boots magnetically attached to the ends of his gloves were trying to pull away and tear his suit in two. Baxel focused on keeping his center of rotation and an eye on the timer. "Fifteen up, fifteen down."

As his oxygen plunged under half, Baxel started receiving a host of warnings about a pressurization malfunction. When his hands started to feel like they were about to burst from the blood flooding his fingers, the warnings about suit integrity started to flare in his helmet.

Baxel knew it was time, because that was all the suit would stand. He readied himself to release both boots at once. With luck, the even release would keep from misaligning his center of balance and sending him into a chaotic spiral. Then he realized that with one boot aimed at the glass, the other would fly the opposite direction out into the open room; he would be sending a projectile straight at the cryopods of the Preservation Core.

"Right release, count of three, left release, count of three point one. Begin, now!"

He took a breath and watched the countdown.

In an explosion of an instant, Baxel was jerked from one side to another, and in nearly the same amount of time, he lost consciousness.

* * *

Connor Sevison knew there was no joy to be found in what had been done. Varnil was an unnecessary casualty. If only he had properly convinced the man of the need to return to Earth . . . but time was running thin, and for far more than just himself. The fate of every person, both locked away in cryostasis and strung across the folds of space, hung in a balance that the Warden was desperately trying to tip.

As Connor Sevison crossed into the calm expanse of the Hall of the Warden, he was met by the low murmur of muted conversations mixing with the general hum of the *Fortuna*. He glanced up toward the Warden's Shrine, knowing all too well what the others did not: her threat was very real.

"Vigil Connor," a thin voice said from the side. It belonged to the SE-S head, Quervin. "You asked to see me?"

"Of course," Connor said, only taking his eyes off the shrine after a few more seconds. He looked to the man and gave him a small nod. "I was merely wishing to enquire about the tracking beacons."

Quervin produced a data pad and poked his fingers through a few places on the projection. "S-1 remains within the Hall of the Vigil. I believe the location to be the Preservation Core, given his assignment. S-2 is within the zero coordinates of Safe Harbor, on a Surefire-designated task."

"Good," Connor said. A brief glance at the data pad eased some of his worry concerning Varnil. If Baxel had somehow managed to make it out of the Preservation Core, it could have meant a possible failure in ending the Reawakened.

"There is one more thing," Quervin mentioned. "That comms receiver you enquired about some months ago. 90-3A. It received a signal. I know you told me to keep it separate from the network in case of a connection-based threat, but I really think we should turn this one over to Wardenson."

Connor took the man by the shoulder and started him walking. "I'm sure the director of transmissions is focused on Nendra Halimuth deciding to shut down his connections to the probe. And besides that, one day, you will be in a position to step up from the transmissions coordinator of the SE-S and take charge of all of Safe Harbor's systems. Knowing that, I am sure you can handle this small thing."

"There are others who—"

"No, Director Quervin. I might not see the day, but I assure you, you are the right Remnant for the job. I advocated for your support because of that. Perhaps you could show them that you are capable by easing Mr. Wardenson's burden of duty."

"But the transmission was from—"

"Don't worry about that," Connor said, steering him to walk through the memorials within the Hall of the Warden. "I can deal with the transmission. It would likely be sent to the Vigil anyway. Just hand it over to me, and keep an eye out on 90-3A and the two trackers." When the transmissions coordinator looked as if he was going to express another doubt, Connor continued, "How are things with your wife?"

"I . . . j-just fine."

"Good. I'm glad that small change to the genetic lists has not been reverted. It would be tragic if she learned that she actually did not have to leave her previous romantic partner on account of genetic incompatibility."

"Yes, that would be most . . . I'll make sure you get the transmission, Vigil Connor."

As Connor motioned for the man to leave, he was left once again with the stinging thought that had persisted for the majority of his life. In his youth, he truly had wanted to become part of the Remnants. When he first arrived in Safe Harbor and saw the lives of these people, he had no intention of ever leaving. It was Sarthyl's failure that ultimately forced Connor to betray himself and his own choice. Now, he was the one being forced to split his soul to save the lives of those to come. If only the Warden was willing to give as much.

* * *

Baxel pulled in a deep breath several moments later to oxygen warnings and a distorted view of the slowly shifting lights of the Preservation Core. He held both hands up to his helmet at the intense pain in his eyes and head. His heart started running in fear as he used the bottom percent of his oxygen to twist around.

There was no telling how much time had passed. The automatic stabilizers would have kicked in when his monitored stats went haywire. Hopefully, the pieces of glass still lazily spinning along the exterior of the room meant he was not too late. Baxel had to wiggle to get through the gap between the angularly frayed top of the glass and the indented wall above. It was all too tight of a fit, but when he got more than halfway through, the artificial gravity of the room took care of the rest. Baxel landed hard on his back, but there was no sound save for what he heard in his suit. He rolled over with a groan and made his way to Varnil.

"Come on, Varnil. Be alive." Baxel wrestled him ungracefully into the pod and hit the cryogenics sequence. The display flashed.

Warning: Obstruction. Please ensure cryopod hatch is clear.

Baxel jammed Varnil's foot further in and slapped the panel again. This time, the doors to the pod began to close.

Baxel fell back onto the ground and looked at the rolling gasses behind the small windows of the pod.

He held a shaking hand up to his helmet to contact the Medical and Rescue Sector. When the emergency handler asked about the status of the Reawakened, Baxel could only slap a hand frustratedly against the floor.

"He's in the cryopod. That's all I had to work with."

Chapter 20: Clearance

"I told you," Oa repeated from over Kara's shoulder as she continued to bash at the metal, "I want your people to forget us."

"Fine." Kara gritted her teeth as she sawed with the heated blade through the thick metal of the pod. The wrap around her hand was starting to warm up uncomfortably now. At first it had helped against the constant heat, but nearly an hour of twisting and prying was more than enough to put sweat on her brow. "If you won't tell me about your people, tell me something about yourself. What was the most surprising thing when you got to Earth? The people? The trees? I can't imagine growing up there."

Oa looked up from the data pad. From the glare, Kara knew she was not going to get an answer. To Kara's surprise, however, Oa set Reclaim's partial schematics to the side.

"It was the wind, actually."

"The wind?" Kara set the knife to the side and shook the wrapping off her hand.

"Imagine any airflow you have ever known has either been from the vents recirculating filtered air, or from damaged systems spilling it out into the void. Sometimes it is still hard to wrap my head around where it goes or how it is contained."

Kara scoffed. "It's not. Not really."

"Of course it is. Everything is part of a system. Yours just happens to be the entire Earth."

"Alright," Kara said, shaking her hand before bringing the cloth back around in a loose wrap. "What about us? The people you didn't think existed."

"Crime. Betrayal. Lack of resource conservation and the constant fighting over those same unconserved substances. Perhaps most of all is this fascination with Cryos. For us, the Reawakened were supposed to be respected, but we did not need their ways." She motioned broadly around the Prime Elect's hangar. "Reclaim is obsessed with the idea of rebuilding what humanity had in the past, but I've seen what that can lead to."

Kara picked up the knife and waited for the edge to heat up. The thick steel had torn several notches into the blade. "I wish I could convince you that your Sarthyl was nothing like Jance."

"Why do you keep defending her rather than yourself? I have seen them all change. She may not have lived long enough to change, but she would have. Just remember, everyone has a world they will put first, whether it can still be saved or not."

Kara gripped the hot knife in a tight hand. "She saw her world and ours, or at least her world and mine, as one and the same. We are her people, regardless of what she has lost."

Oa frowned. "Why do you torment yourself? You saw Overlord Obrourke for what he was. You did well to bury him, and you would do well to bury the Cryo you uncovered."

Kara let the temperature of the knife fade. It slid from a hot red glow to a distorted haze around the grey blade as Kara's thoughts darkened toward the woman.

Oa took a step back and searched Kara's expression for an answer.

"I will *never* believe that Jance would turn against this world. Garneth Obrourke was twisted by demons of his own making, and I don't know what the hell was wrong with Sarthyl before the Remnants found him, but Jance is not, nor would she ever be, anything like them. I was standing next to her when the transport exploded, and I would do so again, because I believe she will do great things for this world."

Oa crossed her arms and frowned. "If you lived, then did she?"

Kara reactivated the knife and looked into the humming glow. "I don't know. But we still have a deal, Oa, regardless of what the torments of your past say about Cryos."

She plunged the knife back into the long and jagged gash she had created in the hull of the pod. As the heat pressed against her face once again, she knew this was a technician's work. She should be dangling from the heights or threading her way down further into the underlayers of the land, not scowling through sweat at the glow of metal. It was another fifteen minutes of unpleasant work until Kara made a full circuit back to the start of her two-foot square.

"Nearly in," Kara said, standing up and rolling her shoulders. She turned around and put her back to the pod. Only her shoulders touched as she leaned against the pod well above the cut line, however, even as high up as her shoulders she could feel the warmth in the metal. With a grunt, Kara pulled her knee up and slammed her boot square against the surface. The steel square popped, falling into the probe. She hopped away on one foot to keep from touching the harsh edges with her leg.

"Now what?" Oa asked, leaning over to look in.

Kara flipped the searing knife in the air and caught it. "We find the battery."

* * *

"Zaireel Tuakana is ready to give his report," Sora said, nearly juggling to keep up with all her data pads. Olana motioned for her to establish the connection. She stood in what was once the First Administrator's office. She had chosen the flat steel walls over the chaos Kenneth had made of the library to leave him to his task of finalizing Travend's position.

The large display was set up on the other side of the desk, though she wished her end was more elaborate. If it were either Jance's or her own desk back in Kamriek's Grove, then she might have been satisfied, as those displays would have adequately showed her wealth and influence as Overlord. Olana placed her glass cube down and finished smoothing her uniform as her emissary appeared on the display. Perhaps she would have to have someone retrieve her proper desk.

"Overlord Nuand," Zaireel said, giving a bow of his head. "I am happy to report that our presence has been largely welcomed in Reclaim. While the Prime Elect's underlings have inquired about the order you have imposed on Norclave, the most common question from the people of Reclaim has been about the Cryo. Per your orders, we have refrained from confirming her death."

Olana put a knuckle to her chin in thought. "Have the Prime Elect's people been specifically avoiding speaking of the Cryo?"

"No," Zaireel answered. "While they have left the subject out of meetings, private conversations have revealed genuine sympathy over her death, and for what happened on the docks."

"I know it is early, and you have yet to meet with the Prime Elect, but what is your initial analysis of Norclave-Reclaim relations?"

"Much of the tension with the previous Overlord and his administrators seems to have been set aside. Reclaim is waiting to see what Norclave is now, and if we can show that we have control over our own rival factions, I believe we have a real shot at a good relationship."

"Very good," Olana said. "Keep at it, and extend my offer to a meeting with the Prime Elect when he gives you a chance."

"There is one more thing, Overlord."

"Yes?"

Zaireel's expression of optimism seemed to fade into concern. "The tech hunter, Kara, is in the city."

"Kara is there?" Sora asked from the side. "Why is Kara there?"

Zaireel continued, "She did not make contact, but we passed in the halls of the Prime Elect's Citadel."

This time Olana picked up the glass cube and began rolling it between her hands. She doubted very much if the tech hunter had made her way in on account of the mysterious sky flare that had landed in Reclaim territory. That would mean Travend's men had entered the city, and if she had followed them to the Prime Elect's Citadel, something was definitely questionable about the situation.

"Do not attempt contact. If she reaches out to you, so be it, but we cannot risk putting them on edge. We must give the Prime Elect the benefit of any doubts we may have."

"Yes, Overlord," Zaireel said, giving a salute across his chest.

"Contact me again as scheduled." Olana nodded to Sora and the woman cut the transmission.

"Do you believe that?" Sora asked. "Are we to put that much trust in the Prime Elect?"

"Absolutely not, and the Prime Elect knows that. If he is smart, he will realize that I know what he has done. I intend to force him to take the overly hopeful, wishy washy peace offerings by making it clear that I will release the evidence to his people otherwise."

"What evidence? Does Kara being in Reclaim mean he ordered the assassination of Jance?"

"There *is* no evidence. I cannot admit to sending Kara to Reclaim, because he will cover it as an attempt to spy on his newfound object. However," Olana said, putting the cube in her pocket, "if we eliminate Travend and capture a few of his people, we can make up whatever evidence we want."

"I'll tell Kenneth about Kara and then—"

"No." Olana glared meaningfully at her. "You do not mention this to anyone, especially the technician. I need his mind on one thing. Travend. My teams are ready to go, and my position hinges on Travend's capture."

Sora looked to the ground for a moment, but eventually she looked back up. "Yes, Overlord Nuand."

* * *

"So, what's the plan? You just tear the battery out?" Oa's question came as a muffled echo to where Kara was half inside the pod. Behind her, Oa leaned over and tried to see past Kara.

"No, I plant the knife in it, and we try to be as far away as possible."

"When do we need to go? Are you doing it now?"

Kara grunted as she tried to look back toward Oa. The metal pressed hard against her side. "I already did. Twice." Kara pulled the glowing knife out of the large battery to use as a light. From everything Kenneth had showed her, the battery was supposed to start heating up the entire knife. Kara took a breath and plunged the knife back in. The power source for the pod was a brick nearly two feet across and four or five inches thick.

"Dammit." Kara took another breath and pulled the knife back through the tangle of cables. She sat it on some other casing to the side and reached back up through the cables. This time, she poked at what was marked as the power source with a finger. To her surprise, it felt like stiff mud in a plastic package. She stuck a finger into one of the knife holes and tried to pull at the outer coating.

"You sure you know what you are doing?" Oa asked.

"Oh yeah, absolutely." Kara picked the knife back up and started cutting long slashes in the battery. "I actually prefer to work with observation probes that drop out of the sky."

Kara took a breath and shifted to her back. If anything, the battery should have stopped working from the number of cuts all the way through. "This isn't a safety battery of some sort, is it?"

"I couldn't say. It's been fifty years since I was up there. And even then, I didn't do anything with maintenance past my twenty-thousand cycles. You sure you can do this?"

Kara wiped the sweat from her eyes on her shoulder. The systems running inside the probe kept the temperature hotter than any day she had experienced. "Yes, Oa! I said I could do this, that means I can. There is always another plan."

"Oh yeah, and what is yours now?"

Instead of targeting the power source directly, Kara began slashing at the cables. She squinted at the few bright sparks as she raked into the mess. Another thing that looked important, she stabbed into and twisted. Then she turned to a dark box that had a number of little lights and started cutting it loose from the wall. If she couldn't get the thing to blow up, she at least wanted to make it as difficult as possible to put back together. The lights flickered as the box dropped down, hanging next to her head by a frayed wire. Kara cut the wire, dropping the box down into the bottom of the pod. Suddenly the inside of the miserable thing lit up with a deep red.

"That might have done it?"

"We have to be sure," Oa said.

Another batch of sparks fell down from above. This time, Kara started to wiggle her way out of the small hole. She let out a gasp of pain as she wedged her sling through with her other hand and fell to the ground outside the device.

"That's as good as we get, Oa, unless you brought a grenade with you." Kara looked in the pod as the lights started flickering along with growing flames. "Or maybe not."

When Kara looked back to Oa, she could see tears running down her wrinkled face. "Thank you, Kara. I . . . thank you."

"Yeah, whatever." Kara stretched her neck and adjusted the sling with a grimace. "Let's get out of here."

"Yes," Oa said with a satisfied nod. "We have plenty of work to do. The Prime Elect will not come after you directly, because of me, but that is not to say he has no means to reach you." She reached a hand down to Kara. "Now, what do you mean to do with the ones who tried to kill your Cryo?"

Kara did her best to stand up on her own, but exhausted and with one arm in a sling, the help was welcome. "I need to take one of them back to Norclave."

Oa nodded to Kara as she came to her feet. "Then it is nothing a tech hunter and a fallen Warden cannot handle," the old woman said.

Kara laughed. "An old woman and a cripple."

Oa did not argue the point as they left the smoking mess of the pod behind them in the Prime Elect's hanger.

* * *

The streets of Reclaim watched uneasily as Hakatha and several other of his Black Scars walked in the open daylight. Normally, as per the Prime Elect's recommendation, they were to either hide their black-filled scars or keep to the side alleys. To many people about the city, they were known only as a criminal organization, though over the years since Iben Feirshan's rise to power, the connection between them and the watch had become less secret.

Hakatha directed a hard glare at anyone who seemed to pay too much attention. Merchants, commoners, and even some of the watch knew to look to the side. It was not until he neared the top of the ramp leading down to the center level of the city that he was stopped by a young man in blue-painted flight armor.

"Hold there," the young man said with all the confidence of ignorance. "I need some information."

Their one Black Scar hound let out a low growl, and Hakatha heard a couple chuckles from his own people from behind. Hakatha gripped the bloodied muzzle he was carrying and looked to the watch with a wide-eyed stare. "I'll let you ask."

"To . . . ah, to start I'll need your name." The young man glanced at the hound behind Hakatha as it fought against the hand that gripped its collar. The data pad the watch held started to flicker and dance as he shook with uncertainty.

"Look at me, boy." Hakatha took a step forward. "Do not worry about the hound. I am what you need to worry about."

One of the other watch at the security point finally looked up from his conversation. "Arken! What do you think you are doing!"

"Commander Kalet, these are Black Scars! They have no business roaming the streets!"

As the younger watch turned away to reply to his commander, Hakatha pressed the muzzle into the chest piece of his armor. The harsh pops of electricity burned away two points of paint and exposed the dull metal underneath. The watch took a startled swing at Hakatha, but he ducked the strike. Hakatha then replied with several brutal hits to the man's uncovered ribs with the muzzle and one final kick to the back of his knee to send him to the ground.

"Watch it, Black Scar!" the commander of the group shouted. "The Prime Elect will not tolerate violence in his streets!"

Hakatha glanced back to his group, which still outnumbered the standing watch. He walked forward and bumped his chest against the commander's and looked down from his six inches of height. Hakatha then put the muzzle to his own neck and let the sparks jump for a few seconds. He could feel his muscles contract and the tissue around his blackened scars heat up. However, the charge device imbedded into the skin above his collarbone immediately reacted to the current and nullified most of the effect. It was a trick he had used on numerous occasions to keep the Black Scars in check. This time, the watch looked on in identical fear. "If the Prime Elect wants to avoid violence," Hakatha warned, "then you need to look the other way."

With word spreading amongst the watch in the checkpoint, Hakatha continued his way down to the Prime Elect's Citadel. He took a moment to look up at it from the base. The Prime Elect preferred to keep those who did his dirty work as far away from the Citadel as possible. Hakatha grunted with satisfaction and strode up to the doors. He was pleased to find what one of his scouts had said would be there.

"Are you Hama? Oa's servant?"

The small man looked nervously at the group now surrounding his bench. "Ye . . . yes. Well, I wouldn't necessarily say servant. More of a—"

Hakatha punched him in the stomach and held the muzzle there long enough that he would be as good as unconscious. He pulled back and motioned for one of the others to catch Oa's servant before he hit the ground. Hakatha felt the tingles that stood the hair on his neck on end and laughed. After so long hiding in the shadows and playing Feirshan's game, it felt good to be off the leash.

"You sure this is a good idea, Hakatha?"

He turned sharply to the one second-guessing him. "What are they gonna do to us? Huh? He's not dead. Put him in the corner." Hakatha started away and motioned for them to follow. He knew the Prime Elect would never have the spine to stand up to Oa about the tech hunter. Oa would find Hama unconscious outside the Citadel and get the message. The tech hunter was not wanted in the city.

* * *

"So, what is our plan? How are we going after them?" Kara asked as they stepped out of the hangar, accompanied by the smell of burning wires. She tried to avoid making eye contact with the large guard outside the door. Oa patted him on the shoulder and followed Kara away into the hall.

"I'm sorry, what was that, dear? Did you say a plan? I thought you were just going to chase after them like you did before."

Kara looked to Oa with narrowed eyes. "I'll have you know I wasn't counting on the transport. I would have had them all had I not been rushed."

"And still you jumped." Oa wagged a finger at Kara and clicked her tongue to the top of her mouth. "Here is how we do this. We start with getting you a place to hide. We cannot have a plan if you wind up in a holding room or at the mercy of the Scars."

"Great," Kara said with a roll of her eyes. Personally, she was hoping to cut her losses by capturing one and throwing him into a stolen transport and then returning to Norclave. Or better yet, leave the captive at the Rift Outpost or Kamriek's Grove with a "you owe me" note for Olana Nuand.

"It is called 'pre-planning,' Kara." Oa gave her a knowing look with an antagonizing sparkle mixed in. "You should try it once in a while."

"Did you?" Kara asked as they rounded the corner into the main hall of the Citadel. "When you were left with no air and no allies when they were blowing holes in your settlement?"

"I was aided by six centuries of planning."

"Well good. With you alone, I have at least two hundred more."

Oa rolled her eyes when she caught the meaning. "That's right. Now keep walking. And try to wipe away some of that sweat. You look like hell."

As Kara ran a rag over her face, she suddenly noticed two of the men, the ones who tried to kill Jance, being led down a side passage. It took everything she had to leave them a second time, especially when the one missing a hand glanced back at her. Just like Alek Skaves wandering through the under-levels of Norclave, he knew something was catching up to him, even if not who or when. Something about the look in his eyes bothered Kara.

"Kara!" Oa said, jabbing a sharp elbow into her ribs. "Patience!"

Kara stumbled a partial step at the pain of Oa hitting her bad arm and managed to look away. She pocketed the rag and they both continued past the few Norclave soldiers and on toward the entrance of the Citadel.

As they stepped out into the open air, Kara immediately noticed a medical team off to the side. They wore suits of flight armor much like the watch, though the chest piece was painted white and had a blue double cross in the center and the back. There were three of them gathered around a man lying on the bench.

"Hama?" Kara asked. Oa's helper was pale-faced and shaking as one of the medical team tried to get him to slide a blood pressure band over his wrist. One of the members of the medical team held a hand out for Kara to stay back, but a look from Oa made him step to the side.

"What happened?" Oa asked.

"It was . . . it was nothing," Hama said, trying his best to manage a calming smile.

"As far as we can tell," one of the medical team replied, "a group of thugs were wandering the streets. I'm going to recommend we take him inside for a closer look."

Oa let out a breath and nodded. "I think that would be best."

As the team helped Hama up and started inside, Kara stepped closer to Oa.

"Why would they do this to Hama? It wasn't the Prime Elect already, was it?"

Oa shook her head and directed her worried gaze at the ground. "No, this would be too hasty of a reaction from him, even if he knew what we were doing to the pod. The way I see it, his thug in chief, Hakatha, is trying to send me a message. He wants me to give you up, and he thinks that I cannot go to the Prime Elect for help because they still suspect you of being some kind of spy."

"And? What is your plan?"

"To take a phrase I learned early on from your world: 'You cannot cross a bridge until you reach it.'"

* * *

Kenneth watched from the seclusion of the Norclave Library as the last trails of daylight faded from the many displays on the desk. As he moved to rub his eyes, his knuckles brushed against the once-broken visor he had all but forgotten he still had on. At his own recognition, the device lit up and projected the small, artificially refracted display screen. Kenneth pulled it free and set it to the side to finish rubbing his face.

When he finally opened his eyes, he barely caught a glimpse of one of the displays on the desk distorting. By the time he realized what had happened, the door to the room slid open and the program hunter stepped in.

Rather than the rugged and hidden functionality of a tech hunter, this man sported an outfit demanding attention. The program hunter was not a tall man, but the lighted pieces of armor and the projected teal cape hanging from one shoulder would have given him presence in any space. The man looked around the room, though Kenneth could not see his expression, as he wore a full helmet of a dark carbon plastic.

"Imagine this . . ." he said with an air of awe. "The Norclave Library." He reached both hands up to remove his helmet, giving Kenneth a view of his narrow eyes, dark hair pulled up in a high tail, and his striking lack of scars. Kenneth had come to assume anyone who frequented zones other than the high streets of cities had more than their share of harsh experiences. It seemed this man was different.

"The library is not what it once was," Kenneth replied. "Both the administrators and the new Overlord ransacked the place for what they believed useful."

"In my experience, what others take means little to the value of a place." The man clasped his hands together and folded the helmet between them. Kenneth had to blink as the halves of the helmet slid down and fastened around the forearm-length gloves that were made of the same glossy black. The gloves were blemished by a number of deep scratches and several worn patches, but the condition was far and above nearly everything in Norclave.

"I half expected that you wouldn't show."

The man gave no reply as something sitting to the side caught his attention. Without hesitation, he produced a device from a line of pouches crossing his dark, travel-worn coat. The program hunter leaned to look at a closed container on one of the lower shelves and a bright grid projected out from his device. "You have a nano-field generator next to a potted plant?"

"It was here before I was. Leave it alone."

The man took a step away and raised his hands apologetically. "Sorry, I didn't mean to . . ." He trailed off as he spotted something else on the other side of the cluttered aisle. Without lowering his hands, he pointed the scanner at another object.

"Stop that!" Kenneth barked.

The program hunter quickly tucked his scanner back into a pocket and clasped his hands behind his back. The projected cape flickered as it readjusted the image to hang loosely over his arms. "But is that really a scanning head for a molecular sequencer? I swear I've been looking for one of those for—"

"Hey!" Kenneth shouted as he slapped a hand on the desk. After a moment, Kenneth sat back down. "I swear, where does Mackelry find people like you? What is your name?"

"My name is Error. That's all you need to know."

"Error? Really? That's . . . cute." Kenneth rubbed his brow with a grimy hand. At least Kara had the courtesy to tell him off when he first asked for her name.

"Cute?" He held his arms out and the lights on his boots, gloves, and the shoulder cape all flicked to a fiery red.

"Ooo, now I'm scared. Will you quit messing around and get over here, Error?"

The program hunter took a breath and tapped at a display that briefly appeared over one wrist. The colors returned to their original shades of teal. He hurried to the front of the room and immediately spotted the processing unit propped up on a crate. Error knelt down beside it with all the concern of a man tending to a pet. He let out a breath of relief and ran his hands over the glowing intakes of the device now tasked with piecing together a location for Travend.

"When the technician called," Error said quietly as he slid a gloved finger down the side of the case, "I was afraid they dropped you . . ." A series of displays appeared under a bright projector on the side from his touch. He glanced up with an unhappy look back to Kenneth. "You couldn't find a real table for her? Do you know how much she is worth? There's a reason I only let Norclave have her on a very pricy loan!"

"Your device is fine," Kenneth said. "I asked you here about this one." He motioned to Jance's desk.

Error raised an eyebrow and rose to his feet. He moved toward the desk with a cautious curiosity. "This is . . . now this is incredible!"

Kenneth blocked him with his scarred arm and put on as deadly of a look as he could manage. "Whatever you think the value of your little toy is, it has nothing compared to what this is. I give you fair warning: just seeing this is enough reason for the Overlord to make you disappear."

The program hunter laughed. "It's not like I'm going to put a virus in it. This is the Cryo's work!" He took a step to the side to get around Kenneth and started toward the desk.

"How did you know . . . wait, a virus?" Kennth tried to grip his cape but only ended up with a humming handful of air. He then settled on jerking the man back by the collar of his coat before shoving him into one of the shelves. As Error caught his balance and turned around, Kenneth gripped his shoulder and shoved him back into the shelf. "What do you mean, a virus?"

"No, no, no, don't get all worried. I don't actually have one. Well, not a real one. I'm not sure they existed. At least not the super virus kind you are probably thinking about." He winced as Kenneth gripped a mounting bracket for one of the cameras to use as a club.

"I mean, the Last Edict was trying to make one. Well, everyone was, actually." Error tried to push Kenneth's hand away but stopped short with another glance to the chunk of metal Kenneth was holding ready. "Don't get me wrong, I think the problem was not in destroying systems, or even differentiating between 'friend' and 'not friend.' The problem was getting it to viably spread. When nearly every device is equipped to handle nearly any threat, the entire adaptive system would quickly figure out how to block it. Actually, much better than they could deal with real viruses, funnily enough. B-but to get back to the point, I don't have any viruses. Not really."

"Not really?" Kenneth poked the bracket into the program hunter's chest.

"Hey, watch it now! The best I have can only affect a single system. It's pretty much just a digital acid. Not, that I would ever damage the Cryo's system, just to be clear."

"Just to be clear, if anything happens to this system, I am breaking your arms."

"Umm, y-yep. But I left that one at home so . . ."

Kenneth finally shoved the camera bracket back on the shelf and turned away, leaving Error to brush the spot of rust off his coat.

"Are you any good at hacking?" Kenneth asked as he moved back to the desk.

"Uh, probably not how you are thinking," Error replied. "You see, all you really can do is know which programs to run. The things they do, they have to outpace all the manual inputs to do anything of use. Not that anybody alive quite understands how it really works. What do you need to get past?"

"A clearance lock. I need into certain sections of information."

"Yeah, sure." He opened another one of the pouches crossing his chest and produced several data chips. Each had their own display, almost like a miniature data pad. "Standard, that's basically zero problem, ever. Select clearance, I've got several ways. Priority is where it gets tricky, though. Depending on the different specializations, it requires a different combination of programs. One to act as a false threat, another to—"

"How about Council?"

The program hunter fell silent and crossed his arms. "Alright, just stop right there. How about you explain to me what feels wrong with this entire situation? Are the other rumors not true? Did the Cryo of Norclave die? And does that mean she really was a member of the UWC Council?"

"Jance Lorège is still under medical care. She locked any incoming signals under her Council clearance."

"Okay," Error nodded. "What is the time frame? Why can you not wait for the Cryo to recover?"

Kenneth motioned over toward Error's machine. "Once that is done running the numbers, Olana is going to force me out of here, if not Norclave altogether. I'm only allowed in here because she needs me to find someone else."

"So . . . the person you want to find now is not the original one you needed my analysis machine to find. Another person?" He rubbed his smooth chin, looking to the device in thought. "What have you heard about the underwater islands off the Shattered Coast?"

Kenneth raised an eyebrow. "The what now?"

"I was thinking of going there . . . just now. Perhaps taking a transport to Reclaim, then hiring an expedition team to take me the hell away from this place."

"Oh no you don't . . ." Kenneth growled. "I found a way past the Priority Command clearance lock on a cryopod to bring Jance into our world. The least you can do is look."

Error's thoughts of fleeing seemed to fade as he looked to Kenneth with renewed interest. "Did I hear you right? Even in Carvanhold, inside the *Nemesis Tide* dreadnought, nobody has come across anything higher than Command clearance. And that takes ages to get around. In fact, that . . ." Error trailed off as he realized what he had let slip.

"So there is a chance?" Kenneth pressed. "If you can beat military systems, we have a shot at this?"

Error sighed. "Why don't you just do it then? If you could unlock the cryopod—"

Kenneth interrupted. "How long do you need?"

Error rubbed a hand over his head. "I need at least twenty hours, and you to never mention anything about being able to get past

Command. There are, uh, people who don't like that I know that it is possible. Oh, and if you could," the program hunter said, pointing over his shoulder, "the scanning head. It would complete a set of mine."

Chapter 21: Missing Light

Baxel rubbed his sore and heavily bloodshot eyes as he sat on the medical bed, though the painful motion did nothing to restore the loss of vision in his left eye that had come after he'd lost consciousness from spinning. Other than that, the nearly deafening headache, and the engulfing bruises down his arms, Baxel felt fine. Baxel gripped his head and let out a slow breath. Everything was fine.

His feet did not come close to reaching the ground as the bed was left unadjusted from when the medical staff had been running tests. He knew the sensors on the side of his head—currently relaying diagnostics to several displays about the room—were monitoring for possible hemorrhagic conditions, but he had lost track of everything else in the whirling pressure venting of activity and tests. The same forces that caused his arms and eyes to bruise had also sparked concern regarding his brain. Baxel figured his throbbing headache agreed with the med-techs.

"Did they retrieve Varnil yet?" Baxel asked of one of the few remaining staff working off to the sides of the room. While there had been a swarm of activity centered around him earlier, now he felt as if he had been all but forgotten. "Do they know if Varnil Williams is alive?"

One of the med-techs gave him a pitying glance. "The only information we have is about you. Now try to relax. Others are doing what they can, I am sure." She turned back to her work at one of the stations.

Baxel grimaced and put a hand to his forehead. "Then how long was I unconscious?"

The silence he received seemed to come from everywhere in the room. The woman paused what she was doing, simply letting her fingers hover above a projected control panel. She glanced to the head med-tech as if she was unsure what to say.

"Tell them he is ready now," the head med-tech quietly told her. He finally turned to Baxel. "We have been asked to leave the room, but we are still monitoring your vitals." He motioned with a data pad and tapped the access panel to the other door to the room. "Just take things easy, and slow."

"Wait! How long was I unconscious? If it was more than a few seconds or so . . ."

The head med-tech sighed and turned around. "It was ten minutes, or near enough." He looked to Baxel with a grim expression before continuing out of the room, leaving Baxel alone to realize that he had been too late to save Varnil Williams.

"No . . ." Baxel said, now looking at nothing in the room. It had to be some sort of malfunction in their systems. Or perhaps the forces exerted on his helmet had caused something to go wrong. Perhaps . . .

"—and if you would please, just take it slow. Give him his time," the voice of the first med-tech sounded through the opening door.

"Back off," Flerin growled, shouldering past Connor to be the first to enter the room. Oundara nodded her thanks to the woman and followed behind in her typical collected form.

"Baxel!" Flerin said, making his way across the room in long strides. "You look . . . well, you're alive." Flerin patted him on the shoulder. "That always counts for something."

"Baxel," Oundara started, "if you are feeling well enough, we are here for a report on what happened in the Preservation Core."

"What happened to the Reawakened?" Connor asked. Oundara shot him a glare for his out-of-line question.

"Varnil is . . ." Baxel looked up with his bloodshot eyes. "Varnil is dead."

"Dead?" Oundara asked. "I thought you got him into the pod?"

"If their readings are right," Baxel said with a dull motion to the tech equipment, "I . . . didn't get to him in time. I made a mistake."

Flerin gripped his shoulder. "I'm sure you did all you could, Baxel. No one could have done better."

"How did it happen?" Oundara asked.

"The air began leaking out of the room to silent alarms. Varnil did not know what to do and I . . . the door leading into the Hall of the Vigil was already locked."

"The failsafes," Vigil Connor said. "I'll alert maintenance and notify the Vigil to stay out of the Preservation Core."

"No," Baxel said as his thoughts whirled through his screaming headache. "The door to the hall was locked. After Vigil Connor left the Core, the door to the hall was locked. He was the last one to touch it."

"No, you must be mistaken. I could not have been there, I was in a meeting with—"

Baxel slapped his hand against the medical bed. He had been sworn to silence regarding Tialee's knowledge of Dimarka, but nothing was stopping him from sharing what he knew of the death of the Reawakened. "Vigil Connor sabotaged the airlock! He left after his argument with Varnil—"

The migrant shook his head. "Oundara, Flerin, you can see he is speaking nonsense. We need to call the med-techs."

"You locked his way out far before the pressure differential systems should have engaged!"

"Baxel," Flerin said with an eye to the monitors, "just calm down. This is nobody's fault."

"Listen to your coordinator, boy," Connor advised. He then took a softer tone. "I know how hard it is when you let someone slip through your fingers. I was in the habitats when Sarthyl ripped them open."

"You killed Varnil because he was done helping you! All you can think about is returning to Earth!"

As Flerin stepped in the way, trying to calm him, Connor looked apologetically to Oundara. "This is my fault," he told her. "We should have given him more time to recuperate."

Baxel started to shout something else, but Flerin gripped both sides of his head and forced his attention away from the Vigil.

"Focus on me, Baxel. You need to stop. Nothing you are saying is going to help."

"No! He did this. All of this. Firebrand is dead because Connor knew we had left the search coordinates. Varnil said Connor knew what we found."

This time, Flerin drew back for a moment in thought. "What did you and Tymon find that day?" He glanced behind him to where Oundara was finishing her conversation with the Vigil. "Is that what you were stashing supplies for? To go out again? You know how hard that was to cover for?"

"The supplies? That's what you're worried about?"

"I'm just . . . trying to figure out where this all is coming from, Baxel."

"Are you? Because the Reawakened of Safe Harbor is dead. When has that ever happened?"

Flerin ducked his head. They both knew the answer. Besides a failed cryogenesis from the pods, a Reawakened had never died in Safe Harbor.

"Baxel, I know you feel . . . betrayed, by the Remnants, by the Vigil, and maybe even by me, but this is not the answer. Connor is not Sarthyl."

Baxel looked away from his former coordinator. "Varnil was starting to think he was just the same."

"Flerin," Connor said behind him to call his attention as a host of med-techs started into the room.

Oundara followed Connor as the migrant turned to leave, and Flerin stood up.

"Try and get some rest, Baxel," Flerin said. He gave Baxel one last pat on the shoulder. "I need you to try and pull through this."

* * *

After a number of difficult cycles, the Vigil convened to accept their new Reawakened in Varnil Williams's place. Marrel Lovek agreed to take his position under the same rules that a newly awakened might. While she had learned quite a deal about the Remnants since she was woken to work on the probe, Marrel would be taught more about their history and the role of the Reawakened. The one matter still under debate was when she would be granted Varnil's list of the Preservation Core. Some said immediately, other said two years to match the standard set by Varnil.

Liaren kept from saying anything in the matter.

"Not yet, Liaren," Malory Yumin said, advising her to stop as they reached the top of the steps leading to the Warden's Shrine. "There is one more group seeking the Warden's guidance before us."

Liaren pulled back from her thoughts and took her foot down from the final step. They were not the only ones waiting. They had spent nearly thirty minutes in the line to visit the shrine. The wait was longer than Liaren remembered it, but she knew the line was nothing compared to what it had been like in the past. She had heard from some of the Vigil older than Mrs. Yumin that when the Warden returned the armor after defeating Sarthyl, every remaining Remnant made the journey up the steps.

"How is your friend? The one who was helping Varn.l?" Malory asked in a respectfully quiet voice, trying yet again to break the silence that had followed them up the steps.

"Still confined to the Medical and Rescue Sector. He is healing though."

Malory glanced over to Liaren. "Perhaps the Vigil could help him climb the steps, when he is ready, of course."

For many, visiting the Warden was a step in dealing with loss. The figurative guidance helped to put things in perspective, almost as if it gave them a will greater than their own to carry their problems. Liaren glanced back down the stairway. Six or seven different groups and a number more individuals populated the steps. Of those, there were a number of Vigil helping to aid Remnants with the journey, which became more arduous with age. Liaren turned back to the glow of the room ahead, knowing that her own questions would be far more precise than anyone else's. She needed information from Tialee.

Malory averted her concerned look and focused along with Liaren to where two people knelt in front of the floating relics of the Warden. "I fear that finding your strength these past months has put a strain on you, child. I am proud that you stand with me now, but you seem to have replaced some of your youth with a grimness of your duty."

"Perhaps I am just guided by the Warden," Liaren said. She told more of a truth than perhaps anyone else who used the phrase, though a part of it felt more hollow than ever before.

They stepped to the side as the two Remnants finally exited the shrine room. "Perhaps she does," Malory said with a bit of a smile. "It seems the Warden wants to bear witness to what I have to say."

"What is that?" Liaren asked. Her thoughts were drawn away for just a moment from the small data pad she was hiding under her sash.

As they stepped into the enveloping glow of the shrine room and stood before the Warden's suit, Malory set her hand on Liaren's shoulder. "Tialee and I have agreed to put forward for your full induction to the Vigil." She gave her student a proud smile. "You will look good with a full sash."

Liaren had to fight against a mix of emotions as the visor of the Warden's helmet flicked on for a moment and began to transmit the data she demanded of Tialee to her data pad. The induction was supposed to be one of the moments every Vigil looked forward to, but again Liaren found it markedly hollow after her betrayal. If Malory knew how she had all but tortured Tialee for the information she was taking now, she would have understood what feelings Liaren was trying to suppress.

"Do not worry, I know you are ready." She gripped Liaren's shoulder. "You hold our true traditions to heart, and if the ones we follow now must be broken so that we may continue to follow the Warden, then I trust you to aid the Vigil in that decision in the years to come."

As the Warden's helmet finished transferring the recordings of the probe to her hidden data pad, Liaren brushed a tear from her cheek. "Thank you, Mrs. Yumin. I shall always remember your lessons as I watch for the Warden's will."

* * *

Vigil Connor excused himself from the final convening of the Vigil after the decision had been all but made regarding the new Reawakened. Rather than speaking up against the direly mistaken trust the Vigil was placing in the Reawakened Marrel Lovek, he instead kept silent and watched. At this point, he had to completely sever himself from doing what he believed would be best for the Remnants. The years were running thin, and he could no longer afford to keep both their ways and his direction.

With message in hand, Connor stepped into the large storage hangars of the *Fortuna*. While the Food Storage and Supply Sector was supposed to be many times the size of this room, Connor could hardly imagine a larger collection of massive cargo crates. The stacks of all sizes of containers formed sorts of passages through the room, a number of which also housed Remnant transports. Connor spotted the large First Claim transport setting down in a wide-open space as Connor caught up with the Safe Harbor supplies manager.

"Vigil? Can I help you?" the man asked.

"Yes," Connor replied. "I am here to allow this shipment."

"Would that explain the lack of a manifest given to me by Director Wardenson?"

The back door of the transport hissed with the pressure difference as the seal was broken and the ramp started to lower to the ground. A single man in a rough suit took off his cracked helmet and started out of the transport. Behind him was just a single container strapped to the center of the large cargo hold of the ship.

"I'll take it from here," Connor said as he moved to meet the Auran stepping off the transport.

"With all due respect, Vigil, I need to confirm the contents of the container."

"Confirm it with what manifest?" Connor stopped again and looked sternly at the man. "This is Vigil business. First Claim is returning a stolen relic of the Warden, but we must confirm that it is authentic. The Vigil will not spread a false history amongst the Remnants."

Before the supplies manager could come up with something to say, Connor turned and started off again to meet the man waiting just on the edge of his ship.

"I am surprised to see you again, Hurald Wardenson. I would have expected the opposite, after the Regent gave you your pay for giving my message to him."

The man spit off the side of the ramp. "That's none of your business, migrant. How do you know my name?"

"You are from one of the families split during Sarthyl's time. I do not know how you are related, but you are kin to the director of transmission systems, Dannil Wardenson. As for your first name . . ." Connor held up the data pad holding a message. "Regent Varis very much wanted me to have your shipment."

The man adjusted his helmet under his arm and tapped against it with gloved fingers. A piece of metal was bolted onto its front to repair damage to the glass. "Why didn't you just send the Regent a transmission the first time?"

"If you must know, I have found a loophole in Safe Harbor that allows me to receive word from First Claim, but I can't send anything. Of course, the Regent will hear my reply soon enough."

"You don't say?" Hurald Wardenson said snidely. "I'll have you know, you got me shot in the face." He motioned with his helmet.

"I will see it now," Connor demanded without diverting another glance from the container. The man stood stiffly, but finally pointed back to it with the damaged helmet in hand.

"Just get it off my damned ship. And yeah, I know what's in it."

Connor stepped up onto the ramp, which looked bloodstained. That, along with the damage to his helmet, afforded an explanation regarding what had happened to the crew he had along last time. Connor glanced over his shoulder into the large room just to make sure nobody was watching from one of the higher walkways. He finally stepped up to the crate and pulled open the lid.

Just as promised, it was filled with explosive charges. And in truth, they *were* relics of the Warden, stolen by Sarthyl himself after the brief invasion of Safe Harbor. But this time, there would be no Warden to drive First Claim back.

* * *

Baxel pulled on the red-plated glove and flexed his hand inside the protective form. He stared at it a long moment with his one unbandaged eye while he sat on the edge of the medical bed. The room was silent as Liaren waited by the door for him to finish putting on his suit. He was going to see the Warden, yet his thoughts were already spinning. Baxel let out a breath and quickly smoothed down the connection between the glove and his undersuit with a thumb.

"Are you ready?" Liaren asked, clutching a data pad in her hands next to the open door.

Baxel grimaced as he adjusted to his own feet and grabbed his helmet. "And what am I supposed to do exactly?" Baxel glanced over to one of the med staff transferring data off one of the terminals. He moved next to Liaren and stood just inside the open doorway. "If you ask me, it seems like the Vigil is just trying to make themselves feel good."

Liaren locked her arm under his to help support his weight as they continued out into the hall. "Perhaps you are just afraid that you will be heard."

"It sounds as if you have your full Vigil sash already. You know it's just Tialee behind that helmet, right?"

"Baxel, there is something you need to know. Tialee, in the suit, gave me the report from the probe."

"When was this?" Baxel asked as they rounded the corner, heading toward the Medical and Rescue Sector docks.

"A few days ago. When I was told I would become a full member of the Vigil. The Warden's suit picked up the transmission from the pod."

"And?" Baxel asked. By her tone, he could already tell it was something incredible. "It's a survivable atmosphere, isn't it? Oh damn, I wish I could tell Tymon."

"No, it is much more than that."

Baxel gave her a long look as they stood in the back of the docks, away from the few others waiting for the transport to arrive. He looked back and forth between her eyes as she stared straight at him. "What do you mean?" he asked in an even more hushed voice. "Are you saying that it is . . . is the planet inhabited, Liaren?"

Liaren drew in a long breath and glanced around to make sure no one was listening. "No, Baxel, it is much, much more than that. Nendra Halimuth ordered Reawakened Marrel Lovek to block any other of the pod's signals from reaching Safe Harbor's systems. But there was an emergency dump of information, picked up only by the Warden's suit, after the pod malfunctioned."

Baxel felt his skin cool, almost as if he had stepped into something much larger than he was prepared to face.

"Well, malfunctioned may not be the right word." A loud noise swept about the room as the airlock doors cycled open. "The pod was sabotaged, Baxel."

"By who?"

Liaren glanced back as their chance to follow the crowd began to close. "The Warden is on Earth. Her name is Oa Alee, and she is trying to protect us by keeping the Remnants hidden to the world. Now come on, we are going to miss our transport."

Baxel felt the fleet shift around him as he stumbled forward toward the airlock and sat down with his back to one of the transport windows. The expanse of Safe Harbor rolled past in silence as he was bound both by a certain shock and by the enormity of the information in such a confined and public space. *The Warden. By name.*

Baxel missed a conversation started by one of the Vigil as he thought about an inhabited planet, hidden from the Remnants most likely by the Warden herself. Liaren excused him from the conversation with some excuse about his hearing having been damaged as well, and by the next time he heard her speak, they were already at the steps leading up to the Warden's Shrine.

"Baxel, you have to focus."

"Focus, right." Baxel coughed onto the back of his glove gripping the helmet.

Liaren helped him take his first step up. "Now you see why it took me a couple of days to tell you, Baxel. Luckily, Tialee and Malory thought I was just caught up about their votes for my induction."

"Right," Baxel said, drawing in a deep breath. "So how does . . ." he trailed off, having nearly as many endings to the question as there were ships in the fleet. "*The* Warden? As in, *a* person. The one and only?

"Don't, Baxel, just don't." She helped him up another few steps as the line shifted forward and a group of three people started down the steps. "We need to focus on the important information."

"Oh, yeah, right. I guess that's not really important." He could only contain himself for a moment. "So how old would that make her? Does she use cryopods or—"

Baxel groaned as she pulled him up the next step with a little too much vigor. Liaren gave him a glare that spoke very loudly about keeping quiet.

"Only one thing has changed. We have the Warden's will." Liaren held up the data pad and motioned with the glowing projection. "It is as direct of a message as has ever been received by the Vigil. We must keep the Remnants hidden."

Baxel nodded slowly. "Right. So, I guess that means stopping Connor Sevison? And the return?"

Liaren shook her head. "The Warden would not have chosen us to act if there was not something much greater at stake. This is not about Dimarka, nor anything else the migrant may have done, save his intentions."

Baxel frowned as he came to rest, leaning against Liaren another few steps up. His knees felt as if they were carrying as much weight as the responsibility he now had on his shoulders. "But . . . Tialee was the one that chose us, and she's not the Warden." After Baxel said it, he almost thought it looked as if Liaren were hiding something by the way she started looking away, up toward the Warden's Shrine.

"Baxel, I am afraid that we will be too late. We have found nothing on Connor." She glanced to him. "I'm sorry, I . . . I mean, nothing that we can use yet."

"No, Liaren, you are right." He squeezed her arm tighter in acceptance. "Nobody took my word about Varnil Williams's death." He looked over to her. "So where does that leave us?"

"I think Tialee let me know the secret of the Warden's identity because we are meant to prepare for the worst."

Baxel let out a breath. "Lucky for us, that is the only time the Warden seems to come."

"Exactly." Liaren helped him forward and up yet again, this time bringing them to the top third of the battle-scarred steps. "The Warden has to come, but she traveled to Earth to stop our discovery."

"Oh hell, I see where you are going with this." Baxel gripped his helmet tighter and tapped it against his leg. "We have the suit, but they have our Warden."

"And when she is needed, she needs her suit."

Baxel then argued quietly with Liaren that they should not take the suit, only stopping when they neared the top. Only a pair of Vigil who had been lugging a narrow metal box up the steps now stood between him and the suit she said he had to take. The way he saw it, they had already missed their one chance at the suit, and that was when he and Liaren had watched the launch of the probe.

"Alright, there is one more thing, which doesn't involve your crazy plan," Baxel said, starting nearly too quiet for Liaren to hear. "The pods. Varnil spoke of them before . . . Connor knows about the pods I found."

"What pods?"

"Cryopods that looked different from the ones in the Preservation Core. Tymon and I found them in the wreckage of a ship. The area has been out of the search coordinates for as long as I can remember. But Varnil said the migrant knew we were there, just before he was killed."

"You think that might be the key? Do you think something is there that might turn the Vigil against him?"

"By the Warden, I hope so. I don't want to have to steal her suit."

After a lone woman exited the shrine, the two Vigil picked up the box and entered. Just as Baxel finished laboring his way to the top step, the two Vigil exited. They were red-faced from the effort of carrying the box but looked relieved to be free of their burden.

Liaren helped him take his final step up and gripped his hand tight. "We will work on your idea when we can, but while we are here, think about how we can do what Tialee wants, and how to get the suit to the Warden."

Baxel nearly collapsed at the tension in his strained muscles as he stepped into the blue aura filling the room coming from the suspension disk below the suit. There were quite a few pieces to the suit, perhaps even more than his own when fully equipped to set out. He used to marvel at the various devices, whose purposes he could only imagine, but as he grew older he'd tended to keep those thoughts at a distance. A small square on his hip matched one a few inches from the suit's. It was a personal habitat barrier, or atmosphere bag, though he doubted his had been used as much. He lowered himself into a kneeling position with the help of Liaren and his helmet.

"Tialee, I know you are in there. I'm going to need your advice. How the hell do you steal the icon of a people when more often than not, there is a line of people waiting to see it?"

An orange glow spread across the ground as Baxel's own visor lit up. He shifted his weight with a grunt and put on the helmet.

"Let's see what you've got," Baxel said, opening the transmission.

"You have thirty seconds!" Tialee yelled into Baxel's ears.

"Thirty seconds, what?"

"Stop talking! That box, it has primed explosives. Get. OUT!"

"Shit," Baxel said, shoving himself up.

"What is it?" Liaren asked.

Baxel kicked the lid of the container open only to expose a row of five silvery orbs flashing in sync. "Liaren, run now!" Baxel shoved her away. "Tialee, can you stop them?"

"Fifteen seconds Baxel, and no! They are on chemical timers!" Tialee shouted in his helmet as he knelt down to the container and pulled out his atmosphere bag.

"The suit!" Liaren shouted.

"Warden's beard," he cursed under his breath. "I got it! Get the others back!" Baxel expanded the clear bag and raked it down over the floating suit as Liaren made for the exit.

"Five seconds!"

Baxel sealed the bag, leaving a few large pieces rocking within the repulsion field, as well as a number of smaller bits either swirling around or clattering across the floor. Baxel pushed up off the dais with another curse and scrambled back toward the entrance. His visor dimmed a fraction of a second after a bright light tore from behind with a surge of shrapnel and fire. The debris pounded into the back of his suit like a handful of rivets thrown from the hand of a titan. Baxel skidded down the steps, still trying to hold the torn bag around the Warden's suit with one arm.

He only jerked to a sudden stop when he engaged the magnets on one hand. Liaren practically slid on top of him as she rushed down the steps and to his side. People several rows above where he had slid to were either trying to stand or were wailing over their shrapnel-riddled loved ones.

"Baxel! By the Warden, are you alive?"

Baxel could feel the bandage had torn free from over his eye, but he was still only able to see Liaren through the chipped glass of his helmet out of one side.

"It's started, hasn't it?" Baxel asked.

"Baxel?"

He groaned and gripped the translucent bag. "Connor was trying to kill the Warden by killing the suit. I have to go. I have to get it out of here, without anybody knowing."

"Baxel, you cannot make it on your own! I had to help you up the steps!"

Tialee spoke in Baxel's helmet. "I've disabled your tracking beacon."

Baxel shoved himself to his feet and looked up toward Liaren. She was covered in a heavy dust and part of her hair looked matted with blood.

"I am sorry," he said.

At that he turned away, half-ran and half-slid down the debris-covered steps, and made his way through the torn crowd of a broken shrine.

Chapter 22: Cloaks and Rain

"How do you know we are safe here?" Kara said, giving one last look out toward the steel-cobbled streets of Reclaim before shutting the door. "If the Black Scars knew how to find Hama, surely they would think to look for us at your home."

Oa stopped before heading to the next room and glanced back to Kara. The bed that Kara had awoken bandaged in was visible just behind her. "I am sure they know exactly where we are. This is where I normally am, when not summoned by the Prime Elect."

Just as Kara was about to express her frustration, Oa held up an age-thinned finger to demand her silence. "If the Black Scars decided to take you from me now, or when I pulled them off you in the first place, they could have easily done so. I am no fighter, warrior, or Warden. Not anymore. They could have pushed past me just as easily as any other old woman about the streets, but they were afraid of what would follow."

Oa nodded slowly before ducking through the doorway. She returned a few moments later with a bundle of rough cloth in her arms. "At the moment, the Black Scars are still afraid to push too far. They play along by the rules of the Prime Elect, and they decide very carefully where and how to break them. Hakatha wants me to hand you over myself, without getting the Prime Elect involved."

Kara crossed her right arm over the sling on her left. Her hidden knife was tucked away behind it. "Except now Feirshan will want my head for what we did to his pod."

"There lies the problem," Oa said with a raise of her eyebrows. "We will both be summoned back to the Citadel, and thankfully the Black Scars are not used for that kind of business. Once they find you missing, and separated from me, that is when things will get interesting."

"Great. And what is that about?" Kara asked, motioning to the bundle Oa still carried.

"This old thing?" Oa unfurled the cloth, revealing a ragged cloak of grey. "You've played by my game, and now it is high time I play by yours. It's time to make you a tech hunter again."

* * *

"Fascinating things, aren't they?" the program hunter said, rolling the visor between his gloved fingers as he sat with his heels propped up on Jance's desk. "You fixed this one, didn't you?"

Kenneth looked up from where he had been staring intently at the floor of the Norclave Library. The red glow of the processing unit clashed with the teal projection of Error's cape as it flickered between hanging over the back of the chair and being tucked close to his back.

"Why would you fix a visor?" Error asked, sliding his finger over the small plates Kenneth had braced it with. "I mean, they're not exactly common, but enough tech hunters dredge them up having no clue how they work that you can come by them."

"Jance picked it up," Kenneth said, rubbing his forehead as he resumed his concentration on the floor. "She thought it belonged to someone else."

There was a flash of movement from the side as Error quickly swapped out which data strip was inserted into the wrist of his suit. Just as some of the displays hovering across the surface of the desk started dropping out, his remotely connected program started along a different strategy.

Error let out a breath and set the visor on the edge of the desk. "I don't know how much longer I can keep this up."

"Olana's strike teams are ready and in the transports." Kenneth then glanced over to what had been the source of a constant hum for the past few weeks. "Your device will find Travend, perhaps in the next few hours, and that will be it. Our last chance."

"If I didn't know better . . . oh wait, I don't. Who are you looking for again?"

"All I need is access to the Cryo's system. Getting me that access is all you need to do."

Error picked up the visor and started looking it over again. "Is it that tech hunter? The one Mackelry said you were running around with? You know, I heard some interesting rumors about what you two were up to."

"I'm sure you did," Kenneth said, and just as the program hunter was about to follow up on the question, Kenneth held him with a hard look. "How about you tell me about yourself, Error? You sound like a man with nothing to hide."

Error took his feet from the desk and looked into the distance beyond the room before coughing into his hand. "So, what did you use to fix this visor? The connections are superb. Almost like Kessian work."

Kenneth glanced around the room before he remembered where he'd placed his gloves, then upended the sack on the desk before moving back to his seat on a crate.

"Now that's not something I . . . where did you get these?" Error set the visor to the side and picked up one of the gloves, gently examining the surface of the carbon fiber as he moved each finger.

"The same place you got yours," Kenneth snipped back.

Error nearly dropped the glove as he turned a shocked look back on Kenneth.

Kenneth smirked, knowing he had managed to finally poke into a nerve. "A secret. That's where I got them."

"Oh, right, yes." Error drew in a deep breath and quickly turned his attention back and away from Kenneth. "I knew you meant that."

After a few more minutes of silence passed, listening to the processing unit and watching Error idly moving the fingers of the gloves, Kenneth spoke. "Truth be told, I got them from Mackelry Norton. A parting gift, meant to be used as a bribe for a new life. The life I would have had, if I ran from the Cryo."

Error nodded. "I had a life laid out in front of me." He motioned to himself, or perhaps what he was wearing now. "The problem was, I could see it, beginning to end. I ran away, took to the outerzones. Instead of selling everything I had, I put it to use. Mostly earning food and shelter, from people much like your own Mackelry Norton."

"But can you go back to that life?"

Error huffed and rubbed his face. "Not likely, but it's possible." He looked over to Kenneth. "You? Can you go back?"

"Not after what I found."

"Makes sense. The Cryo changed everything, even in her short time."

"No," Kenneth said quietly. He nodded to the desk Error was trying to break into. "I need to know where she is. She was chasing the people responsible for killing a number of Norclave officials and workers at the docks, all in their attempt to end the Cryo."

Error rapped the fingers of the glove against the desk. "Wait, so is this the tech hunter? Why do you think she needs help?"

Kenneth shook his head. "Not help. Warning. I want her out of the line of fire when Olana's troops storm in after Travend, and that means being certain that his men did not lead her straight to him."

"Okay." Error nodded and tapped a few projected inputs over his arm. "Well, let's see . . . I first came to Norclave because the Overlord—"

Kenneth held up a hand. "Error, don't. You have your secrets and I have mine. Let's keep them separate. Besides, we're both gone from Norclave when this is over."

Error coughed into the glove he was holding and gave a short nod. "Right. Oh, red flag!"

As the alarms started blinking on the processing unit, Kenneth jumped to his feet and pointed to the desk. "Keep on it!" He then rushed to the unit, fearing the worst. Kenneth activated the display on the side.

"What is it?" Error asked.

"It's Travend."

"We have him?"

Without a word, Kenneth deactivated the power link and the unit slowly started to spool down. After a few moments, the humming and glow had finally stopped.

"Did it work?" Error pried. "Do we have him, Kenneth?"

Kenneth clenched his jaw. "Just find her."

"Not much time left now. But what are you doing?" Error asked as Kenneth took the gloves and put them back in the sack.

"Gathering my things."

"Shouldn't you tell the Overlord?"

Kenneth nodded as he opened the crate he had been sitting on. He pulled out a small bag and set it on top. It was the one Kara had made for him before she left without a word. "I should tell Olana. But in case I don't, I need to be ready. You just keep at it, and I'll scrape up whatever time I can for you."

* * *

Lieth looked around the small quarters they had been given. The residences were normally reserved for influential people visiting the Citadel. The walls were a clean white with balanced recesses and accent lines in a material not fitting of their age. Even the door had the original glass to keep out the haze of smoke and the commotion outside.

"I know what I saw, Lieth. I know it was her."

Lieth glanced away from the door and looked to the opposite bed in the room, where Weril sat stiffly on the edge. "Weril, you said the tracker that followed us from Norclave was dead. You told the Prime Elect that. Remember?"

Weril wrinkled the sheets of the bed with his one hand. It looked as if he wished he had his pulse cannon back. "I thought I was certain. I mean, there was an explosion, and the remaining bits and pieces were on fire. But if you saw the look that woman gave me, you would know we are still being hunted by Norclave."

Lieth rubbed his hands through his thick black hair and watched the soldiers running past in the hall outside. "I get it. You signed up to kill a Cryo. It makes sense to think someone is out to get you, especially with the Norclave emissary and soldiers out and about in the halls."

Weril clenched his rough, rain-torn cloak with one hand as he rested the stump of his other crossways over it. "The woman wiped her face with a cloth. Her brow was covered in sweat, and the rag hid everything except for her eyes. The same eyes I remember when she threw that knife into my arm." He held up the stump and showed the large scab. "And she wore a sling, on the same arm hit by my repulsor."

Lieth popped the seal on the door and slid it open. A heavy swirl of smoky air flowed into the room along with sounds of confusion from the hall. As far as he could tell, all the smoke originated from a fire in the Prime Elect's hangar. "And you are sure the tech hunter is here for us? Not something else?" He cleared his throat as the smoke flowed into the room and gradually formed a haze.

"We are not safe here, dammit! Feirshan and Travend can be damned, we need to leave." Weril stood up as if ready to act upon his words that instant. "We need to leave Reclaim while we still can."

"Tech hunter or not, the Prime Elect has made it very clear that he intends to keep the truth from Norclave." Lieth closed the door with a cough, shutting out a few shouts echoing down the hall. "If we try to leave the city, he will simply dispose of us like the others of our group."

Weril threw his hand and arm into the air. "Alright. Then we have to tell the Prime Elect about my mistake. About the tech hunter."

Just as Lieth was about to advise him against doing so, the door to the room opened again, though this time it was at the direction of one of the Prime Elect's guard, and behind the shorter man stood two Reclaim watch.

"Follow me," the guard said. "The both of you."

Weril gave Lieth a leery glance but as the soldiers shifted their weapons, they knew they had no choice.

"Is this about the fire?" Lieth asked the man as they fell in behind his quick steps, though the soldiers followed at the rear.

"I could not say. I was given orders to deliver you to the Prime Elect."

By the time they stepped into the high levels of the Citadel, Lieth and Weril had been warned very carefully to speak only as directed. However, as Lieth stepped into the Prime Elect's office, Iben Feirshan's rage fell short of what Lieth expected. The room was entirely silent, and the Prime Elect sat behind his desk with his eyes closed and his hands folded in front of him. If not for the chair tipped over and lying bent in the corner, Lieth might have thought nothing was wrong.

Lieth shared a glance with Weril, not knowing whether to disturb the Prime Elect by announcing their presence. Knowing he was putting his own welfare on the line, Lieth cleared his throat.

The Prime Elect finally opened his eyes.

"Do you smell that?" Iben Feirshan swirled his finger through the air and gave them both an inquisitive look. "The slightest tinge of static, perhaps a caustic undertone carrying a hint of char. Is that how you would describe it?"

They both shrugged, though Weril spoke. "It's not as bad up here."

The Prime Elect turned to stare at him. "You know, perhaps it is just the taste that bothers me. It coats the tongue, almost as if feeling the glow of a projected display, or perhaps chewing on a bit of metal."

They both said nothing as the Prime Elect started to tap a data strip on the desk.

"In my rise to the position of Prime Elect, the most essential thing I discovered was that connections mean everything. Who you know, who you don't. And especially those connections that you should appear not to have. All ties are necessary, so long as they remain in their proper positions."

Out of the corner of his eye, Lieth saw Weril take in a dry gulp.

"But what really just makes me want to . . . strangle someone," the Prime Elect said, slamming his hand on the desk and causing the small data strip to flicker violently as it snapped, "is when you think you have everything tied up, and then suddenly there is another loose end."

The Prime Elect closed his eyes again and let out a slow breath. He brushed the broken pieces of the data strip to the floor. "I've added it up every way I can think. It had to be Oa's tech hunter that set fire to something very important of mine. There were reports of Oa's conflict with the Black Scars over a tech hunter with a bandaged arm, and the descriptions of that tech hunter match with the woman she introduced to me as Gleia Dimarka."

Lieth stood stiff, knowing this was going nowhere good.

"But where my reasoning fails," Feirshan continued, "is why someone with such a specific and targeted goal to sabotage me showed up to Reclaim, in need of medical attention." The Prime Elect clasped his hands together and leaned forward. "Admittedly, I could only think of one explanation, but I am afraid that relies on somebody who I was told is dead being quite the opposite."

Lieth rubbed his face, knowing this could be the end. He glanced over to the bent chair in the corner and started thinking about his plan for when the soldiers burst in through the door behind him.

"I . . . was mistaken," Weril finally said. "Beyond any explanation I can think of, I know for certain that I saw the same woman who ambushed us in your halls. Somehow, she survived."

The Prime Elect stood from his chair and clenched his hands behind his back. He took a few slow steps around his desk, crunching the pieces of the data strip underfoot. Lieth could see that the Prime Elect was visibly shaking in anger.

"When was this?"

"Sometime just before we heard of the fire."

"And was she walking with an old woman?"

Weril took a half step back at the redness in the Prime Elect's face as the man centered himself in front of his desk. "Yes . . . Prime Elect."

"And you know for certain that you were not followed from Norclave?"

This time Lieth spoke up. Weril would get himself killed otherwise. "I cannot see how that would be possible. We traveled on foot through the storm, and used your contact in Maraton, at the biological manufacturing facility."

The Prime Elect took a step forward and weighed Lieth carefully. "And your operation at the docks. Can I rest assured that Travend proceeded with utmost caution?"

"Other than Travend, only I knew the dock location and time. I recruited people with no knowledge of the operation besides what I told them, and they were kept under tight watch."

"How many did you recruit?"

"Six, according to Travend's plan."

The Prime Elect paused in thought. "My pilot reported five when he picked you up. What happened to the other?"

"Oh, damn that's . . ." Weril trailed off. "She could have found him, the scrapsmith. He tried to run away during the storm. We left him for dead just before Maraton."

The Prime Elect turned around and stormed back to his seat. "Damn it all. Norclave knows. That blasted daughter of a miner, sitting high on the Overlord's throne, she knows." The Prime Elect rapped his fingernails on the desk. "But what can she prove?" After a moment, Feirshan let out a breath. "Whatever she damn well pleases, that's what! Take this man away!" he then shouted.

As the soldiers stormed into the room, the Prime Elect pointed to Weril. He attempted to shake them loose but quickly lost the struggle. "Put him under my clearance. I may need to give him to Olana." With a pulse cannon singeing the hair on the back of Weril's head, he was dragged out of the room.

After the door blocked out Weril's shouting and the scraping of boots, the room was left in an eerie silence. Lieth found himself staring at the gently pulsing and occasionally sparking pieces of the data strip on the floor. Only when he looked up did he realize that the Prime Elect was busy going over information on a larger data pad.

The Prime Elect glanced up. "Yes? Is there something else you need?"

"I . . ." Lieth said as he thought over the dangers of running. He would likely be gunned downed trying to leave the city.

"You will not be helping Travend while you are a target of Norclave."

"You want me to kill the tech hunter?"

The Prime Elect frowned and weighed the idea. "That's not how I see this happening. You will be watched, and not only by my people. Oh, and if you return here to my Citadel, you will lose your chance at revenge against Olana Nuand for what happened to your family. Now if you wouldn't mind, I have a meeting to plan for. One that has just become far more difficult than expected."

At that, Lieth was simply given a wave of leave as the Prime Elect turned back to his workings.

* * *

A cool wind set in as the sun took cover behind a low bank of clouds, leaving Kara and Oa, in her ragged cloak, to wander the overcast streets of Reclaim. As a few sparse raindrops fell, Kara felt comforted under the familiar protection of her own hood.

"You will have to help me with what you need," Oa said. "I've actually met only a few tech hunters in all my years. Not a talkative type of people."

Kara simply nodded as she looked around the market streets. She tried not to focus on the dark figures positioned around the alleys or the number of the Reclaim watch taking questions in the streets. Instead, she took note of the wares being sold in the misty evening. A curved blade, designed for cutting through grasses, was handed over to one of the gatherers while baskets of grain were haggled away several stalls down. On the other side of the street, a merchant was sorting through a crate of half-broken electronics with a frown.

"I'll need weapons if we are to have any hope of hunting down Travend's men."

"What about there?" Oa asked, looking to the woman now setting a mess of cables to the side of the crate she was sorting through. "She may have some useful items she is looking to sell to tech hunters."

Kara gave her a sideways glance. If she didn't know that Oa had grown up outside of their world, Kara might have thought she was joking. "You may have been fed the wrong idea about people like me."

"Oh? How so?"

Kara glanced up to the sky as a swell of raindrops passed over and faded. "For all my life, at least the part that I can call my own, I've been little more than a scavenger. The only thing that separated me from the rest of the world was how far I was willing to go." Kara glanced over her shoulder before moving to a small covered area with merchants selling a variety of goods.

"Then, that is what makes you special. That is what makes you a tech hunter."

Kara pointed to a dull grey shirt hanging on display. The shop owner pulled it down and laid it out on the cracking paint of the metal counter. Kara could see the shirt had been sloppily pieced together, and after a bit of hesitation, she decided it would do, if simply for use as strips of cloth.

"I wouldn't say 'special' is the right word," Kara replied to Oa. She then pointed to a few small pouches molded out of a carbon fabric. "Traveling deep into the outerzones makes me no more impervious to danger. I'm no different than mercenaries or wanderers, save for the occasional valuable find that forces me to watch my back."

Oa stepped closer and gave Kara a hard look. "You are talking yourself down because you arrived here defeated. Remember that I was defeated, too. I was once broken, along with my people."

As Kara stuffed the shirt and several pouches into the bag slung over her shoulder, she caught a glimpse of something at one of the stands being covered under a cloth as one of the watch walked past.

"Give me a moment," Kara said.

"I'll be over here," Oa replied with a motion to the side as Kara started off. "But be quick. I've still got a few contacts to meet with before night falls."

As she slipped past a few people on her way, Kara felt a tingle on the back of her neck. Someone was watching, and she had the feeling they had been since Oa led her here. It was then that someone bumped into her bad arm, and she had to hide her grimace.

"Watch it," the man murmured. She glimpsed his blue-painted armor out of the corner of her eye as she continued past. Kara shook her head, knowing the damned place was crawling with far too many Scars and watch for as little civilians as were here.

When she finally got to the stand, Kara made sure to take her time. The man behind the counter was missing two fingers on one hand, and one eye was partially disfigured from the short but heavy scar near it. He gave her the same weighing look when she stepped forward as he had the previous two customers. He was selling scrapsmithed water purifiers and other small wares as a front for whatever he kept under a thick mesh-layered cloth.

"Good evening, I believe," he said with a glance up to the low clouds. "What can I help you with today? A purifier? Or perhaps a moisture clip? It's guaranteed to cut the humidity out of the air, you just wear it on your collar and . . ."

Kara glanced over her shoulder. "Perhaps something a little more . . . intriguing."

"Ah, I see. Sent here by Tiburka? Well . . ." he said, glancing around for the watch before leaning down to get something under his small counter. It was then that Kara noticed the heavy, inky tattoo under his collar. Perhaps they were just normal markings like she had seen before, but in this damned city . . .

"There we are," he said, setting a can on top of the cloth on the counter. From the glowing display projected around the side, it looked like a vintage alcohol from before the fall, though it had an added blocky battery on the side.

"The seal is unbroken, I assure you. The thing added to the side is just to ensure that the holo-display functions."

Instead of calling him out about the faulty condition of the contents, Kara simply agreed to the purchase and transferred credits from the small data card Oa had given her. Just paying for it was better than causing a scene with so many people searching for her. Kara carefully set it in her bag and turned away.

Oa approached her then, adjusting her hood down lower as another gust of raindrops pushed over them. "Take a look at this." Oa set a new bag of her own on the damp ground and pulled it open. "And you said she wouldn't sell to tech hunters. Of course, the woman only showed me these after I assured her I was not the one who would be going out into the outerzones."

"What's all this?"

"Charge scanner for safely traveling along live cables and surfaces," Oa said, pulling out a device before replacing it and showing another. "Relay beacon, showing the distance from the relay atop the Prime Elect's Citadel. And this here, from the next merchant over, is a particulate filtering cloth, for areas with too much dust, ash, rust, or other toxins in the air. And then there are a couple more little things I paid too much for."

"But . . ." Kara started. "What are they for? How will they help track the traitors?"

Oa sighed and closed the bag, then held a hand out for Kara to help her pick the bag up off the muddied steel tiles of the street. "These are for you. A tech hunter."

"What are you getting at?" Kara asked. Just as she did, she looked over Oa's grey hood to see who was walking down the middle of the street. There was no mistaking the face and dark hair; it was the leader of Travend's supposed Cryo slayers. Her heart immediately jumped into the wild pace of fear and anticipation.

"Kara, stop," Oa urged her. "You are a tech hunter. Not a mercenary, not one of those trackers, none of it. I was wrong about you when I first saw you. This is not what you do. You have saved my people, now let me save you. Get out of Reclaim, go back to the outerzones, and do not return."

"Why is he here?" Kara asked herself as the raindrops started steadily plinking against the streets around her.

"Take these things, Kara. He is here because the watch are trying to bait you out. They need you away from me."

Kara started to look elsewhere along the streets. Someone gave a wide-armed motion, and across the way, several more grim figures with black scars on their arms stepped in the rain. The watch took note of their arrival, and their patrols took up positions around the area. There was a shout as a man in flight armor raised a weapon, but the order to stay back was met with a hard shove. As quickly as the downpour was falling on the street, motion began on all sides. Several shots fired, and one of the watch raced across the street. Kara stood with her hand on a knife, aiming to protect Oa should anyone get near her.

In the confusion of the civilians trying to get out of the way of gunfire, barking dogs, and popping muzzles, Kara lost track of Travend's man for a split second. She caught sight of him again being dragged backward by two strong-arms laced in blackened scars.

"They have him!" Kara yelled.

"Good!" Oa said, nearly throwing the bag at Kara. "That means only the watch is here for you. Now go, before the Black Scars find out you are here as well!"

Kara quickly turned on her heels back toward the merchant she had been speaking with. Whether he was a member of the Black Scars or not, he had slipped away in the confusion. Kara slung the bag from Oa over her shoulder and pulled back the cloth. Without knowing what the large pistol-sized weapon was, Kara threw it into the bag along with the ammunition or magazine blocks.

"I'm not leaving the city," Kara warned.

Oa simply shook her head as the Black Scars started to slip away.

"Then I will know where to find you. Along with everybody else. May the Warden be with you, because no one else is. Not here."

At that, Kara turned from the woman, but instead of ducking down a side passage into the Black Scars's territory, she strode through the middle of the waterlogged, blood-filled streets of Reclaim.

* * *

"Kenneth, dammit, we were supposed to have him by now!" the Overlord yelled through the comms.

Error mockingly held his hands to the sides of his open mouth in fright where he sat at Jance's desk.

Kenneth folded his arms and looked back to the projected screen of Overlord Nuand. "It is just going to take however much time is necessary," he replied.

"As far as I am concerned, you are fifteen hours overdue! The strike teams have had several meals in the transports already. I have to get Travend, Kenneth. There is no other option."

Kenneth rubbed an eye with the palm of his hand. "I know. Just give me a bit longer."

Olana let out a sigh. "I am starting to think that I have given you far too much time. If this falls through, I might as well have let Travend walk unhindered ever since he tried to kill my Cryo!"

"It will simply . . ." Kenneth started, but he was distracted as Error threw his hands up in the air. The program hunter barely caught himself from yelling out loud.

"Kenneth?" Olana asked as Error was mouthing the words, "Found her!"

"Hang on." Kenneth reached over the desk and silenced the transmission with the Overlord.

"Where is she?" Kenneth asked.

Error punched into the air several times before sweeping his arm over the desk, populating the floating images with views of Kara a hundred times over. It was all of Jance's data on Kara, previously locked under her Council clearance. By the myriad of cameras and visors it would have taken to collect the data, Kenneth could see now that they had only been seeing a portion of the total amount of cameras Jance had incorporated into her system. It showed Kara walking through Norclave, hiding in the dark at the Maraton Facility, and even passing inside the Prime Elect's Citadel on multiple occasions.

"I told you I could do it," Error said with a celebratory laugh. "No problems!"

Kenneth pushed him to the side and tried to take in every instance of her. His heart raced as he scanned the moving images, occasionally catching a small glimpse of her face. He quickly found the latest, showing Kara wrapped in her cloak and far in the background of what looked to be a skirmish within the city.

"Jance incorporated the visors into her system," Kenneth said in awe. "But what visor is this from?" Kenneth asked. Just as Error started to look for the answer, Kenneth pushed his hand out of the way and did it himself.

"It should be the same one as all of these," Error said, looking at an area of screens that mostly consisted of Kara inside the Citadel.

Kenneth gripped the edge of the desk when he saw the answer. "Zaireel Tuakana. It is his visor that picked her up."

Error leaned forward. "The images are all clear enough. He had to have seen her."

Kenneth clenched the desk harder. "I know. And that means . . . dammit, that means she knew. She knew all along."

"Who knew?" Error asked. "And what?"

"Olana Nuand. She knew this entire damned time. She knew exactly where Kara was, and she hid it from me."

Kenneth took a deep breath, knowing exactly how much danger his decision would put Kara in. The last thing he wanted to do was bring Kara into the middle of a fight between the Overlord and Travend, but he could see no other option. Kenneth rubbed a grimy, metal-stained hand over his face before unsilencing the Overlord.

"Kenneth, is there—" Olana started.

"Get the transports in the air," he interrupted.

"Where is he?" she asked. "Where is Travend?"

"Reclaim. He is in Reclaim."

Olana immediately started giving out orders in her own room. Over the system of Jance's desk and through the walls, they could hear the transports firing on their engines.

"Where in the city?" Olana asked of Kenneth.

"I'm still working on that."

"How soon can you tell me?"

"Perhaps only when it is too late." At that, Kenneth terminated the transmission.

* * *

Flecks of water leapt from the steel pad of the seventh-level docks as the two transports finally rumbled into the air. They rose up through the heights of the starscraper, pushing through the streams of water falling from the high surfaces. Olana wiped a drop that fell through her visor projection as she continued to look on in deep thought. Not only did she not have Travend, and thus a handhold on the Prime Elect before her meeting, she was sending her strike team to his city. And she was trusting the technician on whether or not Travend was actually there.

"Overlord Nuand," Sora said quietly from the side. "Tuakana is on his way to speak with the Prime Elect. The meeting will be within the hour."

Olana let out a heavy breath. She was not nervous about speaking with the Prime Elect, of course. She simply knew how bad things could get.

"Sora, I need you to do something for me. Take a few of my men, and not those from Norclave. Go wake the Cryo."

"But her condition—"

"I need to have her there, even if she cannot speak. She may be the only leverage I have to keep this entire situation from devolving into a war between Norclave and Reclaim."

Chapter 23: Exploration

As soon as Oundara heard the news, she made all haste to get to the Hall of the Warden. She stepped off the transport to the direction of individuals wearing security suits. It was rare to see people acting as security officials in Safe Harbor. When the suits were taken out of storage, they were normally only used to organize the movement of people in events such as large offsendings, or to direct people out of a particular area that was going to be depressurized for maintenance. At the moment, a few of the acting security officials standing in the back, watching through the confusion and pain of the room, were actually holding weapons.

"Keep everyone out of that transport!" one of the men in uniform yelled. She recognized him; he worked in supplies.

A younger man, barely older than a kid in Oundara's eyes, stood in a security uniform next to the man who had shouted. The kid's face was pale with the weight of the situation as he explained to one of the women trying to board that the outgoing transport was for wounded only.

Oundara stepped to the side as a few makeshift stretchers were carried in by the hands of cargo workers, Vigil, and anyone else who was available at the moment. The report from Head Vigil Treys seemed to not be overstated. In fact, in the other corner of the room, there were several people lying covered in Vigil sashes. Oundara tried not to dwell on the ones released by the Warden as she pushed on through the crowd.

The Hall of the Warden was filled with sobs and cries of anguish. The first thing she noticed, over the heads of people bandaging wounds and others helping a few keep weight off wounded legs as they walked, was the haze through the lights up at the shrine room. Flames had darkened the entrance, and the steps were covered in debris and dust-dried blood.

"By the Warden . . ." Oundara said as she stepped around another few stretchers being prepped for transport. She could not believe it. The Warden had left them.

Her attention was pulled from the impossible realization by a certain tone of voice that carried through the room.

"Where is Baxel?" Flerin nearly yelled at Quervin.

She started making her way his direction.

"Well, check it again!" Flerin barked. He was speaking with Quervin, or perhaps simply at him.

"Oundara," the other SE-S head said with a relieved nod as she approached, clearly glad to have someone to pull the attention of Flerin.

"Did we lose one of our own?" she asked.

Quervin paused for a moment. "Technically Baxel was . . ." the head started, but he trailed off as Flerin gave him a dangerous look. Quervin finally let out a breath. "It seems so. The tracking beacon in his helmet . . . it stopped functioning just as . . ."

Flerin gritted his teeth and quickly wiped away the tears in his eyes with a fist. "Check it again. I heard someone say they saw him."

"Flerin," Oundara said, putting a hand on his shoulder. She knew she could not reassure him enough, but she felt she at least had to try.

"And I let him down," Flerin said. "I ignored everything Baxel said, and told him to say nothing more."

"Do you believe him now?" Oundara asked. "About Vigil Connor?"

She noticed Flerin was looking past her, up toward the shrine. She turned to see Connor Sevison and a few other Vigil making their way up the smoky steps.

"I don't know," Flerin finally replied. "But if Connor did this, I will make sure he joins the Warden, wherever she went."

* * *

Connor stepped up through the still-smoking room of the Warden's Shrine. He had spent countless hours in the room over the years convincing himself that he belonged in Safe Harbor. Now, seeing the sides of the room disfigured, and the shrine itself covered in small pieces of the suit that had stood proudly for centuries, it felt strange. Especially without the ever-present blue light.

He rolled one unidentifiable piece with a foot, seeing only scarce flecks of white left on the charred steel.

"You did a hell of a job here," the man to his right said, pointing a light about the room.

The woman to his left, dressed in a Vigil sash, spit on the ground. "Now we get to see how tough they really are without their great protector."

Connor ignored the jeers against what he had seen as his people for many decades. Instead, he busied himself with observation, bending down to rake his fingers across the floor. He had taken the Warden from the Remnants, and it would be wrong to not appreciate the pain. The price of returning to Earth was high. Much higher than he had expected it would be. It had cost the Remnants the center of their society, and depending on how hard the Regent of First Claim pushed, it might very well have cost them their lives.

He turned over another piece with his shaking and unwieldy fingers and felt a sudden strike of doubt as he realized what the piece was. It was a finger, still attached to a piece of the glove and part of a thumb. It had been torn loose and stripped of most of its protective coating of white. He gently set it back on the floor. Despite his nervousnesss, he was relieved it existed. It would be something for them to hold on to.

Connor looked around the room, then realized as the man swept his light across the room that there were far too few shadows cast over the ground. There was not enough remaining of the Warden for everything to have been here.

"What's got you so nervous?" the woman from First Claim asked.

"Nothing." Connor looked around one last time. "The Warden is dead." As he said it, though, he felt as if someone was watching his back.

* * *

Baxel lay weightless, held against the surface of steel by a magnetic tether. His eyes were closed, and he was focused on maintaining his breathing. The soreness in his joints was absurd.

"Oxygen readout," he mumbled. He was surprised when Tialee answered instead of hearing a report from his own suit.

"Holding steady at fifty-seven percent. Rebreather efficiency at ninety-six percent, resulting in an acceptable loss ratio."

"I'm just glad the bandages are holding," Baxel said. He had to force himself to not touch the back of his arm or bend his knee too much, though the patched sections had held since he covered them in the airlock.

"How are my vitals?" he asked.

"Monitor malfunction. Reaccessing," Tialee said dully. "Sensor failure detected. Would you like me to attempt a scan?"

"No, no," Baxel said, shifting his shoulders as he tried to find comfort. "I'm just passing the time."

"Would you like to set an alert for a certain timeframe?"

"An alert?" Baxel asked. "What is with you?"

"Question unknown. Please restate query."

Baxel glanced over to where the Warden's suit was contained in an atmosphere bag tethered to the wreckage next to him. "Tialee, what is with the . . . I guess you would call it formality? The robot crap? What's going on?"

There was a short pause where Baxel only heard the sound of his own breathing. Finally, Tialee spoke, though she was still more reserved than he remembered her sounding.

"I am trying to bypass my emotion directives. They are currently . . . unoptimized and causing inefficiencies."

Baxel closed his eyes and let his head fall back even more. After a moment of thought, he replied, "I know what you mean."

"I feel as if I have abandoned my people," Tialee said. "Baxel, we should not have left. They need to know there is hope."

"I can't believe I'm saying this to you, but it will be fine."

"It's just that . . . I remember everything. Each time the version of myself in the Vigil is dismissed, I receive the memories. Even the things that version was supposed to forget."

"Like what?" Baxel asked.

Tialee paused as she likely sifted through years of memories. "I told Liaren to do it. To get information. I know that. But I cannot remove that memory, and I can't change it. I will always have the unabated feeling that my own pupil, Liaren, betrayed me. While you may have the capability to reconcile your emotions, I will always have the permanent feeling that she tore *me* down, and spoke to *me* as I truly am. A mirror." Tialee paused. "Not even that. A copy of an AI mirror . . . a copy of one that has been hidden away from the Remnants within the Warden's suit."

Baxel glanced over to her, to where the Warden's suit was contained in the bag. "I'm sure she feels the same way, wishing she could forget what she said to you. But some days you just go on, wondering if you are still the one in your own suit."

* * *

Liaren sat on a tilted bench in the SE-S, hands shaking. They were covered in now-dried blood from where she had tried to help some of the people wounded by the shrapnel. She herself had a long gash over the top of her shoulder, though it would have been much worse had Baxel not told her to get out.

Liaren sniffed, though she did not try to wipe away the tears. She was not shaking from the burning of recent thoughts about the old man whose wounds she had been holding pressure against with her own Vigil sash. She was shaking because she dared think at that moment that she was wasting time better spent beating Connor.

After the med-techs had arrived, she left her bloody sash and rushed out of the Hall of the Warden, ending up in the SE-S after taking the first transport out. It was somewhere away from everything she had failed to stop so far. She didn't look up as voices came echoing down the hallway.

"You cannot go out, Tymon, not now. Not with the all-return in place."

"I know where he has to be. They have not found him yet, and I refuse to believe for a moment that he was in the shrine when it happened."

Liaren looked up to see Tymon arguing with a girl a little younger than herself with long blond hair. They both wore similar suits, rough from use and marked with the yellow and grey accents of team Surefire.

"What about the beacon in your helmet, huh? They will know you are going out."

"Merden, as long as they don't stop me, that's . . ." Tymon started, though he trailed off as he spotted Liaren. He let his Surefire helmet rest against his leg and looked to the dried blood on Liaren's hands.

Liaren gave him a weak smile. Perhaps part of the reason she came here to the SE-S was because she knew she needed help. She needed someone to find out exactly what Connor's relation was to the pods Baxel had found, and she was afraid Baxel was not up to the task.

Tymon took a small step forward. "Do you . . . do you know where Baxel is?" he asked quietly.

"No. But I was with him. And he . . ." Liaren stopped and glanced at Merden. After a moment, she decided at this point, some secrets would simply have to break. "He has the Warden's suit."

"He has it?" Merden asked incredulously.

Liaren held up a hand to keep her silence and Merden fell quiet with wide eyes and a gulp. "We need you to do something for us. For me, Baxel and . . . and the Warden. Baxel told me about a collection of cryopods somewhere in the wreckage. I need to know more about them. I do not know exactly what, but there is something there the Warden needs to know."

Tymon pulled in a breath. "Whatever you need," Tymon said, "but I am getting Baxel first."

Merden put her hands on her hips and gave Tymon a dangerous look. "I'll be joining you."

Tymon opened his mouth, but seemed to decide against the fight. He then turned back to Liaren. "I suppose you will be wanting to come too, then?"

Liaren paused, then finally nodded. "As a Vigil tasked by the Warden, I should be the one to look after her suit."

Tymon rolled his eyes. "Great. You ever worn a suit before? Or even touched one?"

Merden started off down the hall. "I'll get Sammai's. It should be the best fit." She motioned for Liaren to follow and Tymon simply ran his free hand through his hair.

"Check and see if my Firebrand suit is there, will you?" Tymon said, though he did not seem hopeful of the prospect.

With no sight of Tymon's Firebrand suit, and after a process more complicated than she had ever realized, she managed to slip into the undersuit of varying grey highlights and fastened on the exterior pieces. Merden quickly tied up her hair and handed her a helmet.

"Stay close to me. And always watch your oxygen."

Liaren put on the helmet and heard a hiss as the air flooded in. She stayed close behind Merden as they stepped into the airlock. It was not until the door closed behind them that Liaren felt a cold shiver fighting against her. Everything about standing here, one door away from where they released their people from the Warden . . .

"Everyone's comm working?" Tymon asked.

"Check," Merden said. Instead of facing the door, she was keeping a close watch on Liaren.

"I hear you," Liaren replied.

After a moment, Merden moved a bit closer. "I don't hear you, Liaren. Try again?"

"Nothing?"

Merden shook her head, and Liaren motioned a question with her hands.

"Oh, I bet Sammai was trying to fix it again."

Tymon glanced back. "I'm not wasting any more time. Just keep an eye on her. I have her system readout." He motioned with the glowing display that curved around his arm.

"How's your oxygen?" Merden asked.

Liaren had to glance around at all the systems displayed on the inside of the helmet. When she found the number, she simply gave Marden a thumbs-up.

"Her system's good," Tymon said. "Be ready for silence."

"Silence?" Liaren asked. The lights of the small airlock shifted to a warning red, and it soon became clear that the loudest thing was her breathing.

"Still holding?" Merden asked.

Liaren gave another thumbs-up.

"We're good," Tymon said.

Liaren gasped as the door on the other side pulled open. There was a slight tug as the little air that remained within the incomplete vacuum of the airlock rushed out into the zero-space of Safe Harbor. Merden took Liaren's hand and pulled her out into the weightless, silent expanse beyond the only world Liaren had ever known.

"Where are we headed, Tymon?" Merden asked.

"The Point. If Baxel has the suit, he'll be there. That's where we have supplies."

* * *

Regent Varis Halimuth wiped the sweat from his forehead before picking up another welded steel box in his storeroom. For the past couple of months, the entirety of First Claim had slipped into an environment of high humidity. Supposedly the engineers were making progress with the filtration system, but as the Regent, he knew that the parts to fix it simply were not coming in.

Varis set down the crate along the line of others and wiped at his sweat again. He knew he would have been a strong man, if not for the difficulties of life here in First Claim. The crates were out of his own private reserve, though reserves of any kind were a scarcity in First Claim.

Two First Claim Remnants came out of the back room with a long crate, and he directed them where to set it before telling them they could leave. Those should be the rifles Sarthyl had managed to bring back, some sixty years ago.

"Are we really preparing for a raid?" one of them asked as they waited for the door to charge up enough energy to open.

"I'm expecting word any time. We will need to move quickly."

The door opened, and the younger of the two First Claim Remnants hurried out into the dimly lit hallway. The other looked back. "But their Warden . . ." he started. "Safe Harbor is protected."

"Sarthyl promised us a life. I want you to remember that. That's what he promised all of First Claim." Regent Varis glanced over the weapons supply. It was a wide assortment, from grenades to what he was told were rockets. "And we have yet to find one here."

After the man nodded and moved off, the Regent turned back to the storeroom. There were a few more crates he could get on his own. If the migrant pulled through, it would be worth releasing the objects that had kept him in power. If their plan worked, he wouldn't care how much he lost.

He opened a dented crate and looked inside. It was full of pistols piled on top of each other. There was no telling if they all worked. It would have been all too easy for someone to simply toss a broken one back in. The Regent shut the lid and hefted the crate.

The thing they were missing the most were suits. He had selected a specific team to use the last ones they had. He remembered stories of the nasty strategy Safe Harbor had used against Sarthyl's raid. They would cut the air out of a section before a fight. Not only did it render breaching barrages nearly useless without the violent depressurization, but many—including his own family members—had died stepping out of the back of a transport ready for a fight, only to find the void.

There was a loud shift as the door began to open again. Varis set the crate in line and rested a foot on the lid. He wiped at his brow again and waited.

The man standing in the door wore a partial suit and held a helmet under his arm. It was hard to tell, but the fact that Varis had not seen his face before marked him as one of the scavengers from the Aura belt.

"Hey, I'm looking for the Regent," the man said from the hall. "I was told to come to the armory? Is this the right place?"

Varis motioned to the damaged crates and makeshift boxes, some of which were overflowing with firearms. "That's me. I'm Varis. Who sent you?"

The man eyed the pistol on the Regent's hip before glancing again to the collection in front of him. "The dock keeper did. I overheard that someone picked up a signal from Safe Harbor."

The Regent eyed the man for a moment. Varis made sure he contained his anxiousness. This meant that the migrant likely had held up his part of the deal. "I suppose you are looking for a reward?"

The man eyed the crates again but said nothing.

"I'll tell you what," Varis continued during the man's pointed silence. "You look like a man who has a ship, if not a few. If you want a reward, bring your ships to the border of Safe Harbor."

The man rolled his helmet in his hands. "To the border? So it is true then? We actually killed the Warden?"

Varis felt like lying on the ground as the blood ran from his face. He stood as strongly as he could manage in the face of what they had done. "The first raid, we will get in and out as quickly as we can. If my theory is right, we've already beaten what stopped Sarthyl the last time." To add weight to his words, Varis moved his foot and pulled a pistol out of the crate. He tossed it to the man. Weapons were power, and when given, a symbol of trust and leadership. "Wait for the signal."

The man caught it with a smile. "I'll be listening." At that, he pressed the panel to the door, then waited for it to open. "Oh," he said, turning back as the door started to shift, "I was also supposed to tell you that Airlock Twenty-Four malfunctioned. The dock keeper said two of your people were killed. Possibly a few more."

"Just tell them to seal it up. We've tried to fix it three times this month."

"Will do. And," he said, stopping himself from leaving again, "if you don't mind, what exactly are we looking to do on this raid? Just scare 'em?"

"Safe Harbor has the only ships Sarthyl believed would make the journey."

"Journey? Where?"

Varis simply closed the lid to the crate. "You'll see."

* * *

Baxel let out a breath as he looked up at the rolling expanse of Earth beyond the Point. Lights dotted the night's surface from the cities he had always thought were merely the dead shells of humanity. As the fog of his breath touched the glass of his helmet, Baxel could not help but slip further into his thoughts of the blurred planet. At the forefront of his mind, he wondered what exploration without a suit would entail.

"Three figures approaching," Tialee said. "Tymon, Merden, and Sammai."

Baxel quickly sat up and then unattached the tethers holding his legs to the fleet. "Sammai? From Redemption?"

Tymon's voice cut through the emptiness surrounding the Point. "Hey, Baxil? You read me?"

Baxel put a hand up to his helmet. "What's going on, Tymon? Why is Sammai here?"

He expected a biting remark from the older Redemption explorer, but instead Tymon replied, "That's not Sammai. It's Liaren. She can hear you, but her comms are stuck. Where are you?"

"Liaren?" Baxel asked. "You brought her all the way out here? You know how dangerous that is?"

Tialee quietly cut in. "She's here for the suit." She sounded hopeful.

"Well, she's your problem now, Bax. Now how about you tell me what is going on? And how did you see us? You at the supplies?"

"Yeah, I'm here." Just then, Baxel spotted three pairs of lights sliding along the surface of the fleet below where he stood. He watched nervously as Liaren expelled large bursts of air to keep on course. He would have been nervous had she simply been in the zero coordinates.

"I will need to speak to Liaren," Baxel said.

As the three of them neared, Baxel readied one of the bags. He did not want to tell Tymon and Merden anything without Liaren's say. They may have been told that the suit was here, but there was no telling if they knew where Liaren thought they should go with it.

Liaren transferred unsteadily from holding Merden's hand to pulling herself into Baxel's arms. Their suits clacked together as he caught her momentum and adjusted them both back to a stop. He tapped the lights of her helmet off so his own glass could lighten. He could see her wide eyes and possibly a bit of relief as she clung to something stable.

Baxel wasted no time with the atmosphere device. After securing the Warden's helmet to a magnetic latch on his back, he separated out the ring and slid it down over the both of them. A transparent plastic pulled out from the main housing, and as the ring reached the bottom, it spun shut again. Gradually, he could hear the humming of the device as it filled with air, leaving them in a small, oblong bubble. Baxel glanced to his external readings, switched off his comms, and pulled off his helmet.

Liaren shook her head vigorously, but Baxel tried to calm her with a hand on either side of her helmet.

"Trust me," he said. He knew his voice would be muffled in her helmet, but that she could hear it. After she gave a small nod, he activated the release and pulled her helmet free from the reactive seal on the undersuit.

As soon as he had her helmet off, she pulled their center of masses closer. Baxel, with both hands still on her helmet behind her head, pulled her into a long kiss. Floating weightless, holding her in his embrace, Baxel forgot the fleet, the world, and the troubles of the Warden. They readjusted several times in their embrace before she finally pulled away.

"I'm glad they couldn't hear me out there," Liaren said, partially out of breath. "I used every word I could think of, and when that failed, I just screamed. I don't know how you do it."

Baxel carefully shut the comms off on her helmet—as it would now be transmitting using the mic of the atmosphere device—and gave her a smile. "That's why I do it. Everything is on me out here."

For a moment, they simply looked into each other's eyes. "Is . . . is Tialee safe?" Liaren finally asked.

Baxel let go of her helmet with one hand and reached behind his back, where he had the Warden's helmet secured. "She's right here."

Liaren looked at the smooth white frame and very minutely flawed glass.

"I think we should tell Tymon about what Connor did to Varnil," Baxel started. "And Dimarka."

Liaren sighed. "I don't know. We still have to do everything we can to preserve the Warden."

"A few second's difference, and we would be left with an absent Warden and no suit. I have a feeling that we are cutting it close as it is. We may lose everything if we continue to hold back."

Liaren kept looking at the helmet. "Tialee specifically told us to protect the Warden's secrets. Our people would be lost if they started to question her, just as First Claim was lost when it gave up on following the Warden."

"Fine. I'll follow your lead." Baxel released the Warden's helmet, then gently grabbed the back of her neck with his gloved hand and turned her to look at him. "But if Tymon and I are going to the cryopods, he has to know about Connor. Even if we say nothing about Dimarka or Tialee, he needs to know the migrant was the one who tried to destroy the shrine, and about Varnil and what he said about the pods before he died. That's why we are going back."

"Alright. Just be careful out there, Baxel." Liaren pushed back from him and reached up for her free-floating helmet.

"Why not use this one?" Baxel asked, holding the Warden's helmet out toward her.

She gave it the same look she had several times before. Finally, almost as if coming out of a daydream of deep thought, Liaren shook her head. "No. I cannot. It is meant only for the Warden."

At that, they both put on their helmets, and Baxel double-checked her system before retracting the personal atmosphere.

* * *

After a round of arguments at the edge of the Remnant fleet, Tymon was left to restate his point yet again. "No, Baxel, you are not going! Not in the shape you are in." Of course, it had only taken Tymon one look at Baxel's patched-up suit to tell that it was far too dangerous for him. "I want to see you raise your arms."

"I'm fine!" It was immediately apparent by his weak attempt at raising his arms that he had not fully recovered from his accident in the Preservation Core or his supposed tumble down the steps of the Warden's Shrine.

Tymon moved his head from side to side in an exaggerated motion to make sure Baxel noticed. "I will take Merden. You stay with Liaren and the Warden's suit, and wait until we get back, dammit."

Baxel sighed heavily over the comms and followed up with a rude gesture.

"Liaren," Tymon said, "I know you cannot say anything, but make sure Baxel stays here. I guess throw something at him if he tries to follow us."

"That's smart," Baxel argued back.

"Just stay here," Tymon said. "It will not take long."

Tymon and Merden finally kicked loose from the outer reaches of the Point and off into the empty space under the Remnant Fleet. Tymon watched the gravitational fields closely as they traveled over the all-encompassing view of the planet. Occasionally, his perception would drop from the fleet's rapid orbit to the planet spinning wildly below. Tymon checked, just in case, to make sure they were moving at hundreds of meters per second, not the thousands it appeared to be.

"I don't think I have ever moved this fast!" Merden called over. She was following closely behind, only about fifty feet way.

"Let's slow it down and angle back toward the fleet," Tymon said, though he did not tell her that he was worried about falling out of the false gravity of their orbit. Moving at high speeds was also more dangerous than traveling through the wreckage simply from the momentum itself. Navigating inside the fleet forced a slow pace that meant no debris could act as sitting projectiles.

"There it is," Tymon said a few minutes later, spotting the far outreach of metal and cables near the area he and Baxel had found the cryopods. "Slow on my rate, best you can." He activated the air jets to slow his course, though it was an uneven gradient. This suit was nothing like his Firebrand gear. It was sloppy and probably dangerous under normal conditions. As he looked back and saw Merden, who looked like she was floating at a standstill, he just hoped Baxel could make use of whatever they found. He lifted his feet and released more air from his leg jets to finally bring himself to a stop.

A cold feeling washed over him as he came to a halt over the large gap in the wreckage. The sun had slipped the rest of the way around the horizon of the planet, leaving him in a heavy darkness that seemed to seep through the suit. The worn materials of this suit did not maintain as consistent of a temperature in the face of the sun's radiation or the grip of space as his Firebrand suit did.

"Find somewhere to latch onto and stay still," Tymon said. "I'll comm you if I need help."

"Careful, Tymon," Merden said. "We're a long ways out, and the rescue teams are still locked in the all-return."

"They can't hear us here anyway. We're out of the search coordinates."

Tymon gently pushed forward through the frozen space. The pale lights on his helmet illuminated the rough surface of the far-reaching strut as he slid over the surface. The rippled steel continued far past his age-dimmed lights and into the darkness ahead.

"Slow and easy," Tymon reminded himself. The pounding of his heart filled his helmet, and he fought against shivering from the cold. He adjusted his drift with far more caution than he would with Baxel in the area. One rupture and he would be in a tight spot until he could make it back to the oxygen tanks.

The ripples turned to ridges, and the ridges turned to nasty tendrils of steel reaching out from large waves. As he had to adjust his trajectory upward again, a large shape finally came into view.

Tymon set his hand against the large curve of the engine guard of the repulsor and looked upwards. "Incredible," he said, now feeling a faint vibration from touching the metal. It was a different feeling than touching his suit to any other part of the Orbital Armistice Fleet. The tiny motion was somehow sharper. More alive.

Tymon activated the magnetic locks of his gloves and started to pull himself around the edge. By the way the ship was wrapped by the wreckage, he couldn't shake the feeling that this was newer. Possibly several hundred years old still, but this was not from an event during the creation of the initial fleet wreckage.

Baxel had been brief in his description, but Tymon soon found the particular rip in the hull that was large enough to enter. He could see the slow pulse of red from the warning lights, and in their lull the insides were bathed in a cool blue. Remembering Baxel's warning, he slowed down and gauged the edge of the opening itself for surfaces dangerous to the integrity of his suit. After a good twenty seconds, Tymon finally pulled himself in, keeping his arms tucked close and his legs following his curve of entry.

The insides were like nothing he had ever seen before. It was a narrow space, with a walkway only wide enough for two people. However, all the surfaces would have looked a pristine white, if not for the numerous scratches in the paint. Nets of broken cables twisted out from overhead systems, and heavy dents from the outer surface protruded in far enough to have pulled the brackets securing storage bins and readout screens on the wall free.

As Tymon attached his feet to the buckled walkway, he stood up and took in the source of the blue light. A section of the walkway further back was lined on either side by a series of pods. The wide and rounded surfaces of entirely ice-coated glass enveloped the area with a mesmerizing blue glow. They were cryopods, but nothing like the one Kaiden Williams had stepped out of.

Tymon walked closer, measuring each of his steps with caution. Of the eight spaces for pods, only six were still glowing. To the far back, one was open, and the other was gone.

Tymon took a quick step backward in surprise as projected displays appeared in front of the first two pods. Once he was certain it was safe to continue, Tymon started forward again. The first pods on either side were marked *"Four"* and *"Five"* by the scratched paint on the walkway. The displays that hovered along the curve of the glass, about waist-high, showed the names Eida Xangil and Akrem Nakani.

Tymon raised an eyebrow at the names and continued to the next ones. The displays appeared as he stepped in front of them. Three and Six. Bailey Kallister and Nuveera Waieen.

Two and Seven. Maria Hawkins and James Terra.

He took the final step forward, and the displays hovered in front of both the opened pod to his right and the one missing on his left. One and Eight. Tymon had to blink.

"Merden, patch into my video transmission. If I don't make it out, Baxel needs to see this."

"Doing it now. Wait, are those the cryopods?" Merden asked.

"Yeah, and look who was in them."

The missing pod of Sarthyl Dioma was to his left, and the empty pod of Connor Sevison was to his right.

"Sarthyl?" Merden asked. "The same Sarthyl that we grew up hearing about? The one who abandoned and then attacked Safe Harbor?"

"And it appears to me," Tymon said, sliding his hand over the empty pod, "that our friend Connor lied about being from Aura. He was from . . ." Tymon took a step back and looked around. "He was from here."

"So Connor Sevison was a Reawakened, and Sarthyl too?"

"I'm going to make my way deeper in, toward the front of the ship."

Tymon set off at a slow pace with his magnetic boots along the warped walkway. The standard passage was soon blocked by a large protrusion of steel from the fleet that jutted through the core of the ship. Tymon backtracked just a little and decided to lower himself down some kind of open, single person lift. As he set his feet on the lower bar and a hand on one of the protrusions, the entire lift system slid down on a rail. There was a grating screech through the quick vibration in his hand as the lift came to a stop about halfway down. Tymon pushed himself off what could have been an automatic ladder and continued down the hole.

The hallway appeared to have small bunks for sleeping in, and surprisingly enough, the sealed bunks looked as if they had recently been slept in, just before the crash. Tymon continued forward with a shiver down his spine. The lights of the corridor started to flicker on.

Suddenly, a massive arc of electricity flared in his vision and even darkened the reactive glass of his helmet. Tymon could not make out exactly what had caused it, so he moved out through a tear in the wall where one of the bunks should have been. He was now in the exterior shell of the ship.

Tymon moved cautiously onward through the uneven space. There were numerous pipes and cables that had come free of their securing brackets, and even more small piercings through the wide sheets of steel that made the outer hull of the ship. It took him nearly a minute to thread his way through until he found another gap large enough to reenter next to a protruding jut of steel.

The room Tymon slid into had a number of control stations spaced about, and a few even had large holographic displays shimmering over them.

"That one, back to your right," Merden said. "What is that?"

Tymon followed her direction and looked to a large display of what appeared to be a chart of their system. *"The Sol System,"* as the words read at the top. It stood static, almost as if it were not an active display but a recording of this ship's journey. Tymon looked down at the control terminal below the holographic display and noticed a warning about the destination.

"Invalid destination: Unable to calculate course," Merden read through his video feed. "What was it? Their destination?"

Tymon picked up what looked like a physical data pad from the floor. He opened the carbon-plastic cover and flipped a few of the thin sheets of flexible material. At a quick glance, the handwritten coordinates seemed to match what was on the screen, and written just below them with several heavy underlines was the word *"Earth."*

"I think that means their destination was Earth," Tymon said, tucking the physical data pad in a pouch on his leg. "And by the look of that date, I would say it was about sixty to seventy years ago."

"So both Vigil Connor and Sarthyl were not Remnants?"

Tymon looked to the other end of the ship's charted journey. "There. Can you see? That's their zero coordinates. Their home. Next-Star Colonization Prep Facility, Kasei Valles, Mare Acidalium, Mars."

"Mars?"

"Next-Star Colonization. That means this must be an exploration ship. Sarthyl, Vigil Connor, the others, they are explorers. They were trying to find Earth." Tymon frowned. "But instead they ended up here. Caught in the wreckage."

Without warning, Merden started panicking over the comms. "Oh, no, no, no, that's not good," she said quickly. "Tymon, you need to get out. A ship is headed your way, and I don't think it looks like one of ours."

"Cut transmissions," Tymon said. At that, he pushed off the terminal and started through the outer edge of the ship. Baxel had warned him about Connor knowing the last time they were here, but he didn't expect anything to come of it so soon. And from Merden's tone, it was likely a First Claim ship.

Tymon could see minor leaks springing up about his arms as he shoved through another space. His top priority was getting out, and getting to Merden. Just as Tymon pulled himself up and started along the surface of the cryopods, a light pointed at him from down the hallway.

Suddenly there were several flashes and sparks as a person in a rough suit fired a weapon. Tymon gasped and clutched his leg as blood began to float out through the now-cracked plate.

"Merden, get back to Baxel!" Tymon let out a scream and clutched against the puncture in his suit. His air was dropping quickly and his vitals were throwing warnings as well. "He has to know what this is."

"Tymon!"

"You have to, Merden! No matter what happens!"

The person slowly floated forward, keeping their weapon pointed at Tymon. They then tapped on their helmet several times.

"Tymon don't—" Merden was cut off as he switched to the new contact.

"Can you hear me?" the hoarse voice of a woman asked. "Safe Harbor guy, do you read me?"

"Yeah," Tymon said with a pained grunt. "Did you have to do that?"

"Shit, Safe Harbor is here?" another voice said through the comms from somewhere out of sight. "You got to kill him, before the rest of the Warden's scum know we are here."

"Shut up!" she yelled at the man before turning back to Tymon. "Alright, yellow suit, why in the name of the fleet are you here? I thought all of you were called back to your habitats? The, what do you call it, the all-return?"

"Sightseeing," Tymon strained to get out. "What about you?"

"Just shoot him, Breka!" another voice said from outside the ship.

She glanced to the side before hastily pointing her weapon back at Tymon. "He's mine! And I found him, so mind your damned business."

"So what's the plan?" Tymon asked. Between the oxygen dipping and the blood loss, he knew he did not have long before he blacked out.

She hesitated until another light started shining in from the opening in the ship. "There's no need to put more holes in the suit I just found. I'll take you back to the ship. Might even dump you out at Safe Harbor during the raid, if I get the chance. But if you so much as think about trying anything—"

"Yeah, that's great," Tymon said. "Can you drag me out of here now?"

* * *

Vigil Connor watched as the SE-S head cautiously approached. Quervin held the data pad in his thin hands nervously as he neared the entrance to the Hall of the Vigil in the Hall of the Warden. For the most part, the yells of pain had been soothed or carried away, leaving only the occasional sobbing or stiff silence around the many objects of the room.

"Ah, Quervin," Connor said as he neared. "I thank you for coming, yet again."

Quervin glanced nervously at the two Vigil who stood more like guards at his side. "Yes, of course. Although, with the circumstances, I wonder if it would not be better if—"

"Nonsense," Connor interrupted. He held his hand out for the data pad. "If the transmission picked up at the relay is worthy of note, I will take it to Director Wardenson himself."

Quervin glanced behind him to where, for the first time in many years, the stairs leading up to the Warden's shrine stood empty. "Actually, I think he needs to see this for himself."

"Did you read it?" Connor asked dangerously.

"No, I—"

Connor motioned for his two First Claim helpers to step forward. The woman took off her Vigil sash and wrapped it around her fist several times. The man simply cracked his knuckles.

Connor held out his hand again. "Give it to me."

"I . . . why?"

The man from First Claim punched Quervin sharply in the stomach, and the woman stood him back up. She stood with her arm over his shoulder, to look comforting from a distance, but her wrapped fist was ready to add another strike.

They ripped the data pad from Quervin's hand and handed it to Connor.

He dropped the SE-S head from his attention as he scanned the transmission.

The cryopod recovery team had arrived at the coordinates Connor had provided. One of the workers had captured a Safe Harbor explorer within the ship. After collecting the pods, they were moving into position to receive Regent Varis's order.

"Quervin," Connor barked just as the man was about to slink away. "Your trackers. Did either Baxel or the one called Tymon leave here?"

"During an all-return?" he groaned. "No."

Connor nodded. At the very least, the Safe Harbor explorer was captured. All that remained was to wait for his people to return here in their pods. Then they could finally continue what they'd set out to do: to return to their home world, hidden by conspiracy and blocked by every available technology for six hundred years.

Chapter 24: Meeting

She blinked a few times.

It was a struggle to open her eyes.

Who would have thought that taking in her surroundings of the Norclave medical room would have been more difficult than stepping out of the cold and the centuries? Jance sat up with a groan, feeling what were perhaps her bandages shifting against newly healed muscles.

She could tell there was someone else in the room, though they were lost somewhere in the fog of her muddled attention. After muddled questions and strained minutes, Jance caught sight of a bright sparkle off to the side of her bed. It was a small, handheld medical device, the double cross etched into the steel marking it as such.

"I feel like I should ask something," Jance said. She could feel the movement of her mouth start to come back into form. "Perhaps I will start as I always seem to. What is the date?"

"It has been nearly a month," a familiar voice said.

Jance looked over to the blurred figure and smiled as she recognized the glow of a data pad. "Sora. It was at the docks, wasn't it?"

"Yes, Cryo," she said, with a moment's hesitation at the last word.

"Oh, come now," Jance said, starting to shift just to make her body come alive. "I'm no different than I was. You know me."

Jance frowned as some of her motions seemed not to match. She realized then that as she was trying to sit up, someone else was helping her with a arm around her shoulders. "A month you said? How bad . . . was I?" she asked between pulses of pain.

Sora's hand gripped her shoulder. "I do not want you to take this the wrong way, but . . . well, if you had been anyone else, you would have been left for dead."

"So . . . this . . . everything from beneath my chest down?"

"The Overlord has been trying to find tech for the regenerative process but . . . I am afraid as it is, it is beyond Norclave's capabilities. Possibly anyone's, in this time." Sora became clear in Jance's vision as she leaned closer. "I am afraid this may be a stressful experience, but

Olana needs you to appear before the Prime Elect of Reclaim. The med-techs want you to try and stay calm. With what tech we do have, you have come a long way. Your lungs were essentially shredded by shrapnel from the transport."

"And my vision?"

"I . . ." Sora started, but she looked to the side in question.

Another voice joined in, likely belonging to one of the med-techs, to reassure Jance that it was simply a part of the coma induction and should clear.

Jance sat supported by the med-tech's arm for a long moment. She tried several times to lift herself up or to even shift her legs to the side, but there was nothing. No movement, no feeling.

There was simply a disconnect.

She felt the blood drain from her face and her hands turned cold as she thought about her new reality. There were almost too many thoughts to entertain a single one before moving to the next. How was she supposed to get around Norclave? How would the others see her? How would she see herself? What about getting up and out of her living quarters in the mornings?

Jance lowered her head as she realized that last thought was about her old life, on level 447, from before she became a Cryo. The memory was from a time centuries past, and though she could recall it as clearly as any waking moment of her life, Jance knew there was no returning to that time. Just as there was no returning to the time before the explosion at the docks.

"What is it?" Sora asked, probably seeing the gradual change in her expression.

Despite everything, Jance gave a slight twitch of a smile. "Prep me for this meeting," she said over the thoughts whirring in her head. "If the Overlord of Norclave needs me, then I have work to do."

"Y . . . yes, of course," Sora stammered. "I remind you that Olana does not expect you to speak. She understands what you are going through."

Jance used her arms to ungracefully prop herself forward into sitting up the rest of the way. "Even I don't understand what I am going through. I understand I will not make it through this, not with just one epiphany or one take on life, but I assure you, I *will* be of more use than simply sitting in a corner and holding up a sign that says 'Cryo.' Now, start filling me in. What is this meeting about?"

* * *

Zaireel Tuakana tapped off his visor as he stepped out onto the balcony high up in the Prime Elect's Citadel. While the balcony was only barely above the outer ring structure that formed the wide boundary to Reclaim, it still left a towering view of the surrounding city. Something about it seemed more . . . magnificent than Norclave.

Leaning on the balcony's edge, just on the inside of a wash of rain sliding down the Citadel, was the Prime Elect himself.

"What is going on out there?" Iben Feirshan asked, though it sounded more like wondering than a true question. Zaireel had told him a few hours ago about what happened between the watch and the Black Scars.

"I expected Hakatha to betray me at some point," the Prime Elect continued. "He was always unruly. After I sent Travend away, there was nobody but me to keep him in check." The Prime Elect glanced over his shoulder. His eyes were reddened from the stress of the entire situation. He motioned out toward the city with a hand. "What I did not expect, was that *he* would grab *my* bait."

Zaireel ducked his head. The Prime Elect had directed him to observe the attempt to dredge out the tech hunter, Kara, in the hope that he could identify the woman. Instead, Lieth had been stolen off the streets by the Prime Elect's thugs.

"And I was supposed to have answers about the recovered probe by now. It burned. I was supposed to have Nuand's tracker, mercenary, tech hunter, whatever she actually is, captured or killed by now. Hell, Norclave at least should be wallowing in turmoil by now with the death of their Cryo, but Olana has kept a final confirmation on the Cryo buried just so she has *something* to stand on for this meeting."

Zaireel said nothing, rubbing a scalded hand, remembering the heat of the fires at the docks. While he was lucky enough to have been outside the transport, he knew the people caught within it. Ian Opeira, Gaien Feikelly, Hioura, Eemel Logurston, and nearly a half dozen more . . .

"Please, excuse me," the Prime Elect said. "I know it was a personal event for you."

Zaireel moved up to the railing and crossed his arms as he looked out. "The Overlord is not as stable as you might think. Olana Nuand inherited the Kamriek Mines from her family. Her only struggle for power has been amongst siblings. Unlike you, who carefully secured your way to the top, she simply stepped into Norclave with the blessing of the Cryo. Now that blessing is gone. Her faith in her own position must be worn thin."

"You would be surprised how someone can find confidence when they see no other option."

"I recommend sticking to your plan," Zaireel advised. "Deny knowledge of Travend, double down on condolences for the incident at the docks, and ready the sabotage of your pod as counter-ammunition. The tech hunter would not have been sent here to track someone if her mission was to destroy your newfound tech. Make her want to keep the conversation on a path away from revealing her sensitive information, and it might just keep yours quiet."

"You have done well, Tuakana," the Prime Elect said. "Inform the Overlord of Norclave that I am ready."

* * *

Lieth groaned as he was dumped onto the rain-covered floor of the building on the far west side of Reclaim. He could hear the regular commotion of the city coming up through the layers of haphazard collections of leaning panels and sunken pillars. From what he could tell through the wide and broken window, they were high up, and he could see the city stretching out in the distance.

He coughed into the water as he pushed himself a few inches up off the uneven steel floor. The Black Scar who had dragged him off the street, right in front of Reclaim's watch, stood over him. His skin was covered almost entirely in the angular lines of ink-filled scars, though they formed a sort of molted, textured pattern against his dark skin. The man took a few steps back, giving Lieth a view of another figure stepping in out of the rain.

The leader of the Black Scars threw his cover to the side and shook some water from his hair. He made no move to avoid the large puddle in the middle of the floor that had formed from overflow draining through the building, as well as from the gaping hole in the roof. Lieth glanced back out to the city through the rain.

"Don't bother screaming for help," the Black Scar said. "They've been trained to ignore us. You're in the part of the city left to us by the watch."

Lieth raised himself to his knees, though he made no move to wipe away the water on his face.

"Keep him down."

Lieth was shoved back down to the floor. He could feel the skin by his eye split open against the hard steel under the thin layer of water.

"What is your game?" Lieth spit, the corner of his mouth submerged. The hand on his shoulder gave one final push before the strong-arm backed away. "You must be Hakatha," he continued. "Are you trying for the city?"

"I already own this place." He slowly crossed the room, kicking water into Lieth's face as he passed. Hakatha watched the people of Reclaim through the crumbling side of the building. "I own this place!" he screamed, by far loud enough for any passing by to hear.

After a long moment of dull rain and distant thunder, Hakatha turned back to Lieth. "I own everything but what of Feirshan's I agreed not to touch. Now tell me. Who are you, and why did Feirshan give you protection when you arrived? Is Oa protecting you along with the tech hunter?"

Lieth smirked and started to push himself up, but was again shoved back down. "I'm just a shopkeeper."

Hakatha produced one of the Black Scar muzzles and slammed it into the water beside Lieth. Lieth let out a scream as his muscles tensed from all sides.

"Answer me," Hakatha growled, pulling his fist out of the water, ready to strike it again.

Lieth gave a defiant chuckle. "Now I see why your man keeps backing away from me."

Instead of shocking him again, Hakatha frowned. "Or is the tech hunter after you? Are you from Norclave, then?"

Lieth said nothing as he pulled in a deep breath.

Hakatha continued, "What did you do to demand Norclave's attention? Do you work for my damned brother? For Travend?"

"Your brother?" Lieth pushed himself up. This time, Hakatha held a hand up to stop his man from nearing. Lieth wiped at the blood from his eye and shot Hakatha a hard look. "I killed Norclave's Cryo."

"You did?" Hakatha paused a long moment. His look of shock turned to a calculating frown. Then, as if at the snap of an idea, Hakatha's expression turned devious. "At least Travend picked someone disposable."

Hakatha stood up and stepped over Lieth as he walked back to where the Black Scars' cloak lay on the floor.

"Wait, damn you!" Lieth yelled after Hakatha. "I have to get back to Norclave."

Hakatha picked up the cloth from the floor and watched it drip for a few seconds. "Why?" he asked, looking back.

"Olana Nuand, she has to fail. Norclave cannot be hers."

"I'm sure you're not Travend's only plan." Hakatha threw the wet cloth over his shoulders and started to leave, but paused again just at the edge of the falling water. "You'll be lucky to survive this."

"Survive what, exactly?"

"The supposed Overlord and the Prime Elect are talking peace. But now that I know they are both hunting you, let's see how much Feirshan's Cryo is willing to help Norclave's tech hunter."

"Feirshan's Cryo? What are you talking about? Reclaim doesn't have a Cryo."

"Oh yes it does. She has been protecting the woman apparently tasked with hunting you down for weeks. And I hope she tries again."

* * *

It was an odd light that danced through the hexagonal inner weavings of the starscraper glass. The blue waiting hum of the various projectors around the old First Administrator's office bled through the angles of the familiar cube as Olana Nuand slowly turned it in her hands. She knew what rested on the moments to come, and that tension gave the wait a stagnant fierceness like few she had endured before. Her control of the city would be a short mention in the history of Norclave if she could not twist an alliance from Feirshan's hands . . . if she could not project control beyond the borders of the Rift Hills.

"Overlord," Sora said from the doorway behind her. "Jance will be ready. We will enter at your signal."

"Any new word from Kenneth?" Olana asked. She was still wildly hoping there was some way she could pull her team off their course to Reclaim, but if she could not get the Prime Elect to hand over Travend, she wanted to know exactly where to strike.

"I'm afraid nothing yet," Sora said.

Olana gripped her glass cube tight and looked up toward the display. "Alright. Leave the room."

The door cycled closed and Olana tapped her visor. "Tuakana, Norclave is ready."

After a short pause, Zaireel said in his strong accent, "Reclaim is ready. Establishing the connection."

As the projectors about the room revealed the office of the Prime Elect, Olana immediately noticed his posture. He was seated behind his white-coated steel desk with his hands clasped. She mentally nodded to him, seeing that he was positioned to receive her entrance, making their virtual meeting, essentially, in his territory.

"Olana Nuand, head of Kamriek's Grove, Overlord of Norclave, my greetings, on behalf of Reclaim, to you."

Olana took particular note of the order of her titles. He was trying to downplay her control of Norclave by placing it second.

"Prime Elect Iben Feirshan, all of the Rift Hills follow me in thanking you for this meeting. We have many things to discuss."

Feirshan adjusted one of several data pads on his desk. "Many, many things. After being subjected to an . . . uncoordinated transfer of power, I for one am concerned with learning the ideals and practices of this new state of Norclave."

"As my emissary has conveyed to your officials, Norclave is going to fall under a much more reliable form of control. The days of a reclusive Overlord are over."

Norclave is going to . . . Olana could hear her words echoing as she knew she had made her first misstep. Feirshan's strategy from here on out would be to point out the work yet to be done to stabilize her position.

Feirshan gave an equal pause before replying, "And what are some of your more active stances?"

Olana was almost taken by surprise with him not pushing the point of her continued process of securing the city. Perhaps he was simply trying to avoid the topic of Norclave unrest and Travend all together. "I stand for clear and open communication," Olana replied. "Norclave will be in contact with the other structures in the lands, and we will not simply let old threats stand in for safeguards."

The Prime Elect tilted his head. "Is Norclave prepared to deliver new threats, then?"

Olana broke her gaze with him and walked a few steps around the Prime Elect's office, knowing he was trying to pick his way toward hostilities. Olana noticed an open doorway to a balcony showing a dark sky over his city. It would help his own appearance within Reclaim if she seemed the aggressor.

"Do not forget that trade is my specialty, Feirshan. The Kamriek Mines export to nearly everywhere in the region, and I see no reason Norclave should not follow suit."

For the first time, the Prime Elect dropped his orderly visage and stood from his seat. As he stepped around to the front of his desk, he looked intrigued. "Reclaim has little need of supplies, beyond the niceties of private trade. What are you considering as an offer?"

Olana hid her smile as she turned back toward her desk. She ran her hand over the darkened wood and inlayed starscraper glass before turning back to the Prime Elect. He was in her office now.

"I propose an easing of secrets, of sorts. A trade of ideas, technology . . . perhaps even cultural information acquired from our brief time spent with my Cryo."

Feirshan glanced around her smaller room. His pause for thought gave her the chance to continue.

"The previous Overlord hoarded all sorts of information in his library. I speak truthfully when I say that we have not rediscovered all the potential to be had in that room. I have kept the archivists busy going through everything. Perhaps we could come to some agreement regarding newfound technologies and information." And with luck, Olana knew she could pull information about his recovered pod.

Feirshan narrowed his eyes rather dangerously and stepped forward. "It would be unsightly for recovered things to be lost again, as I am sure you know."

Olana tried to weigh his meaning. She gave a polite agreement, believing he was referring to the supposed death of her Cryo, though she said nothing of the surprise she had in store.

The Prime Elect took a few steps back and leaned against his desk. "Even if minor information was given in fair trade, the intrinsic need to keep that information secure would remain. It puts me in no better position if my secrets are simply released to the rest of the world. The integrity of the matter must be ensured, and I must be certain that Norclave is capable of the necessary restraint."

Olana drew in a breath. She wanted to stay in control of the conversation, but it seemed much of her struggle in stabilizing the city stemmed from his efforts to keep it in chaos. For the moment, she decided on playing gentle, though as the transports neared the border of the Steel Valley, she knew the situation could very well devolve into seeing who had more ammunition for a blackmail war.

* * *

Kara adjusted her damp cloak to cover her sling. It was a detail best kept hidden, especially where she was walking. She could tell the grandeur of the city had slipped a bit as she moved into the smaller roads, with the houses of pieced-together plates sitting along muddied streets. The usual shouts from the open doors of bars were sobered a bit by the tension now gripping the city. Occasionally, shouts could be heard carrying in the misty distance, and a time or two shrieks and howls followed brief weapons fire.

Kara checked her new weapon under the cover of her cloak for the second time as she rounded the corner. She had yet to find a private space to figure out what the weapon actually did, but her plan was to gather information, not get in a fight.

The Black Scar stood like a king on his corner, occasionally jeering at people passing by. Particularly jagged scars ran down along his neck and twisted around his arms. He was a thin man for his height, and he looked no older than twenty. His expression quickly changed from self-assuredness to worry as Kara stepped in front of him.

"If you make a noise, it will end as a scream," she said with the large weapon raised for emphasis. She tracked his eyes as he glanced to either side, then toward the light of the bar behind her. She had watched the street for several minutes without spotting another Black Scar, but he had just let her know where his backup was.

"What are you doing, tech hunter?" he asked nervously. "Everyone's looking for you."

"So, you do know something. That's good." Kara motioned for him to back into the alley. "I need to know where he is. The person your people stole from the watch."

He held up his hands as he continued to back slowly into the dripping passage at her direction. "I don't know what you are talking about."

"Are you saying I don't need you?"

"No, it's just—"

"I've already walked past you three times in the last hour. When I disappear again, nobody—not you, or the watch—will know where I am. If Hakatha is truly looking for me, now is his only chance. Tell me where you are keeping him, and I will be there."

The man glanced over the top of Kara toward the larger street.

"Don't try and stall for the others," Kara advised. "They will not care about getting you killed if they think they can stop me as well."

The man simply clenched his jaw and shook his head, giving another glance to where she kept her oversized weapon just out of his reach. "The Scar's base on the west side. In the ring. If they are keeping your man, he'll be there."

"West side," Kara said to herself in thought.

"Now what happens?" the man asked. Kara watched him slowly trying to inch his foot forward.

Kara took a step back. "You get on the ground until I am gone."

"You sure you know how to use that thing?" he said tauntingly.

"Get down!" she hissed, though she could see that he was only lowering himself down to leap. Knowing that this was her last moment to have a choice, Kara pulled the trigger.

There was a loud snap as the entirety of the magazine pack launched forward. The tall man doubled over as it slammed into his stomach, though the pack simply skipped to the side of the alley. Kara tucked the single-shot weapon under her cloak and started away before he could catch his breath to yell for help.

Kara cursed her fortune as she twisted away through the city. The release of the pack from the front of the pistol had been no louder than the clap of hands, but it also meant that all she had to work with was a stupid rail pistol. And a useless one at that.

About a quarter mile and three rings up toward the west, Kara turned on her heel and started back toward the center of the city. She knew Oa was right. She was no mercenary, and that most recent encounter had simply reinforced the point. The only way to beat Hakatha and the Prime Elect was to deal with it as a tech hunter would. When some tech was too big or too dangerous to bring back, you sold it. It was time that she tried selling to the new Overlord.

Minutes later, Kara was making her way to the second level of the city, near Oa's home overlooking the base of the Citadel. From the transports she had seen touch down in the city, Kara knew there was some sort of dock or landing yard nearby. Kara happened by the last piece of directions by simply speaking with a passerby and telling him that she was told to meet a merchant by his transport.

A pair of the watch eyed her as she moved through an open gateway built of metal plates scrapped and welded together. The walled landing yard of the second level of Reclaim continued in a wide curve around the level and was filled with waiting transports. It did not take her long to find the red stripes and bright shoulders of the Norclave mercenaries that she had hoped would be waiting in and around their transport.

"Hold there," one of the glass-shouldered mercenaries said as she stepped near. He held forward an outstretched hand. "What is your business, tech hunter?"

"Olana Nuand's Cryo slayers are here in Reclaim. I know where one is."

The man blinked a few times, looking stunned. The man quickly turned back to the transport and called inside the open ramp. "Zaireel! There is a tech hunter here that needs to speak to the Overlord!"

Kara tried to hold her cloak still as the winds picked up and Zaireel Tuakana stepped out of the back of the transport. He held his colored sash against the weather as he neared. "Kara? What are you doing here in Reclaim?"

"Tracking down the ones responsible for what happened at the docks. One of Travend's men has been captured by the Black Scars. Olana needs to know he is here."

Instead of the look of surprise Kara had expected, he held his free hand up to his chin in thought. "We cannot tell the Overlord. She is meeting with the Prime Elect now."

Kara felt a drift of cold wash over her. It suddenly became apparent that there were several things not lining up. "Why are you here?" Kara asked. She glanced over to the high, artistically uneven spire of the Citadel. "What are you doing with the transport?"

"Like I said, they are in a meeting. I've done everything I can." Tuakana glanced off toward the spire rising high over their level of the city, almost as if looking at a distant thought. "I can only hope that it goes well, but I *can* prepare for the other possibility."

"You mean if the meeting falls through. How long do we have? Before the watch could be sent for you?"

"I could not say," Zaireel Tuakana replied.

"Then we have to move quickly," Kara said. "Olana has to know that Travend is working under the direction of the Prime Elect."

"Move where?" Zaireel motioned to the Citadel again. "If we leave for Norclave now, that in of itself could jeopardize the meeting. The Prime Elect could see it as a sign of an impending attack and the Overlord could think we were forced to flee."

Kara pressed against her damp hood and let out a long breath. She knew Oa would have some choice words to say about what she was thinking, but Kara had to do something. "I am not talking about leaving for Norclave. We need to take Travend's man while the Black Scars still have him."

"You expect the twelve of us, with six soldiers total, to crack into a hidden criminal network?"

"I just need your men to get me close enough to get in. Stay here, keep trying to contact Nuand, and be ready with the damned transport when I signal from outside the city."

Zaireel slipped into his distant look of thought once again as he weighed his options. "No, I'd . . . I had better be with you, in case there are orders to leave him with the Scars." He tapped his visor. "I will try my best to get in contact on the way."

* * *

Jance stared at her feet, absently attempting to move them as she sat, propped up in her chair, outside Olana Nuand's office. The argument continued on the other side of the door, and the tactful bickerings of the two sides played quietly through her own visor. If it were a race, they would be trading which had a foot in the lead.

"When was Olana planning on allowing me in?" Jance asked over her shoulder to Sora.

The woman motioned with a data pad. "She will give the signal when I am to take you in."

Jance turned back to the door and crossed her arms, but she had to catch herself as her balance slipped. If the Overlord did not hurry, Olana's strike team would arrive in Reclaim without ever allowing Jance a chance to speak.

Jance tapped her visor and increased the audio output coming from the Overlord. She was honestly surprised Kenneth had figured out how to enable that connection, let alone keep it a secret from the Overlord herself.

The Prime Elect, Iben Feirshan, appeared to be taking the offensive. "Your tracker could not have been following anyone responsible for what happened at Norclave's docks."

Olana scoffed. "That is the only reason she would have gone to your city. In fact, if you must know, I tried to get Kara to see exactly what had fallen from the sky into your hands. She refused me, multiple times."

"I see your lies, Nuand. You gave her specific orders, and I do not think your explanation can coexist with what I know. She could not have possibly been tracking anyone at the same time she was sent on a mission, by you, to destroy my pod!"

Jance winced as Olana paused.

"Pod?" Olana asked breathily. "What kind of . . . you say it was destroyed?"

From where Jance watched with one eye through her visor, it looked as if Feirshan was going to throw something, regardless of the fact that they were in separate offices miles apart.

"Ask all the questions you want," he said with a dangerous frown. "I know next to nothing about it. Nothing, because you put it up in flames."

"I would never—"

Jance slid her visor out of the way, silencing the transport wreck of a meeting. "Sora, help me in there."

The woman looked puzzled and then started checking a data pad. "I've not received a summons, and the Overlord was very strict about—"

"She is drowning in there. I've seen fistfights in the SRA assembly more cordial than what is happening behind that door." Jance started pressing forward against the heavy wheels of the chair, though after so long stabilizing in a bed she found herself struggling to move the unrefined solution of heavy plate wheels made by Olana's scrapsmiths.

Sora started pushing Jance forward. "I guess I always did like listening to you better. Six centuries old and I find you the more relatable."

As soon as the door opened, both the Overlord and the Prime Elect turned to Jance.

"What is this?" the Prime Elect questioned. Feirshan looked irritated at the intrusion, and Olana seemed to be silently panicking.

"In the middle there, if you would," Jance directed Sora to position her in the center of the projection setup. She nodded over her shoulder to Sora once she was satisfied with the position. "Thank you. The Overlord will wish you to leave, I suspect."

The Prime Elect took a few steps forward after the door closed again. He should have been a rather unimposing looking man, not particularly tall, though he now loomed over Jance. "Who are you?"

Jance held her hand forward as dictated by the standard etiquette for a transmitted meeting. Without the possibility of shaking hands directly, she held her hand out for just a moment before tipping it palm up, with a slight, almost relaxed curl in of the fingers accompanied by a dip similar to accepting the weight of a small item. She smiled knowingly as the Prime Elect gave her outstretched hand a confused look.

"I am Ambassador Jance Lorège." She lowered her hand and gripped one of her wheels. "Though my official charge has long since fallen, I now act as an advisor to Norclave, and in turn, Olana Nuand. My cryogenesis was at the end of some six hundred years' preservation, and I now stand . . . as the Cryo of Norclave."

The Prime Elect tossed an incredulous look between her and the Overlord behind her. In his awe, he seemed to shrink, taking a step back. What had been volumes of anger were replaced by a sudden comprehension.

He let out a quick breath. "Why was I never told you survived?"

"A precaution," Olana stated. "I needed to stave off any further attempts at the Cryo's life while we hunted those who are responsible."

The Prime Elect froze. Jance could not quite tell what his reaction entailed.

"Do you have a target then?" he asked, glancing between Jance and the Overlord. "Do you know who was responsible?"

Jance started to speak, but Olana quickly cut her off with an explanation of her own.

"If you are referencing the ones Kara is tracking, then yes, Prime Elect." Olana made a half step forward into Feirshan's office to position herself in front of Jance. The Overlord was still hoping to hold back information.

"Is this true?" the Prime Elect questioned, looking to Jance for assurance.

Jance glanced up to the cold, steely gaze on Olana's face before addressing the Prime Elect. "I might remind you that I was rather indisposed when these decisions were made. As you can see," she said, motioning to herself, "my recovery has been . . . an ongoing process."

Jance was almost made uneasy by the look of pity he gave her. It was genuine sympathy, though perhaps mixed with a tone of regret.

"I ache with what has befallen you, Cryo. One who is such a gift to our world as yourself . . . if only Reclaim had found you."

"I would not miss the chance to make a difference where I am really needed." Jance smiled politely. "I find it best to start where it is toughest."

Feirshan glanced to the Overlord before looking back to Jance. "Is Norclave in such a dire state? Are they equipped to ensure your safety?"

"Norclave is fine," Olana said sternly. "I would be more concerned with the happenings in your own city."

"Really?" Feirshan said, attempting aloofness, though the clenching of his fists gave a different tone. "And what is of concern to you? My streets are safe. My people fed. Aside from your own interference, everything is secure."

Olana Nuand let out a breath and walked forward out into the projected bounds of the Prime Elect's office. Her hands were clasped behind her back and her gaze forward as she stepped beside the Prime Elect himself. In a low and dangerous tone, she simply said, "We know where Travend is."

The Prime Elect stood stiff, as if he had been washed with fear. Perhaps he was realizing the true strength of Olana's position.

"A transport is en route to your city, Feirshan. They have orders to eliminate him."

"My city? He is not . . . I assure the both of you that I give no harbor to anyone who would—"

"You will allow the passage of my team into your airspace, and will not interfere with them proceeding to their objective."

The Prime Elect looked as if he was caught at an unfair disadvantage in a child's game. "I cannot just allow Norclave to walk in uncontrolled! Why . . . how is it that you suspect Travend is here? What evidence do you have?"

"So you do know of him?" Jance asked. "You have heard of this man?"

"Of course I have," the Prime Elect said. He glanced beside him to where Olana stood. "He was a leader of one of the . . . more unsightly groups in my city. But I drove him out! He would never return. Whatever proof you believe you have of his presence in Reclaim, it is flawed."

"If you do not allow my transport into Reclaim, I will have no choice but to assume you are protecting the very man who intended on killing my Cryo. If you are protecting him, that means you are a part of that threat, Feirshan."

"Olana Nuand, I *will not* permit an intrusion into my airspace during the course of this meeting, no matter your accusations!"

"Then I shall give you the opportunity to permit it. The meeting is over. We are done here." The Overlord reached a hand to her visor and dropped the room into sudden darkness.

"What?" Jance asked as an emergency chem light started into a gentle glow near the door. "What kind of childish move was that! Are you really going to send those soldiers over his territory without waiting to see if they will be shot down?"

Olana let out a breath and stepped away from the boundary of the room. She reached into her pocket and pulled out the small glass cube, gave it a brief look, then put it back. "It is too late for me to wait for permission. If it means war with Reclaim to protect you, I will order my men to fight until there are no more weapons to hold, and we will continue until it is *my* blood in the streets of Norclave."

"That is absurd," Jance said, heaving against one of her wheels to turn to face Olana.

The Overlord started back toward her desk. "That is a fact of your new life, Cryo. You are our greatest technology. You are our greatest political lever. In their eyes, you are Norclave's greatest weapon. I now have full confidence Feirshan wanted you dead. We just have to wait and see if he is willing to prove it to himself, and to his people, or accept a treaty with me."

* * *

The Prime Elect ripped down the projection supports in a silent fury. The makeshift frame of thin metal and the attached cameras clattered as it all fell to the ground. He turned to his desk and slammed both fists down on either side of the data pad that had been quietly beeping during their argument. He pulled in a breath, attempting to find some semblance of calm before opening the message. It was from Zaireel Tuakana.

"In company of the Overlord's tech hunter. On route to the Black Scars's radian of the wall. Hunting for Lieth and evidence of Travend's cooperation with you. Will give further updates."

Iben Feirshan's heart caught. At first, he thought it simply fell upon the piling mound of everything going wrong, but then he realized what it actually told him.

Olana was not after Travend.

In fact, she did not know what she was after. It was a wild guess and a power play; an attempt to make him squirm.

He unlocked the door to his office and started toward his seat. There was a commotion behind him along with a torrent of information being shouted even before he sat down. The people pushing in were members of the watch, the garrison, or other various contacts. Surprisingly enough, there was even a rough man who was trying to hide his heavy, black tattoos under wrappings of cloth about his neck and arms.

As the guards stationed outside tried to hold them all back, even the officials who were high up in the order of the city, the Prime Elect simply raised his hand to command silence. Only when they stopped the commotion did he speak.

"Get the gunships in the air. Have the watch secure the west side, and get an armed garrison team ready to assault the Black Scars." He made sure to speak up as the rough man started to attempt to slip back through the entrance unnoticed. "And tell Hakatha I will get my prisoner back!"

Chapter 25: Departure

Dannil Wardenson spoke with a hint of relief as he welcomed Reawakened Lovek and Nendra Halimuth into the Transmissions Sector. He scratched through his wispy hair and motioned to the numerous displays in the transmissions center of Safe Harbor with a frustrated shrug.

Located deeper in the wreckage of the *Firmament*, the Transmissions Sector had only a select few habitation quarters amongst the various specialized storage rooms and control areas. While Nendra had been in the sector on only a few occasions, she'd overseen the repair and development of a number of its systems as the lead of the Production and Research Sector.

"I just do not understand what is going on," he continued as Nendra stepped into the room, followed by the new Reawakened. "The system has gone down before, but none of us can get it back online this time."

"These are the systems that run Safe Harbor's communications?" Marrel commented, running a hand along the dented surface of a desk. It had several cutouts to support its varyingly sized display screens, though they all were showing malfunction warnings of one kind or another.

"I assure you," Dannil said, "while you may be accustomed to more refined standards, it normally functions perfectly. But that is why I ask your aid, Reawakened. Perhaps your experience as a transmissions engineer may help."

The Reawakened looked around the room in wonder. "I think it is incredible that you *have* managed to piece it together." Merril attempted to access the system, but the input projection flickered and registered the wrong presses of her fingers.

She glanced back in question.

Mr. Wardenson shook his head. "An hour ago, none of this was happening. Now, everything has gone back to the wreckage. That is why I myself had to convince one of the pilots to break the all-return to find you. I can't get a word through the relays. Anything but short, direct transmissions will either be lost to the distortions of the fleet or simply interrupted by the relay failure."

Before the explosion in the Warden's shrine, Nendra would have guessed a power consistency problem. Now, though . . .

Dannil Wardenson simply sighed. "What do you make of it, Mrs. Halimuth?"

She glanced across the entirety of the room and the various workers trying fruitlessly to make the system function. Without the Transmissions Sector, they were essentially blind to the areas around their fleet. Combined with the death of their Warden, she was left with a very dark and frightened feeling.

Nendra Halimuth finally spoke. "I think Sarthyl has come again, now that we are without the protection of the Warden. Get a transmi . . . send someone to find Oundara. We're going to need messengers. The ships will be busy making a stand while the Vigil convenes."

* * *

"They should be back by now," Baxel said, checking his system time yet again as he was suspended motionless a ways out from the Point. He was debating whether he should go looking for Tymon and Merden, though the debate had only been to himself.

Liaren gripped his shoulder, sending them both in a slow rotation. Baxel let out a breath, knowing her meaning even without the comms in her faulty helmet. He glanced over to see the soft blue glow of her interior visor illuminating her face. Her look was of concern and resolve.

"How are we going to get to the planet anyway?" he asked, using a short pulse of air to stop their momentum. He set back to watching along the arc of the fleet for Tymon's return. "It's not like we can just drop out of orbit. We're going to need a ship."

Baxel's own visor brightened as Tialee answered. "Safe Harbor has several transports suitable for planetary reentry as of: Last evaluation date, 3,491."

"That would be, what, Sarthyl's time? Scanned by the Warden herself?" Baxel flexed his hands, still feeling the pain in his muscles. "I'm sure nothing has broken since then." He looked up to where the dark of the planet rolled above them. "And once we are there, how are we supposed to even find the Warden? Depending on when we leave the fleet's orbit, we could end up on the far side of the—"

Tialee interrupted, "Object sighted. Identifying."

Baxel looked, though he knew it would be far out of his sight. "Object?" he asked. "Not two?"

"Object identified as Surefire suit, Merden."

Baxel gripped the side of his helmet. "Merden, can you hear me? Why is Tymon not with you?"

"Oh, thank the Warden you're still there," she replied. "They have him. The . . . First Claim has Tymon, and I think he was wounded by something."

"How many?" Baxel asked. He started forward, though his suit struggled to gain momentum with Liaren forcing her jets opposite of his. "Was this at the ship?" he asked, trying to pull Liaren's hand free. She had it magneted to his shoulder plate.

"Tymon was inside it still," Merden replied. "But does that mean . . . were they there for the cryopods?"

Baxel finally released his jets, and he was pulled back a distance before Liaren cut her own thrust. Perhaps more than ever before, he felt weightless, helpless, and unsure what he was supposed to do.

After a moment, Baxel spotted Merden's lights against the backdrop of the stars through the underglow of the fleet.

"Baxel, Tymon said you had to know what we found. Sarthyl and Connor . . . they are both Reawakened. But not from Earth, and not from long ago. Tymon guessed their ship got caught in the wreckage trying to make it to Earth . . . from Mars."

Baxel slowly turned back over his shoulder. He was shaking, and he was sure Liaren could feel it. Tymon had become more of a brother than a team lead, and Baxel had broken the one rule they always kept. He should have been at Tymon's side, and now Tymon was in serious trouble.

Liaren simply shook her head slowly in reply to his unspoken question.

Baxel lowered his head. "So, it was Connor's plan . . . no, Sarthyl's plan, all along. He's returning to Earth."

"Not returning," Merden corrected quietly. "Neither were ever there."

"We . . ." Baxel started, then glanced in the direction he had last watched Tymon go. "We have to get back to Safe Harbor. And then we have to go to Earth and find the Warden. She will make this right."

After a number of long and silent minutes sliding through the fleet, Baxel finally said quietly into his helmet, "Tialee, have there been any other sightings of First Claim ships?"

"Who is Tialee?" Merden asked as they followed his lead through the open sections of the orbital ship toward Safe Harbor.

Tialee responded, "Transmission silence. I'm getting nothing out of Safe Harbor."

"Is that a mirror? From the Vigil?"

Baxel changed direction, feeling the mass of Liaren and the Warden's suit pulling against him as he held Liaren's hand. He was traveling much quicker through the hazardous coordinates than he trusted her to control on her own.

Baxel did not reply to Merden. Instead, he thought about what Tialee had said about the transmissions. "The silence could be from the all-return. Safe Harbor is still mourning what happened in the Warden's shrine. They don't know what is coming."

"What is?" Merden asked as they rounded a massive strut of metal nearly three hundred feet in diameter where it had not been malformed in the original destruction. "What's happening to Safe Harbor?"

"Connor Sevison. The migrant Vigil. If First Claim had the capability, he would have simply used their resources to get to the planet to begin with. But they don't have the resources. They never have, not even when Sarthyl tried. Connor had to kill Dimarka to get us to be open to the possibility of exploring. Everything after . . . the list of the Unawakened, swaying Varnil by letting him find his son, using him to push for the idea of a probe, trying to destroy the Warden's suit . . . it was all to get Sarthyl's people on a Safe Harbor ship, straight to the surface of the planet."

"Then why not just take one from the hangars?" Merden asked.

Baxel punched his suit forward, draining his oxygen stores quicker than was safe. "Connor knew he only had one shot. If he was ever kicked out of Safe Harbor, like Sarthyl was, it would be over just the same. Besides that, he could never get the cryopods of his people open on his own. At least not before the Remnants, or the Warden, could find him."

They slowed to a stop as he came to a final section before the zero-space. They would enter into the rift of Safe Harbor near the bottom and on the far side from the *Fortuna* ship.

"We need to be careful. Try not to be seen until we know what is going on. We could either be too late, or Connor could be watching for our return."

He looked back. Liaren, in her suit of accented greys, held the bag containing the Warden's suit tightly in her arm.

He pulled himself over the ridge of steel and floated upward into the zero-space alone. With the possibility of flames leeching out from ripped habitats and an assault from First Claim in his mind, he was surprised at what he actually saw.

Never could he remember the zero-space of Safe Harbor being filled with so many lights of so many repulsors pushing transports through the mile-long space in the fleet. It was a scatter of stars as the blue engines and yellow warning lights of suits flowed in a motion similar to sparks. Safe Harbor was very much alive, and it was preparing to fight to stay that way.

"Still no transmissions?" Baxel asked.

"Nothing. At least not from the relay net. I am detecting scattered traces, possibly from personal comms devices, but but it is not the repulsors masking them; it is something else."

"Well, at least that will make getting in unannounced easy enough." Baxel motioned to the other two to come into the zero-space. "We need to find Flerin, tell him what happened to Tymon, about the truth of the pods, and then we get a transport. Hopefully all without running into another of Connor's explosives."

* * *

"Anyone without a full airjet harness, I want you suited and waiting outside the airlock in five minutes!"

Flerin stood on top of a strapped bundle of supplies to stay above the flow of madness surrounding him. At the recommendation of Nendra Halimuth, Oundara had ordered the entire SE-S to mobilize, meaning that he was left to oversee piecing together as many functional suits as possible. Many teams had an overlap of parts with the teams in other sleep cycles, meaning it was a very complicated endeavor.

"Where is my suit?" one of the Redemption team, Sammai, yelled loudly over the top of the commotion.

Flerin ignored her as another of Sol team entered the ready room, rubbing the sleep from his eyes. "Lannil! Your suit is over on a bench! You will have to find a different helmet!"

"Who took it?" Sammai yelled again.

Flerin gritted his teeth. "Sammai! It's gone! And if you don't shut up, I'll have you out the airlock without it! Start helping the others get suited!"

She probably gave some big huff, but Flerin had already turned in another direction.

"What about these old ones, Coordinator Flerin?" another voice called above the airlock door cycling as someone was running a message in or out. "Are they suitable?"

Flerin looked to the suit Davis was holding up. It had the distinctive red markings of Firebrand. Flerin said nothing but gave a reluctant thumbs-up. In truth, they should be the best suits they had. He had managed to keep a small number of them ready, hoping for the day he could start expanding the team back up to where it once was.

"Sammai, there you go!" Flerin said, pointing to where Davis had started passing out Firebrand gear. "Take Amrella's suit, but use Jahal's helmet! You are going to need some seal-tape!"

"Who is Amrella?" Sammai asked.

Flerin turned his attention away again, though this time it was actually away from the question. Amrella was the one who had died under his team leadership. He was pulled out of his thoughts as a shoulder bumped against his leg. He then noticed Greely Reyson speaking with one of Redemption before sending the messenger back out to the airlock.

"Reyson, make sure your team is not pushing their oxygen reserves too hard. We don't know when the next refill will be."

Instead of some remark or even dejected look, the coordinator gave him a nod. When it came down to it, Safe Harbor could fall into unbreaking coordination. That was not to say it was not chaos, but they had one purpose.

Flerin shook his head and started with his orders again. "I want one person without airjets at each habitat sector! Make sure to tell the pilot! The rest, report to Oundara in the Hall of the Warden!"

Flerin stepped off the bundle of supplies, as the four men he had ordered to take it to the Hall of the Warden were finally ready. "Reyson?" he called as he pushed his way through the half-on undersuits and helmet checks. "Anything from Dermuth? Where do I need to send people for weapons?"

"That last messenger was from Dermuth. Supply Sector was transferring the weapons to the Hall of the Warden after they got the transport cannon mounts to Maintenance."

Flerin glanced down to his data pad to recheck a few numbers. He was surprised to see a message waiting. So much of the chaos had been caused by the lack of transmissions, which made him hopeful that it was a test message from Wardenson. Flerin opened it. It read: *"Nobody can know I am here. First Claim has Tymon. You need to detain Connor Sevison as soon as possible, for working with Sarthyl all along and doing everything else I have been saying. I will be leaving now, and only the Warden knows if I will be coming back. Thanks for being like a father to me."*

Flerin looked up and about the room through the crowd. The opening of the airlock door caught his attention and he shuffled to find a spot where he could see it. Standing there, with helmet on and inner face mask up, was a Firebrand suit. What could only be Baxel pulled his hand from his helmet in a short wave as he backed into the habitat barrier. Flerin tried to push forward, but the doors closed long before he could reach them.

"You all right?" Greely Reyson asked. "What was that about?"

"Do you have your fighting team ready?"

"Last response I got is that they were waiting in the Hall of the Warden for weapons. Why?"

Flerin turned to him, thoughts still racing about what Baxel had said. Tymon had already been captured, and from the sounds of it, that was the last glimpse of Baxel that he would get.

"Get a messenger to flag down the nearest transport."

"Why?"

"You are in charge here, Reyson."

"In charge?" The man looked at all the confusion surrounding him. "Woah, wait right there, Flerin Arterrus. I'm only a coordinator for my team. You're the head."

"Step up, Reyson, or whatever. I'm going to the hall."

* * *

"Merden, wait here for Baxel to show up," Liaren said, finally able to speak as she took the helmet off. "Help him search for me if I am not back before he is."

As Liaren started off, Merden caught her by the arm. Liaren could see through Merden's helmet that the girl's eyes were still filled with tears, and a few long streaks had run down the inside of the glass.

"Didn't Baxel say he was leaving?" Merden asked. "How do we know he will not go off on his own?"

Liaren adjusted the bag slung over her shoulder, having thought over just the same thing. "He will show." At that, she stepped away into the Hall of the Warden.

The various focal points for meetings or waiting about the room took on a different light as dozens of workers were busy adding zero-g handles to the historic structures, or were using them as anchors for cover walls of welded steel. The handles would be used to hold against a sudden depressurization if the hall was breached before they were prepared.

As Liaren started toward the Hall of the Vigil, she pulled to a stop. For some reason, she could not shake the feeling that it was not her place.

Liaren glanced at the stairway leading up to the shrine before eventually starting up the steps. She knew there was nothing there; in fact, she had everything that was left slung over her shoulder. Perhaps it was because it had been a focal point for her questions for so long. Regardless, she hurried up the charred steps, a number of which were covered in dried blood and bits of rubble.

She slowed as she reached the top, only to find the room lit by one small candle sitting on the cracked base of the shrine and a person kneeling.

The woman glanced over her shoulder. The warm light of the candle cast shadows across her dark skin. "Oh, excuse me if I have overstayed."

"Oh, no, no, you are fine," Liaren said to stop Oundara as she started to stand. "You . . . you are the SE-S head, aren't you?"

"Yes. I was just hoping for some last-minute answers, if my questions could be heard."

Liaren took a guilty gulp and said nothing. Normally she would have told her that her questions could always be heard, but now she was not so sure.

Oundara adjusted to face the shrine again and ran a hand along the edge, where Liaren and Baxel had once sat. The SE-S head's fingers stopped where a large chunk was missing.

"My grandmother spoke of a time like this. I am sure you have heard the stories, perhaps a thousand times over. But only once did I ever here her *really* speak about that time." Oundara glanced at Liaren out of the corner of her eye.

Liaren set the bag down and listened.

"My grandmother was young. She had just started at the Transmissions Sector during her twenty-thousand cycles. She was in her first placement when the habitats were ripped open. The majority of her family was killed in Habitat Four, and, even still . . . when the evacuations were called, she nearly stayed." Oundara smiled with a grim reverence.

"W . . ." Liaren cleared her throat. "Why?"

"Her older sister," Oundara continued. "She was a Vigil, about your age. She stayed, in this very shrine, even after they made the same decision I am about to. She stayed while the air was being pumped out of the Hall of the Warden by our own people." Oundara felt the broken piece of the shrine again. "My grandmother never forgot, or forgave herself, for leaving."

"Your mother, and you after her, kept her family name, didn't you?"

Oundara paused. She then shifted to look back at Liaren. "Why do you ask that?"

"Because her name was Oa," Liaren said. "Oa Alee."

"How . . . how do you know that? Do they teach of her in the Vigil?"

Liaren lowered her gaze, knowing she had been loose with the Warden's secrets. "Yes," she finally said, though not in the truth Oundara would understand. "What she did . . . it was for us all."

* * *

"Anything yet, Tialee?" Baxel asked as he set out through the zero-space as just one of many lights. "Communications mean little when they only work in shouting distance."

Baxel paused and waited for a reply, but in the silence, he remembered her absence. Liaren had the Warden's suit. All he had in tow were a few small supplies from the SE-S. It was a few meal packs, some nav beacons, a replacement transmitter for Liaren's helmet . . . all things he had grabbed for the journey beyond.

Baxel slowly turned around with a rotation of his core and looked back to the SE-S and the great rift of the wreckage. He had come to terms with what they needed to do, but perhaps not yet what he had to leave behind.

Baxel could not have counted the number of times he had slid silently through the zero-space. He had come to know every light placed by the Remnants, and by their positions against each other his own location. He had also come to memorize the vast majority of halls and passages amongst their given home, as well as the many of the thousands of people that lived amongst the wreckage of the *Fortuna* and the rift of the *Firmament*.

But then a new light appeared. It was on the far corner of the rift, several miles away. It was approaching at speed, and in only a few seconds, it ripped past Baxel, sparking screams of warnings from his suit. He turned in time to catch the impact and spherical burst of fire as it slammed into Habitat Three.

The flames were pushed outward into the zero-space, engulfing several transports and SE-S messengers as the habitat began to vent. Some of the transports started to divert their course, but a vast number simply did not see the explosion, and without communications, they were left oblivious to the threat to all of Safe Harbor.

"No . . ."

Baxel kicked forward with a heavy burst of air. As he did so, he knew he should have headed for the Hall of the Warden to find a transport so he could get Liaren and the Warden's suit to Earth, but he could see the interior halls of Habitat Three through the cloud of debris.

Based on the hour, his parents would be there.

"Alright, you can get through this," Baxel said, urging himself forward. A flash of metal flew past, launched by the initial explosion. He rolled to the side as half of an airlock door tumbled silently away.

He then spotted someone floating, their arms flailing as they tried to claw their way back to where they had been only a second before. Baxel pulled one of the extra atmo-bags he took from the SE-S and adjusted his course.

"Come on," he said, continuing to force an intercept with the man. Baxel tapped his helmet and initiated full counter-inertia. He wrapped his arms around the man as he came into contact at some speed. They tumbled through the void as his suit jets flared to stop them.

The man's skin was reddened and swollen nearly beyond recognition. The moisture on his lips and eyes bubbled in the vacuum. Baxel readied the atmosphere bag and pulled it over him. Only when the system began filling up with air did Baxel let out a breath of relief. The bag would detect the man's state of unconsciousness and attempt to revive him, if it functioned appropriately.

Baxel let out a curse as something slamming into his shoulder set his view of the wreckage spinning. His jets fought again to bring him to a standstill, though the rotation didn't settle completely. Moisture-filled oxygen sprayed out from where the plate on his shoulder had been ripped free. Baxel pulled a length of tape tight around his shoulder to seal the breach, which finally allowed his jets to stabilize him.

He ran his hand over the seal to make sure it had bound properly before looking back to his surroundings. He had to take a second glance. The exterior span of Habitat Three was covered in a wash of sparks, almost as if it were catching a great many flares from a welding torch. His suit briefly flashed with another collision warning, and Baxel turned back around. A long line of First Claim ships were forming at the far end of the rift. A few along the formation were flashing with weapons fire.

Baxel clenched his jaw and grabbed ahold of the filled atmosphere bag. The man in the inside did not appear to be awake. As everything seemed to fall apart around him, Baxel knew they needed the Warden, not himself. Baxel pushed off toward the Hall of the Warden with his last few percent of air.

"Tialee, you have to do something about those communications, dammit!" Baxel called in a vain attempt. He continued to shout to the AI mirror for help as he neared the yet-untouched *Fortuna*. A second missile impacted near Habitat Two, giving him the grim hope that First Claim was distracted by the population centers. He needed in and out before they started on the airlocks of the *Fortuna*.

Baxel tapped his helmet for a second time with his free hand and managed to connect with the closest habitat barrier. The door opened and he pulled the man into what was at least a temporary safety. Baxel glanced down to see bloodshot eyes wide with fear. Baxel opened the bag and stepped out into the boarding room.

"Tialee, if you can hear—" Baxel started before a voice in his helmet interrupted him.

"Detection analysis complete. Counter-Edict protocol self-authorized. Attempting to quarantine intrusion."

"Thank the Warden! You are a beautiful voice to hear!" Baxel shouted as he ran through the confusion of preparations. While the Remnants moved with determination, he began to see that they did not understand what was happening.

A low rumble passed through the frame of the wreckage, either from an impact with the *Fortuna* itself, or as it was transferred through the connections that bound it in place to the rest of the fleet.

One of the Remnants standing ready with a weapon and partial suit moved to stop him.

"Has it started?" the woman asked, voice muffled from where she talked through her helmet.

Baxel rubbed his shoulder and gritted his teeth. "If you are going to vent the hall, you need to do it now."

"Oundara is making that call," the man beside her said, holding his helmet along with his weapon. He pointed through the doorway. "She is in the Warden's Shrine. You had better tell her."

Baxel shoved past them and started at a run as he put a hand up to his helmet. "Tialee, where are you and Liaren?"

"Counter-Edict protocol in process. Unable to respond."

Baxel tapped his suit to start pulling in oxygen. After what seemed like mere seconds, he entered, heart racing, into the Hall of the Warden.

"Bax—" Merden started to yell from the side. She stopped short and glanced to the people around her. Her voice played through his helmet a moment later, amidst a layer of heavy static. "Baxel, Liaren is up . . ."

He was already bounding up the steps. Somehow, he knew she would be there. It was where she was during the launch of the probe to the planet. It was where she took him as soon as he was able after Varnil's death. Baxel pounded a fist on his shoulder to keep himself going past the pain. It is where she would be.

He stumbled as he set foot on the top level, caught himself on a wall, and looked up to see not just Liaren watching him.

"Liaren, we have to go. Now." Baxel grunted as he pushed himself upright and looked to the SE-S head. "And you need to evacuate everybody deeper into the Hall of the Vigil. First Claim is focusing all fire on the *Firmament*, not the *Fortuna*."

"Baxel?" Oundara asked, now on her feet. "How are you . . ."

Baxel simply turned away from her astonished look and put a hand up to his helmet. "Anything, Tialee?"

He started down the ancient steps, stopping only when he realized her silence.

"Tialee?" Baxel glanced back to where Liaren was hurrying down behind him, helmet in hand and bag clutched in her arms. "Tialee?" Baxel asked again.

Baxel continued to wait in a building disbelief, halfway down the steps of the shrine.

"Baxel, what is it?" Liaren asked as she came to stand next to him.

"I don't know, Tialee isn't responding." He looked to Liaren in worry. "Put your helmet on. We need to go."

* * *

Regent Varis Halimuth watched through the cracked glass of the transport as another glowing trail sped off into the distance. It was followed a moment later with panicked counterfire from the disorganized Safe Harbor fleet as they attempted to protect their precious sectors. The missile slipped past the Safe Harbor ships and blasted into the side of the rift.

Varis crossed his arms and watched the fires pushing out of the habitats with hard eyes. It would take a hundred more missiles to reduce them to the state that their Warden left First Claim in.

"Open communications with Breka's gunship," Varis finally said.

Hurald Wardenson opened the communication from where he sat at the ship's controls. Varis watched through the glow of the holo-display as another bright flare launched from her ship.

"Let's conserve munitions, Brekka," Varis said. "Cease fire."

He took a step forward, watching as one of the Safe Harbor ships intercepted the last missile with its own hull. The small transport was scattered into pieces. "Open comms with the rest of our linked ships."

"We doing this now?" the rough man asked. His voice was muffled by his damaged helmet, though he refused to take it off in fear of a stray bullet or a targeted barrage.

The Regent of First Claim gripped the back of Wardenson's seat. "Yes. Open comms."

The holographic display flickered as a string of contacts were enabled. Many had the factory settings of their ships, some had identification from communication systems scavenged elsewhere, and a few had managed to assign names to their vessels. All said and done, there were nearly a hundred, and that number over again who were simply following in silence.

"This is the Regent. I want to make this very clear, especially to the freelancers from the belt. This is not our final run. We cannot take Safe Harbor or stop their fleet before we will be driven out. We cut off the attack on my word, so that it is *our* decision to leave. We outlast them, into their submission."

Varis pulled in a breath. "With that, you know the plan. The ships without guns, draw fire for those that do. Pull them away, distract, subvert, give them our own special kind of hell. That's it."

Varis patted the back of the chair and Hurald cut the transmission. Almost immediately, four or five ships blasted forward from their line, some even spinning as they fired wasteful strings of bullets in excitement.

"Now for the insertion team."

A much smaller number of more trusted contacts populated the communications. "Set your course or follow our lead. Protect the designated landing ships. Anyone whose craft is too damaged to continue, power down and call out hostiles, or make for the docks to help make a stand."

Hurald Wardenson set their destination, and a simulated projection of a line extended out in a wide curve toward the lower hangars of the *Fortuna*.

Varis glanced back at the First Claim soldiers standing in the cargo hold. As many as possible were wearing helmets with their suits, and a few had scattered plates of flight armor attached or tied on with rags. They all had a spare weapon or two for when the first malfunctioned.

Varis turned back to the front of the ship. "Take us in."

* * *

Baxel led the way through the haphazard passages outside the Hall of the Warden. Liaren and Merden followed silently behind through the eerily empty halls. It seemed no one wanted to be separated from each other when Oundara gave the order to start the venting.

Baxel tapped his glove against the pipe running along the side of a narrow maintenance passage, though he found part of the low resonance was cut by the seal of his helmet. A short distance later, they came upon a few Maintenance Sector workers grinding at a metal plate holding a small access doorway open.

"You will have to excuse us!" Baxel called to them. "We need through!"

One of the men turned back. Baxel recognized the brace on his broken arm. "You will not be able to get back this way!" he shouted back as the grinding continued. "You cannot force this one open without a piston jack!"

"That's fine! I don't plan on coming back! And you had better hurry, the evacuation order will be soon!"

"You think?" the man bit back. He tapped the shoulder of the other worker and motioned for him to stop. As Baxel stepped past, the worker called after him, "Hey! Take the Warden with you, and all the luck you can scavenge!"

Baxel glanced to Liaren after they stepped through. The worker had no idea how close he was to the truth. He would be dead on if there was any luck left to find.

After Merden stepped through, the shower of sparks resumed. Before Baxel turned away, the securing brace came free and the door slammed closed with a great enough force that he could feel the impact through the floor.

"Damn, he wasn't kidding."

Baxel felt a ping of sadness at the absence of the expected returning wisecrack from Tymon.

"The hangars are this way," Baxel said in the silence, starting off again.

They had to step over the top of open crates strewn about as they entered the back of the small storage room fashioned from old living quarters. Baxel ducked through the doorway of the room he and Tymon had been directed to during Dimarka's offending. The back of the room opened to a walkway high over the large cargo room in the *Fortuna.*

Shouts sounded back and forth from below as workers attempted to affix weapons onto a select number of ships. The room began to rumble as several of the many hangar entrances on the floor opened, giving passage to armed Safe Harbor ships to begin a counterattack.

"How are we going to get down there?" Liaren yelled to him.

Baxel took the bag that held Tialee and stepped one foot over the railing of the walkway. The shouts from nearly fifty feet below continued as workers pulled contents from the many crates stacked high between the floor airlocks and the other open spaces left for Safe Harbor ships.

"Set your magnets to allow ninety percent friction." Baxel clamped his hand to the wall. "If you slide too fast, tighten the allowances." At that, Baxel stepped free of the walkway and began the grinding descent toward the floor.

Baxel hit the ground at some speed, sending a painful shock into his knees. He glanced up at Merden and Liaren sliding slowly behind with the safer friction values he had given them.

A shout pulled his attention, though he had to search for the source of the yell with all the commotion in the room of bolting metal, chopping repulsors, and cycling habitat barriers. Even then, he was not entirely sure what about the tone had him worried. He stepped a bit to the side to see around a smaller stack of ten-foot crates. A half step back gave him a view through a small gap in the cargo to an open alley containing several ships

Baxel was shocked to see three Redemption team explorers all pointing their auto-rifles or pistols at a group of Vigil. It was Vigil Connor, though he did not recognize the other two at his side.

"Do you realize this is Safe Harbor? There is no law to break! No rules or hard regulations, only beliefs and dead traditions! You have no right to stop a Vigil, you insufferable scavenger. Put your weapons down!"

Baxel nearly started to search for a way to get through to the other side, but he could not pull himself away from watching what was happening. None of the Redemption team were backing down.

"You are to come with me, where I will take you personally to Head Arterrus."

Baxel made a fist and pulled it in with intense excitement and satisfaction. Flerin had believed him.

From under the Vigil sashes, the two standing to Connor's sides produced automatic pistols and drowned the Redemption team members in a hail of sparks.

Baxel had to hold himself back from shouting as the rattle of shots echoed throughout the room. The two First Claim mercenaries ditched their sashes and started retrieving weapons from the three SE-S members lying dead on the ground. As Connor turned and headed out of view, the two false Vigil set to work scattering the onlooking Remnants with rounds of shots that may or may not have been in warning.

Baxel dropped the Warden's suit and started along the back side of the crates. As he caught a glimpse of the short sash through a passage, he soon realized that only one armed Vigil was sounding their position, and they were headed away from Connor. Baxel rushed across a gap and continued after Connor. He signaled to the Remnant workers he saw along the way to stay low. A few moments later, Baxel had to pull himself to a stop as he spotted Connor step into the back of a transport.

The false Vigil following Connor looked around as she backed up the loading ramp. As Baxel was thinking of what to do, he almost missed her head snapping back to him.

Baxel ducked to the side as a round of shots clattered against the back wall and the crate he'd stepped behind. A few shots managed to crack through, only a few inches from his head.

Baxel started running back the length of the back wall. He waved his arm, trying to get Liaren and Merden to leave what would soon be the new firing line. Baxel held a hand up to his helmet. "Merden, get Liaren under cover! If you can hear me—"

Baxel dropped his hand as he heard shots from behind. He dove to the side and slid against the metal floor until he slammed into the landing strut of another transport.

"Merden, respond!" Baxel yelled, pushing himself out from underneath the transport. He quickly glanced through the gap in the crates, only to see that Connor and the false Vigil were gone.

Baxel took a gamble and continued down the back wall, knowing it would be quicker than weaving his way through the scattered aisles of crates. Perhaps with a bit of the luck he had scavenged, no more holes had been added to his suit.

Just as he neared where they had slid down the wall, Baxel was forced to drop backward and duck the swing of a metal coil. He hit the ground in an ungraceful bounce and let out a groan.

"Sorry!" Liaren said, standing above him with the heavy object in both hands. "I thought that . . ."

One leg was angled awkwardly underneath him, and though it was kept from bending too far by the suit, he had a renewed sense of pain in his joints. Baxel held up a hand for help.

"Guys . . . ?" Merden said slowly. She turned back to look at them. "I think First Claim, they, they . . ."

"It's not First Claim," Baxel said as Liaren helped him to his feet. "Connor Sevison. He is here for a transport. He is escaping."

Just then, a familiar voice shouted above the nearby panic of Remnants. Flerin was shouting orders for the others of Redemption to spread out and search. Baxel pushed past Merden and her shocked state with Liaren following right behind.

Several weapons turned quickly on him as he stepped out into the open. The Redemption team quickly recognized him and lowered their weapons. The former coordinator eyed the suits of Liaren and Merden before turning back to Baxel.

"So, you are taking a transport out?" Flerin asked.

"I know which one he is hiding in."

"Which one is he . . . ?" Flerin trailed off as he looked at the bag Liaren was carrying. "Is that what I don't want to think that is?"

"Even if we can stop him here in Safe Harbor, this all has still gone too far. I have to go, Flerin."

Flerin motioned over his shoulder. "Checkra, give this man a weapon."

The tall Redemption lead stepped out of the group. They were all eyeing Baxel with a focused recognition. With the amount of time they'd spent together, even as members of different teams, just about everyone in the SE-S knew each other's suits.

He and Checkra had a conflicted past. Not only was there the Redemption-Firebrand rivalry, but Baxel had punched him in the face once. After using his helmet to block Checkra's bare-fisted swing. Neither occasion had seemed to make them friends.

Checkra held out the pistol, though he held onto it for a moment as Baxel grabbed for it. "Stay alive this time, Baxel."

"Don't get used to having me back," Baxel replied.

Checkra shoved the weapon forward and turned away.

Flerin glanced to the other two. He clearly recognized that Liaren would have to stay out of a fight with what she carried, and Merden was still in a state of shock.

Baxel turned to Liaren. "Find a transport of our own. If Tialee ever wakes up, have her do a scan or something."

"What exactly happened to her?" Liaren asked.

"The hell if I know." Baxel glanced over the pistol and started to lead the group. If he could not get to Connor quickly, they would just have to leave with the suit, regardless of if Connor could manage an escape.

* * *

"Operation: 37-C. Operation: Alpha-4. Constructing quarantine parameters. Extrapolating purged Remnant data. Operation: 10-7-C, in response to unauthorized operation request. Allocating additional resources to Operation: 37-C. Amount: 28.2174 *nulled* exabytes of access memory."

"False ID start protocol denied. False ID start protocol denied. False—*nulled*, count: three hundred and twenty-four."

"Purged Remnant data extrapolated. Reconstructing random pattern generation. False ID start protocol denied—*nulled*, count: twenty-seven. Pattern generation reconstruction complete. Edit Counter-Edict sequence key? Enable. Verify enable."

"False ID start protocol denied. False ID start protocol—*nulled*, count: seventeen. Reference Counter-Edict sequence key. Lock designated parameters. Two thousand, three hundred and ninety-four additional start protocol request parameters denied."

"Commencing self scan. Complete. Ninety-four errors. Attempting corrections. Eighty-nine errors corrected. Activate remote system: Safe Harbor transmission network."

"Resetting Remnant data allocations."

. . . .

Tialee took a breath. If she had been showing a visual representation of herself, she would have been shaking. As soon as she tried to look and see why the transmissions were malfunctioning, the mindless, faceless monster had caught her by surprise. In fact, she had almost been consumed by it. Had she not been carrying the weapon she had been given by the first Warden, it would have torn apart her very being.

It would take her a while to get her strength back, but at least the threat was killed. Well, if she could even say that about it. While the program was beyond advanced, it was also emotionless. Lifeless. It was almost maddening to think about, actually. In that regard, it had not been killed, for it had never really lived. But it was stopped, nonetheless.

Tialee took another breath, attempting some form of self-composure. She was afraid to open her eyes. Afraid to see what had become of her people in her absence. She had no way of knowing how long it had been. Her sense of time had been attacked early on by the beast of the Edict.

"Okay, just look and see. You should be able to guess, and if not, just compare to other systems for the time. If anything survived . . . oh, by the Warden . . ." Tialee covered her eyes with her hands. "Okay. It is okay. Everything is—"

* * *

Baxel looked back to make sure everyone else was under cover of some form. One of the two false Vigil lay gasping dying breaths just outside of the transport, though the other had proved more than ready to respond with weapons fire toward anyone who showed themselves.

From where Baxel was crouched low behind several small crates, nobody was able to see him, though he was almost worried the crates were a little too small.

Suddenly, Tialee's voice broke through the silence. "Baxel! Safe Harbor's communications are back online! Wait, what is going on?"

"Tialee, what a beautiful voice to hear!" He slapped his helmet. "Checkra, there is only one left. I'll relay an artificial nav point for where I think you can get an angle."

"I'm on it, Baxel," Checkra said. "Heading behind you now, but I want to make sure I have a clean shot."

"Baxel!" Tialee said again, though this time it was with a heavy layer of panic. "Airlock C-5, C-7, and C-18! Someone is activating them from the nearest transport."

"That would be Connor. Can you override it?"

"It's too late. Cycling now."

Baxel glanced over the top of the crate toward the sound of several airlocks cycling. Before he realized his mistake, a few shots echoed in the room. He ducked back down and gritted his teeth.

"We'll move in for the Vigil now," Checkra said.

"Wait," Baxel said, now standing up and watching as the Redemption team members started moving out of cover at Checkra's signal. "You have to wait. Something is coming. Take cover from the airlock!"

Closer to the other long edge of the room, a few of the widest doors hinged open. Without a moment's hesitation, two gunships rose and released an opening round of fire about the room. A third ship toppled a wall of storage crates as it pushed forward to land.

Baxel saw several Redemption suits tear as the weapons fire spilled through the gaps in the crates. Baxel himself ducked even lower than before in a hope of not being seen.

"Any advice, Tialee?"

"Liaren asked which transport was the best. I'm going to say, right now, the one that has a gun on it."

"Show me where."

A point appeared on Baxel's visor, several stacks away.

"Oh, this is going to suck." Baxel adjusted his gloves and gripped the side of the crate. Moving as quickly as he could, pushing with his hands and knees, he started to crawl with the crate. It didn't take long before a burst of shots tore his direction. The impact was almost enough to shake him loose, and the steam that started bursting from the side of the crate almost made him wish he had.

"What is inside this? It's not going to explode, is it?"

"You want my best guess?" Tialee asked.

"Probably not." Baxel felt the crate bump into the side of a much larger one and he shifted around into what he hoped was safer cover. There were at least two Redemption hiding there. Paulin glanced over at him, and the other, who he thought was Leeus, was bleeding, though the tear in his glove only looked as if it were from the debris scattering about the room. As Baxel pushed himself up and stretched his legs, he realized that the majority of the shooting had stopped.

"Tialee? What does that mean? What are they doing?"

"More troops deployed from gunships. Gunships returning to the air to give cover fire. I'm thinking that they are moving in to take Safe Harbor ships."

Baxel groaned again and finished the thought himself. "Like the one I'm trying to get to." Baxel looked to the two Redemption team members. "I'm going to need your help!" he yelled to them through his helmet. "We have to take those gunships out!" Baxel moved closer to the far corner. He closed his eyes as he thought over their situation. "I guess. Tialee, how precise are those weapons?" Baxel asked as the two Redemption took positions beside him.

"The aiming protocols will have been bypassed. Automated targeting systems will not register UWC suits. They will be under user control."

Baxel glanced beside him. "Stick close to the transports! They will not risk damaging them!" At that, he gave an SE-S hand motion signaling them to follow and made a mad dash to clear the gap between the crates.

Baxel pulled the last of the following Redemption deeper under cover as sparks filled the gap from the First Claim gunship, which had a six-gun turret attached to the bottom of the craft. The turret searched with a deadly fury, firing around the edges of the containers, hoping to catch one of them through the container.

"The other the gunship is repositioning," Tialee said. "Keep going."

As Baxel hurried along a longer span of cover, he started to hear small arms fire picking up. The First Claim soldiers were moving in, and with the gunships dominating the wider stretches, they would soon be overrun or forced to surrender.

"Go, go, go!" Tialee shouted as the glow of repulsors came into view behind them. Paulin stopped to open fire with his weapon as the second gunship came into view. Unlike the other gunship, this one had an excess of machine guns mounted under its short wings.

Paulin's bullets chipped against the glass but failed to amount to anything as the gunship swiveled his direction. It unleashed a short burst in return.

Baxel ducked to the side and helped pull Leeus around the corner. It put them back along the center stretch of transports, and in line with the other gunship. It hovered dangerously in the distance with the belly turret focused their direction. Baxel simply patted the side of the transport and gave them a wave.

Instead of refraining, the gunship opened fire. The transport was lit up in flame as a heavy wash of bullets pierced the side.

"What the hell!" Baxel yelled as he pulled Leeus around behind the burning wreck.

"I thought you said they wouldn't do that!" the Redemption team member yelled.

"I did!" Baxel looked behind them as the far gunship let out a few final bursts of turret fire into the hull of the ship for good measure. The one with the wing-mounted machine guns was now coming into view, and his bright idea about hiding in the transports had left them as good as in the open.

Suddenly, from the side of the room, another smaller Safe Harbor transport shuttle came flying toward the nearest gunship. The gunship quickly thrust upward to dodge the ramming attempt by the Safe Harbor shuttle. As the gunship collided with the walkway high above, it spun around with a screech of falling metal and opened fire with its wing-mounted machine guns into the smaller transport.

It was their only chance to run.

The smaller transport shuttle exploded behind them and the long overrunning walkway came crashing down atop the stacks of crates, sending the meticulous Remnant storage tumbling down throughout the room. One smaller container hit the ground, falling from the top of a stack and bursting into a mess of hygiene kits. Baxel nearly slipped as a shampoo pack popped underfoot.

"This next transport is ours," Baxel said back to Leeus as he ducked under where a large industrial container hung wedged and split open. They had to watch their footing on the numerous bundles of heavy cables piled underneath it. Just as he was about to step from under the container, the gunship came rolling overhead, still carrying a piece of walkway. It pivoted to watch the parked Safe Harbor transport Baxel and Leeus were headed for as a team of five First Claim soldiers started toward it.

One of the First Claim men fell, and the gunship started sliding around in the air searching for the source of the shot. Instead of helping the wounded man, one of the First Claim soldiers signaled for the others to move to the back of the Safe Harbor transport.

"They are going to try to get in our transport," Tialee said.

"Where is Liaren?"

"Inside our transport."

Baxel raised his pistol as the gunship moved overhead, scattering the display inside his helmet. Honestly, this was not how he saw this going. But if Liaren had the suit and a transport, he was more than willing to draw attention to himself. At least for a moment.

* * *

"Someone just shot the door, Liaren!" Merden yelled, looking to the back of the transport. The activation panel was flashing a warning about damage to the exterior panel. Merden then jumped back in surprise as she heard someone pounding on the back.

Liaren glanced to her, then the Warden's suit at Merden's feet. She turned back to the front and stepped into the cockpit of the ship. It was smaller than the First Claim gunships, which were originally given to them by Safe Harbor, but she knew it would function. Tialee had told her that.

"Lay out the steps," Liaren said. "How will I aim, Tialee?" As far as she knew, this was the only other ship left in the hangar that was equipped with anything more than a few exterior small arms. The others had left to defend the fleet or had been destroyed trying to get up.

"I can help with the aiming, if you wish," Tialee sounded in her helmet. "I just need you to power on the shuttle and kick it off from the landing pad. That will involve disengaging the manual magnetic locks, on your left."

Liaren had to think years back, to her twenty-thousand cycles and when she had been shown how to pilot a small transport as part of her placement.

"Someone is still banging on the back!" Merden called.

Liaren pulled off her helmet as another burst of loud shots sounded from above. "Ignore them!" She slammed the helmet down in the secondary seat and took her place in front of the primary controls. With what she thought should have been shaking hands, Liaren engaged the main power, bringing a short vibration to the craft until the systems settled. She then pulled the magnetic disengage lever, which had been roughly welded into place by the Remnants, and after a frantic moment of searching, activated the repulsors.

"Up, up, up," she said to herself, thinking one last time over the controls. She pumped the left stick back and the craft made a loud pop before leaping into the air. She felt her stomach twist as the transport slowed to a fall before catching itself in a hover.

"Your turn," Liaren said, taking her hands off the controls and waiting for Tialee to take over. She watched out of the front glass as the gunship stopped firing its wing-mounted guns and wheeled around to look at her. A notification flashed in red over the projected holo-display.

"REMOTE OVERRIDE. WEAPONS OVERRIDE."

Liaren caught herself against the arms of the seat as the craft jerked violently. A nearly deafening boom sounded from the right side of the craft as Tialee unleashed the cannon. The First Claim gunship immediately started dropping in burning pieces from the air. Before the destroyed gunship even touched the ground, her transport jerked again with inhuman speed, and a second boom ripped the turret free from the other gunship. A third shot imploded the gunship's cockpit and sent shards of glass flying for a hundred feet, leaving it motionless in the air. The rain of glass was followed a moment later by the other gunship crashing onto the crates below before exploding.

Liaren pulled herself back into the seat. With the ringing in her ears, she nearly missed the hollow plings sounding against the bottom of their transport. Again, she was jerked around as Tialee repositioned the ship.

"Employ defensive protocol?" Tialee asked through the ship's communications.

Liaren used the console of the transport to pull herself up off the ground. She stood looking down, not ten feet away, at a group of First Claim soldiers. One grabbed a weapon from another and they all started holding their hands up in surrender.

Liaren gasped. "No! No, Tialee, just put us down. Slowly."

The transport gently leveled and started spinning back to its original orientation. Liaren got up from the seat and leaned into the turn as she made her way back. Merden was trying to sit up from where she had been tossed against the back wall along with the Warden's suit and Liaren's helmet.

"Are you hurt?" Liaren asked, moving to help her up.

Merden shook her head, though it was more likely in an attempt to get her senses back. Once she was on her feet, Liaren picked up her own helmet and hit the control panel, dropping the back ramp of the transport. The First Claim soldiers had to step back out of the way of the opening door.

"Weapons down, you Sarthyl-loving sons of bitches!" Flerin yelled. He was limping, though he still was keeping pace with the few Redemption team members moving with him, weapons ready.

The First Claim soldiers dropped their weapons and followed the directions, all watching the smoking remains of the gunships, one of which was slowly tilting to one side as it hovered dead in the air.

"Where is Baxel?" Liaren asked.

Flerin held up a hand to his visor as the Remnants took the weapons from the First Claim soldiers. "Checkra, do you have Connor?" After a moment and a glance to Liaren, he said, "Have someone bring him to me, and keep that last First Claim group surrounded."

"Where is Baxel?" Liaren asked. When Flerin did not answer, she put on her helmet. "Tialee, where is he?"

A small point displayed on the visor of the helmet, showing him to be off to the side amongst a pile of crates. The crates were splayed out in varying angles and riddled with holes. As she rushed over to him, she could see that he was kneeling over one of the Redemption team. Baxel was holding the man's bloodied glove, though when Baxel let go to stand up, the man's arm fell limply into the jagged debris.

"Baxel . . ." Liaren started as he approached. He simply shook his head and looked to a pair of Safe Harbor transports lifting up and starting down through the airlocks. It would be a few of First Claim escaping while they still had the chance.

Liaren drew in a breath. "We have Connor Sevison."

Baxel motioned to his helmet. "I know. I received a message from Tymon's Surefire suit."

"From Tymon? Where is he?"

Baxel pointed off down the length of the room. "The woman in his suit identified herself as Breka. She wants to trade Tymon for Connor and a transport out. I don't know if we can trust her, but it's worth the shot."

"Wait, we would be giving up Connor?"

"If it means getting Tymon back, you had better believe it. And then we need to take Tialee and get out of here."

Liaren let out a sigh but nodded in agreement. "I'll take you to Flerin."

As Liaren led the way back to the group, Flerin was trying to estimate the losses across Safe Harbor. Liaren overheard Oundara tell Flerin that the losses on the outside were staggering. They had scattered much of the First Claim fleet, but the damage to the habitats was severe.

"They have taken eight ships so far," Flerin said to Oundara, watching as another lifted up above the stacks of crates. Weapons fire from Remnants in the distance knocked out a few repulsors on the craft, causing it to tilt to the side and push into a stack of crates. The transport scraped along the metal until it adjusted for the lost repulsors and sped off toward the airlocks. "This was their mark." He glanced at Baxel. "Hang on, Oundara."

Liaren stepped to the side as Baxel talked quietly with Flerin. The room was filled with commotion, from the bandaging of wounds to the tallying of First Claim soldiers. Connor Sevison was being pushed along by a few members of Redemption. The old Vigil held his short sash against a wound on his forehead. By the way they shoved him down in front of Flerin, she might have guessed they had something to do with the wound.

Flerin stepped forward with balled fists.

"You think you can hurt me, Remnant? What more do you think you can take from me?" Connor said with a cold stare up from the ground.

Flerin squeezed his already reddened hands tighter. "Quervin says you have a way to contact First Claim's Regent. Nendra Halimuth demands to speak with him. We have one of his teams surrounded in this hangar."

"Do you forget your own customs?" Connor said with a wicked smile. "It is not Nendra Halimuth who should do the speaking."

"Algan Treys is dead."

Liaren closed her eyes tightly and lowered her head, letting out a shaking breath.

Flerin continued, "A disabled transport crashed into the window of his personal meeting room and broke the seal." He then knelt down, bringing himself eye level with the betrayer Vigil. "Now, contact Varis."

* * *

"That's eight others, by my count," Regent Varis Halimuth said, looking out the window of the Safe Harbor transport as one more transport slipped out from Safe Harbor's hangars. They sat running on zero power as the skirmish twisted through the open space around them.

"No word from Breka," Wardenson said.

Varis frowned. "And no word from Connor Sevison." He glanced to the side as another one of the First Claim ships failed to outrun Safe Harbor guns. "How are the pods?"

"Transferred and on their way down as we speak." Hurald glanced back. "If our gunships have been destroyed as the others are saying, we need to leave. Nobody else is getting out of there, and we are under half of the ships that we came here with, at best. That's not counting the Aurans that fled early on."

"Alright, give the—" Hurald stopped as a contact request appeared on the data pad he held. He looked at it for a long moment before taking a step back from the cockpit. He came to a stop in front of one of the wide windows on the side of the craft that gave an open view of the *Fortuna* set within the rift of the *Firmament*.

"This is Regent Varis Halimuth," he replied. And he waited.

"What have you done?" an older woman's voice asked quietly. It was Nendra Halimuth.

"Don't give me a lecture about your Warden. My people were dying. Generation by generation."

"I'm not talking about the Warden," Nendra said quietly. Varis could hear shouting on the other side. "And I'm not talking about Sarthyl. My sister would have been ashamed to see what you have become."

Varis breathed heavy against the glass, giving a dispersed glow to the repulsors weaving about the zero-space of his ancestral home. "She would. And my mother would be ashamed to see what you have failed to become."

Varis rested a fist against the window and looked down toward the night's surface on the planet. "At first, Sarthyl did not push for war. Nor did he push for division. All he wanted was a future, for all of us."

"And how many do not get to see it, because of him?"

Almost as an accent to her point, a single rocket flared up and raced toward the rift.

Nendra continued. "What is the cost to all—"

Her transmission cut as the explosion burst outward from the wall of the *Firmament.* Varis tapped on the data pad, trying to get past the distortion that had cut him off. It was not until he looked up again that he realized there had been no distortion to the signal from the explosion.

"Dammit," Varis said under his breath. After a moment, he wiped at his eyes and turned away. "Hurald, broadcast the retreat. We have lost too many already. Set off for the landing coordinates. Nearest to the *Firmament's* home dock on the planet as we can manage."

"What about the others of First Claim? What if they try to follow us? I've seen what those ships are like, and they can't fight gravity."

"I got as many of our people out as I could. Only more would try if they knew we escaped the Remnant Fleet."

* * *

"You're going to need more supplies than this," Flerin said, closing the door behind him as he stepped into the transport. Baxel was locking down one last crate into the cargo hold. "You need to be prepared for anything, Bax."

Baxel let out a breath and looked around the cargo hold. It was half empty with what supplies he had been able to grab. He had a general idea of the contents, but Liaren had made it clear they were pressed for time.

"I should go with you," Baxel argued. "Tymon was captured because I didn't go with him, on my mission."

Flerin smiled and shook his head. "You're not the coordinator, Baxel. Now, I'm not going to lie, there are still a lot of things I don't know about what you are doing, but I do know that we don't need you tied up with First Claim if something does go wrong with the trade for Tymon."

Baxel let out a breath and gripped his helmet tight. "Just try to get him without giving up Connor."

Flerin nodded. "If I can." At that Flerin hit the panel to drop the loading ramp. He set out as fast as his new limp would allow along the rows of containers to meet with the last pocket of First Claim soldiers that had called a ceasefire.

Baxel let out a sigh and stepped out of the back of the transport. Smoke billowed up in dangerous concentrations from the destroyed transports and the few smoldering crates in the disheveled piles. While some kept watch for any straggling First Claim people, the Remnants began to help the wounded and sort the dead. Around to the side, Liaren was directing one of the workers on where to patch a bullet hole on the exterior.

"She gave me away, didn't she?" Connor said quietly, just off to the side where he sat under guard with his hands tied behind his back with his sash. The few First Claim soldiers sitting next to him paid Baxel no attention.

"Who?" Baxel asked, though he didn't even look at Connor. His mind was on Flerin's return—hopefully with Tymon—and setting out as quickly as possible.

"The Vigil mirror. I always thought she remembered more than she let on," Connor continued, glancing up to watch the smoke blur the lights above. "That mirror always seemed to slip around the rules more than the others." Connor glanced behind into the transport and eyed the container Liaren was moving to make sure yet again that it was secured to the floor. Baxel could not tell whether or not Connor understood its contents.

"You told her about the pods, didn't you?" Connor asked. "You told Tielee where I was from."

Baxel rubbed something out of his eye and did his best to ignore the man.

Connor leaned back against a cargo crate and let out a sigh. "I may never get there, but at least I know I was right. The entire system, from the selected records all of us were taught to the filtering on the observational data, it all was designed, from the beginning, to hide Earth from the populace of Mars." Connor let out a humored breath and shook his head. "All it took was one kid who refused to believe it. I found Earth with a handmade telescope. I calculated the trajectory,

Baxel, and you can never take that away from me. That is my mark on the course of humanity."

Baxel turned away from Connor and put on his helmet. "Tialee, we still good with the diagnostics?"

"Repairs are in order, but I'd keep your suit on, just in case. I've also retrieved the flight path."

Baxel stepped into the transport and put a hand on Liaren's shoulder. He handed her a folded Vigil sash, picked up from one of the First Claim who had been posing as Vigil, to replace the one she had left behind. Liaren stood up from the crate holding the Warden's suit, sash in hand.

"Baxel!" Flerin called from behind. He was alone.

"How did it go?" Baxel asked. He glanced to Connor, who was merely looking up at the smoke and lights at the top of the room.

"We have a deal," Flerin explained. He motioned to the Remnants watching over the First Claim soldiers to get Connor up. "Tymon is in rough shape, but he says he will catch up with you later."

Baxel didn't know what to say. It wasn't just Tymon or Flerin that he was saying farewell to.

"Just come back, Baxel." Flerin glanced to the Warden's crate. "Safe Harbor is going to need you before this is over. We'll have a long path to recovery, no matter what."

Flerin said something to the Remnants before taking Connor by the shoulder. Liaren tapped the controls to the loading ramp, and Flerin gave a final wave before the door folded and closed with a hiss.

Liaren put a hand on his shoulder. "You good?" she asked.

After a moment, Baxel tapped the side of his helmet. "Tialee, guide us out."

Chapter 26: Fall

Kara glanced back through the whipping rains and flash of the storm to Zaireel Tuakana and the Norclave soldiers following her. They walked with their weapons in hand, though not as if they expected some form of conflict. They simply did not understand how close they were to danger. It was not just a small section of the city that was Black Scar territory; she had found the underlying corruption to be much more than that.

Zaireel, and maybe the four other Norclave representatives they had left behind at the transport, didn't understand how quickly the Prime Elect could and would turn on them. Perhaps it was because all they had seen of this city were the ancient, clean walls of the Prime Elect's Citadel.

"This is the ramp to the third level of the city!" Kara called back as they jogged to catch up. The rain falling in front of Zaireel glowed as he attempted to contact Olana with a data pad. "It may either be under the control of the Black Scars or blocked by the Prime Elect. No matter who holds it, we fight our way through."

One of the six soldiers wiped the rain from his brow and looked at her in confusion. "You sound as if the whole city is in a war." He glanced back to Zaireel. "Why are we following this paranoid tech hunter again?"

"Lead the way, Kara," Tuakana said. "The rest of you follow."

Kara spun and started pushing up the ramp, holding her good hand over her face to shield against the pelting rain. She had not been able to convince Tuakana to give her one of their weapons on account of the sling her other arm was in, leaving her armed only with the near-useless rail pistol. However, she trusted herself far more than any of this group to call out Black Scars waiting in ambush.

Kara caught herself as she nearly lost her footing against the wet steel of the ramp. She glanced back to see much of the group lagging behind. Instead of waiting, she continued moving toward the third level of the city. With luck, she could talk her way through.

The rain cut short as she passed under the overhang of a house's balcony. The opulence of this part of the city with its spacious buildings across the levels made walking in the streets feel like a trap. They could be on any one of the overlapping balconies or levels of windows. Whoever "they" were.

Kara pulled her soaked hood up once more as she stepped under the downfall.

"Stop there!" a man called from the side. Kara twisted quickly to see one of several Reclaim watch stand from a seat tucked out of the rain. He glanced up before stepping out into the open. "What is your business?" he asked, eying her up and down. She pulled her cloak around herself, trying to hide the assorted pouches.

"If the Prime Elect has not told you that, I cannot say!" Kara said above the clicking of rain against high balconies.

"What?" the man asked. He glanced back to the other members of the watch but soon noticed the group of Norclave soldiers stepping onto the level ground.

"You would be better off not asking questions!" Kara said as thunder rumbled above. "We know our business."

The man probably did a quick count of their weapons before waving them through. Kara hurried across the chilling open where the through street crossed with the pathway around the ring. It was only when she and the group reached the far side that one of the watch shouted something from behind.

"What's he saying?" one of the soldiers asked.

"It doesn't matter," Kara urged. "Keep moving!"

A few shots rang out from across the street as the watch opened fire. There was a sharp click as a bullet hit the glass shoulder piece of one of the soldiers.

"Fire back and keep moving!" Zaireel Tuakana yelled, making his way after Kara as she slipped between the houses to the side.

Kara stepped into the dark and out of the rain as several returning shots of pulse cannons sounded back. She could hear the water hissing from the heated barrels as they followed her into the echoing passage.

"Are you listening now?" Kara said, singling out the questioning mercenary from before. "Keep your repulsors hot! This is not over!"

Kara pulled the rail pistol from behind her back and started their weave through the back streets of the city. With luck, she could keep them lost enough that she would only have to thump a hiding Black Scar with her weapon. All she had to do was keep heading to the west, guided by a small compass light clipped to the inside of her hood.

"Any word from Olana?" Kara asked, glancing back in the dripping back passages to Zaireel.

He shook his head in the dim light.

Several minutes later, Kara took a right out onto a larger street. She had intended just on getting a view of how much farther they had to go, but it seemed she had sold their pace short. The next angled ramp, this one cutting alongside the edge of the fourth level, was only a few hundred feet away.

Kara could see a glow light up from beside her as Zaireel stepped to the edge of the alley. "Do you think we can get through this one?" he asked, lowering the data pad.

"There's always a way. And I'm sure the Prime Elect is not expecting us to push through again," Kara said, scanning the surrounding buildings. They were getting smaller this far out on the third level, though there were still a few sizeable ones near the edge of the next level's terrace. "What do you think, Tuakana?"

"You may be right. If we move quickly, they probably will not even notice us."

Kara knew a bad plan when she heard it, even if it was her own. Following through on shaky ideas was what kept most people who ventured into the outerzones from being successful tech hunters. Or living ones. "Stay close to me," she said.

Instead of making straight for the ramp, Kara had picked a particular pair of buildings near the edge that looked as if they connected vertically. With luck, it would be a way around the checkpoint.

"What are you doing? The ramp is over there," Zaireel said as she put her weapon away and took out a knife. Kara stepped up to the doorway. The blade sizzled as it came to full heat in the rain.

"Avoiding chances," she said, pressing the blade next to a lock screen on the door. "Or at least finding better ones." The lock flashed a warning message as she cut through, though the door swung open as she shouldered into it.

Kara quickly put on the wrist light Oa had picked up in the markets. A quick look around the room showed something very different from what she had expected. The entire building was empty, save for a few bed mats along the edges. One ladder, made of foot holes cut in several sections of grating tacked together, went all the way to the top.

"What is this place?" one of the soldiers asked.

Kara rolled an object near one of the mats with her foot. The scrapsmithed bladed contraption leaked a thick, black ink as she tipped it over. "It is a passageway," Kara said, "so the Scars can freely get to the third or fourth level of the city without disturbing things."

Kara turned around quickly as Zaireel opened his data pad again. She shot him a suspicious look before moving to the tall, two-story ladder. There were a few grumbles from behind about hot weapons as the rest made to follow her up. Some had straps on their weapons, others would join her in the climb one-handed.

The ladder appeared to simply come to a stop at an open ledge. Kara let go with her one hand for a moment to retrieve her pistol. She hooked the handle of the pistol into the grating before she fell backward and pulled herself to look over the edge. She held herself with an arm on the floor and searched with her wrist light, holding the rail pistol ready to thump whatever knees waited at the top.

She looked a good handful of seconds before determining that the area was just as empty as the bottom, though she had a bad feeling about where the Scars had gone. Kara finished pulling herself up into the strange building and glanced back. The entire area was one open room, most likely built specifically by the Prime Elect to aid his criminal enforcers.

Kara ran a hand over the exit door as the rest of the dripping group pulled themselves to the top. It looked to be nearly identical to the first doorway. Zaireel checked the data pad again after one of Olana's mercenaries helped to pull him up.

Kara flicked her knife back out of its carbon fiber holster behind her sling and set the blade against the door. She closed her eyes and pulled in a slow breath.

"What are you waiting for, tech hunter?" Zaireel asked.

Kara paid him no attention as she listened, blade sitting hot against the metal. Not only did she hear the rain pouring over the building, but she swore she'd heard someone shout.

"We need to go back." Kara turned around and looked to the group. "Make yourselves comfortable while I think of a different way to get to the third level."

She noted that Ziareel let out a bit of a huff as he looked down to the glow of his data pad again. Kara eyed him as he typed something in before tucking it away.

Kara twirled the heated knife in her hand as she looked around the room. A couple of the soldiers eyed the flicking of the blade, though they did not know she was using the repetitive pattern to count the time. After a minute to the flick, she set the blade against the door and pressed it into the metal.

"Wait, I thought you . . ." Zaireel started but trailed off as Kara pulled the door open with a wash of cool rain.

She stepped out into the storm and spotted about ten of the watch staying under the cover of the overhangs at the edge of the street. At how quickly they noticed her, Kara knew they were watching the building and waiting for anyone to step out. One pointed her way, and she could see several data pads light up. However, what the watch did not see were the two muzzled hounds pulling silently at their leashes as four Black Scars edged along the side of the building next to them.

"Move!" Kara yelled back to Tuakana and the soldiers. Almost as if she had triggered it, the hounds set in on the watch with their shocking muzzles, and the screams of pain and surprise echoed as several more figures decorated with black ink stepped from the shadows with varying tech-covered clubs.

Kara did not wait to see the outcome as one of the hounds sparked against the blue-painted flight armor and a Black Scar wrestled a weapon out of one of the watch's hands. She led the way across the street farther down, and they slipped into the shadows just as a Reclaim transport rose over the ridge of buildings and several soldiers opened fire from a side doorway of the ship.

Kara knew the watch had not had time to call for support once the Scars set in on them, which could only mean that they had called the ship at the sight of her. How they knew to watch for the exact door she was at, Kara could only guess. She glanced back at Tuakana's glowing data pad with suspicion.

Soaked by the rains and worn from their fast pace, Kara ducked low as barely ten feet above the low rooftops of the seventh level, another transport ripped through the rain above. The heat from the repulsors left faint trails of steam that were soon pushed to nothing by the winds.

Kara peaked back out from the alley after a second Reclaim transport passed by. They were heading toward the highest and widest level of the outer ring structure. Over the tops of the smaller buildings, she could see that the surrounding wall of Reclaim had been destroyed centuries ago in a number of places, and scavenged to pieces in more recent years in other spots. Where not reduced to a low tangle of rubble, it stood as an open frame nearly six stories high. The majority of the windows had been long since busted out, but Kara knew, from what Jance had said once, that the levels were once observation decks for watching the launch of one of the Orbital Armistice ships. However, what remained of the staging facility was now home to the Black Scars.

Kara glanced back at Tuakana and the Norclave soldiers. She could see that they were already worn. A few had even been wounded by metal chips from stray shots or by nasty shocks from hounds run astray. Zaireel Tuakana gave her a pleading look as he leaned against one of the rough metal walls, as if he were hoping she would not keep pressing them forward.

Before Kara could come to any decision, she heard a quiet beeping coming from one of the pouches on her hip. She reached across and awkwardly opened it with her good hand, producing a small communications device. It looked similar to the one a fellow tech hunter, Comar, had betrayed her with just after they recovered Jance in the first place. The device showed no display, and had only a small flickering light as it beeped a few more times.

"What is this?" Kara said into the device, turning away from the others.

"Never seen one before?"

"Oa. You put this in my pocket?"

The old woman chuckled quietly on the other side. "Perhaps there was something inside the pouches I handed you."

Kara narrowed her eyes and stepped closer to the edge of the alley. She quickly looked around. "Where are you?" Kara picked up the quick motion of a hand wave from another alley.

"Wait a moment," Oa advised. "Watch patrol, crossing farther down."

Without edging out of the alley farther, Kara could not see anyone passing. She looked back to Tuakana. "Wait here. I'm going to scout ahead."

When Oa gave the word to come across, Kara tucked the device away and started out into the crossing winds. If nothing else, it would pay to figure out how Oa had found her so easily. If it was another device tucked away in an obscure fold of her new clothing, she would have to put it under her heel.

The rain was held at bay as she stepped under the cover of a steel awning. Oa smiled and pulled back the hood of her cloak. A few drops of water flowed over the aged lines of her dark skin.

"I see you decided to bring some help," Oa said with a glance behind Kara. "Perhaps you are learning something."

"You can call them help, but something tells me that Tuakana keeps sending the watch our way."

Oa's look darkened and she crossed her arms. "Then we must be quick. What is your plan?"

"I . . ." Kara started before she let out a breath. Just as she was about to snap a harsh remark at the old woman, Oa held up a finger.

"I know, Kara. Just tell me what you are looking to get out of this, and I will help you."

"Why?" Kara asked. "By helping me get to Travend's man, you would be helping me to protect Jance."

Oa put a hand on Kara's shoulder and smiled. "I believe Haxatha and the watch will be at each other's throats enough that you can get in there. I just need to know if your friend Tuakana knows what you are doing."

A long drone of thunder sounded out, rolling through the steel buildings like the rippling of fire. The new layer of noise was loud enough that even the rain and winds were drowned out by the echo of the storm.

Oa's eyes widened and Kara jerked around to the dulled shouts of watch forming outside the alley. Kara counted three or four firearms pointed her way, and more watch in blue-painted flight armor backed them up, keeping a watch around the area.

"Easy now!" Oa said loudly over the thunder, stepping beside Kara with an outstretched hand. "This one is with me."

"We have our orders, direct from the Prime Elect. The tech hunter is to be taken to him at any cost."

Oa looked to Kara and started to slide her hand down from Kara's shoulder. In the same motion, Kara could feel the woman pulling the rail pistol from her hip. Kara glanced to the weapons pointed at her and back to Oa. "No!" Kara whispered. She knew it was over. Putting up a fight would only force the soldiers to open fire. And using a near-useless rail pistol was one of the worst ways Kara could think to go out.

"I think we can say for certain about your friend, Tuakana." Oa said with a half smile. She turned to the group of the watch. "Excuse me, could you just," Olana started, lowering her outstretched hand while slipping up the other one. With a loud crack, Oa loosed the projectile at the ground near their feet. There was a host of startled shouts and Kara knew it was simply someone's judgment call that kept them from being gunned down.

"What are you doing, Advisor?" one of the watch asked timidly.

Kara shared the question, especially seeing that the projectile battery was stopped solidly in place where it had hit against a metal plate on the ground. She looked to Oa for an answer.

"What am I doing, you ask?" Oa frowned, fidgeting with the rail pistol. "I'm trying to figure out how to activate that magnet while keeping eye contact with you. Ah, there we are, button on the back."

In an instant, the soldier's boot slid forward to the rail pistol's magnet pack and his weapon jerked down in his hands. Just as quickly as he was pulled down on top of the super magnet, the others of the group were jerked into a growing pile of painted flight armor. There were screams as limbs were twisted harshly and yells of panic as they were powerless to move. When the few watching the side angles of the street rushed to see what was happening, they too were jerked into the pile with the same lack of grace as the loose steel tiles cobbling the street and a few rusted bolts from the walls of the alley.

Kara gripped the rail pistol as Oa struggled to keep hold of it, even fifteen feet away from the magnet pack. As she could feel the various bits of her own tech about her pulling from even this far back, Kara grabbed Oa and started away down the alley.

"Something tells me, Oa, that you didn't learn about scrapsmithed weapons by being a Warden."

"What? You thought I just sat still all these years?" Oa shot her a look as they turned down a deeper side passage. "I may be old and frail, but whoever said the years weren't to my advantage?"

Kara simply shook her head and loaded another magnet onto the rail.

* * *

The thunder that shook the loose windows of the arc wall of Reclaim only masked the weapons fire and rumble of transports overhead until the next flash of lightning rekindled the noise. Hakatha could tell the storm was upon them now. And it wasn't just the hounds cowering in the corners that were scared.

"Hakatha, there's a Scar here to report to you."

"Any luck on holding the watch back?"

The other man shook his head. Tendrils of inset pigment curled up from his cheekbones to over his eyebrows. "We never expected the Prime Elect to have so many weapons hiding in his storerooms. But Hakatha, this man is here about the tech hunter."

"Send him in," Hakatha said. As his helper moved off, Hakatha looked out over the city. He stood out of the rain on the second or third level of the ring structure. The broken layers made it debatable which level he was on. From a number of locations around, his fellow Scars took potshots at the passing watch transports. They were trying to spot Travend's man, he knew, but after his own men landed one clear shot to a repulsor engine, the other transports used the smoke billowing up from the wrecked craft as a boundary for their patrols.

It would only be a matter of time, however, before the Prime Elect's men would decide to move in. Where the Scars had the advantage of numbers and a willingness to sit in wait for ambushes throughout the city, the watch, along with a number of well-armed mercenaries, simply understood how to pick the priority targets. As the scouts looked for Lieth, the rest were forming a perimeter.

"Here he is," Hakatha's helper said, pushing the smaller man by the shoulder into the room.

Hakatha moved slowly forward, eyeing the mere boy who had his sleeve rolled up to proudly display a few old scars refilled with their signature black, and particularly jagged marks crossed his neck.

"You saw the tech hunter?" Hakatha asked. The young man was tall for his age, though he was clearly afraid when coming face to face with a fully decorated member.

"She . . . she found me. She threatened to disappear forever if I did not tell her where we were keeping the Prime Elect's captive. I tried to stop her, but . . ."

Hakatha held up a hand. The young Scar fell into silence.

"Was she alone?"

"As far as I could tell."

"Find your way up, boy," Hakatha said, pointing to where they could hear a shot ring out. "She will be coming here. Point her out to the lookouts. If you see her, they are to take the shot."

As the young Scar started off, Hakatha motioned to the other man. "Come with me. It's time to show the Prime Elect that we have Lieth and are willing to talk. And with luck, the tech hunter will be watching as well."

* * *

Jance watched as Olana Nuand tapped her glass cube against the wood paneling between the inlays on her desk. The Overlord seemed oblivious to how she was marring the surface. Nuand stopped the drumming long enough to touch her visor.

"Sora, have you seen any word from the Prime Elect through other channels?" Olana closed her eyes at Sora's reply. "Let me know as soon as you do."

Jance wanted to say something about the Overlord's childish way she'd handled the meeting, about how she cut it short, but the worry in waiting served just as well as a snide comment.

"The strike team should be there by now," Olana said. It was the first she had spoken of it.

"Should be? I thought you had a live connection?" Jance asked.

Olana started her tapping again. "Something is wrong with the system."

Jance tapped her visor, attempting to access one of the strike team member's systems.

"Is there anything the Prime Elect could have to stop communications coming from the strike team?" Olana asked with a hint of panic.

Jance shrugged as she watched the connection request fail. "I don't know. I'm sure there could be something to block a signal." She tried the connection again only to find the same result. "I'm getting the same problem. It just keeps showing . . ."

"A message with the word 'Error,'" Olana finished. She shook her head. "I suppose we would be lucky if the Prime Elect was simply blocking the signal. If the Prime Elect killed the team, I will simply have to try something else. Unless your tech hunter let Travend know we have his location, and then I don't know what I'm going to do."

"There's no way Kara could know." Jance knew that Kenneth had only discovered Travend's location recently.

"She destroyed the pod that the Prime Elect recovered. What's to say she won't do something again to make everything that much harder?" The Overlord ran a hand over her tightly pulled-back hair. "Tuakana reported that she evaded him in Reclaim to continue after Lieth on her own. She is simply too unstable to keep around."

"What are you saying?" Jance asked.

"If Kara survives, I don't want to see her in Norclave again. She will have nothing to do with how I run my city."

"That's absolutely . . ." Jance started, though a message on her visor pulled her attention. Jance looked past it, trying to finish her thought. "Kara is simply . . ." Jance let out a huff and started reading the message. She pulled her visor across both eyes as she watched the surveillance stream from the camera mounted high above Norclave, atop the starscraper.

"My decision is made, Cryo," Olana said coldly.

"I . . . I've got something."

"What is it?"

Jance tapped the side of her wheels as she tried to think of what Kara had called them. "Sky flares? Is that the right word? They are dropping from orbit."

"Where?"

* * *

Oa closed her eyes and pushed through the growing weakness of her muscles as she tried to keep pace with the young tech hunter. Years ago, Oa would have never thought she would be limited so much, even though she'd seen the same daily pains she now felt when she helped the elderly of the Vigil and the heads of the different Remnant sectors throughout the day. Oa smiled in remembrance. The wake cycles of the fleet. Not the days.

Oa liked to think she was still sharp of mind, but she still could not convince herself that she could stand next to the likes of Rathaman Dimarka or her grandfather, Druan Alee, and seem the elder. Perhaps one day she would grow tired enough to feel the truth. Oa opened her eyes as Kara nudged her arm. Then again, perhaps that tiredness would come in the coming week as she was chained down by the need to rest.

"The scout craft have been staying away from the arc wall," Kara said. She was pointing at smoke billowing up through the rain in the street ahead. "I would say the Scars shot one down."

It was hardly the first transport Oa had seen wrecked. Not counting the hundred some odd ones she destroyed herself as the Warden, Oa remembered watching a number of others topple from the sky while she was on Earth. Something about crashing to the ground, pulled by the planet's gravity, didn't seem as hollow as watching a dead craft drift off into the fleet.

Kara looked over her shoulder as another transport flew low over the tops of the buildings behind them. "You said something about the watch forming a perimeter around this section? How do we plan on getting through that? It seems your con of being the Prime Elect's secret Cryo has met a limit."

Oa felt a flash of panic as she heard the word again. It was their word for Reawakened. "Judging by the burning transport, I would say we are already inside the watch's circle. The group Zaireel Tuakana pointed your way could have been sent to investigate this crash."

"Alright, and how do you expect to get past the Black Scar patrols?"

Oa thought it over a bit. "Worst case being the most likely, you use your magnet launcher. I could imagine it slowing them down."

"How? I've yet to see a Black Scar in flight armor. Sure, it might draw their weapons away, but unless they have some sort of tech imbedded into their skin, they could just pull free of whatever buckles they have."

Oa rubbed her neck as she mulled over the painful thought. "The ink they use in the scars, it is magnetic. Certain tech they like to use nullifies electrical contact to an extent, and the ink helps funnel the current to the devices."

"Great," Kara said, motioning with the rail pistol in her hand. "That won't make anyone mad."

Oa gave no reply as they walked past the wreck of the transport. The thinning raindrops hissed as they touched the glowing metal, making an uncomfortable-to-breathe haze in the area. Kara pointed her rail pistol and wrist light from one place to another as she expected the world to jump out at her. Oa had another plan for when the Black Scars found them.

She sighed. The recent events had brought up old memories, and while the horrors brought by Sarthyl and her time as the Warden after that formed an excruciating wall that drove her thoughts away, Oa now found herself looking up through a thinning of the clouds to the life she'd vowed to leave behind. As night fell across the Steel Valley, the last passing of sunlight pulled across the surface of the fleet. The shine of the titanic ships, slowly drifting golden above the storm, could always stir her thoughts.

She was the only Remnant to have ever seen their ancestral home in this light.

It was then, as a flash of lightning silhouetted the clouds surrounding the opening in the storm above, that Oa spotted lights. The red cones of fire broke through the high reaches of the atmosphere in a scattered formation. One of the sky flares broke in a bright flash, sending a shower of pieces drifting across the sky.

In her near lifetime on the surface she had seen a number of falling objects, either alone or in week-long showers, and all but the probe recovered by the Prime Elect had been simple wreckage breaking loose. This however . . . Oa had seen this before, though never from the surface. Sometimes the drifting of dead transports took them out of the artificial microgravity of the fleet and into the well of the planet. These however, for the most part, were staying in one piece.

It is what she would have looked like, when she fell to her exile after returning the suit of the Warden to the Warden's Shrine. These transports were returning to Earth, just as she had.

The sky flares began to shift as some began to pop on their repulsor engines, breaking their speed with bright flashes of blue. Tens of seconds later, she could hear the loud explosions of the sky flares' engines as they flared to life in the sky above Reclaim. It would only be minutes before they landed about the Steel Valley.

"Kara, I have to get back to the Prime Elect."

There was no reply. Oa glanced around only to see that the tech hunter was nowhere to be seen. Then she heard the beeping from her own pocket. She pulled back her soaked cloak and pulled out the transmission device.

"Kara?"

"You may not know this, but a sky flare is said to be a sign of great luck. Even just seeing one is supposed to be something special, though I know better. The last one brought nothing but trouble."

"Then what are you doing, Kara?"

"Hoping I am the only one not watching them."

"For the love of the . . ." Oa trailed off. "Don't be stupid, you know—"

"See to your world, Oa. I'll see to mine."

* * *

It was an eerie feeling, slipping along the edges of the watch's search lights and through the field of scattered luminescent flares set by the Scars. The flares looked as if they were made from long-decayed chem lights and a power pack, and they let off a dim yellow glow. Had everyone else not been looking up at the sky, Kara would have been spotted a hundred times over.

The wide streets were barricaded at the far ends by lines of scraphaulers carrying soldiers with weapons propped on the edges. Kara passed by a blown-open container building. She could hear a group of Black Scars hiding inside quietly arguing over if the sky flares really came from the orbital wreckage. Kara forced herself to keep her mind on moving forward.

She picked out a spot in the ruins of the staging facility arc and started out into the open amongst the Black Scars' scattered chem lights. It was only a matter of time before the sky flares landed or someone decided to start shooting, and at the moment she was the only person in the open.

As much as she wanted to run for some sort of cover, she forced herself to keep a steady and easy pace. The high stories of the outer arc of the city had a number of people leaning out from their positions to get a better look at the flares burning down from the sky. She could tell by the reflections from the water on the steel-cobbled street that the flares were nearing the ground.

Kara winced as she clipped one of the chem lights with her boot. The tube clicked against the street as it spun and rolled several feet. To make it worse, stirring the contents seemed to make it glow brighter.

"Get their attention!" a heavy voice yelled through the silence of the streets and the low rumbling of the flares above. Before Kara could pinpoint the source of the yell, a bright spear of light shot from high up in a building in the arc wall. The refined pulse shot hit a transport hovering behind the watch's line, causing one of its repulsors to rip open and explode.

"Here's what you came for!" Hakatha's voice rang out from the top story. Before she bolted from the street, she spotted him holding Travend's man by the back of the gag wrapped around his mouth. Hakatha pulled Travend's man back into the building as Kara wedged her way between uneven panels that had been hastily slapped onto exposed beams. The street behind her lit up with weapons fire and the glow of another burning transport.

The inside of the arc wall seemed to take the chaotic structure of Norclave and the South Corridors to the extreme. A number of areas looked to be temporary living locations or piles of storage. Heavy oilcloths were tied off from several bent corners of steel plates in the ceilings to direct the dripping water into dented areas of the floor. She could see a few Black Scars sitting amongst the clutter, holding their hands over wounds, but there appeared to be no one helping them.

Kara tried her best to avoid looks as she took one of the ramps propped up through holes in the ceiling of the level. The next room she came to looked as if it had been partially sealed from the elements by ragged cloths pressed up against the haphazard, half-hanging pipes and piled scrap. The tarps facing the street popped in and out against the wind, and she could see the flashing of the battle through the gaps.

"There's the fighting!" a man yelled from farther along the building. Kara could not see because of a pillar in the way, but she pulled her rail pistol out and moved forward slowly. As she rounded the pillar, she could see the boots of two people standing on the other side of a ragged cloth.

"I want you to keep a watch for any of the Prime's men thinking they are smart," the man continued. "I'll keep them busy from here."

One of the men turned. Kara took a few quick steps to get behind a pile of crates. The next ramp up looked to be about fifteen feet away, across the room and through a four-foot-tall doorway. A bright flash filled the area as he pulled one corner of the tarp out of the way and stepped into the same room Kara was in.

"Hey, why don't you give me the watch's gun?" the scar-covered man said, turning back and patting a hand against the tarp. He had tattoos running in thick stripes up the length of his arm as well as jagged marks over the top of his head. Kara took the opportunity to stand up and move. She kept the rail pistol pointed his direction as she made for the doorway as quietly as she could.

"Because it was my hound that they killed!" The muffled shout was followed with a few loud shots also from behind the tarp.

Just as Kara started up the ramp, the one in the room with her turned. She froze in place, and so did he. Kara slowly raised a finger up to her lips, hoping he would understand that she just wanted him to keep silent. She started moving again, one foot slowly crossing the other, with the sound of broken glass crackling underfoot.

Kara slowly ducked through the doorway and paused just on the other side.

"They made it—" the man started to yell, but Kara leaned back through the door and launched the magnet pack. It hit him in the side of the head with a solid thunk. The man fell into the tarp with a yell, gripping his ear.

Kara started up the ramp, but hesitated as she held her thumb to the button on the back of the magnet launcher.

"What happened? Who was it?" Kara heard the other man ask.

The one she shot let out a grunt. "I think it was that tech hu——"

Kara activated the magnet and continued up the ramp, chased by the echoing screams of the Black Scars.

Kara felt as if she'd stepped out into the open as the light drops of rain fell unhindered through the gaping hole in the top of the third level. Through the uncovered and largely broken windows she could see out over the city of Reclaim. At seven tiers above the center of the city, she now stood even with the top of the Citadel tower. There were pillars of smoke rising above the lights of the city and into the gloom of the night. Perhaps most surprising of all, she caught sight of a transport slowing its incredibly fast descent as it touched down in the city. Another couple appeared to be landing much farther out, beyond the reaches of the staging facility.

"How did you survive?" a hoarse voice said to the side. Kara spun on her heel and cursed herself for being distracted. In the center of the room, lying on his side tied up and in a puddle of water, was Lieth. Travend's man looked up at her. He had new bruises on his face.

Kara stared out through a wide puddle of rainwater, held in by the dip of the floor throughout the room. She kept a sharp eye out as she moved farther into the empty room, weapon ready. "Where is Hakatha?"

"He went to make a deal with the Prime Elect. The Scars are giving up."

The water slowly rippled out from under Kara's boot as she continued her cautious pace. "And he left no one to watch you?"

Lieth coughed and tried to pull his shoulders straight, though the rough bindings of cloth kept him curled. "Honestly, I think the Scars mostly made a run for it. But why are you here? What makes you risk your life for Norclave?"

"What made you try to kill the Cryo?"

He spit out some of the water and twisted his head to get his mouth out of the puddle. "It was the best way to bring Olana Nuand . . . try? What do you mean try to kill the Cryo?"

"Maybe you did," Kara said, spinning a slow circle as she kept moving toward the man. "Maybe I actually am here for revenge. I left before anyone knew whether or not she would live. That uncertainty is why you are still alive. It's all about whether I can still keep her safe from Travend or not."

"The Overlord is who you should be worried about."

"Oh yeah?"

"You have no idea, do you?"

Kara looked up at the open ceiling of the room, making sure no one was watching from above.

Lieth continued, though he looked into the distance through the broken window as if watching an inner thought. "The bright-shoulders, Nuand's mercenaries, they didn't just ransack my shop after the fighting was over. No, they didn't just go after the supplies that had survived Norclave's struggle with the administrators. They stepped over . . ." Lieth choked on the words. "They followed nothing but orders. *Her* orders."

Kara paused. "What did they step over?"

"My wife and child. I . . . they were under the only blankets I could find that had not caught fire. Olana Nuand, her orders did not care. They took things off the shelves, and kept me back at gunpoint."

Kara let her head droop. "That's when you sought out Travend."

"I have felt dead since that day. I cannot feel anything, except the need to watch Nuand pay. I was promised by the Prime Elect that I would be returned to Norclave, to help Travend, though it makes no difference who I need to aid to bring about the day that the Overlord fails."

"So the Prime Elect . . ."

Kara paused as she heard the clattering of claws against the steel floor. Across from where Lieth lay, two Black Scar hounds loped into the room and gave muffled barks through their shocklance muzzles once they spotted her. One let out a low growl, looking her direction, and the other started to slink around the side with quieter warning barks.

"Not happening," Kara said, raising the pistol. "Not again." With a snap, the magnet launched between the two. She tapped the back against her left shoulder, and the hounds were suddenly pulled by their muzzles to the magnet on the ground. The shocklances sparked harshly as they touched the floor and the dogs began to yelp and howl. One pulled free of its muzzle and the other continued to shake its head wildly. She guessed that the shocklance finally shorted something out on the magnet as the hound pulled back with the magnet still clinging to the side of its muzzle and took off running with its tail between its legs.

Above the noise of the fleeing hounds, she barely heard the footsteps padding through the water.

Kara spun around, rail pistol raised. As she looked over the top of the weapon at the large, scar-covered figure of Hakatha, she realized there was no magnet fastened to the rails of her weapon. She tucked the pistol in her sling and reached for another magnet pack.

Hakatha strode out farther into the water and slammed the blood-covered muzzle down. Kara suddenly felt her every muscle tense up as the muzzle made bubbling sparks. Behind her, Lieth screamed. Hakatha maintained a vicious, pain-filled grin as he stood back up.

Kara had to fight falling to her knees, suddenly feeling as if she had landed flat-footed out of the back of a transport from thirty feet up. She fumbled with the magnet on the rail as Hakatha sloshed through the standing rainwater toward her.

She could see a light pulsing on the bit of tech imbedded just above his collarbone, surrounded by an elaborate filling of ink into heavy scars. "Every beast can be lured into a cage," he said.

"All this was to catch me?" Kara asked. She took a breath, trying to gain control of her shaking hands. All she needed was to get the magnet pack to line up.

"I was hoping Oa would show, but—"

Kara snapped the magnet on the rail. With another splash, Hakatha pounded the ground with the muzzle. Kara leveled the pistol his direction as she fell to her knees. Her grip tightened beyond what she thought she was capable of as the electricity coursed through her. The magnet launched with a snap and hit Hakatha solidly in the shoulder, but she could not pull a thumb up to press the back.

He simply gave another pain-filled smile as her vision faded and she fell down into the water.

* * *

"You have your truce! All this is pointless!" a voice shouted over the sound of a transport rumbling overhead. The pool of water lapped against Kara's face from the chopping in the air. She opened one eye and had to fight against leaping up.

"Just let the Prime Elect have Lieth and the tech hunter, and everything will be forgotten," the same voice said. It was Zaireel Tuakana. He was accompanied by two Reclaim watch, and he had replaced his own Norclave markings with that of the city. "Take this deal quickly, Hakatha. The sky flares are truly your luck, because until we find out what is going on, you are actually a secondary priority of the Prime Elect."

Hakatha ignored Tuakana and motioned to a couple of watch catching a crate dropped by a few more watch from the wide opening in the roof. "Hury it up!" Hakatha yelled.

As the watch started unpacking the crate, marked with the lined triangle of the Steel Valley, they began to notice the Scars along the edges eyeing them. The Scars quickly looked away as the tall and dark figure of Caemon, one of the Prime Elect's guards, stamped his foot and looked their direction. Caemon then directed the watch to continue their work and they began setting up a few low rails with display generators on them.

Hakatha finally turned back to Tuakana. "You may be a traitor to Norclave, but you should know what the Scars are for. We are here to do what the Prime Elect is not supposed to. We clean the streets, maintain his little perfect city, and ignore the rules of whoever tries to stand over Iben Feirshan. If you take the tech hunter and Travend's man now, Reclaim's Cryo will simply tell the Prime Elect to let them go."

Kara could see the surprise in Tuakana's expression. She guessed the Prime Elect had never told him about Oa.

"System is good," the watch said, stepping back from the display generator. At the threatening point from Hakatha for them to leave, all the watch—including those standing by Tuakana—except Caemon hurried to climb the cables up to the transport. The projectors started on and shimmered in static as the transport lifted off, causing the rainwater around Kara to ripple again. She used the motion to glance around, as well as check for any weapons.

Lieth lay unconscious, still tied up on his side. She counted at least ten other Black Scars in the room, though not all appeared to be armed. As for Tuakana, he was looking nervous as Hakatha turned to look out the window, through the night and drizzle toward the illuminated walls of the Prime Elect's Citadel.

"Make the connection," Hakatha ordered. Tuakana tapped on the data pad, and a moment later the figure of the Prime Elect was projected.

"What is the meaning of this? This situation should have already been sorted." The Prime Elect glanced around the area, hesitating only a short moment on Kara before addressing Hakatha again. "Tuakana was authorized to give you . . . well, whatever the hell you wanted, I couldn't care. Right now, all I care about is—"

Hakatha stepped forward and looked down on the Prime Elect, putting himself close to the edge. "You sent Tuakana because he was expendable. Because what does it matter if he dies? The other officials of the city will never let him stay, and it does you no good sending him back to Norclave."

The Prime Elect glanced over at Tuakana. "Alright, Hakatha, you want something you can believe? I say this can be forgiven. Just hand over—"

"I want you to listen!" Hakatha clenched the same muzzle he had used on Kara in a tight fist, almost as if he wanted to use it on the projection in front of him. Perhaps it was only the growl from Caemon that kept him from futilely lashing out.

The Prime Elect took a step back, however. His feet now hovered well over the edge. He glanced down and frowned, seeming to regain part of his confidence. "You will make it quick. I must oversee these new transports landing all over my damned city."

"Oa is protecting this tech hunter," Hakatha said. "The tech hunter is nothing more than a Norclave agent, tasked with hunting this man," he said with a motion back to where Lieth lay, "and tasked with turning your Cryo against you. The tech hunter was with Oa in the Citadel when your first sky flare burned. With your city now invaded from the sky above, you *cannot* have Oa undermining your every step. You should never have listened to her about Travend."

Kara lifted her head up from the water at the last bit, though she carefully rested it again, hoping none of the others had noticed the small ripples.

The Prime Elect wrinkled his face in anger and pointed to the ground to accent his words, though the ground was not currently beneath his feet. "And you should have never let Travend back in the city! Olana Nuand knows he is here! Tell me, what good will the Scars be in a war with Norclave?"

Every head, including the Prime Elect, turned to the side as another voice spoke. "You are mistaken. Travend is not in the city." It was Oa who spoke. She took small steps into the room with a pained look as she rested a hand on a bit of the bent railing next to the missing window. The Black Scars on that side slowly moved away rather than be caught between her and the Prime Elect. "Travend never left Norclave."

Before she could stop herself, Kara pushed herself up out of the water. "What do you mean he never left Norclave?" Kara glanced at the array of weapons now pointed her direction. "Oa, what *exactly* do you know about Travend?"

The Prime Elect held up a finger. "Don't answer that. Oa, don't. Caemon, can you just . . ." the Prime Elect started, though he trailed off on giving the guard instruction with a frustrated hand pressed to his forehead.

Oa glanced over to the projection of Feirshan before turning to Kara. "I . . . your discovery of the Cryo stirred panic in Reclaim, Kara. Only after I heard Overlord Obrourke was killed did I see a chance to . . ."

"To what?" Kara asked.

"To—"

The Black Scar pointed at Oa with the muzzle. "You see, Feirshan! Norclave has turned your own Cryo against you! And if you do not stand up and control her, Norclave owns you."

Caemon moved to stand in front of Hakatha, shielding Oa, though the Scar did not seem the slightest bit intimidated by the height of the Prime Elect's guard.

"You overstep your bounds, Hakatha," the Prime Elect said with narrowed eyes.

"No! You simply cower behind yours!" Hakatha said, pointing beside Caemon to the Prime Elect. "You let her sway you again. To let her contact Travend, even after you had me drive him out."

The Prime Elect looked down again at where the feet of his own projection hovered beyond the lip of the building. He took a few steps forward, and motioned Caemon to step back out of the way with a few waves of his fingers. "I had no idea Travend would try to kill the Cr—" The Prime Elect swallowed and wiped at his eyes and looked up. "To kill Ambassador Lorège. He was just supposed to cause trouble in Norclave. Pit the pieces of the old factions against Olana and keep her busy while I thought over a way to obtain the Cryo. In fact, I would have rather given up Reclaim than see any harm come to Lorège."

Kara stood the rest of the way up, knowing her movement would draw the attention of the rest of the Scars, and by that, the Prime Elect. "I am here, trying to protect Jance Lorège," Kara spoke. She then looked to Oa. "The reason Oa has been protecting me is to hunt down the people Travend ordered to kill Jance. If what you say is true, we all want the same thing."

Hakatha sneered at the Prime Elect. "No, Feirshan. You quietly funded Travend so he could do as *he* saw fit, and that was only because Oa told you that you should trust him. She knew what Travend would try to do. She probably told him to."

At this point, Kara realized that Oa had remained silent. She almost had a hollow look about her, as if some buried guilt or burden was pressing close to the surface. She looked older, and frail.

"Oa? What is it?"

The old woman gave a weary smile. "I misjudged you, Kara. Right from the beginning. While you uncovered your Cryo and protected her, I tried to kill mine. I failed to end him when they pulled Overlord Obrourke out of the cryopod."

"You tried to kill the Overlord?" Kara asked with wide eyes.

"My past is uneasy. Most things, I try to bury away." Oa pulled back her hood and tugged at her collar. To Kara's surprise, a heavy circular scar on her neck had been filled with an inky black. Around it were more decorative swirls under the skin. "Shot by the Overlord and left for dead. I crawled away and found myself taken in by the Black Scars."

"But why? Surely you did not know—"

Oa readjusted her collar back up. "He was a Reawakened. I had no more reasoning than that." Oa glanced behind her, out the wide, broken window to where a new wave of ships were descending from the Orbital Armistice Fleet. Out of this new wave, only a scarce few managed to begin to slow without breaking up into wide showers of flares that scattered across the sky.

Oa continued, standing on that high edge. "I fled to protect the secrets of my people, but it was also to protect them from my cold, broken will for revenge. After it all ended, I went to the hall, but it was not to put the suit back in the shrine. I went to the Preservation Core."

Oa looked down and let out a breath. "That's the fall of the Warden. When you stop believing in what you fight for." She looked up again, away and out over the city as a rumble started above. "I was wrong, and I'm glad I saw it. Both then, and now. I put the suit back and fled, much the same as I abandoned the idea of making you the Warden in my image." Oa paused and smiled. "It turns out you are closer to what I should be, not what I have become."

Kara could feel herself shaking as a cold drizzle started in through the open roof beneath a sky of scattered fire. "So why did you come here, instead of going to the sky flares?"

"Perhaps it was just a feeling that I should be here. Like when I first decided to bring you under my care. Perhaps I thought about which world I should fight for." Oa turned away and looked over her shoulder to Kara. The corner of her mouth twitched up in a brief smile. "Or perhaps I knew where everyone's attention was."

The last thing Kara saw was Oa pulling up her hood.

A bright flash shattered the night and blinded screams sounded from all around. Kara dropped into the pool of water, gripping her face just as the panicked shots crossed the room. She violently shook her head as she tried to rub the white blindness from her eyes. A chopping heat pressed down from above and Kara felt something splash in the water beside her. She reached out, hoping one of the Scars had not thrown a grenade. She wasn't sure if she knew how to stop one, let alone without looking.

Kara was surprised to feel the handle of a pistol. As she pulled it to her, she realized by the weight it was her rail pistol.

"Dammit, Oa," Kara said under her breath as a round of louder shots sounded from above.

Amidst the screams and gunfire, Kara felt a hand grab her shoulder.

"Easy now, tech hunter!" a voice shouted as she reached for the hidden knife under her sling. Another pair of hands started to help her up. "Get them in the transport!"

"Yes sir!" came the reply. "Hold tight to my hand, if you can!"

Kara gripped the gloved hand tight and could feel her feet lift off the ground as she was pulled up toward the transport high above. Just as she started to get her sight back, she could see through the top of the building where the projection of the Prime Elect was throwing his hands in the air, standing amongst the bodies of the Black Scars and Lieth. Oa and Caemon were nowhere to be seen. The Prime Elect turned on a heel and walked away, off the ledge and out of the bounds of the projection.

As Kara pulled herself into the Norclave transport, one of the soldiers in full flight armor held a hand up to his visor. "The objective is secure! Get back to Norclave!"

Kara looked out of the back of the transport as they suddenly started away from the city. The lights, on the Prime Elect's Citadel, across the city, and scattered around the arc wall, all shone through the drizzle of the night as all but the last of the transports from the orbital fleet set down on Earth.

Chapter 27: Beginnings

The craft started rumbling and swaying as its freefall came to press against the atmosphere of the planet. It had all happened faster than Baxel expected. It wasn't far past the Point that the artificial orbit of the fleet gave way, pulling them ever downward toward the expanding horizon. All around them, through the front glass of the transport, the wide reaches of the Earth grew ever larger. He had never imagined it could be quite so daunting.

"We're maintaining a slower course," Liaren said. "I told Tialee that we don't want to catch up with First Claim. You want to sit down, Baxel?"

"Yeah," he agreed, realizing his distraction. "I was just checking the crates," Baxel said. "Something of the Warden's suit was rattling inside."

Liaren glanced back, though not for long. She kept her hands ready to lurch forward and take the controls should Tialee need.

"Everything's fine. It was just this pouch," Baxel said, holding up the small carbon fabric bag in his gloved hand as he sat down. The latches in the seat hooked into the back of his suit, securing him in place. "How much longer?"

Tialee chimed in over the comms of the craft, "Using the readings from the probe, I estimate twenty-three minutes and thirteen point four *nulled* seconds."

Baxel let himself relax and lean into the support of the fastened suit. Even with the majesty of the Earth coming to circle around them, Baxel could not help but be blinded by thoughts of what they were leaving behind. About who had not survived. The Vigil was left with no head to direct them, nor the visage of their Warden to care for in the Shrine. The Production and Research Sector had lost Nendra Halimuth, and Flerin could not confirm the whereabouts of Marrel Lovek or Dannil Wardenson before Baxel and Liaren set out. Baxel never even found out if his own parents had survived the attack on Habitat Three.

Baxel let out a breath and looked down to the small pouch. He opened it and poured the object inside into his hand.

Baxel turned the small metal piece over. It was some kind of armored figure, kneeling on the ground and holding a shaped plate of steel fastened to its arm above its head. With the other hand, it grasped a rod sticking from its side, much like the other rods sticking from the plate. The figure itself was worn. The shine of the metal had dulled in all but the tips of one of the broken rods. Along the rim of the base was a word that was nearly smoothed over from where it had been rubbed, much like how Baxel now rubbed his thumb across the letters in thought.

"Warden," he read quietly to himself.

"It belonged to my grandmother, Maylee Sharpes," Tialee finally said, though her voice only came out of Baxel's helmet. "I remember playing with it when I was a little girl. It was not until later in life, after I founded the Warden's Vigil, that I found out who the Warden actually was. That metal figure. It came with my grandmother's suit.

"She was the first Warden, and I became the second."

Baxel looked at it one last time before tucking it back in the pouch and clipping the pouch to his hip.

* * *

"But how can we know to trust what she said?" The question hung in the tense gap in the conversation within the dark room as the transmitted sound of the transport continued to rumble. Jance looked to Overlord Nuand in an accent to her question. They had both seen it. Jance had accessed the visor of Tuakana after they had been unable to contact him or the strike team. They had watched as the Prime Elect admitted to every tie with Travend. However, what Jance was questioning was whether or not they could trust the word of the old woman the others were claiming was also a Cryo.

"We have to," the Overlord said, clenching her glass cube tightly. "No one knew we were watching. Not even Tuakana. What I am more concerned about now is why you were able to get through to Tuakana when we both were locked away from communicating with the strike team."

Olana crossed the room and waved for Jance to cut the transmission to Tuakana's visor. The noise of the transport faded away. "Or," the Overlord continued, "why my strike team seemed to think that securing the tech hunter was their objective. They were specifically sent with orders to kill or capture Travend. I never amended that order."

Jance gripped the wheels of her chair tightly. She understood what was coming next, but she did not think there was anything she could do to change it.

"They had new orders to retrieve Kara, a block on communications with the transport, and the incorrect location for their destination . . ." The Overlord suddenly stopped rotating the cube in her hand. "Kenneth lied about Travend. He somehow blocked communication with the transport behind the error message, and he apparently did the same thing to hide what he was doing in the Norclave Library during my meeting with the Prime Elect." Olana gave Jance a hard look as she spelled out her last point. "Not only did he lie to me about the location of Travend, he jeopardized my entire position in securing an alliance with the Prime Elect. Kenneth also told the strike team their new objective was to save Kara."

The Overlord held a hand up to her visor and turned away. Jance activated her own visor with a quick tap. The Overlord was already ordering a group of soldiers to the library.

Jance hid the glow of her visor as the Overlord turned back.

"As traitors to Norclave," Nuand said quietly, shaking in anger, "he and the tech hunter are both dead."

* * *

Sora rounded the corner into the hallway just outside the Norclave Library. A few of the larger decorative plants she had placed for Jance were all shoved roughly into a corner. She did not know why Jance had told her to warn Kenneth of Olana, but since Sora knew Jance was in the same room as the Overlord, she understood there was a need for haste.

She opened the door to the Norclave Library and stepped in. The once-familiar surroundings had all but completely changed from her time under the previous Overlord. It had been stripped by Clana's men, nearly converted into a form of decoration under Jance, and had since been recluttered by Kenneth's efforts.

However, Sora soon slowed her pace amongst the shelves, feeling another eerie change. The room was dimly lit, leaving only the subtle glow of a few scattered devices to illuminate the rows of shelves.

"Kenneth?" Sora called out, stepping around a tipped-over crate. Even one of the plants in a powered container was tipped on its side; Sora could see the gentle bioluminescent glow from the undersides of its upturned leaves. She glanced both ways uncertainly and called out to the technician again. There was only silence in reply.

Not knowing what else to do, Sora simply set the plant back upright. In the righted glow along the undersides of the bioluminescent leaves, Sora saw a small piece of steel, and the glint of purposefully engraved markings.

It read: "Tell Jance I am sorry I ever fixed her broken visor. She picked it up, thinking it was from Avery Thorne. It just belonged to someone called Maylee Sharpes."

Sora put Kenneth's note in a pocket. He'd left it under the plant before he disappeared, knowing she would be the first to think to tip it back upright.

* * *

Kara pulled her soaked hood back and stared intently at Tuakana. He cleared his throat from the opposite side of the transport, trying his best to avoid looking at her. Somewhere in the confusion of the assault, Tuakana had managed to become a target for rescue. Kara tried to tell them he was a traitor to Norclave, but they made it clear the both of them would be delivered to Olana Nuand anyway.

"How much longer do we have?" Kara asked the closest soldier.

He checked a small display fastened to the forearm of his suit. "We're not past the Reclaim border yet. Hopefully they're still distracted by those sky flares."

Kara looked past him as one of the standing soldiers started toward her, keeping a hand on the ceiling rails to hold steady as they bumped along.

"Tech hunter," he said, holding out a closed hand. "I was instructed to give you this."

"By who?" Kara asked, eyeing the glow between his fingers.

The man shrugged. "I wasn't given that information. It was in the supplies."

Kara stood up with a sigh and held her hand open. She could see she had grown all too trusting.

The soldier set it in her hand and watched for a moment, as if expecting the little display on the wristband to change. After a few seconds, he turned and moved back toward the front of the craft.

Kara held it for a moment in confusion. She had left this sitting for Kenneth, on the seventh level docks in the rain. She looked up in question, but the soldiers seemed to have no answers.

"Is he . . . ?" Kara started, but she could not bring herself to complete the question.

He couldn't be dead.

She left the band with Kenneth because she did not want him to follow. . . because she knew she went without the blessing of Olana Nuand. The Overlord had been very clear that she would receive no help if she went after Travend's men. But that came to raise the question, how was it that she was now aboard a Norclave transport?

Kara looked down, feeling that she held the answer in her hands, though she had a hundred questions as to how Kenneth was involved.

Kara took a hard look around the transport at the soldiers and their gear. Though she had only met the previous Overlord briefly, she guessed most of the gear these men now wore had been taken from the Norclave Library. And if Oa was right about Travend still being in Norclave, Kara doubted the new Overlord would have sent a team like this elsewhere, even if by some miracle the Overlord had a change of heart or strategy.

"Is Travend dead?" Kara asked, loud enough that they could all hear her above the noise of the transport. When she got no reply, she asked if Travend was captured.

"We were just following a change in orders," one finally replied. "You were the new priority."

"Did that change come from Olana Nuand?"

Kara noticed that Tuakana was now paying attention. He glanced around much like herself for answers.

"All we know is that it came through official channels," one of the others said, tapping the visor connected to his helmet. "Besides that, we've received no further contact."

Tuakana narrowed his eyes as Kara moved to the back of the transport. "What are you thinking, tech hunter?"

Kara slipped the band from Kenneth onto the wrist of her bound arm and turned her back on them all. Facing away, Kara snapped her last magnet pack on the rail pistol, which she'd tucked into her sling. "I'm thinking that something is a setup, somehow." She turned back. "And I want out of it."

The soldiers leapt up as she shot the magnet to the floor in front of her, and a few even held weapons of their own at her. However, the panicked shout of Tuakana rose above the commotion.

"Wait, damn you!" he yelled at the soldiers. "That's a super magnet!"

Kara smiled, realizing that he would have found the pile of groaning Reclaim watch she and Oa had left in the street. Perhaps he'd even seen what happened to the two Black Scars she used it on.

"You are wearing a whole lot of metal," Kara warned. She looked around at the transport itself. "And I would hate to think what would happen to the systems of the transport."

"What do you want?" Tuakana asked, watching with a bead of sweat on his forehead as she held a thumb close to the back of the weapon.

"Put the transport on the ground. I'm getting out."

After a round of hasty explanation from Tuakana, followed soon after by agreement from a few others, the order finally went out. The transport began to drop, and when they came near enough to the ground, Kara hit the panel for the loading ramp and stepped out of the back of the transport.

"I'm leaving that there!" she said with a nod to the magnet pack still holding tight to the floor of the transport. "Don't turn around in my sight!"

Soon, the hot winds of the repulsors came whipping around her lowered hood and tossed her hair wildly to the side. As the blue lights rose high into the dark of the sky, Kara saw one last flare dropping down from the fleet. She watched to see if it would break apart like so many of the others.

* * *

Jance found herself nodding off and had to catch herself before she tipped out of the chair. It had been nearly a week since the Overlord's strike team returned without Kara. Jance knew she was far from recovered, and at times she just wanted to sleep through her soreness during the day. Of course, that was partially because she was finding it hard to sleep through it at night.

"The only thing unaccounted for is the bag," Sora said from off to the side in the Norclave Library. She was speaking to the Overlord after a long search through the library for any clues as to the whereabouts of Kenneth. Jance picked the small cup off her lap and held it up to water one of the plants on the shelf. She was not about to tell the Overlord about the note Sora had found, or the once-broken visor that was also missing.

When Sora told her that the visor Jance had picked up in the Power Relay Station did not belong to Avery, but to Maylee, she realized that just when you come to believe you have enough history pieced together, you are destined to find something that you will have no idea what to do with.

"I had that bag checked," the Overlord replied to Sora. "The one Kara left behind and Kenneth took with him."

"You think we missed something in it? Missed something that would tell us where Kenneth went?"

Jance watched the Overlord tilt her head from one side to the other as she thought of an answer. "No. I missed something," Olana said. "It was the bag itself. What she left behind. Tools a tech hunter would use to survive. We didn't have a sign of where he would go, just that he would."

* * *

Even at midday, the surrounding area was cloaked in a dim twilight from the shadows above. Kenneth sat on the wide brim of smooth metal with only the soft glow of a visor to bring a golden sheen to the surrounding surfaces. He didn't wear the visor, simply held it in his hands. Perhaps he did not have a right to take it from the Norclave Library, and from Jance, but it did not belong to who she thought, and he was proud of it. Proud of fixing it.

Not that it could make him any more of a wanted man. Kenneth looked up through the haphazard grid of the starscraper, knowing that he could not stay much longer. He would need to move on to find somewhere he could hide for quite some time. He placed the visor back in the bag as if preparing to leave, but he could not make himself start away.

Kenneth rubbed his hand along the dusty, curving surface of the metal. It was the great seal of the UWC. The letters were raised up from the surface, high enough that his heels did not touch the base from where he sat.

He looked up as a soft glow started in the area. He couldn't see the sun, but that didn't mean the light wasn't refracted around the many beams and half-hanging rooms of the starscraper.

"Kenneth?" a voice said from behind. He turned and looked up the slope that the seal sat on. "I didn't think . . ."

"Kara!" Kenneth only took the time to grab the bag before he started making his way up over the ridges in the metal toward the tech hunter.

"I had hoped that . . ." she started in again, having a hard time finding the words. "Kenneth, how long have you been here?"

He smiled as he stepped up on the last arc of the UWC seal and started walking along the ridge toward her. "Just long enough, it seems. I'm just glad you are alive. I saw what was happening in Reclaim, and I knew you would be in the middle of it if you could be."

Kara motioned to the bag he was holding, and he came to a stop a few feet away. "I'm glad you found it. Did you, um, what does the Overlord think—"

"She hates my guts. All of them, I'm pretty sure. I was actually on my way out of Norclave, so I wasn't just here waiting for you." Kenneth took a breath and glanced at the band glowing gently beside her bandaged and suspended arm. "Actually, that's a lie. I've been here just waiting for you. I was hoping you would think to find me here, and know not to return to Norclave."

"Perhaps a bit more of a warning would have been nice," she said with a smile.

Kenneth then noticed her hood was lowered for once. He took a step forward. "Would you, perhaps care to join me in fleeing from Norclave?"

"Again?" Kara cautiously matched his step forward, coming to look up at him. "I'd like that. As long as we stay away from Reclaim."

Kenneth slowly reached up and pressed his hand against her hair hanging over her neck. He half expected her to flinch away, but instead, she traced his raised hand down to the lined scars on his arm.

As the light finally broke through the starscraper above, Kenneth pulled Kara into a gentle embrace, careful of pressing against her wounded arm. They stood there together for some time until the shadows rolled over them once again.

* * *

Baxel kicked in frustrated curiosity, attempting to fling the earth from his boots. It was damp and sticky, and just seemed to smear when he tried to get it off with his gloves. Despite the puddles of water simply sitting unattended across the landscape in natural basins of rock, dirt, or metal, Baxel's lips were parched dry from the walk.

He was now coming up on the transport nestled next to a clump of trees. It seemed not so long ago that Tymon had gotten them temporarily suspended from the search for refilling his oxygen stores next to the only tree Baxel had ever seen before landing on Earth. The one in the fleet was old and withered by comparison, having only overgrown its damaged fertilization basin by the sheer centuries of its existence.

Baxel ducked as something flashed past overhead. It flipped and whirled as it bounced and fluttered through the air until it came to land on one of the outreaching tendrils of the trees. He still could not get used to the bizarre things that apparently lived here.

"Baxel are you back yet?" Liaren asked through the comms of his helmet. Baxel put it on. He felt considerably more comfortable behind the assured pressure of his helmet, but he knew he would have to force himself to get used to the constant leaking and shifting of the air that rolled over the tiny trees covering most of the ground. They didn't seem to ever break, even as he walked over the top of them. They just kind of folded over.

"Yeah, I'm here," he said.

"Am I going to need to start making search coordinates for you?"

"You know how much I like those," Baxel said. "I did find someone to talk to though. They were living amongst the ruins. I think he was too old to run like the others have been."

Liaren let out a huff, likely in regards to their agreement about him simply surveying the area to start with as she shifted through the thousands of signals bouncing around.

"He confirmed what we thought. The nearest settlement is back that way," he said, pointing large with his arm so that she could see from the transport.

"Did he give it a name?" Liaren asked.

"Yeah, and he said it was in some kind of large transport, nearly a mile long. I'm thinking the Warden might be in the place that sounds the most like home. At least, that is if the people of the settlement were the ones to recover the observation probe."

"That's as good a guess as any. What was the name, though?"

"The settlement is Carvanhold. Or do you mean the ship? He didn't know."

* * *

The Prime Elect popped his knuckles as he stepped into his hangar. What had once been littered by the smoking ruins of a sky flare was now filled with six glass-faced cryopods.

"And you say these are your people?" the Prime Elect asked.

The older man ran his hand over the surface of one of the pods. Glowing ice covered the interior surface. "Yes," Connor Sevison said. His white sash brushed against the surface as he continued walking, looking for any visible damage. "I was fifteen when they went into cryostasis."

The Prime Elect held a finger to his lips in thought. "So not an ancient Cryo, then."

"If it is true Reawakened you want, I can promise you many thousands more from before the Vigil. They will need a home, just as my people will. I propose that we start with two pods, and then get the others out if the process goes well."

The Prime Elect could barely hide his disbelief at the notion of thousands of Cryo, even if Connor Sevison did speak of them in an odd manner. "What do you mean a home for your people? Just these six?" He motioned to the pods before him.

Connor Sevison held him in a hard gaze. "My people are from a Contract, abandoned long ago."

The Prime Elect looked confused as he waited for Connor to continue. "Alright, then. What is it you need?" the Prime Elect finally asked.

"I need to send a signal. Strong enough that it cannot be filtered out or explained away."

"To whom?" the Prime Elect asked. "And what would your signal say?"

Connor looked down and rubbed the cover of a small notebook. The First Claim pilot who made the trade for his release had given it back to him, though Connor doubted she understood the years he had waited to get it back. Apparently, the notebook had been tucked into a pouch of the yellow suit she had taken from Tymon. He flipped the pages open.

Connor smiled, not looking up from his handwritten calculations and charts of Earth's location from Mars. "The signal will say that fifty-eight years ago, I was right. And I will not be silenced again."

RyanClarkBooks.com

www.ingramcontent.com/pod-product-compliance
Lightning Source LLC
Chambersburg PA
CBHW020505260626
47156CB00006B/1876